He's a hı
but she's the r

OB........ U LDGE

For the first time ever, all three origin novellas in the Elemental Legacy series are available in one volume, along with a bonus novella, *The Bronze Blade*.

In *Shadows and Gold*, driving a truck full of rotting vegetables and twenty million in gold across mainland China wasn't what Ben Vecchio had in mind for summer vacation. If he can keep Tenzin's treasure safe, the reward will be worth the effort. But when has travel with a five-thousand-year-old wind vampire ever been simple?

In *Imitation and Alchemy*, all Ben wanted was a quiet summer before his last semester of university. All Tenzin wanted was a cache of priceless medieval coins that had been missing for several hundred years. And some company.

In *Omens and Artifacts*, Ben needs a job. A *legendary* job. Finding the lost sword of Brennus the Celt would make his reputation in the vampire world, but it could also draw dangerous attention. The Raven King's gold isn't famous for being easy to find. Luckily, Ben has his own legend at his side.

OBSIDIAN'S EDGE is an anthology of previously published novellas in the Elemental Legacy series by Elizabeth Hunter, USA Today Bestselling Author of *Midnight Labyrinth*, *Blood Apprentice*, and other works of fiction.

PRAISE FOR THE ELEMENTAL LEGACY SERIES

Midnight Labyrinth is non-stop adventure filled with humor, romantic tension and the rich texture we have come to expect from Hunter.

— The Lit Buzz

Ms. Hunter's writing is flawless, impeccable, and truly captivating. It's like coming home every single time and hanging out with the gang, or in this case the new gang.

— Kat's Corner

While the treasure hunt is very entertaining, it's the emotions between these two, what's being said and left unsaid that is very powerful. ...this is Elizabeth Hunter at her best.

— Nocturnal Book Reviews

OBSIDIAN'S EDGE

AN ELEMENTAL LEGACY ANTHOLOGY

ELIZABETH HUNTER

To everyone who wanted more of Ben and Tenzin,
I blame you for this.
—EH

For the beginning seems to be more than half of the whole...

— Aristotle, Nicomachean Ethics

FOREWORD

Seven years ago, I wrote these words at the back of *A Fall of Water,* the fourth and final book in my very first series, the Elemental Mysteries.

"Tenzin?"
"Yes?"
"I'm bored."
"Me, too."

I had no idea that these words would be the inspiration for a series that has taken me around the world on research trips, sold thousands of books, and attracted love and attention from so many diverse corners.

I think it's fair to say Ben and Tenzin are not bored any more.

It wasn't something I'd planned when I first wrote a skinny twelve-year-old boy in *This Same Earth,* but Ben has grown into a character I love just as much (and probably more) as any other featured in the Elemental universe.

This series has traveled across China, though Italy, into the

United Kingdom, and back to New York where Ben began. It has descended into caves and crossed oceans. Ben and Tenzin have recovered gold, found treasures of all kinds, and acquired more than their share of sharp, pointy objects.

We've met new friends and run into old ones. There has been drama, comedy, and even some tragedy.

In short, this series continues to be my all-time favorite place to hang out as a writer, as well as a place that presents me with fresh challenges every time I return.

I hope you enjoy this special edition of the Elemental Legacy novellas, grouped together for the first time and including a bonus novella, *The Bronze Blade*, which is Tenzin's origin story. (Please be aware that *The Bronze Blade* is not for everyone, so I ask that you read my forward at the beginning of that volume.)

For new readers, *Shadows and Gold* is a great place to start with these two characters, who were introduced in the Elemental Mysteries series.

For long-time readers, welcome back.

Elizabeth Hunter
October 2019

SHADOWS AND GOLD

Traveling to the most remote region of China certainly wasn't what Ben Vecchio had in mind for his summer vacation, but when Tenzin suggested a quick trip, he could hardly turn down a chance to keep her out of trouble and practice the Mandarin he still struggled with in class.

Driving a truck full of rotting vegetables and twenty million in gold from Kashgar to Shanghai was only the start. If Ben can keep the treasure away from grasping immortals, the reward will be more than worth the effort. But when has travel with a five-thousand-year-old wind vampire ever been simple?

"ARGH!"

Tenzin looked up from her book to see Ben tearing at his hair, his elbows planted on either side of what she knew was his Mandarin textbook.

"I'm never going to get this," he said.

"Yes, you will."

"No, I'm not. It's the tones. I can't seem to get the tones right, and they're going to kick me out of my next class if I can't get them right."

She knew that wasn't good. Chinese was his minor field of study. Political science was his major at the university, and Chinese was his minor. At least she thought that was how it worked.

"You need to practice more." She spoke to him in Mandarin. "From now on, I'll only speak to you in Chinese. That will help."

"Please don't," he said in English.

"I don't understand what you're saying," she answered, smiling. "I do not understand English when you are speaking it."

"You are full of shit," he said in Mandarin. Or at least, that's

3

what he was trying to say. Ben was right. He really needed practice.

Just then, an image on the television caught her eye. "Ben, turn that up."

He glanced up, confused. "What?"

"The television! What is this program? Turn the volume up."

She stared as the sound grew on the screen in front of her. Images of crumbled brick and construction equipment filled the screen. Men wearing hard hats and pouring concrete.

"Where is that?" Ben asked.

She whispered, "Kashgar."

This was not good.

"Where?"

Familiar mud roofs and bright doorways. Streets filled with colorful dresses. The images on the screen flipped through her memories along with the fragrance of saffron, charred lamb, and dust.

"Where's Kashgar?"

She leaned forward, ignoring Ben and listening to the narrator.

"In the old town, ancient mud brick homes are making way for modern reconstruction, though the government is quick to reassure both citizens and visitors alike that the unique character of this historic city is central to the improvement plans for the special economic zone that is planned."

"Shit."

Ben frowned at her as an image of collapsed walls flashed across the screen. "Why are you so freaked out? It looks like those places were about ready to fall in. Can you imagine how many people might get hurt? Kids might live in those houses."

Tenzin stared at the familiar old streets, tapping her foot. How safe was it? She hadn't moved that cache in several hundred years, but if they started tearing up enough old streets...

Plumbing lines. Foundations. Modern wiring went underground, didn't it?

"Shit," she muttered again.

If only Nima was still alive. She was always better at making these arrangements. She'd need Cheng's help, but he owed her more than one favor. Nobody moved things by horse or wagon anymore. She'd need... What? A truck? A boat? Cheng had many boats. He could probably get her a truck, too. Then there was the new government to deal with. Human governments liked forms and fees. Tariffs and taxes. There would probably be checkpoints, but she could deal with those.

Irritating humans.

"Tenzin, what are you scowling about?"

She glanced at Ben. Back at the screen. A government spokesman was speaking to a reporter.

Speaking *Mandarin.*

She would need a truck, a boat...

And a human.

What was the American phrase? Something about a lightbulb?

Tenzin looked at Ben. Then she looked at his textbook, still laying open on the table in the den. A smile turned up the corner of her mouth.

She asked, "When does your school start?"

Ben was looking at that book again, chewing on his thumbnail. "Next semester starts... Uh, middle of August."

That was months away. Plenty of time. She stood and walked over to him, slapping his book closed.

"Hey! I was trying to—"

"Study, yes. Admirable. But you know what would be better?"

His eyes narrowed. "What?"

"Practicing Chinese with real Chinese people."

"Aren't *you* a real Chinese person?"

"Define Chinese. And person."

He paused. "I see your point. Why are you—"

"I need to make a quick trip to Xinjiang."

"Where?"

"It's a province in China. You can come along."

His eyebrows went up. "Really?"

"Really. Don't you think that would be better than studying from books?"

He sat back, suspicion written clearly on his face. "I guess I could stand to practice—"

"Excellent! Just see to your visa and I'll take care of the rest."

She walked from the room, mentally composing a note for Caspar to send to Cheng's secretary. She'd need to tread carefully. The last thing she wanted was to end up in the old pirate's debt.

"Tenzin?" Ben called from down the hall. "What are we doing?"

"Going to China."

"For?"

"To practice your Chinese, of course!"

Ben muttered something she was pretty sure he had not learned in a textbook.

1

Ben Vecchio landed in the Ürümqi Diwopu International Airport at ten in the morning not knowing what time it was or what time it was supposed to be. Despite its vast territory, the entire People's Republic of China was on one time zone. Beijing time. You might be in Yunan province, Xi'an, or the Tibetan plateau, but you were still on Beijing time.

He roused himself and, ignoring his snoring seat mate, shoved his way into the aisle to grab his bag from the overhead bin. Personal space, he had quickly learned when he landed in Asia, was not a universal value. He stretched his cramped legs and barely winced when the formidable grandmother in front of him knocked him on the jaw with her suitcase.

She said something to him in what he guessed was Uyghur. She said it again, scowling at his clueless look.

"I'm sorry. I don't understand," he said in Mandarin, the language he'd been practicing for three years.

Three years and he was still struggling. For the perfectionist he'd become under the training of his adopted uncle, Giovanni Vecchio, it was unacceptable. Ben was hoping this trip would finally cement the language in his mind. Flip whatever switch was holding him back from true fluency.

The old woman gave him an odd look. She cocked her head and looked him up and down. Frowned again, then turned her back. Ben cautiously glanced around the plane, only to realize something astonishing.

He blended in. That's why the old woman had given him a strange look. She had expected him to understand her.

Taking a deep breath, the tension in his shoulders relaxed, and Ben felt more at ease than he had in days.

"*Xièxiè,*" he murmured to the pretty flight attendant as he shuffled off the plane, hiking his backpack on his shoulder. He strode through the heated tube of the jetway, wondering how hot it would be outside.

It was late summer, and Beijing had been an oven he was happy to leave. He wanted to go back to the city when he had more time—the energy had been intoxicating—but maybe he'd pick spring. Or fall. Maybe even the dead of winter. Anything but the end of June. But Ürümqi was higher elevation and inland. According to what he could find online, Ben was expecting weather a lot like Los Angeles. Warm during the day, but cooler at night. Nothing near the sauna-like conditions of the Chinese coast.

He checked the forecast on his phone as he walked. Mobile phones were as common in China as they were in Southern California, and everyone he'd seen, from the flirting schoolgirl to the Buddhist monk in saffron robes, had one. The vampires, of course, would not.

But so far, he hadn't seen too many of them.

Being a human raised by vampires had its perks. He had sole access to the computer and assorted electronic gadgets in the household. He had little to no supervision during the daytime. And he'd been raised in the kind of luxury since the age of twelve that most of the world could only dream of.

Of course, he'd been under threat of death from his aunt and uncle's enemies for just as long.

By the time he was fourteen, Ben Vecchio knew how to wrestle an opponent twice his size to the ground. By the time he was fifteen, he could shoot an array of firearms, fence with reasonable skill, and use a knife to kill someone in complete and utter silence.

He'd killed a man at sixteen, but it hadn't been silent.

In the five years since it happened, Ben managed to avoid violence whenever possible. And other than an unfortunate run-in with some Russian-Mexican earth vampires, he'd managed pretty well. He liked the rush, but at heart, part of him was still his mother's son. Being noticed made him squirm. He enjoyed surprising people. Flirting around the corners of their awareness until he won. It didn't much matter what he won. Money. Girls. A stupid bet. Ben liked winning, but he didn't like attention.

Which made traveling in Asia something of a shock.

As he walked to collect his bag, he noticed it again. No one looked. No one stared.

"Maybe my favorite place in China so far," he muttered.

It was an uncomfortable thing for him, to be so visible. And in China, he was visible in more than one world. Being the adopted son of two prominent immortals required a visa of a completely different sort than the official government variety. His Aunt Beatrice was the one who'd contacted the Elders at Penglai Island with the information he'd be traveling in their territory "for educational purposes." Since his aunt had been given the title of scribe on Penglai Island, her word was good enough.

Giovanni had still warned him.

"That region is unstable in the immortal world. It always has been. Be careful. Even the Elders keep vampires in Xinjiang on a very long leash. Don't draw any attention to yourself and don't piss anyone off."

He'd only spotted two vampires since he'd arrived. Once at the airport in Beijing and once outside his hotel. Then he'd caught a plane for Ürümqi and hadn't seen one since.

Of course, the sun hadn't gone down yet.

He wasn't quite sure what anyone knew about Tenzin. Tenzin was, as always, vague in her movements. But Ben knew her sire was one of the Elders, so he figured she'd be okay.

For once, it wasn't the vampires making him feel out of place for being human.

His looks—fair skin with an olive undertone, dark curly hair, the thick-lashed brown eyes his mother had given him—marked him from everywhere and nowhere when he was traveling in much of the world. He could be Italian, French, or Middle Eastern. South American or Greek. It was a convenient appearance he'd come to appreciate as he grew older.

He'd been stuck just around six feet for two years, so he figured he'd finished the growth spurt that hit him in high school. Not bad, considering his bastard of a father was a midget. His mother had claimed her brothers were tall, regal men who charmed the beauties of Beirut.

His mother had claimed a lot of things.

But Ben's everyman appearance did nothing for him in China. He was a Westerner. Everyone looked at him. Many gawked. A few even took pictures of him instead of the old palaces the one day he'd spared to visit the Forbidden City.

But in Xinjiang...

The more he looked around as he waited by the luggage claim, the more he realized that many of the men here didn't look Chinese. There were plenty of Eastern Asian looks, but there were Central Asian features, too.

A lot of them.

And... a lot of the Uyghur language.

He'd been sleeping most of the flight, but the more he listened, the more he heard a language he had no idea how to decode.

"Well shit," he muttered. He'd come to practice his Chinese, only to find out half the population didn't seem to be speaking it. As he walked through the arrivals gate, he heard very little Mandarin at all. The people greeting friends and relatives appeared to be predominately Uyghur. A few Chinese. A few foreign business people. But his flight seemed to be mostly a mix of Central Asian looks and languages.

He sighed. "Tenzin."

Go to Xinjiang to practice his Mandarin, huh? Typical.

Ben grabbed his bag and walked toward the exit doors.

He should have known better. After all, Xinjiang was the Uyghur Autonomous Region. For some reason, he figured everyone would still be speaking Mandarin. Because it was China, and everyone spoke Mandarin, right?

His aunt and uncle would say this was why proper prior research was so important.

Lesson learned, Gio.

The intense summer sun hit him the minute he stepped outside. Ben knew Tenzin was in the city, but he had no idea where she was staying. She'd left him a note the day after she suggested he come to Xinjiang with her. The note was... well, also typical Tenzin.

Ben—

Meet me in Ürümqi in two weeks.

Stay at the Sheraton. The beds won't be horrible.

I'll meet you there.

Tenzin never signed her notes because he knew her handwriting—when she wasn't forging something—and who else would suggest he randomly fly to the most remote city in Asia?

Three old women carrying lighters approached him as he walked down the steps.

"Lighter?" they asked. "Five *kuai*." One asked in Chinese, the others in what he could only assume was Uyghur.

He shook his head. He wasn't even a smoker and he knew that was a rip-off. He might blend in more in Xinjiang, but he still had "foreigner" written all over him to the street merchants.

Street merchants were smarter than most. The former thief in him knew that.

Two of the women wandered off when he shook his head, but one cackled at him and said in Chinese, "One then. Just one *kuai*."

"One, I'll buy." He pulled a small bill from his pocket. Having fire came in handy whether you smoked or not.

"You speak Chinese?" she asked, handing him one of the less worn lighters. "You are young! You are American?" She glanced at his bag. "English? Where are you staying? You need a car?"

"I speak Chinese," he said. "I'll take a taxi, thank you." He took another step toward the taxi line.

"Bah." She frowned and stepped to block him. Not too forceful, but just forceful enough. She was good. "Bad drivers, every one of them. My grandson is here. He'll take you in his car. Only twenty *kuai*."

"You don't know where I'm staying."

"You stay in the city center?"

He didn't want to tell her exactly where, but he scanned the parking lot and saw a young man in a newer car watching them hopefully. He was about Ben's age and didn't look Chinese.

"I'm staying downtown," he said.

She nodded. "Twenty. It's very fair."

"And?"

"And nothing. He is a good driver. You will call him if you need a car again in Ürümqi."

Ben glanced at the boy again. He didn't know how long he'd be staying. Didn't know where he'd be going. A taxi would take him to the hotel and drop him off after he paid the meter, but someone his own age looking to make some extra money might be a good resource. Money he had. Familiarity with the city, he didn't.

He adjusted his backpack and scanned the area for pickpockets. Still no sign. The soldiers with automatic weapons by the door probably discouraged them. There would be easier pickings in the marketplace.

Ben asked, "Does your grandson speak Uyghur?"

"Of course. And Chinese. And a little English. He's very smart. He knows the city very well. You speak English?"

"Yes."

She nodded and herded him toward her grandson. "You practice then. You speak Chinese to him. He speaks English to you. Yes? Good."

Ben smiled and let her herd him. They passed the line of taxi drivers who yelled at the old woman. She ignored them and led him toward the parking lot, where the young man was waiting with a smile and an open car door.

"This is Akil. He is a student at the university. And a very good driver."

Akil held out his hand. "Very nice to meet you," he said in English.

"Nǐ hǎo ma?" Ben asked.

"I am well," Akil responded in Chinese as he took Ben's suitcase. "And you? Where can I take you today?"

The old woman had wandered away, no doubt to sell more

13

lighters or find more passengers for another "grandson" who was also the best guide in Ürümqi. He shouldn't be so cynical, but life had taught him that very little was ever as it appeared. Akil seemed to know a couple languages, his car was well-kept, and he didn't have the darting eyes of a con. Probably, he was just a student looking for some extra cash. Ben was more than happy to give it to him, rather than one of the hard-eyed taxi drivers.

They settled in the car and Akil turned up the air-conditioning, though the weather wasn't unpleasant. A little warm, but dry and breezy.

"You can take me to the Sheraton," he said.

"Ah, a very nice hotel." Admiration was in Akil's eyes. "And near the museum. Do you prefer to speak English or Chinese?"

Ben smiled. "What's your best language?"

"Uyghur," he said with a laugh. "But then Mandarin. School, of course."

"Are you in university?"

"Yes, in Qinghai. I am studying agriculture."

"Really?"

"Yes," Akil continued in flawless Mandarin. "It is very important. My family has orchards, but we want to be more modern. To make our farm more successful."

"Cool," Ben muttered.

"Cool," Akil copied him in English, grinning.

Ben smiled back. "How old are you?"

"Twenty-two. And you?"

"Twenty-one."

"What is your name?"

"Ben."

"Welcome to Ürümqi, Ben."

"Thanks."

"Why do you come to Xinjiang?" Akil asked in English.

"I'm meeting a friend here."

"Is he Uyghur?"

"She's... sort of Chinese. But she lives in Los Angeles now."

"Los Angeles!" Akil exclaimed. "Hollywood. This is where you live?"

"Yes, but I'm not in Hollywood. I'm just a student, like you."

"What do you study?"

"Political science and Mandarin. I thought it would be good to come to China to practice speaking Mandarin."

Akil started to laugh. "You came to Xinjiang to practice Chinese? Why didn't you go to Beijing? Or Xi'an?"

"I'm starting to think my friend had ulterior motives."

"I think you are right."

Fifteen minutes later, Akil dropped him off at the front of the hotel, ignoring the dismissive look of the doorman in attendance. Ben caught it, but the man was nothing but politeness for Ben, whom he greeted in English.

"Checking in?"

"Yes, thank you." The doorman whisked his bag away as Ben turned to pay Akil.

"Here." The young man handed him a card. "If you need a driver—"

"I'll call you," Ben said. "For sure. Any suggestions until I meet my friend tonight?"

"The museum is good," Akil nodded down the street. He'd pointed it out on the way to the hotel. "You can walk there. There are signs in English, which isn't common in Chinese museums. It will give you a good idea of the area's history. And there are the mummies."

"Mummies?"

Akil smiled. "Yes. They're famous. The Loulan girl. You should see them. And if you need a driver or an interpreter—"

"I got it." Ben held up the card. "I'll call you."

Akil held out a hand. "Stay cool," he said in English.

"You too."

He walked into the dry air conditioning of the hotel lobby and glanced around.

Clearly new, the Sheraton in Ürümqi was probably built to appeal to business travelers. Akil had told him that Xinjiang was one of China's fastest growing provinces, even though it was the most remote. The farthest west province of the People's Republic bordered Mongolia, Russia, and Kazakhstan, and more than one guidebook said it had more in common with that Central Asian country than it did with the rest of Han-dominated China.

Ben knew it was a diverse region, dotted by some of the most ancient cities on the Asian trade routes.

He just had no idea why Tenzin wanted him there.

2

"Hello," Ben said to the girl at the front desk. Despite her suit, she looked younger than he did, but her manner was completely professional. He gave her his most charming smile, hoping for a reaction. After all, it was summer break. He was on vacation. A guy could use a little fun.

"Can I help you, Mr. Vecchio?"

The desk clerk answered him in English, but he continued in Chinese.

"How are you today?" Something. Anything?

"Very well, sir. How can I help you?"

And nothing. She was the picture of efficient professionalism. Oh well.

Ben had settled into the hotel and debated whether or not to go out in the city or sleep. Being raised by the nocturnal had given him the ability to sleep when he needed to, but he was still affected by jet lag. He had decided to stay up, hopefully stave off the worst of the exhaustion, then sleep in the afternoon. He didn't know when Tenzin would show up, or if the vampire would be forthcoming about her real motivations. But he knew she wouldn't show up until the sun was down. He had to be on his toes so he decided to sleep later.

"I have a few hours before I need to meet a friend," he told the clerk. "What would you recommend that is nearby?"

She pulled out a small map in English. "The Regional Museum is very good. There is an excellent exhibition on the Silk Road, which is of course very important the history of Xinjiang. There is also shopping next door." She held a polite hand toward the attached luxury mall, which held zero interest to him. He could get all the same things on Rodeo Drive.

"You're the second person to recommend the museum." Another smile that affected her not at all. "I think I'll go there."

"If you take your passport with you, they will likely waive the entrance fee. Since you are a visitor."

"Thank you."

"Of course."

Waive the entrance fee? That was a new one. So far, he'd had to pay to get... well, just about anywhere. Even the *hutong*, the historic neighborhoods in Beijing, asked visitors who were walking through to pay an entrance fee. Was it legal? Who knew? But everyone did it, so Ben didn't argue.

Walking through the luxury mall with its glowing six foot ads and discreet security, Ben started to feel conspicuous again. He saw a few tourists surreptitiously snap pictures on their phones, which made him grit his teeth. It was habit to avoid the camera by now. Giovanni and Beatrice kept a few pictures in the house, but when you were immortal, it was best to not keep around photographic evidence of how much you didn't age. The human brain could convince itself of almost anything—like when the neighbor who had lived quietly in the house down the street didn't look a year older than he had ten years ago—but photographic evidence was harder to dismiss.

He reached the end of the mall and left through the soaring

glass doors. New construction surrounded him. He slipped on his sunglasses and scanned the street to find the best place to cross, following the old women who were selling baskets of plums.

According to Akil, Ürümqi was divided between the Han neighborhoods and the Uyghur ones. The museum was in a mostly Han area, but he still saw an intriguing mix of faces. Xinjiang was becoming more and more interesting the longer he visited.

He passed through security at the museum, then walked up the steps and into the cool interior. A glowing map of Xinjiang spread in front of him, and curious groups of Chinese tourists gathered around it, taking turns pressing the lights that high-lighted the various routes of the Silk Road. He turned left to follow the crowd.

Ben took his time in the exhibits. He had at least three hours to kill, and the museum looked like it would eat up more than enough. As he toured the hall highlighting the various ethnic groups that made up the province, he scanned the crowd. No one was following him. Other than a few curious glances, no one seemed to pay him any mind.

Nothing suspicious.

He heard a small group mention the mummies that Akil had spoken of, so he followed them.

Up the stairs and around the atrium, Ben headed toward another hall.

The minute he stepped inside, he could feel her.

Tenzin.

She was there. He didn't know how. Or why. But some sixth sense alerted him. It had always been that way with her.

"The Tarim mummies of Xinjiang—" A tour guide caught his attention as she stood before a glass case. "—are only some of the evidence that this province has been continually occupied for over four thousand years. DNA evidence suggests that the mixed populations of the Tarim Basin had origins in Asia, Europe, Mesopotamia, India, and many other regions. This evidence confirms ancient Chinese historians who reported tribes who appeared to be European passing through and even inhabiting these areas. There were reports of tall men and women, with blue and green eyes. Red and blond hair. Even full beards." The group laughed quietly. "As you can see, the population of Xinjiang continues to represent this diversity."

A shadow passed to his right, and Ben walked into another room.

Tenzin was a day-walker. While most vampires needed to sleep for most of the day, a few did not. Beatrice said it was because Tenzin was so old, but Ben knew other old vampires who needed to sleep. Tenzin wasn't like them. She was just as active during the day as humans were. She just couldn't go out in the sun. As long as she kept out of the light, she was fine.

Was it age or something else? He didn't really know. Beatrice had taken a lot of Tenzin's blood because her father and Tenzin had been mated, so Beatrice didn't sleep much either. It wasn't something his aunt liked and she often spent much of the day meditating in the dark while her mate slept.

Ben had never heard Tenzin complain about it.

He couldn't imagine never sleeping. He loved to sleep. Loved to dream. Missing that would make him a little crazy.

He walked quietly through the hall, trailing behind another tour group, stopping when they did, hanging on to the edge of the crowd, listening and trying to ignore the invisible eyes he could feel watching him. He wouldn't see Tenzin until she wanted to be seen.

Ben wandered to the next room, heading over to the first case he saw with a mummy inside. He leaned over, trying to see her features beyond the glare of the protective glass.

*Qiemo Female Mummy,'*the case read. *The mummy was exhumed from No. 2 tomb. Date: 800 BC. Height 160 cm. She belongs to a mixture of Europoid and Mongoloid traits.*

The mummy in the case was remarkably well-preserved, with a deep crimson robe that was intricately sewn. She had swirling tattoos along her face and four thick braids hung past her shoulders. 160 centimeters meant... He did a quick calculation and determined the mummy was over five feet. Taller than he would have expected.

800 BC.

Ben stared at the mummy, thinking of the vampire he could feel in the air around him, as if her ghost hovered over his shoulder.

What had this woman seen? What had her life been like? How old was she when she died? Had she had a happy life? Someone had taken care when they buried her. Her body was carefully positioned and her jaw wrapped with the same crimson thread her robe was made from. Maybe she was a beloved wife. A mother.

The woman in the glass case was almost three thousand years old. Had Tenzin been alive then? Probably. He didn't really know how old she was. No one talked about it. Then again, no one really knew, did they? Maybe not even Tenzin herself.

He caught a flash of reflection in the glass. A darting glance. A fanged smile. By the time he'd turned around, she was gone.

BEN MADE his way back to the hotel when the sun began tilting toward the horizon. There was a rush of cold air at the doorway to the mall, then the long lit walk past the store fronts. Cartier. Louis Vuitton. Hugo Boss. The juxtaposition of luxury and history was jarring to the senses. He ducked his head when he saw another phone camera pointed in his direction and kept it down until he'd entered the hotel and made his way to the elevators.

Quiet.

Ben took a deep breath and closed his eyes. The elevator sped to the fifteenth floor without stopping, the dinging doors more welcome than any familiar voice. A few more steps and he was in the generic surroundings of a Western chain hotel thousands of miles from home. Door locked. Chain set. Portable electronic alarm attached to the door.

Quiet.

Ben was used to quiet. He often came home to a house where no one was home or no one was awake. It was soothing.

He plugged his phone into his laptop and quickly downloaded the photos he'd taken at the museum, then erased them from the phone. On the off chance it was hacked, no thief would be able to track his movements by his photo history. Then he logged into the virtual private network he used when he was traveling, checked his email and the secure remote dropbox that Gio and Beatrice had set up, before he reset his passwords for the week and turned the computer off.

The security measures were automatic, a routine that had been drilled into Ben as soon as he learned how to work a keyboard. His aunt had more than a passing ability with computers, and she'd taught Ben if it *could* be hacked, it probably *would* be. But that was more of a human threat.

Vampires, on the whole, distrusted technology. Often, the most important messages or communications still made their way by personal courier. Couriers were as well trained as assassins and just as expensive. Immortals on the whole were paranoid about security, and often sired children or kept humans whose sole purpose was transporting information discreetly.

Beatrice's grandfather had a human constantly at his side, loyal to a fault and ready to transport any letter the old vampire might write. Ben knew at least one of Giovanni's regular correspondents who still used wax-sealed scrolls.

There was something to be said for old-school.

He checked his watch and decided to fit in another hour or two of sleep. Ben pulled off his shirt and, glancing toward the sunny window, cracked it open before he went to lay down. Within minutes, he was dreaming.

He woke when the bed shifted slightly.

Ben kept his eyes closed and took a deep breath.

Dust. Honey. Cardamom.

"Hey, Tenzin."

She scooted further over on the bed and he shifted to make room.

"No, really," he muttered, keeping his eyes shut. "Make yourself at home."

"I told you these beds would be comfortable."

"I wouldn't call this comfortable."

"Comfortable for China, then. You're so American."

"You're so intrusive."

"You left the window open."

"I'm on the fifteenth floor."

She just laughed.

"You realize you have boundary issues, right Tiny?"

"Boundary issues?" She bumped her shoulder into the space between his bare shoulders. "Are you being modest again?"

"Maybe."

"Funny boy. It's not like you haven't seen me naked."

He *had* seen her naked. It had been a defining moment of

his adolescence before Giovanni walked out to the pool and lectured Tenzin on modern standards of decency around seventeen-year-old boys. He'd held a grudge against his uncle for weeks.

Ben rubbed his eyes and rolled over. "Hi."

"Hello. How did you like the museum?"

She was wearing her hair in braids which were oddly reminiscent of the mummy he'd seen earlier. He decided not to tell her that. He liked her hair in braids. Tenzin's hair was past her shoulders and thicker than any woman's hair he'd ever seen. Like a black cloud flying behind her when she wore it loose. She often wore it in braids, a habit Giovanni said she'd picked up in Tibet. Sometimes, she tied the ends with brightly colored string that flashed and fluttered when she was in the air. He reached out and tugged on the end of one.

"I liked the museum. It was interesting. How did you get in there?"

"A guard let me in last night. There are some very comfortable yurts in one of the exhibits."

"He let you in? You mean you used *amnis* on the night guard so he would let you in."

"Same same."

"Not really."

Tenzin sat up and folded her legs on the bed as he scooted up to sit against the headboard. He reached for his t-shirt and tugged it on. Ben pulled up his legs and crossed his arms on his knees, settling his chin there as he yawned.

"How old are you?" he asked.

"Old enough to know better and still not care."

He smiled. "No, really."

She cocked her head. "The mummies?"

"Mm-hmm."

"Older. Older than the mummies there."

He mouthed, *Wow*.

"Ancient." She drifted into the air and did a slow roll. "I am an old, old woman."

He loved the way she flew. It wasn't like a bird. Tenzin moved through air as a fish did in water. Second nature. She looked out of place on the ground.

"All right, Bird Girl." He tugged on the end of the loose pants she wore. "Tell me what we're doing here?"

Her eyes flashed to his and she gave him a fanged grin. "What? You wanted to practice your Mandarin, didn't you?"

"Yes, so obviously we went to a place where half the population doesn't even speak it."

"So you can learn some Uyghur, too."

"Tenzin."

She flew up and hovered over him on the bed. "Don't be cross."

"I'm not. I just want to know what we're really doing here."

"I have an errand to run. And I thought you could keep me company."

"What kind of errand?"

She clammed up. Typical.

Ben sighed and leaned back against the headboard. "You know, I heard Xi'an is really nice. And the terra cotta army—"

"All the tourists go to see that. Don't be boring."

"They see it because it kicks ass, Tenzin."

She sneered. "It's packaged history."

"So is any museum. What are we doing here?"

"I just have a few things to take care of, then we can—"

"Tenzin."

"I'll let you know when you need to know."

"Listen," he growled as he leaned forward. "You needed *me* here, otherwise you wouldn't have suggested I come. So tell me now or I'm out of here."

She said nothing, hovering with her back against the far wall, a petulant expression on her face.

He shook his head, swung his legs over the side of the bed and walked to his suitcase. "Packing now. I'll see you back in LA."

"Benjamin—"

"Nope. Done now."

"Don't be like this."

"Like what?" He unplugged his laptop and slid it into the case. "Impatient with your pathological secrecy?"

"You're being immature."

"Nice try, playing that card." He pushed down the loose pants he'd been wearing to sleep and pulled on jeans. "But it stopped working a few years ago. This is not me being immature. This is me being sick of your shit."

"Ben—"

"Xinjiang isn't top on my dream destinations list, so if you don't want to tell me—"

"I need to move approximately twenty million dollars worth of gold and antiquities out of a cache in Kashgar before the old city is demolished."

Ben froze.

"And obviously, I need a human to help me. Since you had time before school started, I thought it would be fun."

She thought it would be *fun*? Of course she did.

He took a measured breath. "Twenty million?"

"Approximately."

"In gold?"

"And antiquities. Some porcelain. Jewelry." She floated down to the edge of the bed. "A few rugs, but those might be damaged."

"Yeah, that can happen with rugs."

She shrugged. "They're silk, so they might still be good. I'm mostly concerned with the gold."

"Twenty *million?*"

"Mostly in gold."

He nodded silently, then went to sit down next to her, rubbing a hand over his face. "When was the last time you moved this cache?"

Tenzin scrunched up her face. "Maybe... two or three hundred years ago? I was still killing vampires with Gio. Sometime then. We had a job in Samarkand, and I had some extra time."

"Of course you did." He cleared his throat. "Two or three hundred years? Are you sure it's still there?"

"There is a family who guards it. They don't know what it is, of course. They just guard it. Nima handled all of that. Of course, I don't know if anyone is paying the family anymore, so they might be gone..." Her eyes were distant for a moment until they snapped back to his. "I forgot about it until that news broadcast."

"You forgot about twenty million in gold?"

She shrugged.

"How many gold caches do you have?"

"You don't need to know that."

Ben took another deep breath and blew it out slowly. "And do you have a plan to get this gold out of the People's Republic of China, who might have a problem with you taking valuable cultural treasures—that are probably worth a lot of money—out of the country?"

She frowned. "But they're *my* treasures."

"I know that, but—"

"*Mine.* I'm the one who..." She considered her words. "...*acquired* them. I stored them. They're mine."

"I realize that, but the government might think differently."

27

"I have a plan."

Ben nodded. "That's good." *Twenty million dollars?* "Plans are good."

Especially when you're trying to move twenty million in gold.

Tenzin smiled. "I know a relatively trustworthy pirate who owes me a few favors."

"A *pirate*? Like, an actual... pirate?"

"Yes!" She seemed delighted. Of course she did. Because pirates were so delightful. "Well, I don't think he's a pirate anymore. Precisely. He's relatively—"

"Trustworthy. Yeah, I heard that part." Ben stood up and raked a hand through his hair. "Is the sun down? I need food."

"Oooh!" Tenzin clapped her hands. "Let's go get noodles. Xinjiang noodles are the best."

Ben grabbed his wallet and Tenzin's hand. "Good to know. We're walking out the lobby. Put your fangs away."

"Relax. Sometimes, Benjamin, you have no sense of adventure."

3

They walked through the market after the sun set, enjoying the smell of spices and cooking oil that filled the air. The night market in Ürümqi was a melange of faces, scents, and colors. Children ran about in brightly colored dresses and shirts. Stylish Uyghur women in intricately embroidered *hijab* surveyed wares with a critical eye. Caps and scarves. Bread and fruit. Everything was for sale in the market that night.

"You fit here," he said, looking around.

"I fit where? China?" Tenzin asked. "I can't imagine why."

"*Here* here. In Xinjiang."

It was true. He'd never been able to place Tenzin's appearance. She was Asian, for certain, but didn't have the typical features of the Han Chinese who dominated the Western view of China. Tibetan? Mongolian was probably closer. He didn't suppose those kind of labels existed in her human years.

Her complexion was pale, but much of that had to do with her vampiric nature. Her eyes were a cloudy grey, but that could have happened during her transformation however many thousand years before. There was no way of knowing what she'd looked like as a human, but she'd been turned in her late teens or early twenties. Of that, he was fairly sure.

And in Central Asia—with its fascinating mix of people—she did, somehow, fit.

Tenzin shook her head, lifting the corner of her mouth in a smile. A hint of her ever-present fangs peeked out. "I don't fit anywhere, Ben."

"Whatever, oh ancient and mysterious one." He nudged her shoulder to head down an alley that smelled particularly savory. "You fit with me."

She raised an eyebrow, and Ben quickly added, "And all the other nocturnal weirdos. You know what I mean."

"I know what you mean. This noodle shop is good." She pointed toward one where a man in a cap was standing outside, cooking skewers of what smelled like lamb over a narrow, rectangular grill. "They have good noodles."

"Is that rice?" There was a large metal cooking bowl, even bigger than a wok, sitting outside over a concrete oven.

"*Polo*," she said. "Kind of like a pilaf. Very common here. Rice, chicken, carrots. It's good. We can have some of both."

She spoke to the man in quiet Uyghur and he held out a hand, guiding them inside where a smiling woman motioned them to a table and seated them with menus that Tenzin ignored. She spoke a bit more with the woman who nodded and disappeared to the kitchen.

Tenzin said, "I ordered a few things. You can try some of everything that way. It's a good thing you like spicy food."

"But did you order *enough*?"

She shrugged. "For your appetite? They might have to kill another sheep."

It was quiet in the restaurant, with only a few tables occupied, mostly by small groups of men. One table was full of children some older women hovered over. They were watching a soccer game on a small television and eating noodles as they laughed and joked. Cousins maybe? Ben knew some of the minority groups in China could have more than one child. Whoever they were, they looked like family and added a cheerful atmosphere to the tiny restaurant.

The walls were decorated with nice artwork in bad frames, but the ceiling was embellished with painted wooden beams that Ben suspected were hand-carved. He and Tenzin drew a few looks, but most of the patrons seemed far more interested in their own conversations.

"This is nice," Ben said, sitting a moment before a pot of tea appeared at the table. It smelled like honey and saffron.

"The food will be good."

"How do you know?"

She smiled. "Because it smells good, silly."

Within minutes, the table was full of dishes. The golden rice dish he'd seen cooking outside, scented by cumin and dotted with raisins and carrots. Noodles topped with lamb and peppers. Small sticks of meat charred from the fire.

"How much of this are you going to want?" Ben asked, his mouth watering.

She smiled. "Not much. Go ahead."

Vampires never had large appetites, but they did eat. Beatrice said that even though blood was all they truly needed, immortals who didn't eat lived with a gnawing feeling in their bellies which was as uncomfortable for them as it was for humans. Since their digestion was slower, they never ate much. Small tastes of things here or there were all they needed.

Tenzin ate regularly, but that was partly because she liked to cook. Ben considered it fortunate that he liked to eat, because he was always available to dispose of the leftovers.

"Oh my gosh," he mumbled around the first bite of noodles.

"I told you."

"I'll never doubt you again."

She smiled. "Really?"

"No, of course I'll doubt you." He set down his chopsticks and picked up the spoon to try the rice. "You can barely operate in the modern world, Tenzin."

She rolled her eyes and took a small bite of a lamb skewer. Ben ignored the eye-roll because they both knew he was right. He may have been young, but he'd assisted Giovanni's butler, Caspar, for years. There were things that had to happen during daylight, and part of his job in the household was taking care of those things. Dealing with contractors and delivery personnel. Going to the market and sometimes paying bills. He'd been helping to run a household since he was twelve.

Tenzin, on the other hand, often had the lights shut off in her warehouse because she forgot to pay the bill. Sometimes, it was days before she noticed. Bookkeeping was not her forte.

"Will anyone understand us here if we speak in English?" he asked.

"Probably not, but switch to Spanish if you want to be careful."

He switched to Spanish.

"So, we're moving a cache of valuables."

"Yes. From Kashgar."

"Which is close to Ürümqi?"

"It's about fifteen hundred kilometers."

Ben almost spit out his tea. "What?"

"It'll take a day of driving or so to get there. The roads..." She waved a hand. "You know."

"No, I don't know." He pushed back the annoyance. This was Tenzin, after all. The whole concept of driving amused and baffled her. "Why did we meet in Ürümqi instead of Kashgar? I saw connecting flights at the airport."

"Because we have to pick up the truck here, of course."

He took a deep breath and closed his eyes, switching back to English and speaking quietly. "Okay, we're starting from the beginning."

Tenzin frowned. "I thought we were at the beginning."

"Tenzin!"

"Okay. So impatient."

She refilled both cups with tea and spooned a small portion of rice onto her plate.

"The person who is helping me has many shipping operations, including some that use trucks. He owes me a number of favors, so he has arranged a truck for us here in Ürümqi."

"Has he arranged permits, too?" He took some more noodles. "I can't imagine that you ship anything in China without a ton of permits."

She waved a hand. "He assures me that the papers are taken care of and will be with the truck, along with a manifesto."

"I think you mean manifest."

"Yes, that. There will be crates with the truck with vegetables in them. Some of them will be empty. We will use these to pack my things." She ate some of the rice and watched Ben finish off the noodles. He thought about ordering more, but then a second round of meat sticks came to the table.

Score.

Tenzin continued, but switched back to Spanish. "So Cheng has arranged all this here in Ürümqi. He does not have trucks in Kashgar, so we will have to drive it there."

"So, it's a day of driving through what are probably mountains and deserts where I've never driven before."

"Maybe two days," she mused. "I forget you have to sleep."

He rubbed a hand over his face. He needed something stronger than tea.

"Yeah, Tenzin, I have to sleep. So when you say a day of driving, do you actually mean twenty-four hours?"

33

She frowned. "I think that's what it will be. I'll fly, of course, so—"

"Oh no. You're not flying."

She looked up from her plate. "Of course I am."

"I don't think so. If I'm driving a truck to get *your* stuff, then you're riding with me."

"I do not ride in human vehicles," she said with a sneer.

"Then you can sit on the top of the damn cab, for all I care. But you're not flying your vampire butt to Kashgar in a couple hours while I drive a big-ass truck for two days on my own. If you think that's the deal, then I can catch a flight home tomorrow."

She scrunched up her face. "You are not nearly as cooperative as Nima."

"*Nima* had a staff of people at her beck and call, Tenzin." He was really trying to be patient, but sometimes, Tenzin just pissed him off. "Nima probably had contacts of her own, like Caspar does, who could arrange anything and everything for the right price. You have me. Who you dragged out here on false pretenses—"

"What is false?" she protested. "Your conversational Mandarin is appalling."

"Wh—*appalling?*" His mouth gaped. "It is not appalling!"

She said nothing, just sat back in her chair and pursed her lips in silent judgement.

"Fine," he said. "It's not great. I still think appalling is a little strong. But we're not in Beijing or Xi'an, Tenzin. You brought me here so you could have a human to help you get your stuff."

"So?"

He sat back. "So what's in it for me?"

Tenzin mirrored his posture, crossing her arms over her chest and narrowing her eyes. A slight smile came to her lips. Tenzin *loved* to bargain.

"I'll pay you," she said.

"Not interested. I have plenty of money." It was true. The trust fund Giovanni and Beatrice had set up grew every year, and he'd been investing his own money since he was seventeen.

Her eyes lit up. "You don't want money?"

"Nope."

And he had her. A bargain for something other than money was irresistible.

"What do you want then?" she mused. "What does my Benjamin want?"

He said nothing and let her speculate. Ben also ignored her use of the possessive pronoun, because that wasn't somewhere he needed to go just then.

She leaned forward and sipped the honey-scented tea. "Gold."

"The first thing you're going to agree to is driving with me. If I'm in that truck, then you are, too."

Tenzin cocked her head. "This is part of the price?"

He nodded.

"Very well." She kept watching him. "You don't want gold."

Ben shrugged.

"You want..." Then her eyes smiled. "You want something shiny, don't you, Benjamin?"

She did know him, after all.

Ben had lived much of his life with nothing to carry but the clothes on his back and whatever he could fit in his pockets. A psychologist would probably have a field day with his acquisitive nature, but he knew—even before he met Giovanni—he liked nice things. More than once, he'd escaped his parents and spent all or most of the day wandering through the Metropolitan Museum of Art. It was one of the few places in the city he could get into for free. Plus, it was full of beautiful things.

35

Then, he'd met Giovanni Vecchio. And Benjamin would be the first to admit that part of the allure the vampire had was the elegant brownstone he owned in Manhattan. Filled with art, antiques, and books, it was a thief's dream.

And when Giovanni told his new charge he could teach him how to get all those pretty things without the police dodging his steps, Ben listened. And he learned. He already had the skills his mother taught him, plus a hefty sense of self-preservation gleaned from dodging his father. Learning for Ben came easily. But while his Uncle Giovanni's truest love in the world—other than his mate—was books, Benjamin Vecchio's was art.

Paintings. Sculptures. Jewelry of all kinds. The older, the better. And if it had a story attached? Even more irresistible.

So yes, Ben wanted something shiny.

"How much art is there?" he asked.

"Not a lot," she admitted. "But there is jewelry."

"I want my pick. One piece."

"*My* pick. Don't you trust me?"

He grinned. "Not with the good stuff. You're as big a magpie as me. You're talking about two days of driving up to Kashgar. Packing your gold. Then driving all the way to... Where are we shipping this stuff to L.A.?"

"Shanghai. Cheng's boats are in Shanghai."

Ben took a deep breath. He was going to be spending a lot of time on the road. He only hoped the paperwork was as good as Tenzin was assuming. His insistence on her riding with the truck was also a practical consideration. If they ran into any trouble, Tenzin—with her flawless Mandarin and ability to influence human thought with *amnis*—would be far more able to handle the police. It would be up to him to make sure things didn't get unnecessarily violent.

In fact, that had been his stated assignment more times than he could count. He could even hear Giovanni's voice in the back of his mind.

"You'll be helping Tenzin on this, Benjamin. Please try to avoid unnecessary violence."

It might even be considered a motto at this point in his life.

Still, Ben shook his head. He knew he had to be firm. Tenzin would take any and every advantage otherwise. "Tiny, if I'm doing all this driving and packing and more driving, it's my pick. It won't be unreasonable. Don't you trust *me?*"

Tenzin sat back and sipped her tea again. She thought. Sipped some more. Ben was finished talking. He had his pick of a centuries-old treasure cache on the ancient Silk Road on the line. He picked up a skewer of lamb and savored the taste, licking the corner of his mouth when the juices dripped.

"You're right," he said. "Uyghur food is amazing."

"One thing," she conceded. "One piece. And don't piss me off."

He held in the triumphant smile. "Wouldn't dream of it."

"Yes, you would."

"Maybe I'd dream about pissing you off, but I wouldn't actually do it. Not intentionally anyway."

"One piece, Benjamin."

He held out his hand. "You're in the truck with me while we're transporting the goods, and I get one piece of *my* choosing from the cache."

"Agreed."

They shook and then he eyed her plate. "Are you going to finish that?"

"You're a bottomless pit, you know that, don't you?"

"Someone has to finish all this food."

He finished the rest of the food with relish and tried not to show his triumph at the bargain. Tenzin had centuries of treasure in that cache and probably no idea how valuable it was all worth. She didn't read auction catalogues or museum publications.

Neither did most of Ben's friends, but then again, he'd always had unusual interests. He was fine with it.

His best guess was, if Tenzin was valuing the cache at twenty million, it was probably closer to twenty-five or thirty, depending on the condition of the silk. It didn't matter, really. Ben had no interest in selling anything. Whatever piece he chose would be for his own collection.

"You know," she said as she watched him finish the food. "You're the one who fits in here."

He looked up. "Me?"

"You have Persian eyes, Benjamin."

He shook his head. "My mom was Lebanese, not Persian."

Tenzin shrugged. "What does blood know about borders? Persian eyes. You should be happy. They're very beautiful."

"Thanks."

"You're welcome."

Tenzin looked around the restaurant, but no one was staring at them anymore. She leaned back and watched Ben finish his tea. He got out his wallet to pay the bill, wondering if Tenzin was even carrying any modern currency.

Probably not.

Then again, the vampire was going to hand over a priceless piece of jewelry or artwork of Ben's choosing in exchange for his help driving a truck and packing. It may have been more time then he'd planned on spending in China, but how dangerous could it be? All in all, he was happy with the deal.

Dinner could be his treat.

4

It was close to two in the morning—middle of the night for humans, but the heart of the working day for vampires—when they met Cheng's man in Ürümqi. Ben hung back, watching Tenzin from a distance as she talked with the vampire whose eyes kept flicking from Tenzin's slightly hovering form to Ben as he leaned in a small doorway. Ben wore the dark shirt and jeans he'd worn to dinner and carried nothing on him that the vampire would easily detect.

The small knives in his waist had been acquired in the market from a shop above a metalworker who sold copper tea pots on the ground floor. He'd quickly ushered Tenzin upstairs to show her the far more illegal offerings he sold to discreet customers. The revolver on Ben's ankle wasn't fancy, but it was serviceable. As for the more obvious firepower they'd bought, that had been stored back at the hotel. After they left the warehouse where they were meeting Cheng's man, they would stop by the hotel, check out, and get on the road as soon as possible.

According to his phone, driving to Kashgar would take over twenty-three hours, so he was expecting to be on the road for at least two days. Tenzin assured him that the highway was clear, if winding, and they would have no problems traversing it.

Ben knew Tenzin didn't know jack shit about roads, so he wasn't taking anything for granted. Still, she'd also told him that much of the fresh produce in China was grown in the Kashgar region, which made the likelihood of passable roads more probable. From what he could tell, the major highways in China were as good as those in the US. Massive amounts of commodities traveled thousands of kilometers every day by truck. One small vegetable delivery truck would hardly garner much notice.

The truck Cheng had given them told Ben that the vampire who'd loaned it was either a very good smuggler or a very real businessman. Possibly both. More of a delivery truck than a semi-rig, it was small enough that Ben would be able to drive it, big enough to hide the crates that Tenzin said they'd need, and just banged up enough to look like every other truck on the road. No fancy logos decorated the outside, but a very official set of characters and numbers were visible on the back.

He saw Tenzin frowning at the papers the vampire handed her. Would she know what to look for? He'd called Caspar earlier to double-check the research he'd done online. He knew there should be a forged commercial license for him, along with several different permits for each province they'd have to pass through. The paperwork made Ben nervous. There was so much and Tenzin, for all her expertise, was complete and total crap at understanding paperwork. Ignoring her earlier instructions, he walked over.

He spoke in Latin this time. "What is it?"

He held out his hand for the papers, and with an amused look, she handed them to him. They were all in Mandarin.

Of course they were. Shit.

Speaking Chinese was one thing. Reading and writing was

completely different. And Ben's reading definitely qualified as "appalling."

Tenzin barely glanced at him, but continued talking with the other vampire, who held out an envelope. It looked like linen paper sealed in intricate fashion, a distinctive stamp pressed into rich red wax on both sides with a small jade bead making up the center of the stamp. Tenzin glanced at it, then put it in her pocket.

Cheng's man fired off rapid Mandarin that Ben had a hard time following. He thought the vampire was offering to hire them a driver—for a small extra fee, of course—but Tenzin immediately held up a hand.

"No, no, no," she said, more slowly. "I prefer my own driver."

"You don't trust Cheng?" There was a gleam in the vampire's eye. "I'm sure he would prefer his own driver for the truck. A gesture of consideration, of course."

Tenzin's mouth curled up in the corners, her eyes warmed, and Ben had to keep his mouth from dropping open.

It was the most unabashedly seductive smile he'd ever seen on her face.

"Oh, Cheng knows *exactly* how much I trust him. And so do you, Kesan."

Ben recognized the tone of her voice, he'd just never heard it from *her*.

But that smile was unmistakable, and now Ben wondered just who Cheng was to Tenzin.

He didn't think of that part of her life. Or the lack of it. He'd known she'd been mated to Beatrice's father, but it had been a political marriage. Wasn't it? He'd never seen her with a lover. Never seen her even show any interest in a man. Or a woman. Not with that kind of smile on her face.

Her body language still telling a story he wasn't sure he

wanted to hear, Tenzin said, "Tell Cheng not to worry. If we have problems, he can be sure I will have my human get in touch with Jonathan."

His heartbeat had picked up, and he saw Tenzin's head angle toward him. She'd heard it, which meant the other vampire had, too.

Ben cursed himself silently. Any unexpected change in his pulse was something he'd been trained to control since he was a boy. Vampires may seem like genteel creatures, but at the heart, his aunt and uncle had never let him forget they were predators.

And predators chased prey.

"Do not become prey, Benjamin. Because if you do, you will be chased. And you will be caught."

His heartbeat was marking him as prey, and there was no way of explaining his unconscious reaction. Because it wasn't from fear. Fear was something he'd trained away for many years. It was from something far more complicated.

Tenzin's eyes met his for a moment, but he couldn't read their expression. It was dark and fleeting. Then her smile curved again, but it was false. Something inside him screamed and beat at the facade. Tenzin stepped closer and placed a hand on his cheek, rubbing her thumb under his lower lip absently. His pulse spiked again.

"Go wait for me in the truck," she said in soft English. "We'll only be a minute."

He pulled away from her and walked to the delivery truck, not understanding exactly what had happened. He climbed into the driver's seat and slid it back, surprised the Cheng's vampire had even fit in the truck to drive. Then he sat back and stared at the dashboard while his thoughts raced.

Tenzin and Cheng? Who was Jonathan?

Why the hell had she smiled at him like that, and why did the falseness of it grate against his nerves?

Tenzin and *Cheng?*

"He owes me a number of favors..."

Now Ben was wondering what kind of favors they traded.

He shook his head. It didn't matter. It was none of his business. But he couldn't forget her smile.

IT WAS MORE LIKE AN HOUR, and not the minute she promised, before Cheng's associate opened the truck door for Tenzin. She didn't hesitate as he'd seen her do with vehicles in the past. She lifted herself into the cab and settled on the passenger seat.

"I will see you in Shanghai, Kesan."

"Are you sure I cannot send my driver with you?"

"Quite sure."

"Safe travels. We will see you in the city."

Then the door was closed and Ben didn't have time to wonder at her ease getting into the truck. He started the engine and pulled away, pretending to be the professional he was supposed to be. Pretending not to notice the stiff set of her shoulders beside him.

They made it all of five blocks before she said, "Pull over."

He pulled over.

"What the hell was that?"

Now *that* tone was familiar.

He put the truck in park and sat back, but didn't turn to her.

"Explain yourself, Benjamin."

He shrugged.

"I had specific instructions before we left the hotel. Stay back. You're a driver. Not important. Don't make yourself visible."

"I know."

"But you just couldn't help yourself, could you?"

He said nothing. She was right. Even though it grated at the adolescent pride he knew was a weakness, he should have followed her instructions and made himself as inconspicuous as possible.

"Now you are visible. A person, not just a human who belongs to me. Kesan knows you are not only a driver. You are a driver who speaks Latin. Which he might speak, by the way, as Cheng's first is a former English clergyman. He also knows you speak Mandarin, because of the way you reacted to what I said about Cheng. What were you *thinking?*"

He hadn't been thinking. Clearly.

"I don't know."

"You don't? Because your heartbeat told Kesan that you were either frightened, angry, or reacting to something else. Frightened and angry are the worse options, so now, he thinks I've brought my young lover to China into the territory of his master, who has never been known to share well with others."

"And what, exactly, would he be sharing?" Ben muttered.

She was on him in a heartbeat. Clutching his chin to force his face to her as she bared her fangs.

"Your presumption irritates me. Do not forget who I am, Benjamin Vecchio."

Ben stared at her, unblinking, and his pulse didn't trip. It had been a long time since he'd seen her this angry. He took a deep breath and opened his mouth, but she cut him off before he could speak, jerking his chin to the side as she sat back in her own seat. He could still feel the edges of her nails in his neck.

"I don't want to hear your explanation. I expected better from you. You're too smart to act this stupid, Ben. Don't let it happen again. For now, we play things as they stand."

"And how do they stand?" he asked, putting the truck back into gear.

"Cheng will dismiss you. He pays little attention to any humans. That is what Jonathan is for."

"Jealous former boyfriend, huh?" He tried to control the flush of anger he could feel on his cheeks, but knew she probably scented his blood rising.

"Boyfriend is a ridiculous human term for the three hundred year old water vampire who controls the Shanghai Group. And what Cheng is to me is none of your business. Drive."

HE DIDN'T SAY another word until they got back to the hotel. Then, it was terse questions and quick answers. Weapons were packed. Supplies were stowed. He checked out, even though they only had a few hours of driving before dawn. It would be enough to start out of the city; Ben only hoped they could find daylight shelter along the road.

An hour after they'd left the lights of Ürümqi behind, he asked her, "What are you going to do during the day?"

"I think the safest route is to stay in the back of the truck. Find a petrol station or a way station where you can rest. If you sleep in the front, no one will look in the back. I won't sleep anyway, so as long as I stay out of the light, I'll be fine."

"Is there a vent back there?"

"I'll be fine, Ben."

He didn't like the idea of her being trapped in the back of the truck, but then, he pitied anyone who tried to break in. Tenzin was still dangerous, even at noon. The truck came equipped with curtains for the front windows, so he'd be able to sleep on the bench in relative privacy. It was probably a better plan than trying to find a hotel or some other lodging on the road.

"Fine," he said. "I'll look for a rest stop once it starts to get light. I'm getting pretty tired."

He'd had a total of six hours of sleep in the past twenty four hours. Not the worst he'd ever clocked, but not ideal, especially when he was navigating foreign roads in a truck he'd never driven before. One hundred fifty kilometers out of Ürümqi, he was feeling it, and he could see the sky starting to lighten.

"Next place," Tenzin murmured. She'd been silent for most of the trip. Usually, when they were together, it was a nonstop back and forth of jokes and stories. Now...

"I'm sorry," he said, spotting a sign for what looked like a travel plaza. Two trucks in front of him were exiting the highway, so he followed them.

"About what?"

"About earlier. I was trying to help, but I know I messed things up."

Her voice was slightly warmer when she answered. "This can be a very dangerous place. I'm trying to protect you."

"I know."

"It would be easier if you were vampire."

"Not gonna happen," he whispered.

"You're too young to make that decision."

It was an old argument. One he'd been having off and on with her since he was seventeen. One he didn't feel like having at the moment, so he let it drop.

Ben pulled off the road and found a place to park among the other trucks at the road stop. His was not the only delivery truck on the lot, though most were the larger diesel trucks that filled the highway. Still, they were in Xinjiang, so the mix of faces was diverse enough to warrant no second looks when he went in to use the bathroom and grab a bowl of noodles to fill his stomach. There were truckers there, but also many other travelers. Even a

Westerner with a small group of Han Chinese, who looked like they were dressed for business.

No one spared him a glance.

He made it back to the truck and handed Tenzin the tea he'd bought for her.

She was grinning. "Look what I found."

He took a long drink of water and climbed in the truck.

"What's up?"

"Cheng's people are quite clever. That is what is up."

She tugged the curtains closed and pulled away the back cushion on the passenger's side, revealing a hatch about the size of a large dog door.

"What is that?"

"I checked in the cargo area, but you can't see it from there. A false wall! It's been welded in place. You can't access it from the compartment, only from the driver's area."

"A smuggler's hatch? Nice."

She shrugged. "It's always good to have some places that remain invisible from prying eyes."

"Will the crates fit in there?"

She shook her head. "It's about the width of a twin bed, if not narrower. And only accessed by this door. You could fit something small, but it's made for hiding a person."

"Or persons," he said grimly, knowing that more than one vampire was involved in human trafficking.

Of course, a lot of humans were involved in that, too.

"Cheng quit that business many years ago. He does still move some people discreetly, but only those who want to be moved."

He didn't really want to hear about Cheng.

"It'll be a perfect resting place for you," he said, "as long as you don't mind crawling inside."

It was pretty small, but then, so was Tenzin. She grinned

and handed him her cup of tea, then slipped through with the practiced ease of a cat burglar.

"Comfortable in there?"

"It's cozy." She stuck her head through and he handed her the tea. "There is a fan. It's well ventilated. Completely light proof."

"Good." He knew she could take care of herself, but he still hadn't liked the idea of her in the more easily accessed back while he was sleeping. "Escape routes?"

She pulled back, and he heard her shuffling around. "One in the floor and... if I had to, I could punch out the welds on this wall. They're not solid."

"Of course they aren't," he muttered. "You do realize that this is Cheng's truck. He knows that compartment is there."

"I don't sleep, Benjamin." She stuck her head through the hatch. "I'm hardly vulnerable during the nighttime, and I'm not worried about humans during the day."

"No?"

"Cheng doesn't trust anyone who can be manipulated by *amnis*."

"Ah." *Please don't get chatty about Cheng.*

She disappeared back into her bolt-hole. Ben locked the truck doors and cracked the windows, thankful that the air in the mountains was cool and dry. Stuffing a duffel bag under his head, he stretched out as much as he could. His knees were bent, which he knew he'd pay for in the morning, but he didn't have many options.

"I may not trust Cheng," Tenzin continued in a muffled voice, "but he's still quite possessive. He might try to kill me, but he wouldn't let anyone else do it in his territory."

"Sounds like a lovely relationship." He kept his eyes closed and mentally begged her to shut up.

"Relationship is not a way I would describe it."

I don't want to know, he mouthed silently.

"It's been years since I've seen him."

"Goodnight, Tenzin."

"Goodnight." She reached through the hatch and squeezed his hand. The spark of *amnis* was unmistakable.

"Tenzin did you—"

"You need to rest." Her voice was muffled by the steel compartment and the fog of sleep that was quickly descending.

"Tiny, I..."

The world around him turned feather soft.

He heard her whisper, "I would have you rest easy, my Benjamin."

It was the last thing he heard before he fell into a deep and dreamless sleep.

5

Despite Ben's fears, the two day drive to Kashgar was uneventful. Save for the near-constant griping of his travel companion, Ben almost found it relaxing.

"You are a terrible driver," she muttered as he took another hairpin turn.

"I'm not. I'm actually a very good driver." He *was* a good driver. He'd known how to drive a car since he was ten and though Gio had never allowed Beatrice to see them, he'd driven his uncle around long before he had a proper license.

He didn't really enjoy freaking her out. But the upside of Tenzin being a curled ball in the seat across from him was that she wasn't letting her curiosity get the better of her. This was a newer truck and vampire *amnis* would short out the dashboard if she tried to mess with it.

"You're going to make the truck crash."

He laughed. "You're funny."

"No, I'm not. I'm..."

"You're what?" He chanced a glance over, only to see her sitting precariously in the seat, lifting herself in the air every time they went over a bump, clutching the small handle over the door. Her face was still and her teeth were clenched.

"You're scared," he said, shocked by the sudden realization. Tenzin wasn't scared of anything. Not really. She was often cautious, but scared?

"Do you realize how utterly defenseless you are in this vehicle? It is not a van, it is a giant trap."

"How many exits?" It was a game they often played. Tenzin asking him how many ways out of a room or random location. Ben quickly giving her all the available exits, with her usually adding one or two more.

Tenzin said nothing.

"Come on, Tiny. How many exits?"

"None!"

"Wrong. Kick out the front window. One. Break open the side doors. Two and Three. Moon roof." He rapped on the overhead hatch. "Four. In this small a room, four exits is more than enough."

Tenzin glanced speculatively at the moonroof. "It opens?"

He put a hand up and popped it up. It wasn't automatic, but the plastic joints gave easily, allowing a quick suck of air into the cab. He could see Tenzin relax almost immediately.

"Four," she said. "That is sufficient."

"More than sufficient. After all," he said, flicking his eyes toward the now-easy vampire, "you really only need one."

"I wouldn't leave you behind if we fell over a cliff," she said, neck craning to look over the edge of the road through the mountains.

"That's comforting."

"Unless it was you who drove us over the cliff. Then you'd deserve it."

"I'll keep that in mind."

51

~

ANOTHER CITY, another eerily quiet warehouse. Someday, Ben would write a book—probably a very short book—on how universal most cities were. Yes, they all had their quirks, but on the whole, he found them to be startlingly similar. Smells changed the most. This time, when they opened the door, the earthy smell of vegetables met their nose. Ben could see crates stacked on one wall of the warehouse Tenzin directed him toward. He'd pulled into the warehouse and barely stopped before Tenzin burst out of the vehicle, flying up to the rafters of the warehouse and perching there like a very large bird.

"Tenzin?"

"Just let me sit up here for a while."

"Take your time." He went to close the giant door of the warehouse. Light was sucked out of the room as the door rolled closed, but he could hear Tenzin fluttering in the rafters as she stretched her legs.

"You're going to have to find lodgings," she said. "There's not enough time to start tonight. Cheng's man said there is a motorbike in the warehouse somewhere."

He stood, looking up at her and frowning. "So you want me to just run out and find a hotel—"

"Not a hotel. Anyone local will be watching hotels." Her dark eyebrows furrowed together. "What do you call the place where the backpackers sleep?"

"A tent?"

"No, where they go when they're not camping."

"A hostel?"

"Yes." She smiled. "Use one of those. There are probably several, and they are less likely to be watched. Find one near the old city."

"But don't you—"

"I'll stay here," she said. "Plenty of room to fly and the windows have been blacked out."

"Are you sure?" He couldn't see a thing in the warehouse. There was a small light over the door, but once he'd rolled down the door, the space had been plunged into darkness. He had no idea how he was going to find this motorbike Cheng's man had mentioned if he couldn't even—

He tripped over something in the darkness, smashing his shin.

"Ow," he said through gritted teeth.

"Found the bike?"

"Yes." More like, the bike had found him. And it wasn't a bike. It was a scooter. "Tenzin, I don't like the idea of leaving you here."

She found a light near another door and flicked it on. It wasn't much, but it was enough to illuminate the warehouse with a grey light.

"Why not?" she asked. "There is plenty of room to kill anyone who comes after me and you need a bath." She flew down in front of him, her nose slightly wrinkled. "Really. A bath. At once."

He pushed a hand through her tangled mop of hair. "You're looking lovely, too, my delicate Himalayan flower."

Tenzin laughed, the full-bodied burst of sound he loved to hear.

"Okay," Ben said. "I'll go out and find something. I have my phone."

"No hotels."

"No hotels." It looked like there were a few hostels in the old part of the city. "I'll manage. The scooter is mine?"

"Yours. Try not to drive it off a cliff."

"Did I get us here in one piece?" He threw a backpack over his shoulder. It was packed with a change of clothes and a few other essentials. Good thing he traveled light, since his suitcase wasn't going to fit on the rickety old Vespa. "Where do you want to meet tomorrow night?"

"I'll find you," she said. "Get some sleep."

The thought of stretching out, even on a hard Chinese mattress, was appealing. He gave Tenzin a quick nod, then pushed the scooter out the door, into the familiar unfamiliarity of Kashgar at four in the morning. A quick look at the map on his phone, and he was off.

~

TENZIN WATCHED HIM GO, amused by Benjamin's ease on the bike. In the city. Everywhere.

He was an easy travel companion, one she didn't have to worry about taking care of himself. A chameleon who slid into any situation with ease, he was as comfortable in a back alley bar as he was in a five star restaurant. Giovanni had given him part of that, but much of it was simply Ben himself. And though the young man avoided troublesome situations with the caution of a hardened street child, he now had the body and skills of a warrior. Years of training had seen to that.

His reaction to Cheng had been... odd. She couldn't decide if it would be problematic yet, so she didn't spend much mental energy on it. Nevertheless, he had made himself notable, and Kesan would be sure to mention his presence to Jonathan, if not to Cheng himself. Tenzin didn't often travel with humans, so they would tuck the knowledge away, possibly for use at a later time.

Whether Ben drew more attention to himself beyond a passing notice would be something they would have to discuss. Cheng had a habit of considering Tenzin "his" when she was in his presence, and Ben needed to be able to ignore it. Had he been surprised by the idea of her having past lovers? That was amusing. She was five thousand years old. A practical vampire. Lovers could be an excellent way to pass time. She was choosy and discreet, but by no means did she ignore that part of her life anymore.

Tenzin had Cheng to thank for some of that. It was the reason he was allowed his presumption of claiming her. Cheng knew he was audacious, but he winked and smiled his thief's smile. Then she would laugh and allow him to steal her for a time.

Tenzin enjoyed his boldness, though even her amusement had limits. Their intimate relationship was mostly in the past, though Cheng had been more than open about his willingness to rekindle it if she ever desired. She'd never known whether his interest was political or personal. It was probably both, and she could hardly blame him. The canny immortal leader was well aware of her status at Penglai Island, and had more than once flaunted their relationship to tweak her sire. Cheng enjoyed rubbing his success and newly amassed power in the face of the Elders. They were everything old about China, and he was everything new. He reveled in their annoyance.

It was that energy and ambition that had attracted her in the first place. Cheng was so very alive. And when they had been together, Tenzin allowed herself to feel the same way. It was Cheng she'd fled to after Stephen had died. Cheng who had welcomed her black presence and asked no questions, no matter how many crowded his eyes.

Yes, her gratitude to the pirate extended rather far.

How long had it been since she'd taken a lover? Certainly not in the time she'd been in Los Angeles.

Perhaps Ben *had* been surprised.

No matter. He would have to conquer his own reactions, though the fiction she'd created for Kesan would do for now to explain any odd responses the young man continued to have. Ben being her human paramour was a useful lie, so they'd continue it while they were in China, even though the necessity of it annoyed her.

Tenzin wasn't ready for Benjamin to make himself notable yet.

That would come in time. Like Giovanni, he would have to make himself feared if he wanted to live in any kind of peace in their world. But though he was young, she had seen the flashes in his eyes. Seen the grim determination against an opponent. He would never be a man to seek out violence, but he did not shrink from it. He had killed his first man when he was only sixteen. Killed the human in defense of a friend. An honorable first kill. Tenzin held his hand when he grieved his loss of innocence.

He'd only shed tears once.

Benjamin Vecchio would be a formidable immortal. This ridiculous need to cling to his humanity annoyed her.

She spoke her will into the still night air. "He is young. We will change his mind."

BEN STRETCHED out on the bed, which he'd dragged to the window overlooking the street. He propped the blinds open and listened to the morning call to prayer as it echoed down the narrow street in the old city. Though part of the new reconstruction, the neighborhood still held the flavor of the mud houses he'd seen on the road into town. So much of the old city was being demolished to widen roads and create safer housing. He hoped the character of this unique place could remain, because he already loved it.

It smelled of dust and roasted mutton. Bread and sesame

hung in the early morning air. He closed his eyes against the grey light and took a deep breath. The tentative morning sounds started when the call to prayer died down.

As the city started to wake, he dozed.

He'd woken the young Chinese man who ran the hostel with a friend, begging a place to stay for a few days and offering enough yuan to make it worth his time. It was a hostel, but Ben had a private room and a bath, so he couldn't complain. It was basic, but comfortable. And the quiet courtyard outside his room was lined with low tables and rugs. A comfortable place to remain anonymous.

Plus, you could never complain about free wifi.

He closed his eyes and dropped off to sleep. When he woke, it was already dark, and Tenzin sat in the window, perched on the wide ledge. He wondered if she'd flown up to it and if anyone had seen her. She made a picture, sitting there, her tangled braids wild from the wind. Black tunic and leggings. She was darkness in vampire form, her face the pale moon against the black night of her hair.

Ben reached under his pillow and grabbed his phone, snapping a picture of her before she could object.

"Don't."

"Too late." He hid the phone under the sheet that covered him from the waist down. "Did you fly?" he asked, his voice rasping with sleep.

She shook her head. "Dropped from the roof. The roofs here are wonderful. Very easy to run across. If they don't fall in when you land on them."

"I'll keep that in mind."

"Just avoid the older ones," she said. "You were tired."

He stretched up his arms, then absently scratched the line of hair that ran down the center of his stomach. "Exhausted."

Tenzin cocked her head. "You have grown so tall. I forget

57

sometimes that you cannot curl up as I can. The truck must have been uncomfortable."

"It was fine. I'm not that tall."

"Far taller than me."

He was. But then, Tenzin was barely five foot.

"What's the plan?" He grabbed his shirt from the floor by the bed where he'd dropped it and held it to his nose before he grimaced. Nope. Wasn't going to get another day out of that one. The drizzle of a shower last night had cleaned his body, but his clothes were another matter. There were clothes lines in the courtyard, but he didn't know if he had time to do laundry.

"We can walk to the house from here. We'll have to sneak into the old town. Only residents are supposed to go in there."

"Is it that dangerous?"

She shrugged. "I don't know. We'll see. There's no question it will be demolished when the government finally gets to it, and the cache is buried beneath a house. It must be moved. There is no telling what the condition of anything will be."

He rubbed his eyes and started to think practically. "Transportation?"

"We won't be able to get a truck in, but we might be able to pay some locals to help us. Hand carts and the like."

Ben shook his head. "Nothing goes without one of us accompanying it. You saw the crates in back of the truck. What's your estimate?"

"To pack everything?" She mulled it over. "I think... ten. They can't be too heavy because we'll have to carry them."

"That's it?"

Tenzin grinned. "The most valuable things are often the smallest. Size is no guarantee of quality."

He left that one alone. She probably wouldn't get the joke anyway.

"Okay, so we could carry things out with a large cart. I'm guessing small, but heavy. How far to a main road?"

"Not far. A few blocks only. I'll find a driver and... persuade him to stay with the truck while we're loading everything up."

"Persuade" likely meant she'd brainwash one with *amnis*. He didn't have the inclination to argue. To accomplish this, they'd need all vampire tricks available.

"Okay, so tonight we'll—"

"Grab the crates from the warehouse."

"We crate up the gold," Ben said, "then haul it to the truck."

Tenzin nodded. "I'll stay with the truck through the day. You stay here and enjoy a human-sized bed as long as you can. We can leave tomorrow night."

"Fair enough." There was something he wasn't... Damn it, why did she always have to hit him with stuff when he was sleepy or distracted? She did that shit on purpose.

"It's settled." She leaned toward the street. "I'll give you a few minutes to—"

"Wait!" He rubbed his eyes, wracking his brain for the tail of the problem he'd detected. There was something...

"Anyone local will be watching hotels..."

"Tenzin, who's the VIC here?" It was his own shorthand for Vampire In Charge. Because there was *always* a vampire in charge. Some areas had quiet vamps, who looked the other way on pretty much anything. Other areas had micromanagers. But if there were people and resources, there was a VIC. And Ben had a feeling this far west, it wasn't Cheng.

"Tenzin?"

She pursed her lips.

"Tell me it's not someone who hates you."

"This is slightly embarrassing."

"Why?"

"Because I don't know who is in charge here."

"You don't?" That was surprising, considering her memory.

"In this area, it's almost constantly changing. Power struggles are a way of life."

"Why didn't you ask Kesan?"

She looked offended. "And let him know that I do not know who runs this area? Hardly."

"So, rather than look bad in front of someone you mildly trust, you're going into a city and taking out gold when you have no idea who the VIC is *at all*?"

She shrugged. "It's my gold."

"They may not see it that way, since it's been in their territory for over two hundred years, Tenzin."

"No matter. I hardly think we'll arouse any interest."

"Really? You're so full of shit."

She smiled.

Ben groaned. "You're itching for a fight, aren't you?"

"It's been a while."

He sat up and grabbed for his backpack, rifling through to find a clean shirt.

"Fine. Whatever. Don't get me killed and remember the golden rule of pissing VICs off."

"I have no idea what you're talking about."

He leaned forward and grabbed her chin between his fingers, forcing her to look at him. "You break it, you buy it. So unless you want to be the de facto immortal leader of a small city in Central Asia, don't kill anyone, Tenzin."

She pouted. "You really like spoiling a fight, don't you? And this is faulty reasoning. If they try to hurt us, I'm going to kill them. I don't care what happens afterward."

"Why do I even bother?" He went back to his backpack. Yeah, he was definitely going to have to do laundry. "Fine. Try not to kill anyone important."

"Of course."

"Happy now?"

"Always." She leaned over and rolled onto his bed, shoving him toward the edge. "Oh, this *is* comfortable. I'll just wait here while you get dressed."

"Boundary issues, Tenzin."

"What?"

He shook his head and walked to the tiny bathroom, hoping he wouldn't give himself a concussion trying to get dressed. "Nevermind."

6

It was inevitable that everything went to hell the second he thought they were clear.

Ben and Tenzin had made their way to one of the oldest crumbling neighborhoods of Kashgar around midnight, the moon full enough to give them some light, which was good because street lamps weren't something the city had invested in for this part of town. Most of the light came from open doors and a few windows. Many of the houses were already deserted. Mud brick walls lined the narrow streets as they turned and twisted further into the dark maze of square houses.

Eventually, they came to a crumbling wooden gate. Tenzin paused, putting her finger to her lips. She listened for a few minutes. Then, without turning to Ben, she leapt into the air and over the wall. He heard a few steps. A pause. More steps. He was reaching for the door handles when the gate suddenly swung open on squeaky hinges. Ben immediately pulled out the small can of spray lubricant he'd picked up that day to quiet the gate.

"Sorry," Tenzin said. "Needed to make sure we were alone. The family is gone."

"Gone?" His eyes swept the bare courtyard. Though the gate had been in bad shape, the courtyard was neat and relatively intact. Three houses opened onto it, all two story with carved wooden beams supporting the bricks. Numerous windows showed that, at one time, the houses had been showpieces. A covered cistern was in the center of the courtyard and brick planters lined the walls. But all the plants in them were dead. Old vines had fallen over and not even a bird or a rat lingered.

"I don't like this," Ben said.

"I don't know if they'd been paid since Nima died. It's possible they just moved on."

"You have got to get someone hired to take care of your paperwork, Tiny."

She shrugged.

Ben shook his head. "You think your cache is still here?"

"We'll see, won't we?"

Without another word, she walked over to the cistern and pulled open the grate.

"You stored it in a cistern? I thought you said—"

"There is a false wall. I borrowed an earth vampire to dig it so that the water would run to one side while keeping my things dry on the other. He did an excellent job. This area doesn't get enough rain to be a danger." She slipped inside, her narrow body disappearing beneath the earth. Ben tried not to shiver.

"You used an earth vampire to dig it?"

"Yes." Her voice echoed up from below.

"How did you know he wouldn't come back and steal from you?"

There was no sound for a few minutes, and then Ben heard a smashing. Then a crumbling, as if rocks were tumbling down. He wondered if Tenzin would answer his question or just let him wonder. Finally, her dusty face peeked through the hole, hovering just under the surface.

"He wasn't a very nice earth vampire."

"Oh."

She smiled. "It looks like everything is still here. The question is, do you want to start sorting or get the crates?"

"Is there a ladder?"

"Not down here."

He spun around and saw one leaning on the second floor of one of the houses, propped against the roof. Ben walked over and stood at the doorway of the empty house, pausing to listen for any traces of occupation. There was nothing, so he went inside.

Flicking on the flashlight he'd pocketed, he could see it was definitely empty. Dust and a few broken pieces of furniture were all that was left. He made his way up the stairs, a few bits of straw and mud falling as he climbed.

Maybe it was being raised in earthquake-prone California, but Ben shuddered at the thought of living there. The whole place felt like it was about to crumble. He found his way to the walkway that ran around the outside of the second story and found the ladder, carefully lowering into Tenzin's waiting hands in the courtyard below.

"You go get the crates," he whispered. "I'll start sorting."

She nodded and took off into the night, the dark flap of her black tunic sounding more like a night bird than a person. She kept to the shadows, hopping along the roofs of the houses until she was out of sight.

Ben climbed back down to the courtyard, relieved that the ladder seemed to hold his weight, then he lowered the thing into the cistern and took a deep breath.

"Please no rats," he whispered. "Or snakes."

Holy shit.

He'd watched movies. Seen some pretty amazing museum exhibits. But nothing really compared to holding a really large bar of pure gold in your hand.

Holy shit.

It was heavier than he'd expected. Really heavy. The small bars were nothing like the bullion he'd seen pictures of at Fort Knox. No, these were closer to the size of a deck of cards, with just a little more length. There was a symbol he couldn't read pressed into them and pieces had been sliced or chopped off here and there, so they were far from uniform.

Still, that much gold in one place... And this was only *one* of her caches.

The gold bars had been stored in small wooden boxes, crumbled by the inevitable passing of years. Silks, old tapestries, and carpets were piled on top of the boxes, but most of those were molded or moth-eaten. He removed them carefully, placing them in one corner of the small room half the size of his walk-in closet at home. There were a few pieces Tenzin might want to save. Other than that, there were two boxes of remarkably intact porcelain packed in moldy straw, one box that looked like it contained idols of different kinds, and another small box he'd saved for last.

"Oh yeah," he whispered, guessing the small chest was where Tenzin had placed the jewelry she'd mentioned. It was locked, so he took out the set of picks he always carried with him and eased the old latch open, touching the rusted joints with the oil he'd brought. "Come on..."

A click. A crack. And there it was. The lid swung up.

"Hello, beautiful."

There was a jumble of gold chains and loose stones in the

bottom of the box. He saw a ruby almost the size of his thumb. A twisted diadem of some kind. A gold and garnet crown. Earrings, most of them pressed and engraved gold. Chains and bracelets of every thickness and length were tangled in the bottom of the box.

And then there was the necklace.

It was a thick crescent of pure gold that would fit around a woman's neck with a delicate series of chains hanging in back. Tiny twisting depictions of animals with hunters following them in chariots. Flowers and mythical figures he thought were probably griffins. He tried to date it, but he couldn't. He'd have to look it up. It wasn't Egyptian or Greek.

He was going to have to do a lot more reading if he was going to treasure hunt with Tenzin.

"Scythian," came a whisper over his shoulder.

Ben spun to see Tenzin hovering over him with a grin. "You're going to have to work on that. Anyone could have snuck in and knocked you over the head while you were mooning over that necklace. Don't get gold-dumb."

"Sorry." He held the necklace up. "This one. This is the piece I want."

She cocked an eyebrow. "Just like that? You should ask me what the provenance is. Where I found it. Or stole it."

"I don't really care," he admitted. "I want it."

"As I said, it's Scythian. Third or fourth century. Closer to fourth, I think. I found it in Russia."

"Is it mine?"

She looked around the room. "As soon as we get these packed and out of here, yes. I'm assuming you want to keep it with the the rest of the treasure for now."

Tenzin held out her hand and waited.

With effort, Ben held out the necklace, which was already warm from his hands.

"Don't be greedy," she whispered. "It's been around for sixteen hundred years. It's not going to disappear."

He handed it over.

"You have very good taste, by the way," Tenzin said. "This is one of the best pieces in this cache. If I was trading, I'd ask for at least two of these gold bars in exchange."

"Why? It's not half as heavy as one of the bars."

"But the craftsmanship." She trailed her fingers over a line of flowers that decorated the top loop of the crescent. "Keep this one. It's a good piece. An auspicious start to your own collection. I took it in trade from a man I respected a great deal. I'll tell you the story someday." She put it back in the box, examining the open lock with a smile. "But not now. Let's get to work. You climb up and I'll hand you the pieces."

He walked to the ladder as Tenzin bent near the rugs and the silks.

"Have you ever lost things?" he asked.

"Lost? No." She picked up one silk carpet that was only ragged on one edge. "I always find things eventually. Had things stolen? Yes."

"Who stole from you?"

"Remember that earth vampire I mentioned?"

"Oh."

She looked up. "I left him in his element."

Realizing she must have killed the vampire and left his body to disintegrate down in the cistern, he cringed.

"Ew."

She shrugged and went back to sorting through the pile. "Dust to dust. One day, I will be air. Dissolve into nothing more than a drift on the breeze."

"No," he said, not wanting to think about a world without Tenzin. "Forget the breeze, Tiny. We all know you'd be a hurricane."

She laughed quietly, her eyes sparkling in the low glimmer of the flashlight he'd propped in the corner.

"I'll go up and start," Ben said. "It's going to be a long night."

IT WAS HOT DUSTY WORK, even if you were a vampire. Tenzin had a seemingly endless supply of energy, flying back and forth from the bottom to the mouth of the cistern, handing up a few rugs, porcelain bowls and vases, and brick after brick of gold. They worked silently for three hours until the majority of the cache was packed.

Ben distributed the gold evenly between ten crates so none would be too heavy to carry. He'd found a hand cart that afternoon, so while Tenzin sorted through the last of the silks and porcelain, he went to get it from the truck, glad he'd remembered to bring the chalk he used for caving. He marked the path through the old neighborhood with surreptitious white tags at waist level, which allowed him to walk through the maze of old houses and back to the truck with ease. He retrieved the handcart and started back to the courtyard where Tenzin was finishing up.

He drew a few curious glances from windows, but it was three in the morning and most of the old city was asleep. Very few lights illuminated the alleyways or houses. Ben felt utterly alone. Alone was good. When you were transporting a bunch of priceless treasure, company was not a desirable thing.

The city was quiet. So quiet that, when he turned the last corner, the sound of shuffling feet in the courtyard brought him up short. Tenzin didn't shuffle. Mostly, she floated.

Shit.

Ben didn't hear her, but he did hear strange male voices

speaking Uyghur. Someone was in the courtyard and he could hear them opening the crates he'd just nailed shut.

Bastards.

They laughed softly, then he heard one kick something metal. Then came the sound of wood breaking, and Ben knew they'd broken the ladder. More sound of metal on bricks, and he realized the heavy plate would be back over the cistern, trapping Tenzin under the earth.

Not good.

He peeked through the cracked gate and saw three vampires poking through the contents of the crates. One held up a vase as another dug through the straw.

"You're poking through her stuff and tried to trap her underground," he murmured. "You must really want to die."

THE MOMENT the grate fell over the opening of the cistern, the shot of instinctive panic streaked through Tenzin. She could feel the press of the narrow walls around her and, for just a second, the taste of earth was in her mouth.

Tenzin hated being underground.

She narrowed her eyes and eyed the lovely little treasure she'd just unearthed from the tangle of a crumbling tapestry.

It was a bone-handled *pesh-kabz*, a Persian blade she'd picked up in the eighteenth century from a trader on the Khyber Pass. Lovely. Still in excellent condition. And more than capable of taking care of the foolish vampires who'd tried to trap her.

Tenzin floated to the top of the cistern, peeking through the grate to see who was examining her gold.

Where was Ben? Hopefully, by the time he got back with the handcart, she'd have hidden all the bodies. He did get strangely upset when she had to kill people, even if they were vampires.

One of them was muttering and holding out a brick of gold with her mark on it. If they had any sense, they'd realize who it belonged to, drop it back in the crate, and run. If they did, she'd let them live. After all, she was done with this hiding place anyway.

The vampire showed the mark to the one who seems to be in charge. He cocked his head like a spaniel, shrugged, and grabbed the brick, slipping it into his pocket.

Obviously, they were idiots and she was going to have to kill them. Vampires that stupid just made the rest of their race look bad.

SHOULD HE GO IN? Wait outside? Ben was fairly sure Tenzin didn't need any help, and she might even get annoyed if he tried. It wasn't as if the metal grate was that heavy. Maybe the vampires didn't realize she could fly. While Ben debated how much carnage he wanted to witness, he saw the grate begin to move. While one vampire halted what he was doing to look at it, the others had disappeared from his sight.

Oh shit.

They ripped the door from its hinges and pulled Ben into the courtyard. He wasted no time, years of practice kicking in. It was all automatic reaction. As they tossed him into the air, he tucked and rolled, reaching down to the small sheaths strapped to his ankles. Pulling out his throwing knives as he landed, he immediately aimed at the nearest vampire, who was still coming forward, laughing at the silly human they'd caught.

The vampire's scream when the knife caught his eye shattered the moon-lit night. He pulled at the knife, covering his bleeding eye with one hand, while the other curled into a fist. The bloody immortal bared his fangs and charged him, but tripped over a crate as he clutched his face. Ben could see the grate sliding open from the corner of his eye. Like a shadow, Tenzin rose from the earth, grabbing the vampire nearest the cistern by the hair. She cut his throat before he could make a sound. Then, still holding his head as the blood poured down his front, she drew back the dagger and hacked at the vampire's spine. With two heavy thwacks, the body dropped.

The vampire with two eyes rushed to Ben, crouching over him, his fangs almost in Ben's neck before Ben was able to bring his knife up. He forced the blade under the vampire's ribs just as a flying head collided with his attacker's temple, blood and brain matter spattering the bricks as the vampire released Ben.

Ben spit something he didn't want to think about out of his mouth as he rolled to his back, bringing his legs up and punching them into the torso of the vampire still on top of him. The kick drove the dagger in deeper. It caught in the immortal's ribs, and Ben heard a soft crack.

The two vampires were still shouting. Then it was only one. Ben's head whipped around to see the vampire with the bloody eye in a heap on the bricks. This time, it took three thwacks to decapitate him.

Ben felt his stomach lurch.

Then it was done and only one was left. Tenzin walked over, her blood-drenched tunic flapping as she approached him.

"Are you injured?"

"No. Just... trying not to puke."

Tenzin grabbed the last vampire by the hair, batting off the square hat the man wore and bringing up the dagger she held. "Ben, this is a good lesson on why you do not let your blades become dull. Obviously, it creates greater mess when you have to use them and can be to your detriment in a fight."

Don't throw up. Don't throw up.

"Got it, Tenzin."

Ben pulled off his bloody shirt and wiped his face, but he wasn't sure if it cleaned anything or just spread the blood around.

He didn't throw up.

Tenzin flew up, dragging the vampire to the balcony on the second floor of the house. Ben sure as hell hoped no one was looking over the wall, especially since there'd been so much noise. She sat on the edge of the balcony, kicking her legs back and forth and dangling the bloody stranger in front of her.

"Who is your master?" she asked in her most reasonable tone. She was using Mandarin and he wasn't sure why. Tenzin spoke Uyghur. Was it for his benefit?

"Are you going to kill me?"

"Yes. But I will kill you at a later time if you tell me who your master is."

"Eh..."

Obviously, this wasn't what the vampire wanted to hear.

Tenzin explained, "I am very old. So it's quite possible I'll forget about you for decades. Though I will kill you eventually."

"My sire is Aqpasha."

"Well," she said with a snort, "he thinks a lot of himself, doesn't he?"

"What?"

"Nevermind. I am Tenzin. Have you heard my name, even if you obviously haven't seen my mark?"

The vampire nodded.

"Then you know you should never try to take what is mine. Benjamin, there is a brick in one of the men's pockets, grab it please."

"Since you said please..." Ben muttered, rolling his shoulders and trying to ignore the bruises on his back he could feel forming.

"Now, vampire, what is your name—never mind, it is not important and you'll probably lie to me so I can't find you again." She pulled him closer and snarled, "It won't work. I have your smell. So tell me, did Aqpasha send you or were you exploring?"

He muttered something in Uyghur and Ben tuned out the conversation. After a few more pointed questions, she dropped him. The bloody vampire fell in the courtyard below, eyeing Ben with bitter eyes as he pulled out the knife still lodged in his ribs. Ben raised one eyebrow at the vampire as he threw the knife at Ben's feet.

"Pick the knife up, clean it, and hand it to my human," Tenzin called. She was examining the bodies of the other vampires, kicking them to the walls as their blood filled the cracks between the cobblestones, slowly creeping toward the cistern. She picked up Ben's other knife that had dropped near the crates and tossed it to him.

Ben caught it with a wince, slicing his finger open on the edge of the blade. "Careful, Tenzin."

The remaining vampire lunged toward the scent of Ben's blood, but before he could reach him, Tenzin tossed one of the severed heads at the vampire's ankles, tripping him as he tumbled at Ben's feet. Then she flew over, leaned down, and whispered in the man's ear before she cut his throat.

"I suppose it's later."

7

"When are you going to start speaking to me again?" Tenzin asked, sitting uneasily across from Ben in the truck. It wasn't his anger making her uneasy. It was his driving. She was completely at ease with his anger.

Whatever.

"This is going to be a very long trip," she continued, "if you refuse to speak to me."

Ben said nothing. He was pissed. More than pissed. Actually angry. Because they'd killed three vampires who belonged to someone he assumed was important, they'd sped out of Kashgar as soon as the truck was loaded. They didn't go back to his hostel. They didn't see the Apak Hoja Mausoleum like he'd wanted to. They didn't get to visit the market or the central mosque. And all of his things, including his books, were left at the hostel. All he had on him was the bag with his computer, wallet, and passport. And his weapons.

Fucking Tenzin.

It wasn't the first time she'd pulled him into some shit she dreamed up or sought out. And while she'd saved his life, he was fairly convinced a little strong-arming and verbal intimidation of the VIC would have avoided the entire mess. But why find the vampire in charge and negotiate when you could just kill a bunch of people you didn't care about? And if your traveling companion had a little brain matter splattered across his face and had to knife someone in the gut, what was the big deal?

She settled into the seat across from him and Ben kept driving. By his calculation, they had a little over two hours of full night left. Then, Tenzin could crawl in the cubby hole for the rest of the trip, as far as he was concerned. He had half a mind to leave her in the middle of Xinjiang and fly home. Only the lure of the gold and garnet Scythian necklace carefully packed with the rest of her cache and surrounded by wilted vegetables made him stick with the truck.

Mercenary? Maybe. But then, he was traveling with a mercenary. Tenzin didn't lie about that. Why would she when she enjoyed it?

Ben glanced at her, but her eyes were closed and she was doing the meditating thing she did when she was tuning the world out.

The question of Tenzin's mental state was one Ben had thought long and hard over.

She was crazy. That had never been in question. Ben figured that anyone who'd lived as long as Tenzin and seen a fraction of what he imagined—and Ben had a vivid imagination and a good grasp of history—would be unbalanced. She had moments when he could swear she wasn't even in the room with him. Moments when she'd turn to him and a second of insanity was caught in her eyes. Cold. In that second, Ben knew she didn't know him. Didn't know anything except whatever inner rage forced her to keep living as long as she had.

Then she blinked and she was herself again.

Crazy? Yes. And funny. Sarcastic. Caring. Pragmatic. The

oddest combination of child and ancient he'd ever seen or ever would see.

Ben could accept it, because it was just... Tenzin. If he didn't want to deal with it, he wouldn't spend time with her.

He knew his anger would wane eventually, and she'd have him again. The next time she had some scheme or adventure, she'd lure him into it and he'd go, knowing it would all go to hell at some point and he'd deal.

Because it was Tenzin.

Next to him, she pulled her legs up onto the seat and wrapped her arms around them, settling her chin on her knees as she gazed at the moon. He could see the slight smile curve her lips from the corner of his eye.

"You like the rush," she whispered.

"Tenzin—"

"Someday, you'll stop lying to yourself about it. It doesn't make you a bad person, you know, to like the rush. It makes you feel alive. Reminds you that you are the one who survived."

Ben tried not to think about it. Because then he'd start questioning his own mental state.

"I want to live as peaceful a life as I can in this world," he said. "Picking fights is generally a bad idea for a mortal living with vampires."

"There's a solution to that."

"Not one that I'm interested in."

"Benjamin," she whispered. "Why do you value something that only holds you back?"

I don't want to be like you.

No, that wasn't it. Not exactly. But, he wasn't ready to talk about it. Might not ever be ready.

He took an exit and pulled over. They needed gas and he needed a promise.

He turned to her. "Tenzin."

"Benjamin." She smiled, obviously amused at the gravity in his face. But he was serious. Deadly serious.

"I want you to promise me something."

"That depends on the promise." Her eyes were calculating now.

"Promise me you'll never turn me."

Tenzin's grey eyes narrowed.

"Ben—"

"Even if I'm dying," he said, almost choking on the words. Ben lived a dangerous life and there were no guarantees. Dying young was a distinct possibility. "Even if I'm dying, Tenzin. Do not turn me. I want you to promise me."

She stared at him just long enough to reassure him she'd thought about it. "I promise I won't turn you."

That was way too easy.

Tenzin hopped out of the truck before he could say another word.

"We should get tea," she said. "Then get back on the road. It's a long way to Shanghai."

Night turned into day, then night again. Over and over as they drove across country. The papers Cheng had arranged for them worked. So much that, after the fourth night Tenzin didn't even stay in the truck bed. She'd only had to use *amnis* once, and that had been when the official had been more interested in the lithe young woman traveling in a cargo truck than in checking Ben's papers.

That time, it was Tenzin holding Ben back from violence.

They still drove mostly at night, though sometimes, Ben bullied Tenzin into a daytime drive so he could see some of the country. Five thousand miles. Almost seventy hours of driving, and that wasn't counting traffic. They crossed deserts and climbed mountains. Up and over, the highway often following the same route that caravans had traveled for hundreds or thousands of years. The vastness humbled him.

Jiuquan and Zhongwei, vast spaces and mountains of sand. Guyuan and Xi'an, the Han influence growing stronger. He made Tenzin stop in Xi'an for two days so he could take in a few of the sights, but he could have spent a week there. She buzzed past the ancient belltower at night, scaring the bats, and he jogged along the old city walls as the sun rose. Ben loved Xi'an, but he knew he'd have to come back. The weight of all the gold hidden in quickly rotting vegetables made touring the terra cotta warriors somewhat less alluring.

He'd stopped thinking in English and had switched to Mandarin somewhere in the past week. Tenzin spoke to him only in Mandarin, and his spoken language had reached the point where the officials who examined their papers didn't question Ben, they just assumed he was from Xinjiang, as his forged documents claimed.

"Do they really think I'm Chinese?" he'd asked Tenzin one night, just after they'd passed another weigh station where they'd been inspected.

"They think you're Uyghur. Most of the population here has never been to Xinjiang," she'd explained. "It's the perfect cover for you. They know your accent is different, but they assume it's because you're from so far west. You look Caucasian, but so do many of the people in Xinjiang."

"That's convenient."

She squirmed in the truck. "None of this is convenient. I could be in Shanghai in half the time if I was flying."

"Oh well," he said, slipping his phone into his pocket. "Then I'd be bored."

Tenzin gave him a dirty look, but at least she'd stopped complaining about his driving every second of every night.

"What was that beeping sound?"

"My voicemail."

"Did someone call you?"

He shrugged. "Another message from Cheng's guy. He wanted to know if the papers worked."

"If they didn't, I certainly wouldn't tell Kesan."

"You wouldn't?"

"Not without a knife to his throat."

"You might want to work on your communication techniques, Tiny."

Mountains and villages flew by, harsh terrain gradually giving over to soft green. As they drove, the air grew softer, too. Cold dry nights bled into warmer ones.

Nanyang and Xinyang, where the air became so humid, it wrapped around his throat every time he left the sanctuary of the truck.

But the green. The emerald mountains and hills of Henan province almost brought him to tears, they were so beautiful. There was nothing in his experience that equaled the sheer size and grandeur of the Chinese landscape. Vast was too small a word to capture it. And the people, the cities. Ben didn't think he'd ever been to a country more dynamic. It was ancient and new at the same time.

Somewhere past Nanyang, Tenzin said, "We're in Cheng's territory now."

"Oh?"

"Which means if we have a problem, we can't rely on my connection to Penglai to solve it."

Tenzin's sire was one of the Eight Immortal Elders who ruled Penglai Island near Beijing.

"Tell me about Cheng."

She frowned. "Our relationship—"

"Not that," he quickly interrupted her. "Just him. Is he really a threat to Penglai? I thought the Elders ruled all of China."

She shrugged. "Officially? Yes. But Cheng has been consolidating power for the last hundred years or so. He was a pirate and he now holds vast shipping interests. He's a close associate of Beatrice's grandfather, actually. But he has... what is the word?" She switched to English. "He's diversified now. The Elders consider him nothing more than a nuisance, so they leave him alone as long as he gives them the appearance of respect."

"Does he?"

"What?"

"Respect them?"

"He respects their power. But he has no interest in their traditions. I think he considers them the old China. And he is the new."

"That makes sense."

She grinned, and her fangs pressed against her lips. "Things are much more interesting in Shanghai then they are in Beijing."

"So does Cheng like you because of *you*, or because liking you pisses your sire off?"

"For me, of course." She propped her feet up on the dashboard. "I'm wonderful."

"And so humble."

"I never understood the purpose of humility. It seems too close to false modesty for me."

"And you have neither."

She gave him a guileless look. "I have very little of any kind of modesty. You know that."

Time to change the subject.

Ben stretched his arms up. "I'm so ready to be out of this truck."

"Only one more night," she said. "Then Shanghai."

She sounded excited, so why did he get the sense she wasn't looking forward to it?

Tenzin hated Shanghai. She hadn't minded it so much several hundred years ago, when it was just a port town, but it had grown so crowded. Skyscrapers towered over the city. The skyline was constantly changing. There was no quiet. No rest. It was build the new and damn the past. Part of its energy appealed to her. She couldn't deny that. But there were simply too many humans. A lush menu if she needed to eat often, but as old as she was, Tenzin needed little blood to survive. The blood of her own kind was far more nourishing to her anyway.

It didn't escape her notice—or the notice of the Elders—that many of the younger immortals in China flocked to Shanghai, eager to enjoy the more lax supervision of Cheng's patronage. He was going to have to be careful eventually. She didn't want to be the one to remind him. Then again, if Tenzin remembered correctly, pragmatism was Jonathan's job.

Tenzin was loath to bring Ben among Cheng's people when he'd already attracted Kesan's attention. The wily river vampire would have told Cheng about the human she'd brought with her. Told him Ben was more than a lackey.

Inconvenient.

But not insurmountable.

Cheng still owed her a number of favors. And their continued friendship was one of the things holding the Elders back from interfering with his business. Her father considered Cheng one of his daughter's odd friends, which was fine with

Tenzin. She had many odd friends. So Cheng could only push her so far. But if he started threatening Ben...

Tenzin realized that if it came down to alienating Cheng or Benjamin, she'd alienate Cheng first.

"Hmm."

Ben heard her and asked, "What?"

"Nothing."

He muttered something under his breath, but she couldn't be bothered to listen.

Ben was an amusing human, but why would she alienate Cheng for Ben's benefit?

Well, Cheng *was* immortal. If he became angry with her, she had plenty of time to make amends.

Ben was *not* immortal. And he belonged to Giovanni, who was hers.

Giovanni, who had also extracted a silly promise from her years ago about not turning Ben if he didn't wish it.

She'd promised them both. Silly boys. Didn't they know she lied when it suited her? That was the thing about having mostly immortal friends. You had lots of time to assuage their anger should it ever crop up. Ben, for instance, could barely remain angry with her for a week.

A week was nothing. Giovanni hadn't spoken to her for five years once. It had been mildly annoying, but she forgave him.

THE NEXT NIGHT, Ben took Tenzin's directions when they finally left the main highway and drove to an industrial area south of Shanghai. He could see the lights of the city in the distance, but Tenzin said the ship would leave from the commercial port and not the city that sat on the mouth of the Yangtze River. He was itching to see the city, but he was also eager to hand over control of the cache to someone who'd get it on a ship heading to the States.

"Turn right here," she said, looking at the directions Kesan had given her in Ürümqi. "And then left at the light."

"Are we meeting Cheng here?"

"No. We're dropping off his truck. His manager will see that it gets on the cargo ship once we do. I'll inspect it before the container is sealed. Do you still have the inventory?"

"Yep. And pictures." They'd done a proper inventory just outside of Jiuquan. He'd intended to do it sooner, but Tenzin didn't want to take any extra time when she didn't know who they might have pissed off in Xinjiang. Jiuquan was well within her sire's territory.

"Pictures?" She smiled. "How convenient. It will be much harder for him to lie to me then."

"Do you *expect* him to lie to you?"

"Of course."

"Maybe you need to reevaluate your friendships, Tiny."

"Why?"

Ben shook his head and just kept driving. Far be it from him to question the twisted morality of vampires.

After he made the left at the light, he was forced to stop. The turn had taken him into a bank of warehouses, and there was a human guard standing by a locked gate.

Tenzin popped her head out the window and barked, "It's Tenzin. Open the gate. Jonathan is expecting me."

The guard either recognized her face or her name, because the human reached back into the small booth and pressed something that made the gate swing out. Within minutes, they were driving through the warehouses.

"Where to?"

"I have no idea. Just keep driving. I think these are all Cheng's. Jonathan will find us."

He didn't look like a "Jonathan," but a wind vampire swooped down and hovered next to the truck, motioning Tenzin to follow him. He led them down a narrow alley until Ben could see a figure looming at the end of one row. Tall and lean, the vampire had the glowing pallor of a man who'd been light skinned in life and was almost translucent in immortality. He was definitely not Chinese.

"Is that Jonathan?"

She nodded.

Jonathan wore a black trench coat despite the heat, and a thin blue scarf around his neck.

"He always wears the scarf. Don't ask," Tenzin said.

"Got it."

Vampires were, almost to a fault, eccentric in some way or another. A scarf in tropical humidity was hardly the weirdest thing he'd ever seen.

Then she said, "Don't speak."

"Okay. Don't kill anyone."

She threw back her head and laughed. "I suppose we'll both have to just do our best."

Ben had to smile. And he was still smiling when he stopped the truck and climbed out. Jonathan raised a single eyebrow, the hollows of his cheeks shadowed in the glow of the headlights. He was handsome in that thin, European way a lot of vampires had. Tall and dark haired, the vampire's eyes were shockingly blue, even in the low light of the industrial complex. He glanced at Ben for only a second before he turned his eyes to Tenzin. Beyond the facade of indifference, Ben could see the wary intelligence in his eyes. This was no overconfident flunky.

"Tenzin," he said in a perfect British accent. "How lovely to see you again."

"You too." She jumped up and executed a few somersaults in the air, stretching herself after the cramped truck. Jonathan looked at Ben. Ben looked back, glanced at Tenzin flipping herself end over end in the air.

Ben shrugged. "She doesn't like vehicles."

"I imagine not. And you are?"

"Speechless until she kills someone."

"Dear Lord," Jonathan said. "You *must* be Vecchio's ward."

"I couldn't say."

Tenzin flew down and landed on his back, wrapping her arms around his neck from behind and her legs around his waist, careless as a kid asking for a piggyback ride.

"He's mine," Tenzin said. "Don't try to steal him."

Jonathan's expression didn't change a bit, but he said, "Tenzin, I've heard an odd rumor about some immortals going missing in Kashi."

"Kashi?"

Ben said, "It's the modern name for Kashgar, T."

"Oh! I have no idea what you're talking about."

"I do believe that Cheng would agree with you. Most vehemently. You have absolutely no idea what could have happened to them. Any rumors to the contrary are the vampire version of urban legends."

Ben said, "She probably has a few of those floating around already." He glanced over his shoulder. "No pun intended."

Tenzin rested her chin on Ben's shoulder. "Odd place, Xinjiang. All sorts of people pass through there. Highly uncivilized."

Jonathan asked, "Didn't you live there for several hundred years?"

"Of course I did. I love it. But unfortunate incidents happen."

Frustratingly polite irritation. That was how Ben would classify the expression on Jonathan's face at that moment. "I distinctly remember Cheng making a request for no 'unfortunate incidents' to occur during your travels in Xinjiang."

Ben said, "She's very bad at following orders."

She pinched his lips together. "So are you. It's done, Jonathan. Get over it. Especially because I have no idea what Cheng could be talking about."

"Right." Jonathan glanced back at the truck. "What a delectable scent, my dear. I'll have our people clean it out and pack the crates in the container. The ship leaves in two days and will be in Long Beach twelve days after that. I trust you have people on the other side who can take care of things there?"

"I've already talked to Ernesto."

"Excellent." Jonathan was all business. "Then we will have everything ready for you to inspect tomorrow evening. The container will be sealed in your presence and then loaded that night. Do you have your own inventory?"

"My human does."

Jonathan nodded. "Then I'll take you to Cheng as soon as the truck is secured."

"No."

A shiver crept down Ben's spine when Jonathan turned. "No?"

"I'm tired and I stink. I want safe lodging for me and my human tonight. I'll meet Cheng tomorrow. At sunset, if he wants. But surely he won't want to greet me when I still smell like rotting vegetables."

Jonathan didn't say anything. Clearly, this was not the plan. But Ben was guessing Tenzin outranked Jonathan *and* Cheng in whatever intricate political and social construct was in play here. They could hardly refuse her request without offending her.

"Of course," Jonathan finally said. "We will make arrangements—"

"I have my own accommodations arranged," Tenzin said, still perched on Ben's back. "I simply want to know that my human can move freely within the city during the day if he wishes."

"You may depend on it," Jonathan said smoothly. "Cheng's hospitality is renowned. I hope your human enjoys Shanghai. Shall I arrange a vehicle?"

"Please."

Within minutes, Ben was driving a car that Jonathan had procured for them. He didn't speak, just took the keys and sat in the driver's seat while Tenzin got in the back. She was far more comfortable in a vehicle now. Not a bad thing.

"I'll show you where to go," Tenzin said, as she settled into the plush bench of the black Mercedes sedan. "This is much nicer than the truck."

"Most cars are nicer than that truck."

"Hmm. Curious."

"Tiny, you realize this car—"

"Will be tracked somehow. Yes, I know. We're not going very far."

"You do remember I can't fly, right?"

She laughed. "We're in Shanghai, Benjamin. There are far better ways for you to travel."

8

Ben woke to the sound of lapping water under his window and the voices of old women in the courtyard, laughing as they hung the laundry. It was early. Way too early.

They'd arrived in the small water town late last night after dumping the car not far from a freshwater lake west of the city.

Tenzin and Ben had walked to a boatyard near the lake and "borrowed" a narrow wooden vessel reminiscent of a gondola that Tenzin piloted across the still water. Night birds called and the moon was high. As they navigated the dark canals and tributaries on the outskirts of Shanghai, Ben felt as if they were the only two beings on earth.

They approached the water town from the lake and turned down a wide canal, slipping under an arching bridge before they made their way into the village. Lights grew fainter and canals narrower. There were no cars. Few humans. It was deep in the night. No one gave them a passing glance.

They docked the boat near a bridge and climbed the stone steps. Ben heard fish jumping behind them. He said nothing, thoroughly exhausted by days of travel. He followed Tenzin as she led him down one street and across another bridge. On the other side, she stopped in front of a square set of doors and knocked softly. Blocky characters hung over the door. It was a boarding house or hotel of some kind, but when an old woman answered the door, Ben realized it was no ordinary hotel.

The old woman bowed deeply to Tenzin and stammered something in a language Ben didn't recognize. Tibetan, perhaps? Like Tenzin, her hair was worn in many braids. When she bowed, there was a slight tilt of her head to the left as she bared her neck. A subtle gesture Beatrice had explained to Ben before he left for Asia.

A tilted bow was a mark of respect and an acknowledgement of a vampire's immortal status. The human who bowed that way was acknowledging the vampire and also submitting to his or her bite, should the vampire need to drink. It was meant to be respectful and welcoming, but the tilted bow of the woman with silver-threaded braids made Ben shudder. She was old. She looked like someone's grandmother. Surely Tenzin wasn't going to bite her.

The old woman smiled up at him, and Ben realized he was being introduced. He stepped forward and held out his hand. The old woman took it and pulled him through the gate and into a courtyard lit with candles. There was a large pond in the middle with channels cutting through the cobblestones that led under the house. Ben realized the pond must connect with the network of canals that ran through the town. Gold fish darted in the shadows thrown by the candlelight.

The old woman showed Ben to a small room where a maid was already turning down the bed.

"You can stay here," Tenzin said. "Jinpa is a relative of Nima's and her house is under my sire's protection. We are completely safe, so you'll be able to rest."

He eyed the dark windows in his room. "And you?"

"There are light-safe rooms for me." She gave him a slight

smile. "Clean up and get some sleep. You look exhausted. There are many shops here. Some that cater to Westerners. We'll try to find some clothes for you tomorrow."

He'd been wearing the same set of clothes, alternating with a pair of too-short sweatpants and a few t-shirts he'd bought in Xi'an, for days on end. New clothes would be more than welcome.

"I'll see you tomorrow then."

"Have Jinpa show you to my chambers before sundown. We need to talk before we see Cheng."

"Right." He didn't want to think about that meeting. He was hoping to skip it altogether. Why on earth did he need to be there for Tenzin's meeting with her old boyfriend? He blinked as the exhaustion started to really hit.

"Sleep, Benjamin."

She didn't need to use *amnis*. As soon as he'd taken a quick shower, he slept, and he didn't wake for hours. He felt the sun come up, warm stripes cutting across his back. He heard the water lapping below the house and the old women laughing as they worked. He roused himself enough to close the blinds before he stumbled back to bed.

He slept. He dreamed. And in his dream, he flew over mountains like none he'd ever seen, soaring into a black-dipped night. He saw the moon shadows of white birch groves from the sky, swooping down to trail his fingers in the frigid stream that cut through them.

He heard her laughter behind him. Above him. At his back.

Her lips were on his. Cool. He tasted honey and tea. Her mouth was at his neck. Her body brushed his. Her mouth... He could feel her. Feel the pointed pressure. His heart raced in anticipation.

Her mouth was at his neck—

"Benjamin."

He woke with a gasp, Tenzin hovering over him as he lay tangled in the sheets. The heated dream caused his face to flush as he pushed her away.

"Dammit, Tenzin." He shoved up to sitting and gathered the bedclothes around his body. He'd been so exhausted the night before, he'd tumbled into bed naked. He didn't even own a pair of pajamas anymore, because he'd left everything at the hostel in Kashgar. "Get the fuck out. I didn't invite you in my room."

She frowned. "It's almost nightfall and you still hadn't come to me."

"Yeah, I was tired." And turned on. And he really didn't want her to see the evidence. Could he have no privacy? Just a little was too much to ask?

"Did you sleep all day?"

"Yes, I did." Dammit, but she was irritating sometimes. "Apparently I'm a weak human who hasn't had a good night's rest in weeks. I can't imagine why the hell I'd want to actually sleep when I finally got into a comfortable bed."

Tenzin's face screwed up in confusion. "If you slept so much, then why are you so cranky?"

"I'm not cranky!" He took a deep breath. "Boundaries, remember? I'm... naked. And still waking up. And you were just —" he held a hand inches in front of his face "—right there when I opened my eyes. You surprised me. I'd appreciate a little privacy. Will you leave, please?"

"We need to talk before we go."

"Yeah, I remember. Give me a few minutes."

"I'll need to bite you. And then find you some clothes, since you didn't go out today and yours are all wet. Jinpa washed them not realizing you didn't have any others."

"Yeah, that's fine. I'll hit the shops—wait. What?"

Did she just casually mention biting him like he was some kind of bowing servant?

She shook her head. "No, *I* have to go to the shops. You don't have any clothes, remember?"

"Yeah, that's not gonna happen."

"But you need clothes." She looked confused. And kind of adorable. She was going to drive him insane.

"You're not biting me, Tenzin. You can, however, buy me some clothes." He turned and tried to tuck the sheets around himself. He scanned the room. Yep, they'd taken everything. Even his underwear. Couldn't they ask? Or did they just assume Tenzin called the shots and he was a servant, so there was no need to ask his opinion about anything?

Thousands of kilometers of driving. No sleep. Stupid dreams, and then Tenzin talks about biting—

"But Cheng will think you're my human lover," she insisted. "That's what we want him to assume so he'll ignore you. One bite would be sufficient. It won't hurt."

"I don't care! You're not biting me." He didn't know why he was so angry. It probably had something to do with weeks of culture shock, uncomfortable beds, and being really really hungry.

Not just for food.

"Forget it, Tenzin."

Her mouth curled down into a frown. "But if you were my lover—"

"Are we going to have *sex* because Cheng thinks I'm your lover?"

And fuck. That train of thought was not helping the situation under the sheets.

"Of course not."

"So we're just going to lie and expect him to buy it?" Ben reached out and grabbed her hand, pulling her hard into his chest. "Even though you obviously don't smell like me?"

"What are you doing?" Her face had gone totally blank.

Ben rolled them over so that Tenzin was laying on the bed under him. Now they both looked pissed. That seemed fair.

"You're saying you need to bite me because Cheng would assume a human lover would feed you. Well, I'd smell like you too, Tenzin." He lowered his face to hers. Ben could feel her gather in a breath. He was frankly amazed she hadn't punched him yet. "And you'd smell like me. Not just my blood, but my skin. My sweat. *Everything.*"

"You're being an ass."

"Am I? Did I break into your room while you were sleeping?" The sheet was still wrapped around his waist, but that was pretty much the only thing separating them. She had to feel him.

Tenzin glared. "I don't sleep. And if you broke into my room, I'd hurt you."

He lowered himself so his chest was pressing against hers. "Isn't turnabout fair play?"

"A bite isn't the same as—"

"I don't give a shit what you think or don't think it is. You're not biting me. You want to pretend we're lovers?" He propped himself up with one arm and reached for the knife under his pillow. "Here's your pretend bite."

"Benjamin!"

Her hands came up, but Tenzin didn't stop him when he pierced the skin of his neck with the tip of the blade, just where her mouth had been in his dream. Two quick flashes of pain and he could feel the blood well.

Tenzin's eyes dilated. Her mouth fell open and her fangs

glistened. The piercing pain at his neck did nothing to quell his reaction. It was automatic. He grew harder. His pulse roared.

He could feel the outline of Tenzin's slim legs trapped between his own. Could feel the gathering power of her anger. Her grey eyes flicked to the wound on his neck and a drop of blood fell, staining the sheet next to her.

"There's a pretend bite for your pretend lover," he whispered. "Go ahead. Have a taste. But do not ever casually mention sinking your fangs into me again."

Tenzin bared her teeth. Then, before he could blink, her mouth was at his neck. Ben felt the light pressure of her lips. Closed his eyes when he felt her suck his skin into her mouth. Her tongue swept out, licked the wound clean, then it was gone.

She was gone.

Ben rolled over, the sheet still tangled around his waist, his back against the pillows, and his body showing no signs of settling down. Sweat dotted his forehead, not only from his anger and arousal, but also because it was late afternoon and the room was sweltering. His heart was pounding and he could barely catch his breath.

Tenzin stood at the door, her face impassive.

"I closed the wounds. Cheng would only expect scars anyway."

"Fine."

"I'll go out and get some clothes for you."

"Good."

She glared, clearly displeased that Ben wasn't cowering before her obvious anger. Well, too bad. She could learn to knock.

Ben sat up and let the sheet fall, stretching his arms across the carved wooden headboard and crossing his long legs at the ankles. He didn't look away when she glanced down. Let her look. He was sick of it. He wasn't a teenager anymore, and it was time she realized it.

"Fine," she said. "Boundaries."

"Boundaries are good."

"I'm going to buy you some clothes."

"Clothes are good, too."

It was probably childish, but he smiled a little when she slammed the door.

I<small>T WAS</small> ten in the evening when the knock came. Ben was sitting in a small room off the courtyard, reading a book someone had brought him. It was a travel manual in French, but he could read a little of it. And something was better than nothing, especially with Tenzin ignoring him.

He hadn't seen her since their confrontation in his bedroom. She'd sent one of the women of the house to find clothes for him, so he was dressed in jeans and a t-shirt. He was walking around barefoot, though. They couldn't find any house-slippers his size. He ignored the knock, but heard the women rushing through the courtyard to answer whoever might be calling.

Ben was embarrassed by his anger, but not by anything else. He shouldn't have lost his temper, but it was high time Tenzin stopped treating him like a child she could boss around. Yes, he still had a lot to learn, but he wasn't Tenzin's property or her employee. And if she continued the way she had been, she'd lose any and all respect for him.

That wouldn't be good for either of them.

Tenzin needed a few people around who weren't afraid of her. Most people were either so awed or so frightened that they treated her like a mythical being, not an actual person. He and his uncle had talked about it.

Giovanni said the death of her mate, whatever their relationship had been, had opened Tenzin up in ways he hadn't seen in hundreds of years. She'd become more human. More aware of the world around her. Less remote. More curious.

Ben didn't want her to lose that. Ever. The older the vampire, the more removed they usually were from the world around them. And however complicated their relationship might be, Tenzin was one of his best friends. He didn't want to lose her to the cold distance of immortality.

"You must be the human," a voice said from the doorway.

Ben looked up. "You must be the pirate."

Of course he would look like a pirate. Of course. The vampire he assumed must be Cheng was of medium height and medium build, but his body was lean and his face must have been very tan in life. He was ruddy looking, even as pale as he was. He had a rakish grin and spoke in perfect English. He wore a trimmed beard and his shirt was open at the throat. He even had shoulder length hair pulled back by what looked like a leather strap.

"All you're missing is the eyepatch," Ben said.

"You know, it wasn't because we were missing eyes." Cheng toed off his shoes and sat down in the low chair across from Ben. "It was a battle tactic. A way of making sure our vision could adjust quickly going from full light on deck to darkness below. I believe military special forces often use the same technique even today."

And he seemed cool, too. Asshole.

Ben held out a hand. "Benjamin Vecchio."

The pirate took it. "Cheng. Just Cheng."

"Like Cher?"

He leaned back and threw one hand up in the air in a flourish. "I prefer Madonna."

Ben couldn't stop the smile. "Is she expecting you here?"

"She knows I know of this place. So probably yes." Cheng looked around. "This is a comfortable house. Its mistress is under the direct protection of her sire. She knows I would respect that."

"Would you?"

"Yes." Cheng smiled, his fangs sneaking down. "I'm reckless. Not stupid."

"Hmm."

They sat in silence for a few moments. Ben didn't speak, but he didn't keep reading his book, either. The two men sat across from each other, drinking the tea that Jinpa had brought and sneaking measuring glances at each other.

"Jonathan told me you were her lover," Cheng said. "This surprised me, so I wanted to meet you. Obviously you are not."

"Oh?" Cheng could assume whatever he wanted. Ben wouldn't say either way until he heard from Tenzin. Where the hell was she, anyway?

"I do know you're the nephew of the two scholars from California. You're gathering your own quiet reputation in our world. I noticed. Somewhat impressive for a human."

"Is that so?" He sipped his tea. "How audacious of me."

Cheng burst into laughter. "I can see why she likes you."

"Why are you here?"

His eyes flashed. "To see my woman, of course."

"I'm here."

She spoke from behind him, but Ben forced himself not to turn. Tenzin walked around the couch and Cheng rose as she approached. His friendly gaze turned predatory as their eyes met, and Cheng whispered something only vampire ears would be able to hear.

Tenzin walked up to him and rose to her toes, kissing him full on the mouth as Cheng wrapped an arm around her waist. The kiss went on long enough that Ben forced his eyes away.

"I missed you, cricket."

Ben looked back. Cheng's hand was on Tenzin's cheek and she held the front of his shirt, clutching it in her hands.

She said, "I missed you, too."

"You wait too long to visit me."

"And you never visit me, so you cannot complain."

Cheng shrugged and smoothed a hand over Tenzin's hair. "You know how busy I am. And I do not want to intrude."

"I will tell you if you are unwelcome."

The corner of his mouth turned up. "I know you will." His eyes flicked to Ben. "Your human is interesting."

Tenzin finally looked at him. Their eyes met over her shoulder and locked. The stormy grey was cold again. He met her gaze, chin lifted, and forced a small smile to his lips.

She turned her eyes back to Cheng. "He's not my human. Come, we'll speak on your boat."

He's not my human.

It was exactly the point he was trying to make. And somehow, it still stung.

9

Tenzin ignored the laughter in Cheng's eyes as he guided her to the small vessel he used to reach Jinpa's home.

"What is going on there?" he asked.

"Nothing that concerns you."

They both sat, Tenzin in the bow and Cheng at the stern. He put a hand in the water and used his amnis to force the boat away from the dock. They drifted slowly out into the moonlit canal, then farther to the lake. She watched with pleasure as he stripped off the shirt he'd put on to visit the house and held out his arms.

"Come."

She floated to him and settled between his legs as Cheng slid down and arranged the pillows he'd brought to cushion their bodies from the wooden hull of the ship. He'd been a man of the sea as a human, but one who liked comfort. To this day, his quarters were lush with silk cushions and down filled blankets. He collected riches from all over the world, not simply to cache them as she did. No, Cheng enjoyed luxury.

His bare arms settled along her shoulders. "When was the last time you were touched?" He held up a hand when her mouth opened. "And don't lie about that boy. I know you haven't been with him."

She thought about Ben's brash anger in his bedroom. About the weight of his body over hers. The taste of his blood and skin. She pushed the thought away.

"The last time I saw you." She allowed her head to rest on his chest. Allowed her back to arch as his fingers stroked along her spine. "I've been busy."

"Years, cricket." He brushed the braids away from her neck and kissed her there, his fangs carefully pulled back. She'd never allowed him to bite her. "You must not go so long between visits if I'm the only one you trust this way."

"You assume, Cheng."

"We've both seen what happens when the old ones become too removed from life."

"I don't like it when you lump me in with them."

"You're better," he murmured, still touching her. He was a tactile man, and she suspected he always had been. She allowed it because a part of her knew he was right. "Before Stephen—"

"I'm better. I don't want to talk about Stephen."

"Do you ever mention his name to anyone else? Or only me?"

On the boat, like this, they were honest with each other. Their bodies and minds accepting. Cheng had always preferred to have her that way. The water at his back and the wind at hers. Perfect congress, he called it. The wind upon the waves. She couldn't count the number of times he'd taken her in the water.

"I'm tired of talking about Stephen," she said. "Touch me and don't speak, or I'll go back to the house."

He chuckled. "So bossy. I'm not the one who angered you. Don't take it out on me."

"Fine. You may speak. But not about Stephen."

"Benjamin Vecchio, then."

She scowled and called up a gust of wind, knocking him out of the boat and into the water. When he rose above the surface, he was laughing.

"Oh, I missed you, cricket." Cheng climbed back in the boat. "Tell me your stories. Who have you fought lately? Other than the three idiots in Kashgar."

"They tried to bury me and steal my gold. I only intended to kill two of them, but the other tried to bite Ben. What was I supposed to do?"

"Who did they belong to?"

"Someone named Aqpasha."

Cheng frowned. "This surprises me. Aqpasha isn't a bad sort. Just young. His people are inexperienced, but not unintelligent."

"I did him a favor then, to kill the ones who were."

"Curious."

"Why?"

"I've had some dealing with him. And you are not unknown. He's rough. Young. But he's exhibited a canny ability to give lip service to the Elders without endangering himself or his sphere of influence." He stroked a hand down his face, squeezing the water from his beard. "This disregard for you surprises me. Perhaps they were rogues."

"I don't really care that much."

"I do. A power vacuum in Xinjiang could cause a political shift. Arosh has been very quiet in the west, but I've heard rumors that make me think he is waking."

"I'd be more concerned about your own people."

His hands froze on her shoulders. "Who?"

"Kesan."

He turned her around. "Why?"

She liked that about him. Cheng didn't automatically dismiss her because she wasn't as familiar with his people. He was smart and always willing to use her as a resource if it worked to his advantage. It was one of the most attractive things about him.

"It was the way he watched Ben in Ürümqi. Ben spoke up, but Kesan had already noticed him. Had already decided to mention the human with me. How many times did he mention that I'd brought a human lover with me to China?"

"Several."

"And how many times did Jonathan?"

"None. Jonathan knows what you do is none of his business unless it affects me."

"Jonathan is loyal. His interest is in making sure his sire is well cared for and protected. Kesan is looking for weaknesses and wanted to see what kind of reaction you'd have to the idea of me bringing a lover. He hoped to provoke you to jealousy. Did he?"

The corner of his mouth curled up. "I can't tell you all my secrets, can I?"

"I don't want to talk about Kesan." She turned and pulled off her tunic, leaning her bare back against his chest. "We can speak of it later." She took Cheng's hands and crossed them over her front, breathing in his scent. The old familiar feel of his arms. The blood that still pulsed in his veins when he was aroused. She felt his heart beat once against her cheek.

Tenzin couldn't remember the last time her heart had moved.

"What are you doing in Los Angeles, Tenzin?" he murmured as he lifted her arm and laid a kiss along the sensitive skin of her wrist. "What occupies you there?"

"Let me guess. You think I should be here with you."

"Yes." He curled over her, molding Tenzin's body to his. "With you as my consort, we would be unstoppable. Ancient and modern. No one could challenge us."

"I hate Shanghai."

"I wouldn't ask for your blood," he said, ignoring her. "We are not that. But I care for you. You know this. We could do such great things."

"I like America."

"You have to be bored out of your mind."

"I'm not. I have good friends there."

"Like Benjamin Vecchio?"

"Yes."

She could feel him smile against her back. "Then why didn't you simply call him your friend?"

"I did."

"You didn't."

Was he *trying* to irritate her?

"Kiss me," she said. "Or I'll fly back to the house."

Cheng shook with silent laughter, but he kissed her. His lips were firm on her back. Tenzin turned her face to take his mouth and she could feel the scrape of his beard on her skin.

Lovely.

Tenzin forgot about everything while she kissed him. The rough texture of his beard against her mouth grounded her. Her mind was anchored in her body. She felt every nerve ending. Every stretch of her muscle and bone, bending for him. Moving in concert with Cheng's body.

This was what she'd been missing.

Too often, her mind broke free. Too often, she felt the black night dissolve her from the inside out, as if she had lost the substance of herself and existed only in her element.

"Be with me here," Cheng whispered. "In this moment. Are you with me, cricket?"

"Yes."

She closed her eyes and let her body exist in his hands. For just a little while, she could be his.

~

TENZIN WAS SOAKED to the skin when she returned to the house. Her face was flushed. From what, he didn't choose to think about.

Ben took one look at her and stood. "I wanted to apologize for losing my temper."

Her eyes held nothing. He didn't know what he was waiting for. Some kind of acknowledgement. Some acceptance. Something?

Nothing.

Well, he'd tried.

"Goodnight," Ben said, turning to walk back to his room.

"Ben."

He stopped, but didn't turn. "What?"

"I accept your apology and offer one of my own. You are correct. You are not a child."

He turned. "No, I'm not."

Tenzin cocked her head. "To be fair, I have never thought of you as one, even when I probably should have."

"When was that? When I was sixteen? I was already driving, paying bills, and killing people when I was sixteen."

"I suspect you were no more of a child at sixteen than I was."

What had her life been? Ben wondered if anyone knew. Did Cheng know? Had she confided in Stephen, her dead mate? Giovanni or Beatrice? Was there anyone who understood the wells of darkness behind her eyes?

Tenzin stepped closer, and Ben's eyes scanned the darkness of the courtyard behind her.

"He's not here," she said. "He went back to the city."

"Nice visit?"

"A necessary one."

All sorts of sarcastic retorts rung in his head, but he kept his mouth shut. It was none of his business.

He looked away. "If we don't need to go anywhere tonight, I should to go sleep. I'm still catching up."

Tenzin took a step closer. From the corner of his eye he watched her. Saw her eyes fall to his neck, where the marks she'd healed were still an angry red.

"Do you want to be my friend or my lover, Benjamin?"

He blinked. "What—"

"When I introduce you to Cheng's people tomorrow," she said, as cool grey eyes met his own. "When we are traveling together. You do not want to be known as my human, which is acceptable, but leaves you in an unknown role. So, friend or lover?"

He knew she would lie to suit herself. Knew it was only a question of how he wanted to be presented in her world. It didn't mean anything. Not really. Still...

"Friend," he said in a low voice. "Always your friend."

She nodded and moved to walk by him. Ben caught her wrist, bothered that the last time he'd touched her had been in anger.

"Come here," he said, pulling her closer.

"Ben—"

"For me. Come here."

She only came up to his chest, but he leaned down and wrapped his arms around her, not caring about the damp clothes or her soaking wet hair. He just needed her to know.

"Your friend. Always."

She didn't raise her arms. Didn't return the hug. It was okay, Ben told himself. It wasn't about that. He held her for a few more moments and felt a single beat from her heart before he let go. He stepped back, brushed a thumb over her cheek, and tried to ignore the blank expression on her face.

"Goodnight, Tenzin."

∾

WHEN HE WOKE the next afternoon, the sun still slanted through the windows of his room. Ben took a moment to open his blinds, lean out the window, and enjoy the view.

This, he thought, was the China of postcards and kung fu movies.

Sloping tile rooftops and willows hanging over the water. Boats filled the canal below his window, pilots calling and laughing to each other as everything moved through the water. Fruits and vegetables. Bags of fish. One boat full of what looked like piles of laundry. Then there were the tourists. So many tourists. Mostly Chinese. The now-familiar sounds of Mandarin echoed through the air. Ben thought he was starting to recognize a few of the different accents; the native population of the lively water town was easy to understand.

Zhujiajiao was one of the few river towns that had lasted into the twenty-first century. Graceful stone bridges arched over the main canals that ran through the town. It still got by without cars or motorbikes, mostly because of the patronage of the many tourists who visited from Shanghai. There were a few streets he'd visited the night before that hawked the regular tourist junk, but they were clustered near the main bridge. It was easy to lose the crowds on quieter streets like the one where Jinpa's house was located.

Sadly, it was only mildly cooler on the water than anywhere else in the Yangtze delta. Which meant the old water town, like the rest of greater Shanghai, was a furnace. Sweat plastered Ben's dark hair to his forehead, so he took a quick shower and dressed in a pair of linen pants and a loose white shirt that were a little cooler than his jeans and t-shirts.

Curious what was going on in the rest of the house, he slid the door to his room open and stepped into the central courtyard.

"Good evening, Benjamin," Jinpa called from across the way. She was sitting at a table near the open kitchen door, shelling what looked like peas. "Some tea?"

"Yes, thank you." He'd give his right arm for a tall glass of iced sweet tea, but hot was how they drank it in China. He'd almost gotten used to drinking steaming beverages at all hours of the day and in all kinds of sweltering weather.

Almost.

Jinpa handed him a steaming mug with a smile. "You are looking for Tenzin?"

He hadn't been, but would Jinpa actually tell him where her rooms were?

"I had something I wanted to talk to her about. Is she awake?"

She was always awake, but he had no idea if Jinpa knew that.

"Come," the old woman said. "I show you to her room."

Frowning, he followed. If this was the kind of security Jinpa offered...

But maybe Tenzin was the only vampire who ever stayed there. Maybe she owned the house, for that matter. Ben had no idea. He'd spent more time sleeping than anything else. Had Tenzin brought other humans here? Had Giovanni visited? Jinpa was Nima's family member, a niece or cousin of some kind, and Nima had been Tenzin's human companion for over sixty years. It was possible that Jinpa kept the house for Tenzin alone.

Following a narrow passageway, the old woman led him to an arched doorway with red lanterns hanging on either side. A dark green door with brass handles stood beyond the gate. Jinpa motioned to the door, then disappeared quickly, leaving Ben at the entrance to Tenzin's room.

He stood shuffling for a few minutes. She'd be awake, for sure. Tenzin didn't sleep. But would she answer a knock? It couldn't be open.

On a whim, he pressed down on the latch.

The door opened.

Well shit. What was he supposed to do now?

"I don't sleep. And if you broke into my room, I'd hurt you."

"I guess I'll find out," he muttered.

Ben pushed the door open and stepped through, closing the daylight behind him. Immediately shrouded in darkness, he grabbed his phone from his pocket and switched on the flashlight. The room wasn't a room, but a suite. Maybe a whole other house, in fact. He stood in an entrance hall lined with intricately carved wooden screens. A formal sitting room was on the right and another room with various musical instruments was on the left, filled with low couches. A tea service was set out.

You could have heard a pin drop.

"Tenzin?" he called in a quiet voice. She'd hear him, even if he whispered.

He walked through the music room and through a doorway where a faint light shone. When he stepped through, he realized it wasn't a light, but the heavy grey of a series of alabaster doors that must have opened onto an interior courtyard. The sunlight through the doors filled the room with an indirect light tolerable for an immortal. Clever. Each door stood at least eight feet tall, the translucent stone thin enough to reveal a faint glow without allowing any damaging sunlight. At night, the doors could be pushed open to allow the evening air to cool the rooms. A massive dragon was painted in one set. A phoenix on the other. The four doors stretched across the space illuminating the room in grey shadows.

"Tenzin?"

When he turned, he realized the wall behind him was filled with bookcases.

"Hello," he muttered. "Someone's been hiding all the books."

Ben bent down and tried to read some of the titles. Most were in Chinese, but there were a few in English. He was so absorbed in searching, he didn't even hear the approach.

He did feel the cold metal at his neck, though.

"I told you I'd hurt you if you broke into my room," Tenzin said, floating down to perch on his back.

Ben stood up, Tenzin still clinging to his back, her knife pressed to his throat.

"If we're comparing the situations, I'm not in your bedroom. And you're not naked."

"How do you know?"

He reached up and tugged the sleeve he could feel at his neck.

"Are you going to take the knife away from my carotid now?"

"Your pulse isn't even elevated," Tenzin said, resting her chin on his shoulder. "That's rather extraordinary for a human."

"What can I say?" Ben said, hand darting up and grabbing her wrist, twisting it until she released the blade. "I have interesting friends."

Tenzin laughed and jumped off his back, walking to a lamp in the corner and pulling a cord to flood the room with light.

"Cool place," he said, looking around.

It was a house. Not a large one, but a beautifully decorated one. He could see the door to what he assumed was a bed chamber on the other side of the library. To the left, another door that was closed.

"Yes, I like this house," Tenzin said.

Ben nodded toward the doors. "Those are amazing."

"They are, aren't they? A little joke from my father when he heard that Cheng and I were together. He thought it was amusing."

"Those are a joke? Tell Zhang he's got my name for any and all gag gifts in the future. Those doors are beautiful."

"They are. Are you feeling better? You look more rested." She motioned to the low couches in front of the bookcases. "Did you want some tea?"

"Is it cold?"

She grinned. "I'm afraid not. That is one thing I do miss about America when I'm not there. So much wonderful ice."

He frowned, suddenly realizing why her house felt so different from the rest of the compound. "But your rooms are cool."

"Oh yes. I had air conditioning added years ago. Yours is the only bedroom that hasn't been updated yet."

"You know—" Ben sat back and stretched out his legs. "—sometimes I go days and days harboring the illusion that you're nice. Then I'm reminded you're not. You're really mean and I don't know why I put up with you."

"I thought it would be a more authentic Chinese experience without the AC. Plus, that room does have the best view of the canals."

"Small blessings." He leaned back, closed his eyes, and decided to just enjoy the cool air while he could. "What's on the agenda for tonight, Tiny?"

"I thought we'd go into Shanghai. Eat some fish. See the lights. Maybe help Cheng lure a traitor into the open before he steals my gold."

Ben paused, thought, then gave her a nod. "Sure, that sounds fun."

10

Shanghai. Was. Amazing.

The lights. The people. The towering skyscrapers, their tops so high, they were hidden by the fog that came off the ocean at night. Dinner boats and freighters passed between the Pudong and the Bund, crossing the divide of new and old Shanghai.

From the banks of the old town, Tenzin and Ben watched the lights of the new city flash and flicker, leaning over the railing on the riverbank.

"The best way to see the lights," she said, leaning close to him, "is from the air. When the fog is in and it's dark. No one can see you if you're flying up there."

He smiled, imagining her playing in the forest of skyscrapers that rose across the river. The crowds and traffic below oblivious to her joy.

Tenzin smiled, her fangs flashing briefly before she closed her mouth. The crowd of humans was too thick along the Bund, the older European side of the river. Tourists from all over the world came to see the grandeur of Shanghai. But even in the rush and bustle, Tenzin was forced to hide, her ever-present fangs forcing her to hide her playful smile from the world.

"What?" she asked.

He leaned over, bumping her shoulder with his own. "The world misses out, not getting to see you smile."

She rolled her eyes. "Sentimental boy. Have you liked your trip to China?"

"It wasn't exactly what I expected."

"Far more exciting, I'm sure."

He laughed, shaking his head as he said, "I don't know why I ever try to predict how things will be when I'm traveling with you. But I love China."

"You'll come back, then?"

"Oh yeah." He scanned the crowds. "Though I might make my own itinerary next time."

She turned and leaned her back against the railing, watching the mass of humanity rush by.

"Is it very different?" he asked.

"Always. This place... It is always changing. And yet, it never really does."

"History repeats itself?"

"Constantly." She blinked and looked up at him. "But I can still be surprised by the most insignificant things. I am a fortunate person."

"So am I."

"Are you? Sometimes, I imagine you wish you lived a more ordinary life."

The corner of his mouth turned up in a rueful smile. "What's ordinary?"

"True. You and I, we are good at this."

"Good at what?" Ben caught a flash of face. A familiar face. The woman was passing the small cart selling cold drinks on the corner. He'd seen her before. She'd been outside the small restaurant where they'd eaten two hours before. Coincidence? He didn't really believe in coincidence anymore. He caught Tenzin's eye and jerked his chin in the direction she'd gone.

"You see her, too?" Tenzin asked.

"Mmhmm." He didn't stare. In fact, Ben looked away, throwing a casual arm around Tenzin's shoulders to lead her away from the railing. Three tourists quickly rushed in to take their place. "What were you saying? What are we good at?"

"This." They continued walking, staying close in the press of the crowd. "We work well together, Benjamin. Over by the pharmacy."

"I see her." He was careful to walk slowly. To anyone looking on, they were two young people out for an evening stroll. "We fight almost constantly."

"Only about unimportant things."

"She ducked into that restaurant. And I'd hardly call your lack of respect for my personal space unimportant."

"Personal space is a very Western concept, you know. And I have an idea."

"Can we talk about it after we figure out why that woman was following us?"

"If you're having trouble concentrating, I suppose so."

It started to rain, a thin drizzle of warm water falling from the sky. Umbrellas popped open on the sidewalk, almost impaling both Ben's eyes before he could duck away. The woman following them was Chinese. Young. Her hair was hidden under a plaid cap, and if he hadn't been raised to respect his own paranoia, the girl would have appeared like any of the thousands of fashionable young women walking along the Bund that night.

"There," he said, spotting the flash of her cap.

"No, there." Tenzin tugged on his arm. "She gave the hat to someone else. Watch the way she walks. The way she holds her handbag. Caps and scarves are too easily discarded. But humans have a far more difficult time changing their stride."

"Got her."

They walked more quickly, following the pretty human into one of the large pedestrian streets lined with shops. Flying lights spun above them as street vendors shouted out to the children holding their parents' hands. Tempting them with flashing laser pointers and spinning whirligigs. Ben almost lost sight of her, but she ducked down a side street and caught her heel in a crack of the pavement. She paused and threw a cautious glance over her shoulder before she dove into the alley.

She's definitely spotted them.

He felt Tenzin floating a little off the ground, and he squeezed her hand. "Not here."

She muttered something under her breath, but followed him. She probably wasn't able to see the woman, but Ben, being almost a foot taller than her, hadn't lost their tracker.

"Was this part of your plan?" he asked. "To draw some attention?" They were getting closer to the alley.

"Yes. I was expecting someone else, though."

"Kesan?"

Her head whirled around. "How—"

"Who else knew we were retrieving something in Kashgar? I was mad at the time, but really, we hadn't been in town long enough for rumors to have reached the VIC. Kesan tipped someone off. And whoever is running Kashgar would be smart enough to send more than three guys after you. So Cheng's guy tipped someone off, but he didn't want them to succeed."

No one had come out of the alley, and no one else had entered. It might be a shortcut to another street. It might be a passageway between buildings. It might be a trap.

"Is anyone looking?" she asked in a whisper as they turned the corner. It was utterly and completely black. The unnatural

glow of the city lights had thrown the space between the buildings into deep shadow.

"If they are, it's too dark to see anything."

There was a fluttering at his side and Ben knew she'd taken
to the air. A few minutes later, there was a scuffling sound.
Then Tenzin marched out of the alley with the unconscious
young woman thrown over her shoulder.

Ben sighed. "So I'm supposed to carry her back to the car
like that? Do you *want* me to get arrested?"

"Don't be silly." She hovered a few feet off the ground.
"Take the car. Drive to the docks. I'll meet you there."

"Okay, but—"

She was already gone.

"Tenzin!" he hissed, looking for a trace of her in the shadows. "Tenzin?"

Ben sighed and walked out of the alley, grabbing his phone
and wondering if there was any way to put a GPS tracker on a
vampire.

Two hours later, Ben was sitting in the car, staring at the
locked chain link fence surrounding the destination his GPS
had led him to. Not surprisingly, the port of Shanghai was
massive, and he had no idea where he was. The phone rang. He
was hoping it was one of Cheng's people, but he saw his uncle's
number pop up instead.

He picked up the phone and answered. "Hey."

"Ah. Excellent. You're not dead," Giovanni said, the slight
echo telling Ben he was on speaker-phone. "Injured?"

"Nope. Kinda lost. But no major injuries so far."

"Yes, she forgets the entire world doesn't see things from a
bird's-eye-view at times."

His head fell back on the headrest. "So she's always been like this?"

"As long as I've known her, yes."

"And you worked with her for how long without killing her?"

His uncle chuckled. "No one forced you to go, Benjamin."

"I know." He looked around the empty parking lot. "I guess it's more interesting than spending every night at clubs and hooking up with... actually, clubbing sounds pretty good right now." He scraped a hand along his jaw. "I miss air-conditioning. And Mexican food. I'd kill for a really cold beer."

"When will you be home?"

"As soon as we get this cargo on the ship. Which is supposed to be tonight. I'll call the airline in the morning."

"Let us know when you'll be back."

"Will do." He yawned. "What time is it there?"

"Six in the morning. I'll be going to rest soon. I was just wondering how you were doing."

Well, Gio, I've lost all my possessions, I'm pretty sure I still smell like rotten carrots, and I stabbed a vampire in the eye while he was trying to kill me. Then I practically assaulted one of your oldest friends when she interrupted me having a sex dream about her.

"It's been... great," Ben said, clearing his throat. "Now, if I can just find Cheng's docks, it'll be even better."

"Why don't I have Caspar text you or email you Jonathan's contact information? He always keeps a human secretary close by. He'd be the one to help you. So, you've met Cheng?"

"Yep. And Jonathan's number would be great." Ben did a mental fist pump. What was he thinking? He should have called Caspar to begin with.

"What did you think of Cheng?"

"He looks like a pirate. I'm considering sending him a parrot for Christmas. Or Chinese New Year. Whatever. Hey, could you get me that number?"

"Oh yes. Of course. I'll let you go and have Caspar send it right away. Stay safe, Benjamin."

"Night, Gio. Give B my love."

When Ben finally pulled into the parking lot near the private docks where Cheng loaded his ships, Jonathan was waiting for him.

"Where is Tenzin?" Jonathan asked.

"No idea." He got out of the car and grabbed the messenger bag that was still hanging on. It was the only thing that had stayed with him the whole trip, and its comforting weight bumped against his hip. "She's not here?"

"No."

Thinking of the human woman she had to be carrying, Ben said, "Well, that's... not good."

"I would agree with you. Come."

The tall Englishman led him through security, past the maze of containers, and into the open, where a pier that looked more like a giant road seemed to lead straight into the sea. Beside them, the hull of a freighter rose in the night, lights lit and cranes roaring as they loaded the massive ship. An almost empty container holding ten small crates stood in the open. Cheng and another figure stood nearby, a black car parked a little distance away.

Cheng nodded as they approached. "Mr. Vecchio. How are you tonight?"

"I'm well." Ben glanced up, but Tenzin was taking her time appearing.

"I believe you know Kesan," Cheng said.

Ben held out his hand, but the vampire ignored it. "We met in Ürümqi. Nice to see you again."

Kesan only lifted his chin, his black eyes gave away nothing. If he was concerned to be there, it did not show.

"So," Ben started, shuffling a little. "Should we get started?"

Cheng asked, "Did you not want to wait for Tenzin?"

He let his eyes go to Kesan. "We ran into a little trouble in the city. I'm sure she'll be along shortly. In the meantime—" he nodded toward Jonathan "—we can get started on the inventory. I have it with me."

Jonathan said, "Excellent. Let's begin, Mr. Vecchio."

"Please, call me Ben."

"Gladly." The two men, mortal and immortal, headed toward the open container. Jonathan spoke under his breath. "Do you speak Latin, by chance?"

"I do." He switched to the ancient tongue that had become a second language since Giovanni had adopted him. "I'll assume we're avoiding Kesan's ears. What's going on?"

"Do you know where Tenzin is?"

"There was a woman following us in the city. We cornered her and Tenzin took off. That was over two hours ago."

"Not good."

"My thoughts exactly."

They ducked into the container and Ben knelt down to pick up the pry bar set by the crates. He took the printed inventory and set it out next to his phone. He and Jonathan started to unpack the wooden boxes and check the inventory to make sure both matched up.

"Are there gold bars in each crate?"

"Yes," Ben said. "We had to carry the crates. There should be about twenty or so in the bottom of each. Then porcelain packed on top. Then jewelry."

"Right." He dug through straw, still speaking in Latin.

"Cheng has suspicions about Kesan. That is why he's here."

"Tenzin and I had the same suspicions."

"They must have spoken about it the other night. It's possible he was the one who sent those three after you in Kashgar. These are beautiful. Very old." Jonathan was holding one of the palm size bars in his hand. "What do you estimate?"

"About two kilos each. And I think it's more probable than possible. He was the only vampire in the region who had the connections and the knowledge of where we were going."

Jonathan shook his head. "What would be his purpose? The vampires who attacked you might not have known their opponent was so formidable, but Kesan did. He knew Tenzin would kill them."

"But maybe not before they killed me. Which would piss her off. And who would she blame if something like that happened?"

Jonathan shrugged and continued to stack small gold bricks. "The vampires who killed you?"

"With the right rumors, she might be tempted to blame a former lover. Especially if he's known to be territorial."

The Englishman gave Ben a grim smile. "If he thought that, Kesan does not understand the nature of Cheng and Tenzin's relationship."

"Does anyone?"

"Good point. My God, this jewelry is exceptional. These are museum quality."

"Silly vampire," Ben said, taking a Byzantine sapphire and gold necklace from Jonathan and marking it off on his inventory. "The best pieces are never in museums. If Tenzin wanted to sell this, it would never even see an auction."

"Cheng doesn't appreciate antiquities unless he can sell them, unfortunately."

"Poor you." Ben grinned. "We like the pretty stuff."

Jonathan sighed and handed over a leather sack of gold coins. Ben poured them into his hand and counted them. It was tedious work, but he didn't mind. The treasure had been out of their control for over twenty-four hours. More than enough time for a thief to take advantage. He wouldn't rest easy until the crates were sealed, the container was locked, and the ship was at sea.

He glanced over his shoulder. Still no Tenzin, but Cheng and Kesan stood watching them. Ben's eyes met Cheng's before he looked away. The vampire looked bored, but Ben was guessing it was a carefully built facade for Kesan's benefit.

A few minutes later, Ben heard footsteps on the roof. He looked at Jonathan, whose eyes were already on his sire. Cheng stood, hands behind his back, face lifted in a smile as he looked at whoever had landed on the container over them.

"Looks like someone finally joined us," Ben said, carefully setting down the necklace he'd been wrapping and stepping out of the container with Jonathan at his side. He swung the giant metal door closed, then locked it with a padlock he'd brought with him. He didn't know what was going to happen, but he had a feeling that inventory would have to wait.

Tenzin stood, toes hanging off the edge of the container, the woman who'd been following them glaring at her side.

"Kesan!" she called. "I have something of yours."

Without a warning, Tenzin threw the woman into the air, straight at the vampire who bared his teeth and took a step back. Cheng was the one who caught the human, tossing her to the ground as her scream cut off. Jonathan darted to his master's side, but Kesan's eyes were on Tenzin, glaring at her. Ben saw the glint of silver at his waist. The slight twisting of the vampire's torso.

Without another thought, he reached for his own blade and sent it flying into Kesan's eye.

11

At the human's scream, dockworkers and security officers came running. A small crowd gathered in moments. Tenzin landed on the ground near him. His hand was already drawing the second blade.

"Stop," she said, putting a hand on his. "Cheng wants to make an example of him."

Ben glanced around at the crowd. Mostly humans, but with a number of vampires thrown in to spread the word. All had their eyes trained on the two vampires circling each other, one with his hands in the pockets of an eight thousand dollar suit, the other holding his eye as blood dripped down his face.

"So, Kesan, you thought you would betray my friend?"

"She has no loyalty to you," Kesan hissed.

"And you do?"

Kesan said nothing, and Ben knew the vampire had underestimated the old pirate.

"I faced a mutiny once," Cheng said, stepping close to Kesan. "Do you know who won?"

"You," the other vampire muttered.

"No, actually. My crew did. I learned a valuable lesson that day." He grabbed Kesan around the throat. "Kindness gets you nowhere. Only cruelty is remembered."

Cheng threw Kesan to the ground and calmly took off his jacket and handed it to Jonathan. The crowd around the two immortals had begun to call out, clearly ready for the fight. Ben started to step away, but Tenzin put a hand on his arm.

"Wait. We must watch. We're his guests. This is as much for us as it is for his people."

"I have no desire to watch him chop some guy's head off, Tenzin."

Her eyes gleamed. "Cheng doesn't like to use weapons."

Ben's stomach turned over when he heard the crack of a fist against a jaw. Cheng's laughter rose above the cheering crowd. He forced his eyes back to the center of the circle.

Kesan was fighting back, but he had no chance against the stronger vampire. Cheng had stripped down to bare skin, the humid air of the river clinging to his chest, making it look as if the immortal was drenched in sweat. In reality, vampires didn't sweat. But for water vampires, humid air was a boon, the element suffusing the air and giving them even more strength.

"What is Kesan's element?" Ben asked her.

"He's an earth vampire."

"I was guessing that based on the panicked way he's eyeing all this asphalt."

Earth vampires needed bare earth to draw strength, which was one of the many reasons they avoided the city. Kesan hadn't expected this ambush from his employer.

"Was the girl the one who drove the truck to Ürümqi?"

"Yes. She's his servant. He didn't think we'd turn down the offer of a driver. He planned to use her to steal my gold. She was going to seduce and kill you. Kesan thought I would blame Cheng and he could use the loss of face to grab more power for himself. How did you know she was the driver?"

"I remember thinking how weird it was that the seat was so far up when I got in the truck. Thinking back, someone a lot smaller than Kesan must have been driving and it must have been a human, because the dashboard wasn't shorted out."

"You're very observant."

"I try." He winced when he saw Kesan's head snap back so far a human would have been dead. It wasn't easy to kill a vampire. You had to sever the spinal cord completely. Snapping it would cause paralysis, same as in humans, but that would heal unless the spine was completely severed. It was one of the reasons swords and knives were still so popular.

This wasn't a knife fight, however. This was pure brutal rage directed at the vampire who had pissed Cheng off.

"He's enjoying this, isn't he?"

Tenzin shrugged. "He could be called an exhibitionist. He knows his people enjoy it. So this idea I had—"

Ben sucked in a breath. "Is he actually going to—"

"Probably."

Cheng gripped Kesan around the neck in a chokehold, the other vampire scrambling to release the iron forearm at his throat. If Cheng wasn't going to use weapons, that meant to make an example of Kesan, he'd have to...

"Ugh," Ben muttered. "Gross."

"Yes, that's one word for it."

Ben still faced the crowd, but he let his eyes leave the two fighting figures under the lights. He saw a figure squirming out of the crowd, trying to remain inconspicuous.

"Oh, look who wants to get away," he murmured.

The human who'd been following them in the city—the one Tenzin said had been hired to kill him—moved the same way, even when she was backing away and hoping no one would notice her. Ben stepped away from Tenzin, who was watching Cheng fight, and stepped into the shadows.

No one was stopping her.

Tenzin asked, "Want some help?"

"You watch Cheng. I've got her."

"Careful. She bites."

The woman might not have been a vampire, but she was no innocent. She crept to the shadows and fled, running into the night and away from the growing crowd.

Ben chased her.

As he fled deeper into the labyrinth of containers, he tuned out the sound of the shouting and grunting crowd, focusing on the single panting breaths of the human who was trying to escape. Part of him was reluctant to chase her. She was human. Who knows how she'd been dragged into this world? Maybe she was like him.

No.

"*She was going to seduce and kill you. Kesan thought I would blame Cheng...*"

Well, that just pissed him off.

He ran to the end of one aisle, only to turn left and slam into something that crushed his nose. The woman must have grown tired running from him. She stood at the ready, palm out, his blood wet on her palm.

He winced and spat blood from his lips.

"Ow."

"So you were the one I was supposed to kill." Her eyes were narrow and appraising. She spoke in clipped English. "It wouldn't have been that bad, I suppose."

"Am I supposed to be flattered?"

He ducked right and raised his hands. She didn't have weapons. Not that he could see. It didn't seem fair to reach for his.

The woman smirked. "Aren't you cute?"

"If you think I have any American reservations about hitting girls, you obviously don't know who my sparring partner is."

Two quick jabs to her left and he'd clocked her on the jaw. Her head snapped back, but she used the momentum to spin around and duck under his arm, jabbing a sharp fist into his left kidney.

Ben roared in pain and snapped his head back, but she was too short to make contact. He stuck out his foot and she didn't jump fast enough. He hooked an ankle around her knee, throwing her off balance. She came down hard, the air leaving her lungs as he bent down and straddled her. She spat in his face and tried to twist away, but he had the advantage. She was no match for him once his weight was on her.

The woman's eyes darted to the knife he carried on his left side. "So you're going to kill me now?"

"No." Stymied on how he'd control her, he spied a length of frayed twine, oil soaked and kicked to the side of one container. He leaned over and grabbed it. "But I can't have you running around."

She squealed when he flipped her over and pushed her face into the dust. She let loose with a string of Chinese profanities.

"I can understand all those, you know," he said with a grin. "I can even pronounce most of them now."

"Fuck you!"

"That word is universal, isn't it?"

"You bastard!"

"Yep. Right in one." He frowned and twisted her hands behind her back, securing them with the twine and mentally thanking the boring weeks in the Cochamó Valley where he'd had nothing to do but help the cowboys with the horses and cattle.

He learned a lot about knots that summer.

Ben dragged the woman up to standing and pushed her in front of him, starting back toward the sounds of the fight.

"You're going to hand me over to Cheng?" Her voice was wavering now.

"I'm guessing you get some kind of paycheck, right?"

"Yes."

"And if the vampires here are anything like the ones I grew up with—"

"I didn't have a choice!"

"Yeah, you seemed really conflicted back there when you broke my nose." Ben scrunched up his face. He could already feel it swelling. "Anyway, I'm guessing you received pretty fat paychecks and the name on those paychecks was Cheng's. So, since you're his employee, I'm turning you over to him. What happens after that is none of my business."

They reached the pier. Kesan and Cheng were still fighting. Tenzin caught his eye and gave him an amused nod where she stood by her container.

"If I could," the woman spat out, "I would stab you with my heel right now, you stupid boy. Then I'd kill your little girlfriend."

"I'm feeling so torn about handing you over to Cheng now."

Just then, a roar rose from the crowd. There was a shout. A wet ripping sound. Then a blood-soaked Cheng lifted Kesan's mangled head from the center of the crowd.

Ben felt ill.

The blood drained from his face and his stomach twisted. The woman turned to him. For the first time, he saw fear in her eyes.

"They're monsters," she whispered. "Every one of them. No matter what face they wear. You and I both know it."

"Yes, they are," Ben said, suddenly exhausted by it all. "But you and I both chose to play with the monsters, didn't we?"

He wanted to go home. Wanted Isadora's chile verde. Wanted to watch a dumb action movie with Beatrice. Wanted to hear Giovanni lecture him about his grades.

"Besides," he said, pushing the would-be assassin forward. "The worst monsters in my life have been the human ones."

"Is your face okay?"

"Yeah." He wiped the blood from his jaw with the wet towel Jonathan had handed him. Tenzin held out an ice pack. "Thanks."

Her hand tilted his face up. "It's straight."

"Good to know that modeling career is still an option."

"There will be a bump, I think. But you were too pretty before, anyway."

"Thanks." He pushed his face into the cool of the ice pack and groaned. "Okay, I'm done. Can we go home now?"

She stroked a hand through the hair at the back of his neck. "Soon. Can you finish the inventory with Jonathan tonight? I can't access the pictures on your phone without breaking it, and the boat is supposed to leave before dawn."

"Let me find a bathroom. I'll wash up and get it done."

Tenzin nodded. "Give me the key. I'll have Jonathan load the container on the ship. We'll check it there so they can keep working. Then we can seal it and be done."

"Cool."

Ben didn't see the woman in the sterile office trailer they showed him to. He didn't ask. Maybe he'd have nightmares about handing her over, but he didn't think so. She'd have killed him if she'd had the chance.

Jonathan was waiting for him by the time he'd bandaged his lip and cleaned up. There was nothing to be done for the nose except stuff a bunch of tissue up it and wait for it to stop bleeding.

"Hey."

"Shall we?" The tall Englishman still looked as impeccable as he had at the beginning of the evening. A thin red scarf hung around his neck.

"Sure."

They climbed on board the freighter and up to the deck, quickly finding the container in the maze of others loaded on the medium sized ship that would cross the Pacific. Tenzin was waiting, but flew away after she'd handed over the key. Ben and Jonathan worked for another couple of hours, each crate opened, checked and marked. He ignored the bustling of workers around him, the whistles and cranes. He just wanted to get done.

"Well, Mr. Vecchio..."

Ben hammered the last nail in the final crate and looked up at Jonathan.

"Yeah?"

"I do believe we are finished. Does the handling of Tenzin's property meet your approval?"

Jonathan held out a stack of paperwork. Ben took it and skimmed over it, signing the bottom of the top sheet and handing it back.

"It does. Thank you, Mr. ..."

"Rothwell."

"Thank you, Mr. Rothwell. This shipment of..." He flipped through the paperwork. "...miscellaneous holiday decor has been loaded to my approval and handled to my satisfaction. I'm sure Tenzin will be pleased."

"Excellent. I'll leave you then. You and the miscellaneous decor should be in Long Beach on schedule."

Ben chuckled, until he realized what Jonathan had said.

"Wait... what?"

"Twelve to fourteen days, depending on weather. Probably twelve."

"No." Ben shook his head and ran out of the container, looking around him to see nothing but ocean with the lights of Shanghai far off in the distance, obscured by the nighttime fog. "No!"

He was alone on the broad deck of the cargo ship.

Alone. On the deck. Of a cargo ship.

Shanghai miles away.

"Tenzin!"

He looked around. He looked up. But she was nowhere to be found.

"Dammit, Tenzin, this better be a joke!"

Jonathan came to stand beside him, holding out the key to the container. "I can assume this particular part of the arrangement was not properly explained to you?"

He clenched his jaw. "That would be a safe assumption."

"Oh dear. Well, Cheng was quite reluctant to take complete responsibility for it while in transit." Jonathan clapped him on the shoulder then walked to the edge of the deck. "No worries. I understand there are very comfortable quarters for passengers. Quite... cozy."

"I'm gonna kill her."

The tall vampire turned, a smile on his face. "That's certainly not the first time I've heard that. Nor will it be the last, I imagine. Best of luck, Benjamin. I'll look forward to our next meeting."

Then the water vampire stepped backward off the deck, falling into the ocean and leaving Ben staring at the distant lights of the Chinese coast.

EPILOGUE

Beatrice's head shot up from Giovanni's shoulder. They were watching a movie on the giant television in the den and Tenzin was profoundly grateful their faces were not attached to each other as they often were.

"Ben's home!" she said.

Giovanni glared at Tenzin. "I was wondering. His classes start in two weeks."

"He'll be fine." She shrugged. "Sea travel can be unpredictable."

Tenzin was tempted to feel guilty about the storm that had thrown Cheng's freighter off course and delayed it for six days, but after all, she didn't control the weather. She heard the car door slam. Then the kitchen door slam. It was almost five in the morning, so the only people awake were the vampires.

And Ben.

Beatrice yelled, "We're watching a movie, Ben!"

She heard him on the stairs. He must have already been heading their direction.

"You!" Ben stormed into the den wearing ugly blue coveralls and a full beard. "You miserable little troll!"

Giovanni and Beatrice's words of greeting died on their lips.

"How was the trip?" she asked.

"How was the trip?" He raked a hand through hair that really needed a trim. "You mean the two and a half weeks I was trapped on a freighter? Unexpected! That might be the right word for it. Long. Cramped. Nausea-inducing, maybe?"

"I heard there was a little storm."

"You mean the typhoon off the coast of Japan? *That little storm?*"

Tenzin smiled. "Yes, that's the one I was thinking of."

"Do you have any idea how uncomfortable those beds are? I've spent the last two weeks in a room the size of a closet, sleeping with my knees bent every night, puking in a bathroom the size of a *smaller* closet—"

"Don't they call it a 'head' if it's on a boat?" She looked at Beatrice, whose mouth seemed to be sealed shut. "I thought they called it a head."

"Not a single person on board spoke English. No wifi. No books. No music. I've eaten nothing but rice and noodles for two weeks. When I could even keep anything down."

"You like noodles."

"Not anymore! And I don't like tea, either."

She cocked her head. "Or razors, apparently."

"I was supposed to take Jackie to her parents' horrible garden party last week. She begged me to go with her. I *promised*. She's never going to speak to me again. Because it's not like I could call her." He leaned down, hands braced on the arms of Tenzin's chair. "There's no mobile service in the middle of the Pacific!"

She reached up and tugged on the beard he'd grown. "This is nice. I've never seen you with a beard before. It's quite handsome."

"Know what else they didn't have on the ship? Ice packs.

Which sucks when you have a broken nose and are trapped on a ship against your will."

"I suspect they had them, they just didn't want to give you any of their first aid supplies." She pushed his face from side to side. "Still, it appears the nose has healed rather well."

"I am *never* traveling with you again."

"Of course you will."

"I'm never helping you. Never assisting you. Not even an internet search. But feel free to ask, because I'd love to laugh in your face while I say 'no way in hell!'"

"Laughter will not be necessary. Is the gold safe?"

He stood and lifted the battered canvas bag that had miraculously survived their trek across China. "Mine is! The rest of it is your problem. But don't worry, I took an extra couple of bars in exchange for escorting the container. *And* the necklace. So we're square, Tiny. Which is good, because I am never going to tag along on one of your stupid trips again."

"One hundred fifty thousand seems excessive for two extra weeks of work."

"Don't care! Never again. Never *ever* again."

"You keep saying that, but you know you will."

He spun and stalked to the door.

"I'm taking a shower. And sleeping. Probably for a week. If anyone in this house loves me, they can make me a chicken burrito."

Giovanni said, "You do remember your classes start in two weeks."

"I'll be ready for classes. If I can put up with *her* shit, classes will be no problem." He spun around at the door. "Never again, Tenzin!"

"So you said." She couldn't help but smile. His anger was too amusing.

Ben stormed out and stomped up the stairs.

Giovanni said, "Do you think Ben knows he delivered that entire rant in perfect Mandarin?"

Beatrice shook her head. "Probably not thinking about it at the moment."

"He sounds so much better," Tenzin said.

"You're right. He sounds like a native."

"Two weeks with no company but Chinese sailors will do that for you."

Beatrice added, "I imagine he's picked up some rather interesting vocabulary, too."

"True."

Tenzin turned back to the television, where several buildings were blowing up in a completely unrealistic manner.

Ben just needed a little time to calm down. He became so cranky when he didn't get enough sleep.

He could thank her later.

THE END

IMITATION AND ALCHEMY

All Ben Vecchio wanted was a quiet summer before his last semester of university. Was that too much to ask? All Tenzin wanted was a cache of priceless medieval coins that had been missing for several hundred years.

And some company.

Ben Vecchio thought he knew everything there was to know about the immortals of Italy. But when Tenzin tempts him into another adventure, finding a cache of rare gold coins missing since the nineteenth century, he'll discover that familiar places can hold the most delicious secrets. And possibly the key to his future.

PROLOGUE

BENJAMIN VECCHIO SAT IN THE library of his home in Pasadena, studying for his art history final. To say the class was an easy A would be a gross understatement, but the habits instilled by his scholar of an uncle wouldn't allow him to rest for the night until he'd at least looked over his notes.

A small air vampire floated into the room and over the library table, blocking his notebook. She settled on his textbook and waited silently for Ben to acknowledge her.

He glanced up at Tenzin a second before he shook his head. "Nope."

She said nothing, watching Ben with storm-grey eyes that always seemed just a little out of place. Her features were unquestionably born on the steppes of Central Asia. Her full lips remained closed over the lethal, clawlike fangs in her mouth. And her expression? It revealed nothing.

"Whatever it is," he continued, "the answer is no. I can't spar tonight. I have a final tomorrow. And I don't have time to get online and research an obscure manuscript in Sanskrit or whatever it is you want. I need to sleep."

The air vampire continued to watch him silently. Ben

continued to ignore her. Ignoring Tenzin when she wanted something from him was a talent he'd been honing for years.

She had a face that could have been fifteen or thirty, depending on her expression. She'd let her hair grow out to below her shoulders the past few years, so she looked younger than Ben now. If you didn't know who or what she was, she could pass herself off as an innocent schoolgirl.

Well, until she smiled and you saw the fangs.

She used her looks to her advantage, but no matter what expression Tenzin wore, Ben saw millennia when he looked into her eyes.

She ignored his indifference and leaned over his notes. "Why are you studying this? You knew about neoclassicism before I met you."

He grimaced. Modern universities were inexplicable to Tenzin. "I need the credits if I'm going to graduate next winter. I only have one more semester, and I've ignored most of my lower-level requirements."

"Because they are stupid."

"Art history is not stupid."

She flicked the edge of his notebook. "Taking a class where you probably know more than the instructor is stupid."

"Well, they wouldn't let me take the upper-level class."

"Why not?"

"Because I hadn't taken the lower level... Listen"—he sat back in his chair—"do you have a purpose here? What do you want?"

"It doesn't matter." She shrugged. "You've already said no."

"Tenzin—"

"Why are you taking art history?" She stretched out on the table, lazing like a cat. "What does art history have to do with political science?"

"Nothing. It's just part of my— Will you get off that?" He pulled his textbook from under her hair. "I need to study—"

"No, you don't! You've known art since you were old enough to steal it. Do you want some food? I feel like cooking. What would you like? I'll cook food and you can eat it."

"What do you want, Tenzin?"

She rolled over and propped her chin on her hands; her eyes laughed at him. "You already said no."

"Just tell me."

She kicked her legs. "I want to go to Italy this summer."

His eye twitched and he looked back to his book. "No."

"You go to Italy all the time."

"I learned my lesson last summer, Tiny."

"We're not going to China. I want to go to Italy. It's practically a second home to you. You have a house in Rome."

"*Gio* has a house in Rome. If you want to borrow it, ask him."

"You speak Italian like a native. You have friends there. You could visit Fabia."

"Fabia has a boyfriend lately."

"So?"

"Just... no."

She didn't move from her position stretched on the table. Not even when he picked up his notes and stood them up, blocking her face.

"What if—"

"No!" He slammed his notebook down. "No. No. No. I'm not getting involved in one of your schemes. I'm not stealing anything. I'm not pretending to be your butler again—"

"I only told one person that, and I think Jonathan knew it was a joke."

"I do not want to lie to dangerous people. I don't want to run for my life. I don't want to hurt anyone. I don't want to get beat up or threatened or—"

"Fine!" She scowled and lay on her back, huffing at the ceiling. "What happened to you? You used to be fun."

"I grew up, Tenzin. And I realized that I can't live in my aunt and uncle's house forever. I'm twenty-two. I'm going to have to get a job one of these days. And a house. And pay bills." Ben grimaced. "I'm going to have to figure out something useful to do with my life, and I have no idea what the hell that means for someone like me."

He slammed his notes back on the table and tried to concentrate, all the while feeling her eyes on him like a brand.

After a few minutes, she crawled across the table and leaned down to his ear. Tenzin whispered, "Medieval gold coins from Sicily."

He groaned and let his head fall back. "I hate you a little right now."

☿

GIOVANNI was in the den, curled up with a book, Beatrice lying across his legs while she caught a movie.

Ben stopped in the doorway and watched them.

It was a hell of a lot to aspire to. Some days his heart ached watching them. As much as they loved him—and he knew his aunt and uncle loved him a lot—the love they had for each other was so tangible it almost hurt. He couldn't imagine having love like that. If he ever did, he'd grab on to it with everything he had.

Ben would never forget the months they spent in Rome when he was sixteen. When Giovanni had been taken, leaving Beatrice alone. It was the first time he ever remembered feeling stronger than his aunt.

Giovanni looked up with a smile. "Hello."

"Hey."

Beatrice stretched her legs and kicked a pillow off the end of the couch. "What are you doing tonight? Come sit with us."

Ben walked over and sat down. "I was just studying. Two more finals before summer break."

Beatrice smiled. "I'm so proud of you. Have I told you that lately? We're both so proud of you. I can't believe you've almost earned your degree."

He glanced at their loving smiles before he turned away in embarrassment. "Thanks."

Beatrice was thirty-eight now but looked barely older than Ben.

It was odd to realize that in a few years he would be the one who looked older than his aunt. Their relationship was already changing, becoming more friendly than parental. Just another reminder that time was passing.

Too fast, a childish voice whispered inside. *Too fast!*

"What do you think you want to do this summer?" Giovanni asked. "You should do something fun. Beatrice and I are stuck here, working on that damned library theft." He added a string of Latin curses that had Beatrice smoothing her thumb over his lips.

"Shhhh," she said. "You'll shock the boy."

"I don't think that's possible anymore," Giovanni said.

Ben had forgotten all about the library heist when he was thinking about how to sneak off to Italy without his uncle becoming suspicious.

It had been a massive scandal in the rare-book world and had become the bane of his uncle's existence since much of the "uncatalogued special collections" that had been stolen from the Girolamini Library in Naples wasn't actually part of the library but was instead the private collections of numerous Italian immortals. Some of the vampires had stored their private miscellany in the library since the sixteenth century and did not take kindly to humans stealing and selling their treasured manuscripts or personal papers.

Giovanni and Beatrice had been hired by multiple clients to track down particularly elusive items that had made their way onto the black market. The Naples library heist had been keeping them—along with their resident librarians in Perugia, Zeno and Serafina—busy on and off for almost two years.

Ben cleared his throat. "It's funny you mentioned Naples. I was actually thinking of going to Italy for part of my break."

Beatrice frowned. "In the summer? But it's so hot! You sure you don't want to go down to Chile?"

"I haven't seen my friends there since Christmas. And Fabi's seeing a guy she wanted me to meet. So—"

"The house in Rome is yours anytime you want," Giovanni said. "You know that. In fact..." He frowned. "If you don't mind doing some work while you're there, I think Zeno will be in Rome the middle of June working at the Vatican Library. I might have you take some notes to him."

"And that journal we tracked down in New York last month," Beatrice said. "Ben can take that to Zeno too. Collect on that commission."

"Good idea, Tesoro," he murmured, brushing her dark hair from her cheek. "Ben, let me know if you want to borrow the plane. But right now—"

"Got it." He stood when he saw Beatrice turning to her mate. "I know when I'm not wanted."

"Close the door on the way out."

Glancing over his shoulder, Ben saw Giovanni had already pulled Beatrice to straddle him. He tried not to laugh.

Like rabbits, the two of them.

"Ben—" Giovanni pulled his lips from his mate's and

cleared his throat. "I'll let Emil know you'll be in Rome this summer. You know the game. Just make sure you stay out of Naples."

Ben's Tenzin-radar went off. Naples. Southern Italy. Sicily. Very southern Italy...

Medieval *Sicilian* coins, huh?

"What's up with Naples?" he asked, trying to sound casual. "Problems with the VIC?"

"The 'vampire in charge' as you say, is named Alfonso. He's Spanish. Or Hungarian. I'm not sure. And he's..." Giovanni frowned.

"He's nuts," Beatrice threw out. "Completely bonkers. And mean. He hates Emil."

"Ah." Ben nodded. "Big Livia supporter?"

Beatrice said, "No, he hated Livia too."

Giovanni was watching his mate with the focused stare that told Ben he'd forgotten anyone but Beatrice was in the room. It was the vampire hunting stare, and Ben knew if he didn't get out of the den quickly, he was going to see way more of his aunt and uncle than he wanted.

"Just..." Beatrice held Giovanni back. "Stay out of Naples. It's not a good idea right now. The rest of the country? No problem."

"Avoid Naples." He gave them a thumbs-up they probably didn't see. "Got it. Later. Don't do anything I wouldn't do. Except, you know, the biting stuff I don't want to know about."

"Good night, Benjamin."

He shut the double doors behind him and leaned back, letting out a long breath before he walked to his bedroom. "How much you want to bet...?"

☿

THE next night, he was working with Tenzin at her warehouse in East Pasadena. She'd converted most of the old building to a training area, complete with one full wall of weapons. The only personal space was a loft in the rafters with no ground access.

Because the only person allowed up there could fly.

The windows were blacked out, which made life easier when you didn't sleep. At all. Ben didn't know how she stayed sane. Then again, the state of Tenzin's sanity was never a settled subject.

"Look at that." She leaned over his shoulder and reached her finger toward the computer screen, which began to flicker before he slapped her hand away.

"Don't touch."

They were watching a video about Kalaripayattu, an obscure Indian martial art, that someone had posted on YouTube. Tenzin *adored* YouTube.

"But look at those forms," she said. "So much similarity to modern yoga. But more..."

"Martial."

"Yes, exactly. If you could isolate pressure points..."

She started muttering in her own language, which no one but Tenzin and her sire spoke anymore, though Ben thought he was starting to pick up some words. Giovanni theorized it was a proto-Mongolian dialect of some kind, but Ben only spoke Mandarin. He hadn't delved into Central or Northern Asian languages yet.

"If you watch..." She frowned. "The balance. That is key. This is very good. We'll incorporate some of the balance exercises for you since you are top-heavy now."

"It's called muscular, and it's a product of testosterone. I refuse to apologize for that."

"Look." She slapped his arm. "The short-stick fighting. We can incorporate some of those techniques too."

"Are you saying I have a short stick?"

She frowned, still staring at the computer screen. "What are you talking about?"

Ben tried to stifle a smile. She could be so adorably clueless for a woman with thousands of years behind her. "Nothing. Ignore me."

"Oh!" She laughed. "Was that a sexual joke? That was funny. But your stick is not short, Benjamin." She patted his arm. "You have nothing to be worried about."

"Thanks. That's... comforting." He cleared his throat. "So, I told Gio I was heading to Italy for the summer. He said the house in Rome is mine as long as I help Zeno out with some stuff at the Vatican while I'm there."

"That's good." She cocked her head, her eyes still stuck on the video playing. "Can you skip ahead to the dagger fighting?"

"Yeah." He found the section that was her favorite. "So, Tiny, when you said that we'd be looking for Sicilian coins, did you mean we'll be going to Sicily?"

"Don't be ridiculous," she said, leaning closer to the screen. "We're going to Naples. That's where the gold is. Or where it was."

"Of course it is."

"Is Naples going to be a problem?"

"With you, Tenzin?" Ben leaned back and crossed his arms. "There's really no way of knowing."

1

BEN FELT HIS SHOULDERS RELAX as soon as he stepped into the terminal of Leonardo da Vinci International Airport. He walked quickly through the crowd, making his way past the slow-moving early-summer tourists. He'd skipped a checked suitcase—the notes and journal Giovanni had given him were wrapped in the bottom of his messenger bag—so if he timed things right...

He arrived at passport control just before an enormous tour group of Chinese visitors flooded the line. With a few quick stamps and another few rote questions, the girl checking his passport stamped it and waved him through.

"*Benvenuto a Roma, Signor Vecchio.*"

"*Grazie. Ciao.*"

With his name and near-impeccable accent, she probably figured Ben for an Italian despite his American passport.

It wouldn't be far off.

Though his blood was an even mix between Puerto Rican and Lebanese, he could easily pass for an Italian, especially when he grew out his beard, which he'd done as soon as his semester had ended.

Slipping on his sunglasses, Ben grabbed a cab and relaxed into the backseat, letting out a long breath as the taxi wound its way through the traffic of midday Rome. The driver hummed along with the quick jazz on the radio but didn't try to talk to him. Ben gave him an address near the Pantheon and leaned back to close his eyes.

Rome.

Ben smiled. It was good to be back.

Home had always been a fluid concept to Ben. It consisted far more of the people present than any particular location. Home was Giovanni and Beatrice. Caspar and Isadora. Dez and Matt. But home was also Angela, Giovanni's longtime house-keeper in Rome. If there was any city that felt more like home than Los Angeles, it was probably Rome. Some of his happiest and most terrible memories were here.

He started awake from his snooze when the driver stopped in the tiny Piazza di Santa Chiara. Ben paid him and grabbed his bag, then waited for the driver to pull away before he made his way up the side street that led to the house.

After punching in the code for the giant wooden door that shielded the property from prying eyes, he pulled it open, wondering how Angela was coping with the gate when she ran errands. His uncle, being a five-hundred-year-old vampire, tended to forget about things like human frailties and arthritis.

"*Ciao*, Angela!" he called into the courtyard.

He heard a fluttering like bird wings before a tiny woman appeared from the kitchen on the ground floor.

"*Ciao, Nino!*" Angela covered his cheeks with her small, wrinkled hands and pulled him down for a kiss, chattering as he laughed.

Angela had to be in her late sixties, but she still had the bright eyes and impeccable style of a woman much younger. She'd run Giovanni's house in Rome for most of her adult life with a healthy balance of efficiency, warmth, and Tuscan comfort food.

"You've gotten taller since Christmas," she said.

"No. I promise I haven't." He'd filled out a bit in the shoulders, but he was done growing. Almost six feet would have to suffice.

"You're too thin!" She pinched his arm. "Nino, what do they feed you in California? It's not enough. Come." She waved him into the kitchen. "I'm making meatballs for you and Fabi for dinner."

He rubbed his eyes. Now that he was within the familiar walls of Residenza di Spada, he felt the delayed exhaustion hit. He'd bypassed the offer of Giovanni's plane, choosing to use some of his frequent-flyer miles to upgrade to first class, but he hadn't really slept for almost twenty-four hours.

"Angie, I think I might lie down for a little bit."

"Not too long!" The housekeeper was accustomed to international guests. "Sleep for a little. I'll wake you up for dinner. You need to get on Roman time."

"*Si, zia.*"

"Your room is made up. Fresh sheets on the bed and I washed the clothes you left here. Not many summer things, I don't think."

Because he usually avoided the furnace of Rome in the summer. He could already feel his shirt sticking to his back. "I'll be fine. I'll pick up some new things tomorrow."

At least there was no lack of shopping in Rome. It was expensive, but Ben thought the quality was worth the extra cash, and he saved most of his formal shopping for Italian visits.

He walked upstairs and tucked Giovanni's notes and the journal in the safe in the master suite, then made his way to the cool shadows of his room where he toppled face-first into bed.

☿

SHE was playing with the curls of his hair when he woke. Soft humming and the warm smell of citrus and bergamot she'd worn since she was a teenager. Ben rolled over and grabbed Fabia around the waist.

"Gotcha," he said, his voice still rough with sleep.

Fabia laughed as she fell against his chest.

"Bad boy," she said, brushing a kiss against his jaw. "The beard is so sexy. I love your hair longer. You should always wear it that way."

Ben lay back, her familiar weight resting against his body. He took a deep breath and let his fingers trail over her smooth shoulders as Fabi laid her head on his chest and hugged him.

Women were just so... delicious.

Other than friendly kisses and a few teenage fumblings, he and Angie's niece had never been more than friends, but the flirtation of more had always lain between them. Fabia was a beautiful girl. Smart and effortlessly sexy. She'd shorn her red-brown hair into a pixie cut when she entered her graduate program and moved to Rome. It suited her.

"I missed you," she said.

"Why did you get a boyfriend then?" He smiled at her when she looked up. "I can't kiss you—well, I can't kiss you as much—if you have a boyfriend."

"I don't want a boyfriend who lives in California most of the year." She pouted. "I am not made for a long-distance lover, Ben."

"You could move to LA."

"And you could move to Rome."

They both grinned at the same time.

Ah well. Not meant to be, no matter how the chemistry taunted them.

He leaned down, gave her a quick kiss, then rolled her to the side while he went to use the attached bath.

"So how hot is it?" he asked through the door as he splashed water on his face and pulled off his sweat-stained shirt.

"Not too bad yet," she said. "But July is just around the corner."

He walked out and caught her admiring his bare chest with an arched eyebrow.

"I don't have many clothes," he said. "I'll need to go shopping."

"I can go with you tomorrow." She sat up and went to the wardrobe, opening it and surveying the contents with a frown. "You're right." She threw a shirt at him and closed the doors. "Wear that for dinner. It'll do. We're meeting some friends tonight by the river."

"Is the fair going on?"

"*Sul Lungotevere,*" she said. "Good restaurants this year."

During the summer, the banks of the Tiber were taken over by restaurants and vendors who took advantage of the cool evenings to lure locals and tourists to the river. It was a combination of food, drink, and art that Fabi had told him about, but he'd never had a chance to visit.

"You can meet Elias." Fabi fell back on the bed. "I *really* like him, Ben. He's kind. Smart, but not full of himself—"

"Not like me then." He grinned at her as he dressed.

"No, not like you." She rolled her eyes. "He is handsome though. His mother is Ethiopian. He's gorgeous. And so tall."

"You trying to make me jealous?"

"Is it even possible?"

Maybe. He couldn't decide yet. Fabi was an old friend, so it was nice to see her happy. That didn't mean he'd give this guy a free pass because she thought he was handsome. Ben was protective of the women in his life, especially the human ones.

He buttoned up the shirt. "So dinner with Angie and drinks after?"

"Yes. I called Ronan and Gabi too. They're going to meet us. Gabi will want to sleep with you now that you have a beard. Ronan might too. Just warning you."

Ben laughed. "And yet, neither one is my type. It'll be good to see 'em both."

Ben and Fabi's group of friends in Rome mostly consisted of other young people who had—like them—grown up under vampire aegis in some way. Ronan's parents worked for Emil Conti, the immortal leader of Rome and most of Italy, while Gabi's family was involved with the vampires at the Vatican. Gabi and Ronan didn't offer information; Ben didn't ask.

When you grew up with vampires, you learned to be careful which questions you asked.

But it was easy to be with a group of people who understood where you were coming from. Darkness didn't hold the same allure when you grew up walking half your life in it. Their friends understood that.

"So why did you decide to come to Rome in June?" she asked as they walked toward the smell of meatballs. "Not that it's not nice to see you, but—"

"I'm visiting friends." He put his hand at the small of her back and ushered her into the courtyard where Angie was setting a small table for the three of them. "And I'm delivering some things for my uncle. And..." He sighed. "Still trying to figure out what I'm going to do, you know? Sometimes it's easier to think when I'm not in LA."

She touched his jaw in understanding. They'd spoken of post-university plans at Christmas.

"Any ideas yet?" Fabi asked.

"Maybe. Nothing definite. You?"

She shrugged. "I'm an attractive twenty-five-year-old

Roman girl with degrees in archeology and art history. What do you think I'm going to do?"

"Tour guide?"

"Of course!" She smiled ruefully. "If I can build up a good private clientele, I can make a decent living. And I'll set my own schedule. I like that."

"I like the idea," Angela said as she placed a dish of olives on the table. "As long as she stays in the house and helps me here."

Ben raised his eyebrows. "Yeah? Like, permanently?"

"I'm thinking about it," Fabi said. "Zia Angela says she could use the help."

"I'm not getting any younger," Angie chided. "And Signor Giovanni will need another housekeeper when I must retire. It's a good job. And it will keep her busy when she's not leading tourists through the dust."

Ben smiled. He liked the idea. "I think you'd be great here. You already have your own room. Gio and B like you. Perfect solution."

Fabi rolled her eyes. "I haven't decided anything for certain. I like my apartment."

Ben looked around the lush courtyard with the palms and bougainvillea, the fountains providing trickling background music that echoed off the old walls surrounding them.

"Really?" he asked. "You like your apartment better than *this*?"

Angie leaned across the table. "Exactly. Listen to Nino. You live in a palace here. Don't be stubborn. Come work for Signor Giovanni."

"Yeah," Ben said, popping an olive in his mouth. "Don't be stubborn, Fabi."

"You're one to talk, Ben Vecchio, he who likes to pretend he doesn't know exactly what he's going to do after university."

"I have no idea what you're talking about."

"Your uncle has been grooming you as a protégé for years, Ben. Are you really so clueless? He wants you to go into business with him."

Angie said, "Giovanni won't say anything; he doesn't want to pressure you."

Ben winced. It wasn't that Ben didn't know that Giovanni wanted him to work with him and Beatrice. Hell, he'd been unofficially working for his uncle since Giovanni had adopted him. But Ben was resisting it. Mostly because he just didn't know if he could spend the next seventy years sorting through dusty libraries, which—the rare adventure aside—was most of what his aunt and uncle did for clients.

"I'm thinking about it," he said. "Just... pass the wine, will you? I'm not going to decide tonight."

ᚥ

TENZIN watched the small group of young people from her perch by the statue. No one seemed to mind that she'd crawled up the embankment and sat next to the bronze chimera that had been mounted near the steps under the Ponte Cestio.

She caught Ben's expression and smiled. It was good to see him laughing. The past year at university had been stressful for him. He worked too hard to please his uncle. She knew part of Ben still considered any achievement a payment for the life of a boy rescued from the dirty slums of New York.

Ben didn't understand love yet. Not really.

But then, no one did when they were young. She leaned back against the cool stone and contemplated her latest plan to lure him in as a partner. She'd become bored in this modern world, and she needed something to do. Catching up on twentieth-century technology and mastering video games wasn't enough to keep her mind occupied.

No, she needed the rush of adrenaline again. She hadn't felt this restless since the days that she and Giovanni had been mercenaries.

Now *that* had kept her occupied.

But the world had changed. There was no longer any honor in living a warrior's life. Those who hired out their services as soldiers, even in the immortal world, were a different kind of animal than she and Giovanni had been, and she felt no kinship with them.

Ben turned and met her eyes in the low lights that reflected off the river.

Tenzin had a different kind of plan to occupy her time.

He stood and carefully wound his way through the outdoor tables and the small crowd watching a musician. Then he stood under her, his chin just reaching the edge of the ledge where she was sitting.

"Did you think I wouldn't see you there?"

"I didn't think about it. I didn't want to disturb you and your friends."

He held out his hand. "Jump, don't float. Let the humans see gravity."

Tenzin jumped down and let her feet land hard. Such an awkward, heavy feeling. Yuck.

"Do you want me to leave you?" she asked.

"No, you're going to join us for a drink."

Tenzin halted. "No."

"Tiny, Fabi's the one who spotted you. Your cover as an inconspicuous statue has already been blown. You might as well come have a glass of wine."

Tenzin wasn't comfortable socializing outside her close circle of friends, and Ben knew it.

"Just try," Ben said, putting an arm around her shoulders.

"All of them—except the tall Ethiopian guy—know about your kind anyway."

"Fine. One drink. And my Italian is rusty."

"We'll speak English then."

She made her way through the crowd of humans, automatically assessing threats and marking weapons. A surprisingly high number of them for a lazy summer evening, until she realized that two of the tables were surreptitious security for the young people at the table.

Interesting.

The guards immediately took note of Tenzin, and she felt Ben's arm tighten around her. He'd spotted them too.

Sometimes she was astonished by his perception. It was truly exceptional for one so young.

Fabia and Ben didn't warrant security from Giovanni, at least not under normal circumstances. She wondered whether socializing with Giovanni Vecchio's ward was considered something to be cautious about by other immortals. It could also be that there were current threats in Rome of which Tenzin hadn't been apprised. She'd have to give Giovanni a call later.

Until then, a far greater danger awaited her.

Small talk.

"Hey, guys!" Ben said. "This is Tenzin."

She saw the recognition immediately. Young people growing up under immortal aegis wouldn't have any idea what Tenzin looked like, but almost everyone in their world—human or vampire—knew her name.

The ancient one.

Daughter of Penglai.

Commander of the Altan Wind.

Assassin.

Spy.

Tenzin had been a legend before most of the Western immortals took their first breath.

Ben pressed a hand to her back and eased her into a chair he pulled next to his.

Only Ben, his friend Fabi, and her clueless boyfriend were at ease.

"Tenzin, it's so good to see you," Fabi said. "How long are you in town?"

Tenzin smiled. Fabi was Angela's niece. A smart, humorous girl. Ben was at ease with her, so Tenzin could be too.

"I'm here for a time," she said vaguely. "I have some business in the south, then I'll probably head north to visit some property."

She had a house in Venice. It was one of her favorites. Had she ever told Giovanni about it? She couldn't remember. She'd show Ben.

Ben said, "You know Ronan and Gabi, I think. And this is Elias, since Fabi is being rude—"

"*Zitto!*" Fabi laughed. "Sorry, I forgot. I feel like Tenzin must know everyone."

The young man leaned forward and held out a hand. "It's a pleasure to meet you. You're an American friend of Ben's?"

Tenzin stared at the hand for a moment before she held hers out, touching the young human's fingers only briefly so he didn't notice the unnatural chill of her skin.

"I am," she murmured, careful to keep her lips closed and her fangs covered. "It's a pleasure to make your acquaintance."

Ben seemed at ease with the young man. His earlier stiffness had eased the more he talked with Fabia's new friend. If Ben approved of the young man, Tenzin would give him the benefit of the doubt.

Ben quickly led the conversation into a discussion of a current film that had just premiered in Rome. Tenzin sipped the wine he poured for her and smiled, but she avoided speaking. Elias didn't know about immortals, and it was too difficult to conceal her nature from ignorant humans.

Ronan and Gabi's tension eased after a few moments, and soon the young people were drinking, joking, and laughing like the old friends they were. Tenzin, however, watched Ben.

Did he have friends like this in Los Angeles? He must have, but she didn't know them. When she was in LA, she didn't socialize except with Giovanni and his family. It was fascinating to see Ben in his element with the other humans his age.

He was a natural leader. He steered the conversation without effort, probably not realizing the others followed his lead. He was the kind of man other males would follow, not out of fear but because he made them feel a part of something greater. More important.

And with the females... Tenzin couldn't stop the smile.

Every girl Ben met fell half in love with him whether she wanted to or not. He was handsome, yes, but even more, she knew he truly enjoyed women and all their facets.

He caught her smiling at him.

"What?" he whispered.

Tenzin switched to Mandarin. "It was good for you to come here. You will see things more clearly."

"What things?"

She didn't answer him but leaned close and brushed a cool kiss over his bearded cheek. "I told you the beard was a good look for you. All the girls in the restaurant want to have sex with you."

He shook his head. "Seriously, Tiny—"

"I'm going to go. You're going to see Zeno tomorrow night?"

He nodded.

"I'll find you. Good night, my Benjamin."

"Night."

She waved to the others but slipped away without another word. She stepped lightly through the crowd, marking the humans and few vampires who were patronizing the festival that night. She kept her head down, and within moments, she was past the lights of the riverbank. Past the clatter of humanity.

Tenzin melted into the comforting shadows and disappeared.

2

THE VATICAN LIBRARY MIGHT HAVE been the most famed, mysterious library in the Western world, but Ben still thought it smelled like most libraries everywhere. Dust. Mold. A stale smell he associated with institutional cleaners. He leaned back at the table in Zeno Ferrera's workroom and kicked his feet—newly shod in the best Italian leather thanks to his shopping trip with Fabi—on the table.

Zeno knocked them down. "Don't make me beat you."

The surly immortal had worked for his uncle over a year now, but he still held his connections with the church. Zeno had been a priest, and he was relatively young for an immortal, though he had been middle-aged when he'd been turned. He was just over one hundred years or something like that. Ben knew better than to ask.

"Grumpy old man," Ben muttered. "And after I brought you presents too."

Zeno waved a dismissive hand. "The journal will get at least one of our more... persistent clients off my back. He showed up at the library unannounced last week and surprised Fina. She wasn't pleased."

"I'm surprised he's still alive."

"Yes." Zeno drew out the word. "I think he is too."

The grumpy vampire had married the human librarian who ran Giovanni's library in Perugia, and he was rabidly possessive of both the woman and her young son.

"Fina and Enzo coming to Rome?"

"And swelter in this heat?" Zeno asked. "It's cooler at home. And Enzo's still finishing his school term. I think we'll take a holiday to the mountains if the weather doesn't let up. She's been asking for one, and the Naples theft..." Zeno shook his head and muttered under his breath. "It's been driving both of us crazy."

"Was it that bad?" Ben had a hard time understanding his family's obsession with books.

It wasn't that Ben didn't love books. He'd been a voracious reader since before he'd met Giovanni. Books were one of the few cheap and available escapes he'd had as a child. Alcohol made his mother cry. Drugs were expensive and dangerous.

But stories...

He'd split any time he could get away from his mother between the public library and the Metropolitan museum. But he couldn't understand the overriding desire to preserve medieval tax records or Renaissance-era farming manuals like they were made of precious metal.

"We don't know how big the Naples theft was," Zeno said. "That's part of the problem. And it wasn't just books."

"What does that mean?"

Zeno raised an eyebrow. "Valuables, my friend. Artifacts."

Okay, now his interest was piqued. Ben leaned forward. "I didn't hear Gio mention any artifacts. What's missing?"

"We don't know unless a client tells us. And your uncle doesn't deal in antiquities. Only books."

Ben's excitement fled. Bummer. Artifacts would have been

interesting.

"A large portion of the library was uncatalogued," Zeno continued, paging through Giovanni's notes. "Partly because it's so old, and partly because many immortals used it like their own personal storage unit."

"That seems... unusual."

Zeno shrugged. "It's Naples. They're crazy down there."

Ben laughed.

"I can say that," Zeno said, "because I was born there. It's the truth." He tapped his temple. "Everyone from Naples... We're a little off, yes? We like it that way. Keeps life interesting."

"Makes me think I should be hanging out in Naples more."

"No, you shouldn't," Zeno said, shutting him down. "Maybe in another hundred years when there's a different vampire in power."

Ben pursed his lips. "So... when I'm dead."

Zeno frowned. "Why?"

"What?"

"I always assumed Giovanni would sire you. Why wouldn't he? You're his son."

"I'm his nephew."

"So?"

"And I don't want to be a vampire."

Zeno shook his head. "You're a fool."

"No," he said. "I'm just not a romantic."

Zeno threw his head back and laughed. "And what is romantic about this life? Drinking blood? Hiding from the sun?" Then his amusement fell. "Watching old friends die?"

"Exactly. Do you wonder why I don't want it?"

"Yes." The old vampire narrowed his eyes. "Because I see the same thing in you that I could see in myself at your age. You're greedy."

It pricked Ben a little. Made him feel like he was asking for more than his share. He sat a little straighter. "There's nothing wrong with wanting—"

"Don't be offended. I understand it," Zeno said. "I wanted many things at your age. Money. Good music. Cheerful friends." Zeno grinned. "Many, many women."

Ben shrugged carelessly.

"I see much of myself in you, Ben. The same... ambition that drove me. The same greed."

"I don't see ambition as greed."

"I'm not talking about money," Zeno said. "Not talking about anything that... unimportant. I scraped coins growing up. I know just how good it feels to accumulate wealth. But that's not the kind of greed I'm thinking of. You're greedy for time, Ben Vecchio."

Ben stayed silent.

"Time," Zeno said, "is the true treasure of this life. And who is more greedy for time than those of us clinging to the dark?"

"You told me once you didn't want to become a vampire," Ben said quietly.

"I didn't!" Zeno said, sorting papers into a pile that he carefully placed in a grey document box. "I *didn't* want to be a vampire. But that didn't mean my sire was an idiot." Zeno winced. "Unfortunate that I killed him before I knew that wasn't strictly allowed. But he knew I'd come to terms with it."

"Why?"

"Because I was a thief!" Zeno said with a grin. "And a gambler. And because in the end, my sire helped me pull off the greatest heist of my life. *I stole time.*"

☿

BEN was helping Zeno sort letters two hours later when a

timid priest knocked at the door and peeked in.

"Brother Zeno?"

"Why do you bother me?" Zeno roared. "Can you not see that I am working?"

The priest flinched. "There is a... person here to see you and your guest."

"Who?" Zeno frowned. "I'm not expecting anyone."

"She was most insistent."

"Is it my wife?"

"No," the priest said quickly. "Though I have not met the *signora*, I am sure—"

The young man broke off when surprised shouts echoed down the hallway. Tenzin flew over the young priest's head, shoving him down and landing in front of Zeno with a smile.

"Oh," Zeno said. "It's you. I wasn't expecting you."

"Nobody expects me!" she said.

"Or the Spanish Inquisition," Ben muttered.

"What?"

Ben cleared his throat. "Nothing, Tiny. Why are you here?"

She flew over and sat in the center of the worktable as the young priest abandoned the room with relief.

"I was bored. And I wanted to talk to Zeno about Naples."

Ben leaned against the table. "Oh, are we being forthcoming this time?"

She shrugged. "There's not so much mystery. There is a vampire there who wants me to find some old coins for him. I want you to help."

Zeno's eyes shot up. "Who?"

"Who what?"

"Who wants you to find the coins?"

"Alfonso." Tenzin scooted over and swung her leg over the edge of the table, shoving Ben's carefully organized papers to the side. "Who else?"

Zeno's eyes darted between Tenzin and Ben. "And you intend to take Giovanni's son with you?"

"Yes," Tenzin said.

"I'm not Gio's son. And you haven't actually asked me to go with you," Ben said, crossing his arms. "I'm not going unless you tell me the details. And that includes any cross-Atlantic steamer trips I might be unknowingly booked on."

Zeno started laughing.

Tenzin flew behind Ben and perched on his back, hanging her arms over his shoulders. "Don't be mad. Didn't you get an excellent grade in Conversational Mandarin the next semester?"

"Not the point."

Zeno was still laughing. "I want to hear that story."

"It's really not that funny."

Tenzin said, "It really is."

"Tiny, if you want me—"

"I'll give you all the details. I already told you about the Sicilian coins, didn't I?"

"Mentioning a type of coin isn't a story. That's a detail. Is this another one of your caches? Is this someone who hired you? What will I be doing? Will any weapons be involved?"

"Such a pacifist." She sighed. "So boring."

How did she piss him off *so* quickly?

He untangled her arms from around his neck and shoved her away. "Fine. If I'm so boring, then you can—"

"Ask me your questions," Zeno barked. "Then take your lovers' quarrel somewhere else. I don't want to listen to it."

"He's not my lover," Tenzin said. "He's my... life coach."

Ben and Zeno both stared at her.

"What?" she said. "You don't like it when I call you my human, so I've been thinking of other things I can call you instead of that."

Ben could feel the headache starting in his temples. "Do

you even know what a life coach is?"

She threw up her arms. "Does anyone really know what a life coach is? I'm living in Los Angeles. They'll just think I've gone crazy."

"—er," Ben said. "Crazier. And don't call me your life coach."

Zeno asked, "So what are you?"

"I'm..." Ben sighed. "I don't know. Impatient to hear the rest of this."

"Fine." Tenzin hopped off his back and onto the table. "I wanted to ask Zeno some questions anyway."

"Ask me what?"

"About Alfonso," she said. "He's the one who wants me to find his lost Sicilian tarì."

"Tarì," Zeno said. "Medieval tarì?"

Tenzin nodded. "These were minted during the twelfth century by Roger the Second."

"I don't think of Roger as a very Italian name," Ben said.

"He wasn't. He was Norman." Zeno stepped forward. "Truly? Twelfth-century tarì?"

"Alfonso had a very large chest of them. Rare, but I think they have sentimental value of some kind."

Zeno asked, "Was this chest in the library in Naples?"

"The big heist?" Tenzin grinned. "No, I don't think so, but I don't know the details. I just know Alfonso used to have them, and now he doesn't. And he wants me to find them."

Ben was suspicious. "Why you?"

"Because I'm good at finding things." She paused. "And I might have let it slip in some circles that I'd heard rumors about a hoard of medieval gold coins."

Ben's suspicions grew. "And had you? Heard rumors?"

She cocked her head to the side. "Not... precisely."

"It figures," Ben said, gathering up his messenger bag.

"Zeno, do you have any weapons I can use? I have a feeling this is going to be one of *those* vacations."

"I didn't invite you on vacation!" she yelled. "I told you this was a working holiday."

"Yes," Zeno interrupted. "Working in *Naples*. Does Giovanni know?"

"No," she said. "Does he need to?"

"Well yes, because *Alfonso is crazy*," Zeno said. "And you're taking his son there."

"Not his son!"

"Alfonso hired me," Tenzin said. "And I've met him before... I think. I hardly think he's going to hurt Ben or me unless we try to double-cross him."

"Well yes," Zeno said. "It's entirely possible that you will get there and he will decide you have offended him in some inexplicable way and he'll kill you. Because he's *mad*. They call him the Mad Spaniard."

Ben turned to Zeno. "Like... regularly? That's his regular nickname? The Mad Spaniard?"

Why, why, *why* did she think this was a good idea?

"Not all the time," Zeno said.

Tenzin added, "Sometimes they call him the Mad Duke."

"So much better!" Ben threw up his hands and started pacing.

"But I don't know if he was really a duke or not." Tenzin shrugged. "It might just be one of those rumors. And Zeno, Alfonso could certainly *try* to hurt Ben or me," Tenzin said through a wicked smile. "That might be entertaining."

"Not from my perspective," Ben said.

"What do you want to know?" Zeno asked.

"What is his political situation right now?"

"Tenuous," Zeno answered. "But it is always so. His longest-serving advisor is a vampire named Filomena. She's powerful but doesn't seem to want the spotlight. Known to be vicious. You'd like her, I think."

"Because she's vicious?" Ben asked.

Zeno smiled. "Because she's straightforward. Filomena is probably the only reason Alfonso has stayed in power this long. She tempers him. The *napoletana* court is small, paranoid, and insular. Many of them came to Naples before Bonaparte. They don't truly consider themselves Italian, and they don't recognize Rome."

Ben asked, "And Emil Conti lets them get away with that?"

Zeno shrugged. "Naples is not his concern at present, though it would be better if the library theft had not happened. Now people are paying attention to it. Now some of his own people have lost possessions, which is why he's been putting pressure on Giovanni and Beatrice to take on Roman clients. Mostly Conti would like to pretend that Naples does not exist. Alfonso *does* pretend that Rome does not exist. As long as the status quo is maintained, everyone is happy."

Tenzin's head fell back. "The status quo is boring."

"And safe." Ben patted her head. "Remember that part."

"Fine," she said. "So we avoid pissing Alfonso off, keep Filomena in sight if things look like they're going... sideways, find his gold, and get out of there."

"Alfonso is known to be greedy," Zeno said. "If he wants you to find his gold, make sure you don't keep any souvenirs."

Tenzin's eyes went big and round. "Would I do that?"

"Yes," Ben said. Then to Zeno, "Yes, she would. Which is usually why Gio doesn't mind if I tag along on these kinds of things. I'll keep her out of trouble."

Tenzin's impish smile spread.

"Oh yes," Zeno said. "Obviously."

☿

THE train to Naples was only an hour. He dozed in the sun, then grabbed another taxi from the station to Piazza Bellini, just south of the Archeological Museum. It was late afternoon, and the black stone streets of Naples were sweltering. He ducked in from the piazza and entered the quiet, flower-filled courtyard with a fountain at one end. The building was old. The furnishings were modern.

"*Buongiorno*," the hostess at the front desk said when he opened the door.

Ahhhhh.

A rush of cool air. He stood for a moment, eyes closed, reveling in the air-conditioning.

"*Signore?*"

"Hey," he finally said in English. "I have a reservation under Benjamin Rios."

She smiled and answered in English. "Your passport, please?"

He pulled out a passport and handed it to her. Ben wasn't sure why he was using the fake passport Gavin had helped him procure last year in New York. He hated using his father's last name, but it made the most sense. He'd answered to Benjamin Rios for nearly twelve years, after all. Now the name only existed as a useful shadow.

The girl checked him in and handed him the key and a map directing him to his room. It was a small hotel, but it was perfectly located and had terrace rooms, which was necessary when he was traveling with Tenzin.

The hallway was sweltering, but the room was cool. Ben unlocked the french doors leading out to the terrace, closed the drapes, and decided to take a nap.

And woke to Tenzin on the bed beside him.

"This is starting to become a habit when we travel, Tiny."

"You're not naked this time. I checked."

He kept his eyes closed and shook his head. She'd checked. Of course she had.

"This bed isn't as comfortable as your bed in Rome," she complained.

"Yeah..." He yawned and rolled toward her. "I didn't pick it because of the beds. I picked it because it has a private terrace. That way you can come and go as you please. This place seems to be pretty quiet, so I think you'll be okay."

"Awww." She patted his cheek. "You're such a thoughtful life coach."

"Please don't call me your life coach. That would make me feel responsible for any bodies you leave in your wake."

She laughed.

"Are we meeting Alfonso tonight?" he asked.

"Yes. Despite my somewhat flippant attitude with Zeno, I don't want to linger in the city too long. I want to meet Alfonso, make the deal, and fly out of here. We have three weeks, and that should be just enough time if we're smart."

"Want to fill me in?" he asked. "Now that Zeno's not here to tattle to Gio?"

"I will." She frowned. "But not yet. I want to get your impressions of Alfonso's court without any background information. Is that fair to you?"

He shifted on the bed. "I get it. His chief advisor—"

"Filomena."

"Yeah, Filomena. Are we meeting her tonight too?"

Tenzin nodded. "She's the one meeting us at Piazza del Gesù Nuovo at ten o'clock tonight."

"Do we have time to get dinner?"

"Always hungry. Always, always hungry."

☿

SHE watched him as he chatted with an artist and munched on the hot *sciurilli* he'd picked up from a street vendor. She'd sampled a few of the delicately fried zucchini blossoms before she handed them over to Benjamin to demolish.

A group of rowdy street children ran into the square, shouting and laughing. Tenzin watched them spot Ben, his fashionable new clothes and Roman accent making him what the boys thought would be an easy target.

She watched the children slyly kick the ball closer and closer until the artist was yelling at one boy for disturbing his display and one of the others bumped into Ben, the child laughing and apologizing as he dipped into Ben's pocket...

And came out squealing. Ben clapped a hand over the boy's mouth and grabbed him by the back of the neck, dropping the fried snacks he'd been eating as the artist rushed to gather the prints that had gone flying with the soccer ball. Ben crouched down next to the boy, pinching his small hand in his own and speaking fiercely as the boy's cheeks turned bright red.

A few seconds later, the boy was running after his compatriots, who had abandoned him, a five-Euro note clutched in his hand, while Ben helped the artist pick up the last of his prints and a stray dog finished off the *sciurilli* that had fallen.

Ben walked over to a nearby street fountain and washed his hands before he shook them off and walked back to Tenzin.

"Pizza?"

She smiled and shook her head. "What did you tell him?"

"To be more careful choosing his marks."

"You didn't try to warn him away from a life of crime?"

Ben looked down the side street where the boy had disappeared. "I did a lot worse when I was hungry." He nodded toward a pizzeria on the corner. "Come on. I'll buy you a slice. Hopefully this Filomena won't be late."

3

B EN SPOTTED THE VAMPIRE ENTERING Piazza del Gesù Nuovo a few minutes before ten. She was tall, especially for an immortal. With notable exceptions like his uncle, humans turned before the last century tended to be shorter than average. Tenzin was a perfect example. She was tiny, though she protested that she'd been quite tall for her time.

This vampire was wearing high-heeled boots and leggings with a long, sleeveless tunic that showed off lightly muscled arms. Caramel-brown hair flowed down her back, and her skin was pale with a slight pink flush that told Ben she'd fed earlier in the evening. No one turned to look at her as she crossed the square, even though she was wearing sunglasses at night, which made Ben think she was a familiar sight in the neighborhood. Though she looked young, he knew she wasn't.

She was also drop-dead gorgeous.

Ben knew the vampire had spotted Tenzin, who was perched on the graffiti-covered base of the monument in the center of the piazza, but Ben hung back, wanting to observe Alfonso's lieutenant for a few more moments before he drew her attention.

She was confident. He couldn't see any weapons on her, but she approached Tenzin with what could almost be called a swagger.

It was unusual in the immortal world. Though humans rarely noticed Tenzin—which she loved—something about her made most immortals pause. Beatrice had told him once that Tenzin's amnis "smelled ancient," whatever that meant. If he'd been able to detect it like vampires did, he might have been intimidated.

But he was human, so she was just Tenzin.

"You are Tenzin," the vampire said when she reached the center of the square.

"Yes."

Tenzin didn't rise to her feet. Just looked up at the other vampire, squinting a little, her chin resting in her palm.

The street boys who'd been hanging around sank back into the crowds on the edge of the square, leaving the vampires alone, save for Ben, whom Filomena finally noticed. She looked him up and down with an appraising eye.

"I am Filomena. Who is the human?"

"This is Ben, my yoga instructor." Tenzin didn't bat an eye, so Ben didn't either. He just started plotting how on earth he was going to pay her back for that one. Was yoga instructor better or worse than life coach?

To Filomena's credit, she didn't blink. "Will he be accompanying you?"

"Yes."

"Fine." Filomena jerked her head. "Come. Alfonso is waiting."

Tenzin rose and followed Filomena, who led them toward the odd stone building that dominated the square. Covered in pyramid-faced stones, the church of Gesù Nuovo was deserted, visiting hours long past. No matter. Filomena knocked at the

173

wooden door and stood back until it swung open. She passed something to the priest at the door and ducked inside.

Tenzin and Ben followed her, neither meeting the eyes of the human in black robes who closed the door behind them. The heavy thunk echoed in the empty church. It was dark, except for a few candles lit in each chapel.

Baroque art assaulted Ben's eyes. Paintings, statues, and intricate altar pieces. "More" seemed to be the overriding design scheme. Filomena led them down a hallway covered with brass plaques and medals shaped like various body parts. Hearts and lungs. Legs, heads, and hands. The disembodied parts plastered the walls of the narrow hallway, lending a surprisingly morbid air to the holy place.

"For healing," Filomena said when she caught him looking. "Pilgrims come and pray here. They hang medals to ask for healing."

Ben smiled, delighted in the excess. "Does it work?"

Filomena blinked. "Of course not. It's superstition. Humans are very gullible."

He saw the edge of Tenzin's smile when he passed her.

The hallway led to a back room with a hidden door behind a tapestry. Then another hallway and another door. Ben could feel the cool damp growing the farther they traveled. At his side, he felt Tenzin's tension increase.

"Where are you leading us?" she asked.

"Alfonso keeps court under the city," Filomena explained. "He prefers the seclusion."

Only Ben caught the minute falter in Tenzin's step.

"That's unusual, isn't it?" Ben asked, stepping quickly into her silence. "I was told Alfonso was a water vampire."

"He is."

No other explanation came, nor did he expect one. Filomena pressed on, turning corner after corner until Ben was completely baffled. It was a maze, designed to confuse those not familiar with it. Plaster hallways gradually gave way to stone passages. Then Filomena stopped at a wooden door and pulled out an old iron key.

She said nothing as she unlocked the door and swung it open, the damp musk of earth blasting them as an even darker passageway gaped below. Filomena didn't wait for them to enter. She handed Ben a flashlight from a shelf set into the wall and continued down the wooden stairs leading below the surface.

Ben watched Tenzin. Her tension had been steadily growing the farther they traveled. Now her face was a complete mask. Dead eyes. Face devoid of expression. He'd never seen her look less human.

"Tiny?" he murmured.

"Go. I don't need the light."

Something was very wrong.

"Do you want me to—"

"Walk, Benjamin."

She shoved him toward the stairs and followed him, but Ben grabbed hold of one of her cold hands and held it, disturbed beyond reason by the look in her eyes. He walked down the damp, earthen passage leading under the streets of Naples.

Tenzin wasn't claustrophobic. The mere idea of it was ridiculous. She'd comfortably traveled across much of China in a smuggler's hatch once. What the hell was going on?

He refused to let go of her hand, even when she tried to tug it away. Finally she seemed to give up and let Ben hold it as they walked down the stairs, following Filomena into the darkness. The vampire slowed down to allow for the clumsy human to stumble along. The passageway was smooth, but the dirt floor was uneven.

"How do you walk in those heels?" he asked Filomena.

A low laugh. "Natural grace and centuries of practice."

Ben smiled.

He followed her for what felt like an eternity before the earthen passageway gave way to stone again, and he felt the tension begin to ease from Tenzin's fingers. Another turn and they entered an arched chamber nearly the size of a gymnasium.

"What is this?" he asked Filomena.

"One of the catacombs," she said. "Naples has many tunnels. Alfonso has used this system for years. The humans don't come here."

Ben ran his fingers along one wall. "This construction looks Roman."

"It is."

He couldn't help but smile. It was like walking through a ruin, only perfectly preserved from sun and weather. Arches soared over his head along with a series of walkways leading from the second story into other tunnels. There were no electric lights, but torches lit the hall and the air was fresh, so he knew there had to be ample ventilation. He could hear water flowing somewhere. It must have been what drew Alfonso to this place.

Hidden from the sun. No electricity. Secret passages. Underground water.

"It's brilliant," he said under his breath.

Tenzin, seemingly fully recovered from whatever had plagued her in the earthen tunnel, nodded in agreement.

"A most comfortable court," she said. "I am impressed, Filomena."

"On behalf of my lord, I thank you," Filomena said, nodding respectfully toward Tenzin. "The immortals of Naples are very proud of our city."

"As you should be."

☿

TENZIN hated being underground. Absolutely hated it. She couldn't remember the last time she'd frozen as she had on the stairs.

It wasn't the close passageway. It wasn't even the knowledge that they were going beneath the earth. It was damp air. The closed passage. The taste of the earth and rot in the air surrounding her.

The taste of earth in her mouth...

She'd heard ancient laughter in the back of her mind, and the wary creature in her emerged. The gut-deep urge for blood took root, and she concentrated on the pounding of the young one's pulse.

Th-thunk. Th-thunk. Th-thunk.

She followed it in her mind, pacing his steps. Following his blood. But something stopped the creep of amnis before it reached his skin. Some instinct whispered to the feral creature, coaxing it to calm.

They walked into a tunnel built of rock, and the smell of earth receded. The pressing eased on her mind.

There was nothing but the taste of earth that could cause that old reaction to emerge. Tenzin found she was still holding Ben's hand. It showed weakness, but she did not let go until they entered a larger hallway clad in dressed stone, when the rotting earth had receded and her sanity had returned.

Mostly.

Filomena led them under the Roman arches of subterranean Naples and toward her master, who was sitting on a raised dais playing king of all he surveyed.

Tenzin disliked him immediately.

He wasn't a handsome vampire. His face was pockmarked and sagging. His skin had once been olive, but now it leaned toward sallow. A high forehead, arched nose, and haughty gaze led her to believe he was, as he claimed, Spanish royalty of some kind.

Filomena stopped at the edge of the dais and gave Alfonso a short bow.

"Alfonso," she began in English, "I introduce Tenzin, daughter of Zhang Guolao. Sired of air. Mated to water..."

Oh, so he was one of *those* immortals. Tenzin tried not to sigh as Filomena continued.

"...Scourge of the Naiman Khanlig. Commander of the Altan Wind. Protector of Penglai Island. Patron goddess of the Holy Mountain..."

Goddess of anything holy, let it end.

"...protector and scribe of New Spain. Friend of Don Ernesto Alvarez of Los Angeles." Filomena paused. "And... Ben, her yoga instructor."

Ben leaned over and whispered, "You have so many more titles than I realized."

"You have no idea."

"I need to be called 'The Scourge' of something. Just put that in the back of your mind to think about later."

"Maybe the Scourge of the Refrigerator," she muttered. "That would be accurate."

Ben must have realized that a dozen or so vampires were staring at the two of them because he straightened, cleared his throat, and whispered, "Sorry." He stepped just behind Tenzin and to the left, instinctively covering her weaker side.

Tenzin, not wanting to piss off the vampire who would be paying her lots and lots of money if everything went according to plan, inclined her head and said, "Thank you for your generous welcome, Alfonso."

"Welcome to Naples," Alfonso grunted. "It is one of the few civilized places left on the peninsula."

"I have found it remarkably civilized," Tenzin said. "And very rich. In history. And... culture."

And gold, but Alfonso would probably find that crass. There were a few artifacts in the archeological museum that Tenzin was considering liberating from their cases. Some things just shouldn't be forced behind glass.

"As you are here, I assume you received my communication regarding the gold."

"I did."

"The Norman tarì are mine." Alfonso's eyes burned. "Whatever rumors you might have heard, any knowledge of them should be given to me. Withholding information that might lead to their return would be very unwise."

"I have long welcomed," Tenzin said quietly, "the opportunity to assist my... friends in the retrieval of valuable possessions, should those possessions be lost or misplaced." She raised her voice enough for the other immortals to hear it. "But be careful, son of Kato. I do not respond well to bullying."

☿

GOOD Lord, some vampires were stupid, no matter how long they lived. Ben repressed the urge shake his head. Who heard the litany of titles Tenzin carried—*the Scourge of the Naiman Khanlig?* What was *that* about?—and then proceeded to threaten the Scourge?

Tenzin was quietly schooling Alfonso, so Ben made mental notes about the Neapolitan court. Lucky for him, most of these vampires were traditional and completely ignored the human in their midst.

Filomena, he noted, did not. In fact, she was watching him more than she was Tenzin. And the slight curve at the corner of her gorgeous mouth told him she'd like to get to know Tenzin's "yoga instructor" a little more.

Ben returned her smile with a wink.

Filomena's eyebrows rose, but she did not look displeased.

Tenzin was speaking in a lower voice to Alfonso. The two leaned together, engaged in a private conversation. Alfonso scowled, but Ben didn't get the impression he was displeased.

Filomena sidled up to him. "He always looks like that."

"How? Pissed?"

Filomena clearly didn't understand the American slang.

Ben quickly said, "Sorry. I mean angry."

"Ah." She nodded. "Yes, Alfonso nearly always looks angry. And he often is. But I believe he and your pupil are merely negotiating some arrangement regarding the coins she's heard rumors of."

Ben was confused. "My pupil?"

Filomena cocked her head. "You are her yoga instructor, are you not? I admit, I did not know that a warrior such as Tenzin was so spiritually inclined, but I find it inspiring that she is so. She must be very devout to bring you with her, even across oceans."

"Right." Ben tried to look very solemn. "Well, I'm kind of her... spiritual advisor too."

"Of course."

"So you find Tenzin inspiring, huh?"

She blinked. "She is one of the most ancient of our race. A woman of tremendous power and influence."

"And you?"

"I'm young." Her mouth curled into a smile. "But not so young as you."

Filomena's eyes traveled across his chest and up his neck while she let the edge of her fangs peek from her bottom lip.

It was the vampire version of a proposition, and Ben's body responded with enthusiasm.

"Will you be remaining in Naples?" she asked.

I will be now.

Ben forced himself to remember his role. "That depends on Tenzin, of course."

Filomena glanced at Tenzin and Alfonso, who were still locked in conversation. "And you do not belong to her?"

Hell no.

He put his solemn face back on. "I hope you understand that I take my spiritual commitments very seriously. I could never involve myself with someone under my instruction."

Her fangs dropped lower. "I have heard that those who practice the eastern arts exhibit great flexibility and vigor."

Ben didn't even hear Tenzin approach until she interrupted.

"Yes," she said. "Ben is very vigorous. Shall we go?"

He blinked. "What? I... Yes. I mean, if you're done with your conversation with Alfonso. Then yes."

She looked amused. "I am. Filomena, your master said you could see us out. The front door this time, please."

Filomena glanced over Ben's shoulder and nodded at whoever was behind him. Ben was assuming Alfonso, but he didn't turn to look. Yoga instructors wouldn't be that curious, would they?

"Of course," she said, bowing a little as she motioned down a hall that was opposite the way they'd entered. "If you would follow me, my lady."

"No bowing, please. And call me Tenzin."

"I would be honored to do so."

Ben fell in step behind them as Filomena led them down another stone hallway and up a set of torchlit stairs. Within moments, they were exiting through the front of a dimly lit nightclub. Vampire and human patrons turned to glance at them, then quickly looked away.

Once they were out of the building, Ben looked around and realized they were close to his hotel on Piazza Bellini.

"Convenient," he muttered, looking around at the young people gathered across the street. Naples was alive with humans and more than a few vampires. The sound of music and smell of tobacco filled the air. Ben saw paint-spattered artists and earnest students. Young men with slicked-back hair and girls in snug cocktail dresses.

Tenzin and Filomena were all business.

"I'll make contact when I locate the item," Tenzin said. "I would estimate three weeks, but I cannot say for certain. This will require a trip to Switzerland, you understand?"

"Of course," Filomena said. "We all understand the Swiss are... complicated. If he grows impatient, I will remind him of your words."

"Thank you."

"The thanks are mine." Filomena inclined her head. "The tarì are part of our treasury. You honor Naples with your assistance in this matter."

"I look forward to our continued cooperation," Tenzin said. "Ben, let's go."

He followed Tenzin, throwing Filomena one more smile over his shoulder. She returned it before he lost her in the crowd.

"Careful," Tenzin said.

"What?" He stopped looking for Filomena in the mass of people. "Careful what?"

"She's powerful. Ambitious too. And she's playing you."

Ben felt a bite of annoyance. "Listen, Tiny, I'm not a teenager—"

"If you think she doesn't know who you are, you're kidding

yourself." Tenzin didn't look angry, only amused. "You don't actually think Alfonso's second believes I brought my yoga instructor to Naples, do you?"

Well, yeah, but he decided to play it off. "Good. That means I won't have to worry about bending into impossible shapes when we hook up."

Tenzin laughed. "'Hook up?' You act as if you'd be catching a fish on a line. Trust me, if anyone is the hunter in this situation, it is not you."

His cheeks burned. "This really isn't any of your business."

"On the contrary, it is certainly my business." Her face grew serious. "Human girls are one thing, but she's a three-hundred-year-old immortal. Have you had sex with a vampire before?"

He clenched his jaw in an effort to rein in his temper. It worked. Some. "That's none of your business either."

They walked into Piazza Bellini, the crowds of young people no less dense than they had been outside Alfonso's club. Tenzin walked Ben to the gates of his hotel and turned to face him.

"Sex is one thing, Benjamin. Don't let her bite you. We get possessive when we bite."

"Yeah, I know that."

She shrugged. "You'll do what you want. Just remember, don't sabotage this deal with your ignorant libido. Alfonso wants me to find his coins. You help me and you'll get twenty percent of the finder's fee, which is not insignificant."

Sex he didn't want to discuss, but money was always on the table. "Forty percent and I'm an altar boy until after we deliver the coins."

"Twenty-five. You may flirt, but you'd end up being an altar boy anyway. You're too smart to be her plaything."

"Who said I wouldn't be playing her? Thirty percent."

She cocked her head. "Done. I'm going to Switzerland

tomorrow night. Go back to Rome and look busy. Help Zeno in the library. Maybe head to Perugia for a few days of research. I'll be in touch when I need you."

"Sounds like a plan, Tiny." Ben grinned. "Switzerland, huh? Don't forget to take a sweater."

4

BEN SLEPT UNTIL NOON THE next day, then decided to wander around Naples and enjoy some of the street art the city was known for. More than one artist who'd gotten his or her start in graffiti had been signed by major agents in the past few years. It was fascinating to see the blend of styles. Art of any kind fascinated him, but street art, with its inherently fleeting nature, touched something in Ben's soul.

He stood at the mouth of an alley, staring down at a small white figure painted on the soot-black stone of an alleyway corner. The figure was holding a tiny sword high against a flying dragon. A red feather was perched in his cap.

The painting might have been there for months or hours. Who knew when city workers might come and paint over it? Another artist could come and wipe it away with something darker or brighter or coarser or more colorful. But the artist had taken the time, probably in the dead of night, to put her mark on that wall, hoping to touch a passerby. For the moment Ben looked at that tiny figure fighting off the dragon, Ben and the artist were in the same space.

Fleeting.

Like the painting.

Here today. Gone tomorrow.

He was the tiny hero with the feather in his cap, fighting things impossibly powerful. He was the painting on the wall. No grand masterpiece preserved and admired for eternity. His life would be a blink. A quick glance from the immortal pedestrians of history.

No wonder the little figure flew a red feather in his cap. No wonder his sword was held so high.

Tiny hope. Foolish courage.

Ben pulled out his phone and snapped a picture before he continued to walk down the Spaccanapoli, the narrow road splitting the heart of old Naples. He stopped for some gelato, then wandered some more. Bought a few trinkets in a shop. Watched a drummer when he finally arrived back in Piazza del Gesù Nuovo, the spiked facade of the church a reminder of his meeting the previous night.

Naples was... odd. Fiercely different from other Italian cities he knew. Gloriously excessive. He wished that Beatrice could visit. He knew she'd love it.

His phone buzzed in his pocket with a text message from Fabi.

T called the house. She said to make sure you go to the archeological museum before you meet your new girlfriend.

Ben texted back: *Ha-ha.*

??? Do I need to be jealous?

He shook his head. Leave it to Tenzin to try to cause trouble.

No, he texted back. *And don't you have a boyfriend?*

Never hurts to keep your options open. ;) I want details when you get back. Stay safe.

Always.

He pushed away from the wall where he'd been searching for shade and wandered back to the Piazza Bellini. The Museo Archeologico Nazionale di Napoli was only a few blocks from his hotel, and while he'd heard about the mosaic collection there —famous for its detailed relics from Pompeii—Ben had a feeling it was the coins and medals exhibit Tenzin wanted him to visit.

He wandered the grand halls, fanning himself with the museum map. The marble-clad museum was shady, but not particularly cool in the sweltering June heat. Still, he didn't hurry. It was better than fighting the crowds for shade outside.

The Pompeii mosaics really were everything the guidebooks said they'd be, but as he walked up the stairs to reach the gems room, he wondered what exactly Tenzin had wanted him to see. He'd seen more than his share of old currency. What was special about Naples?

The front desk had told him he was fortunate the rare coins exhibit was even open. As he entered, Ben was struck by the sheer number in the collection. Everything from Greek and Roman coins to medieval and modern. One room even contained dies from the old mint in Naples.

Norman *tarì*, Alfonso had said. Ben had looked up Norman *tarì* as soon as he'd arrived back at the hotel, but he didn't notice any in the collection. What he saw was a mix of metals in all different states and a whole lot of empty space as museum visitors took in the more dazzling treasures of the museum.

Norman *tarì*.

What was so special about these *tarì* that Alfonso would risk disrespecting Tenzin to get them back? Did Tenzin already know where they were? Is that why she'd gone to Switzerland?

Ben felt a twinge of jealousy that she'd abandoned him when he felt the bead of sweat roll down his temple. The beard and longer hair might have been a hit with the girls this summer, but he was tempted to find a barber and a razor that afternoon.

Instead, he went back to the hotel, drank two cold beers, and retreated to the shelter of his air-conditioned room for the remainder of the afternoon. When he emerged, the sun was down, the temperature had cooled, and a vampire wearing high-heeled boots was smoking a slim cigarette in the garden of his hotel.

Filomena smiled and blew out a thin stream of smoke. "You're awake."

Ben walked toward her. "So are you."

She shrugged one lightly muscled shoulder and nodded toward the piazza. "Join me for a drink, will you?"

Ben cocked his elbow out and Filomena rose, her boots putting her just a hair taller than Ben as they walked.

"So, Benjamin Vecchio"—Filomena leaned into his side —"what is the adopted nephew of a famed assassin doing in my city with his uncle's old partner?"

He really hated when Tenzin was right.

☿

FILOMENA smiled at him in the candlelight, careful to conceal her fangs even when she laughed. "Was yoga instructor her idea or yours?"

"What do you think?"

"I hardly know. I only know Tenzin by reputation." She gave him another careless shrug. Such a human habit for an immortal. Did she do it out of true habit, or was it an affectation to put her prey at ease? Ben was drawn to her regardless.

They were sitting at a small table outside a quiet restaurant near the waterfront. The moon was high, reflecting off the Bay of Naples as shadowed ships bobbed in the distance. The water-front was busy, but the restaurant she'd chosen was isolated down a small alley, which meant they didn't worry about being overheard.

Ben said, "I think everyone knows Tenzin's reputation."

"Yes." She sipped the red wine. A drop lingered on her lips before she licked it away. "Everyone does. And yet you were raised with her?"

Ben shook his head. "Not exactly. I only met Tenzin when I was sixteen."

"A child."

"Of a sort."

Ben couldn't remember ever feeling like a child. His earliest memory was of his parents in a fistfight, screaming at each other before his father threw his mother into a mirror. It was the sound of shattering glass and the taste of blood in his mouth that had stuck with him. His mother said a shard had sliced his lip. He still bore the tiny scar. And the rest of his "childhood" he simply tried to banish to the murky shadows of history.

"But what a childhood it must have been," she said. "To be raised among legends."

"What about your human life, huh?" He leaned forward, keen to take the attention off himself. "Do you remember... the Renaissance?"

Filomena laughed. "No."

It was a game. Vampires were notoriously secretive about their origins. To reveal their age meant revealing their power. But guessing and riddles were fair game.

"Italian unification?"

"Oh yes," Filomena said, her eyes flashing. "I remember that quite clearly."

"Napoleon."

"You're getting closer," she said, leaning a slim arm on the table, propping her chin in her palm. "You know I'm not going to tell you."

"But you are from Naples."

She smiled and he saw a hint of fang. "Define *Naples*."

Ben gave her a good-natured growl and threw up his hands. "I give up."

Filomena laughed. "You should know better, Benjamin Vecchio."

"Ben," he said. "Call me Ben."

Dark brown eyes appraised him. "And did your friends warn you away from me, Ben?"

"Of course." He leaned across the table until he heard her draw in his scent. He stared at her lips. "You may be a stunningly beautiful woman, but you're also a lethal immortal enforcer, second to one of the most dangerous vampire lords in Italy." He let the corner of his mouth turn up as he raised his eyes to hers. "And I am a mere yoga instructor. I'd be a fool to—"

The breath between them vanished when Filomena took his lips.

Hot. Ben closed his eyes and took her mouth as she had taken his, raising his hand to cup the nape of her neck. His fingers tangled in her thick, caramel-brown hair.

Filomena heated her skin until it matched the flush of his own. She tasted of wine and chocolate and the indefinable taste that was all her own. A medley of scent and flavor and sensation. Her eyelashes brushed his skin as he eased away from her mouth and trailed his lips along the arch of her cheekbone. He followed the fragrance of her hair and the perfumed skin beneath her ear.

Filomena let out a low, satisfied purr and dragged her nails down his neck.

The sharp bite of pain brought Ben up short.

Blood rushed back to his head as he trailed firm kisses back along her chin and up to her mouth again, luxuriating in her taste and the softness of her lips.

Her fangs were fully aroused.

Ben drew away, gently biting her lower lip before he smiled. "You taste delicious."

She blinked slowly. "And you are a cautious man."

He cupped the side of her neck, brushing his thumb over where her pulse would beat.

If she were human. Which she wasn't.

"Mmm," he said on a sigh. "Sadly, I have to be. After all, a foolish yoga instructor wouldn't last long in your world."

"*My* world?" Filomena raised an eyebrow, clearly still enjoying their flirtation. "Is it not your world as well?"

"That's an excellent question."

"One you're not going to answer."

"It's only our first bottle of wine, Filomena. We shouldn't reveal all our secrets at once."

"True."

She shrugged his hand off her neck, so Ben let it fall to the back of the chair in a proprietary gesture that seemed to please the vampire, judging by the smile teasing the corners of her mouth.

"You're bold."

"Am I?" *That's probably why I'm not dead already.*

Lucky for him, she only smiled and leaned against it, willing to play his game for the night. "You're also surprisingly good with your mouth. For a human."

"Thanks. I got kissing lessons from a three-hundred-year-old French courtesan when I was a teenager. I think it helped."

Filomena threw her head back and laughed loudly. She even wiped a pink tear from the corner of her eye before she asked, "Is that true?"

"I'm not going to tell you."

She narrowed her eyes, trying to find his tell, but Ben smiled innocently.

"What?"

"It's a shame I cannot take you as a lover. I don't think either of us would regret it."

He let his eyes trace her mouth, the delectable cleavage she had bared for the evening, and the sweep of her long, muscled legs. "I think regret would be the last thing on my mind."

"This life is long."

He cocked his head. "Not for everyone."

"All the more reason to seize the night."

Ben shook his head and poured both of them more wine. "My friends were right. You are a dangerous woman."

ō

Rome, one week later

BEN KICKED the ball back to Enzo, the boy whooping in delight as he ran after it in the courtyard. His mother, Serafina, watched from the bench near the fountain where she chatted quietly with Fabi as Ben and Enzo killed time before Zeno rose for the night.

The old vampire had finally convinced the quiet woman to marry him the Christmas before, though Fina had protested they should wait until her son was grown. Ben was fairly sure his uncle would have a new immortal daughter once Enzo was an adult. Neither Fina nor Zeno had said anything, but Ben could see how devoted they were to each other. Plus they were both under Giovanni's aegis and invaluable members of his staff.

Fina had brought herself and Enzo to join Zeno in Rome as soon as the boy had finished his school exams for the year. Now the three were residing in Residenza di Spada with Ben and Angie.

Angie, of course, was delighted. Especially since that gave her three human appetites to cook for. Four if you counted Fabi, who ate dinner with them most nights.

"So Fina"—Ben interrupted the women's quiet conversation —"Zeno said you saw Tenzin at the library before she went north."

"Only briefly," Fina said. "I didn't speak to her. I think she only sheltered for the day before she flew away. Though she did take a fifteenth-century manuscript on metalsmithing. Well, the copy of it. I only have a digital scan because the original resides in—"

"Metalsmithing?" Ben frowned. *Metalsmithing?* But why would Tenzin need a manual on medieval metalsmithing if she already knew where Alfonso's cache...

Oh, Tenzin.

Shit.

He should have known.

"Ben," Fina continued, unaware his thoughts had wandered, "Zeno tells me that you and Tenzin are working for Alfonso in Naples. You are being careful, aren't you?"

"Of course." He kicked the ball back to Enzo just before Angie called the boy inside the house to wash up. Ben strolled over to the edge of the fountain and perched on the corner. "What do you know about him?"

"Well"—Fina's prim voice made him smile—"it is rumored that he was part of the Bourbon court, but that is only a rumor. Like many things in Naples—well, and anything to do with immortals, if we're honest—rumors of corruption have followed him over the years. Giovanni is fairly certain he was behind the library theft."

Ben's eyebrows rose. According to what he'd been able guess

from subtle questions to Filomena, much of the unrest in the Neapolitan court was *because* of the library theft. Many of the richest immortals in Naples had lost personal collections that were both valuable and highly confidential. Ben suspected it was one of the reasons Alfonso had risked calling Tenzin.

So if Alfonso himself was somehow behind the theft and hiding it from his own people...

"How sure are you?" Ben asked. "That the theft is because of Alfonso?"

"Fairly sure," Fina said. "Officially, the authorities arrested the former director of the library. He had very suspicious polit-ical connections, and some of the books that made it on the black market were traced back to him. But when I spoke to my friends familiar with the Girolamini Library, they were quite certain there was more to it than one man. There were portions of the collection that had never been catalogued. Parts they were unofficially told to ignore. That had been happening long before the former director came into his position."

"But why would Alfonso want to steal his own people's papers and collections?"

Fabi, who'd been listening silently, said, "Power? Paranoia? Didn't your uncle say he was crazy?"

"Pretty sure Beatrice called him completely bonkers. Gio said something much more polite."

Fina smiled. "That sounds correct. Naples is... Well, it is different. I have always liked the city, but it is unique. Why wouldn't the immortal leader also be unique?"

"So if he was behind the theft...," Ben muttered. "Fina, how much of the theft have you tracked?"

"We're not tracking the whole theft. There's no way. Emil Conti asked, but Giovanni said he would only take on indi-vidual clients with specific items. And only books, of course. Those who lost antiquities have to rely on the human authorities. And most of them..." Fina shrugged. "Well, you know how secretive vampires are. They won't trust Italian police or Interpol."

Ben said, "So if I'm a vampire who lost... a coin collection, let's say"—Fabi shot eyes at him, but Ben ignored her—"you're saying there's no one like Gio who would track that down?"

Serafina shook her head. "Not that I'm aware of. No one with your uncle's reputation anyway. You could hire someone, but we're speaking about priceless artifacts, Benjamin. Many of which would only be legends or rumors to human sources."

"And"—a gruff voice broke into their quiet conversation as Zeno entered the courtyard—"we're paranoid bastards." He bent to press a hard kiss to Fina's mouth. "Are you well this night, my love?"

"Yes, Zeno."

"Good."

Ben cleared his throat loudly, and Fabi kicked him. He ignored her.

"So Zeno, why don't you think—?"

"How would one vampire trust another to retrieve an artifact for him or her without stealing it, eh?" Zeno sat next to Fina while she fussed with the collar of the shirt he'd obviously just tossed on. "Even if you did trust another vampire to find it, that immortal would be a target for the opportunistic ones. There are few vampires like your uncle who have trustworthy reputations *and* the ability to back up their word with power."

"But Gio won't look for anything but books."

"No, and I understand why. To do what we do"—he put an arm around his wife—"you must love it. You must have passion. Because often the work... It is dull, no? So many hours looking for one tiny clue that could lead you to another clue. Dead ends. Destroyed sources. Your uncle loves beautiful things, but he doesn't have the passion for art that he has for knowledge. It would be very convenient if we had someone who did."

Fabi kicked his shin again.

"Ow! Will you stop?"

Fabi just shook her head. "Nino, sometimes your head is full of rocks."

5

R io Terà dei Assassini, 3806 Venezia

"REALLY?" BEN LOOKED AT THE paper in his hand and the key that looked like it belonged somewhere in the seventeenth century. Then he looked at the seemingly incomprehensible address that had been left at the house in Rome the day before.

His low cursing must have attracted the attention of the young man setting out tables at the small osteria on the Rio Tera dei Assassini.

The young man smiled and called out to him, "Are you looking for something?"

"My friend's flat," Ben replied, tugging his messenger bag back up his shoulder and walking toward the waiter, valise in one hand and slip of paper in the other. "This address she gave me... I swear, I'll end up walking into the canal. I don't think it exists."

The young man frowned at the paper when Ben handed it

to him. "I don't recognize this address either. Venice can be difficult. Sometimes the houses aren't marked. This one..." He
craned his neck around the curve of the narrow street. "Yes,
you're right. It should be on the corner next to the canal, but the
number isn't correct."

"Great."

"Try to call her, yes?" The helpful young man smiled. "She
must have written it down wrong."

"Yeah, probably."

"Or she doesn't really want to see you." The waiter laughed.
"Women, no?"

"You have no idea with this one." Ben tapped his leg and felt
the key in his pocket. "I think I'll go try the one on the end.
You're right. She probably just wrote it down wrong. Thanks."

"Come back for a drink if you can't find her," the waiter
said. "Nothing makes us forget them like wine."

Ben cracked a smile. "No such luck. This one is unfor-
gettable."

He wandered down the street and waited, but it was dead
quiet. The street was hardly wider than an alleyway back in
LA. There were no shops and only a couple of quiet restaurants,
neither of which looked like it catered to tourists. In the maze of
Venice, this tiny street managed to be completely anonymous
while only five minutes' walk from the madness of Piazza
San Marco.

"Incredible," Ben said, leaning out over the canal where
gondoliers pushed gawking tourists through the narrow canals.
Some sang. Most chatted on their mobile phones.

Ah, Venice.

He had to admit, the note had been a surprise. What was
Tenzin doing in Venice? What did this have to do with Alfonso's tarì? And where the hell did she expect him to go?

He was leaning on the end of the building, watching the

gondolas push past when an old man shuffled out of the nearest door. It was a green maintenance door with electrical-shock warning signs screaming in yellow and various outlines blocked out. Apparently that doorway was not a good place to walk your dog.

The stocky old man turned to lock the green door and noticed Ben. He scowled, took a moment to look him up and down, then snorted while nodding.

"Okay," the man said, giving Ben a "hurry up" hand as he walked across to the opposite door. "What do I expect? Does she tell me anything? Of course she doesn't." He stopped and turned to Ben. "Do you have the key or not?"

"I think so?" Ben held up the key and the old man nodded and took it.

"Fine, fine."

The old man must have been Tenzin's caretaker. Or... something.

The old man kept grumbling. "'A friend soon,' she says. When is soon? Of course soon is three months later. Because I have nothing else to do but wait for her friends."

"Oh God." Ben had a depressing flash of insight that the old man could very well be a vision of his future. Fifty years from now, his youth gone, still managing to get pulled into Tenzin's schemes. "I need to rethink my life."

The old man opened a heavy wrought iron gate and raised a finger as he squinted at Ben. "Yes. You do. And don't forget to lock the gate on the way out. The code is written on the wall in the courtyard. Five hundred years old and she can't remember a gate code. She has to carve it into perfectly good plaster. Bah." He threw up his hands, let go of the gate just as Ben caught it, and walked away.

"Bye," Ben called. "Thanks."

The old man just threw up a tired hand and kept walking.

"Really, *really* need to rethink my life," Ben said under his breath as he hoisted his bag higher and walked into the entryway of...

One seriously cool house.

"Holy shit."

It was a "house" the same way Giovanni's house in Rome was a house. Just a Venetian version. There were rooms on either side of him, but a wide, open-air hallway led back to a lush green courtyard where an old marble fountain trickled and orange and lemon trees were espaliered along the walls, interspersed with raised beds of herbs and vegetables. Three stories up, arched windows opened over the courtyard, letting in whatever trickle of breeze the sweltering day allowed.

Past the courtyard, a wide entry hall floored in black-and-grey-checked marble led to a private dock with another elaborate wrought iron gate. White marble statues lined the entry, and Moroccan lanterns with brightly colored glass dripped from the ceiling. Ben could hear a gondolier whistling past the gate, but the man paid him no attention as he explored.

"This. Is. The. Coolest," he said. And a pretty brilliant setup for an air vampire. He kept in the shadows of the entry hall and realized that, except for the courtyard, the whole first floor was light safe. No direct sunlight could get in with the high walls and soaring buildings across the canal. At night the private, open-air courtyard would give Tenzin access to the rooftops of Venice while the canal, though not ideal for an air vampire, provided another exit route.

He wandered up a half flight of stairs off the entryway and saw a carved wooden door cracked open. He peeked his head in and saw a fantastic suite complete with a sitting area and small kitchen. There was a bedroom that faced the corner canals and a bathroom with the biggest tub he'd seen so far in Italy.

"Mine," he said, pulling the thick velvet drapes back to look out the windows. "So, so mine, Tiny."

Ben wandered back to the stairwell and up to the second floor, but the massive arched doors were locked. He poked around the ground floor a little more. It was well maintained, had a surprisingly updated kitchen, but wasn't anything shocking. Another bedroom and what looked like a utility room of some kind. Laundry facilities and gardening tools mainly. Ben's suite was the only room with air-conditioning, so he tossed his bags in the wardrobe and collapsed on the bed.

☿

TENZIN landed in the courtyard of the Venice house just after dark to the echo of Louis Armstrong singing "Hello, Dolly!" coming from the hall on the ground floor. The turntable had been dragged out of the utility room and a pile of old records sat on the table next to it. The colored lanterns were lit and the gate to the canal was swung open. A wine bottle was open on the lacquered table, and Ben was lying stretched on the chaise facing the canal, a glass of wine dangling from his fingers as he watched the shadows of the gondolas pass.

She sat across from him and grabbed for his glass of wine, throwing her legs over the round arm of the rattan chair Silvio must have bought recently, probably when she told him to expect guests.

"Does Silvio know you're playing his records?" she asked as the needle started "Mack the Knife."

"Me and Silvio"—Ben held up his fingers and crossed the first two—"we're like this, T."

Tenzin started laughing at the lazy, half-lidded expression on his face. It wasn't often Ben let himself become intoxicated.

When he did, she had to admit she found it entertaining. She sipped the wine and recognized a familiar vintage.

"I see you discovered my wine," she said.

"I moved a few cases to my suite." He sat up and kicked his legs out, grabbing his glass back from her fingers. "I figured you'd want to share. Tenzin, this place is amazing."

She looked around and nodded. "I like it."

"No, no, no. You don't *like* a house like this." He waved a hand toward the canal. "This is *la dolce vita*. This is a house you escape to as often as you can."

She shrugged. "I come here more often than you might guess. Venice is very peaceful at night."

"That's good. I'm glad. I'm glad you come here." He stared at her, his eyes heavy-lidded, his mouth spread in a lazy smile. "Peaceful places are important."

She laughed. "You're drunk."

He slid off the chaise and scooted over to her, sliding his knees across the polished marble.

"Maybe a little." He leaned his elbows next to her and leaned his chin on his hands. "Do you mind?"

She mussed his curls, damp from the muggy Venetian air. "Of course not."

He laid his head on the arm of her chair and closed his eyes. She was a little worried he was going to fall asleep until his ears perked up at the sound of a simple piano melody from the record player.

Ben stood, unfolding his rangy frame with the grace of the slightly buzzed, and held out his hand.

Tenzin shook her head.

"Yes," he insisted, tugging on her hand until she rose to her feet. "You have to."

"It's my house."

"And it's Louis singing 'A Kiss to Build a Dream On.' On a

record player." He swung her into his arms and began to lead her around the entry hall. "In the most perfect house in Venice. We have to dance."

She gave up and let him slide one arm around her waist. "What is this?"

"This is... kind of a drunken foxtrot," he said. "Don't question it. Just let me lead."

She laughed when they slid a little too close to the canal steps and Ben swung her back at the last minute. "Just don't lead us into the water!"

He whispered, "Shhhhh."

Ben kept them away from the canal. They swayed as the song crackled in the air, the singer's voice rasping over the smooth trumpet and piano. She felt Ben sigh deeply and pull her closer as the trumpet rose in chorus. He hummed under his breath and continued to spin slowly around the checkerboard floor. Tenzin heard a gondolier outside singing along.

His voice rose as he passed the dock and spied them dancing. "*Bacialo!*" the gondolier called with a laugh. "Kiss him!"

Before Ben could respond, Tenzin floated up and pressed a fleeting kiss to his open mouth.

"Shhhh," she whispered. "Don't spoil it."

Ben smiled his sweet, lazy grin and turned them in another circle.

It was a crystal moment.

A balmy summer night in Venice, the water lapping quietly at the dock as a beautiful boy danced with her under colored lanterns. A slow turn and whirl that reminded Tenzin she was alive. After everything... she was alive. She tucked the dance into a corner of her mind, next to the scattering of other crystal memories.

A baby's laughter.

The feeling of stars inside her.

A gentle brush of paint over bare skin.

A familiar face stamped on the boy in front of her.

An unexpected dance on a warm summer night.

The song wound down, and Ben dipped her back until her hair swept the marble. He slowly raised her up and hugged her tight. "Thank you," he sighed out, "for making me come here."

"You're welcome."

"I needed this."

"I know."

"Yeah," he said, laying his cheek on the top of her head as "Takes Two to Tango" came on the record. "You always seem to, Tiny."

"That's because I am very old and wise."

"And I'm kinda young and stupid sometimes."

She pulled back and looked up at him. "We all were. Even me."

He shook his head. "Nope. Don't believe you."

Ben started to move her to the music again. The wine must have been wearing off because his movements were just a little tighter, his feet a little faster.

"Where did you learn how to dance?"

"Caspar insisted," Ben said, spinning her around with ease. "Told me I'd thank him some day."

"And have you?"

"Many times. Girls love a good dancer."

"So, are you finally relaxed?"

"That depends." He pulled her to his chest and tipped her chin up. "Are you going to introduce me to your forger?"

Tenzin smiled. "I knew you'd figure it out."

ô

A YOUNGER, less grumpy version of Silvio picked them

up at the dock at midnight. The young man, whom Tenzin introduced as Claudio, kept the boat's motor almost silent until they were well away from San Marco. Speeding into utter blackness, Ben tried not to panic and instead enjoyed the whipping wind on his face as the wood-paneled boat crossed the dark lagoon.

"Where are we going?" he shouted.

"Murano."

"The island of glassblowers?"

"It's not just glass. But the glass helps. Nobody notices his forges there."

Forges. Of course. You couldn't fake medieval coins with a regular art forger, you needed a metalsmith. Someone who could pour the metal and create the dies for the coins. You'd need an engraver too.

"Tenzin?" He switched to Mandarin. "Do you actually have these coins?"

"Of course. I've had them for around four hundred years. Took them from the Neapolitan treasury ages ago."

"So you stole them?"

She shrugged. "Define *steal*."

That sounded like a conversation he'd need more wine for. "The manual you took from Perugia. Was it for your forger's benefit or yours?"

"Mine. Oscar has been doing this for a long time. I just wanted to check his work. Don't mention the manual to him. He'd be offended."

"Wouldn't dare."

The moon peeked from behind the clouds and lit up the lagoon. Ben tried not to notice how fast they were going since Claudio looked bored. This was clearly a familiar route for the young Venetian.

"The museum," she said. "Did you go like I asked?"

"I did."

"Several of Oscar's copies are in there," Tenzin said.

"So he's good."

"He's the best."

Ben could see tiny lights in the distance. The flat outline of Murano appeared in the sliver of moonlight. The small collection of islands had become the home of all Venetian glassmakers in the thirteenth century when they were forced off the main island by fears of fire. Since then, Murano had swelled and waned in power. Now it was part of Venice, but Ben knew at one time it had its own government. Even minted its own coinage.

"How old is Oscar?" he asked.

Tenzin shrugged. "Ask Oscar."

Yeah, that was likely.

"I first heard of him in the seventeenth century," Tenzin said. "He already had a very good reputation as a metalsmith. Water vampire, of course. Most Venetians are. He designed a piece of jewelry for me around the time I bought my house here. We've been... associates since then."

"So he's at least five hundred years old."

"I'd estimate around six. He was young when I met him, but not that young."

Ben nodded and tucked the information away. Venice in the seventeenth century would have been in decline as an economic and cultural power, but it was still plenty wealthy. Tenzin must have paid someone off handsomely to buy a home in San Marco.

"We'll go to his workshop tonight so you can meet him. He told me the job is about half done. He'll need another week at least before we can return the coins to Alfonso."

"You mean give him the fakes?" He shook his head. "Do you really have the tarì? Or was this whole thing a ruse?"

"Would I lie to you? Of course I have them. How else could

Oscar have reproduced them? I like them, and I don't want to give them back. Why should I when I can hire Oscar to make some very nice fakes for Alfonso? I even found some North African gold to duplicate the originals."

"Tenzin, that's not the— Wait, you had a stash of North African gold just lying around?"

"Yes."

He let out a slow breath. "Sometimes I want to be you when I grow up, then I think about your tenuous grasp on sanity and remind myself it wouldn't be a good idea."

She leaned her head back and closed her eyes. The wind whipped her hair around her head. She wasn't wearing braids, so the mass of it rose like a black cloud behind her.

"Sanity," she said, "is vastly overrated."

"Is it really worth pissing off the Mad Duke to keep some old coins? Especially when Gio asked us to tread carefully in Naples? Are they worth *that* much money?"

"No." She sat up and squinted. "That's not the point."

"What is the point?"

"They're mine. I don't give people things that are mine. Especially if I don't like those people."

"But you'll go to all this trouble to forge duplicates for him?"

A smile quirked her lips. "I will enjoy his look of triumph when he holds the fakes. That will be very satisfying."

"Because you'll be laughing internally?"

"Yes."

"You're twisted, Tiny. So very twisted."

"That's what keeps me alive." She leaned forward as the boat approached the islands. Instead of pulling into the main canal, Claudio turned northeast and headed along the outer edge of Murano, slowing to putter past tiny docks where local boats bobbed in the chop. He pulled up to an unmarked set of steps near a redbrick wall.

"Three a.m.?" Claudio asked.

"We'll be here between three and four," Tenzin said. "Is that enough time?"

"Of course." Claudio grinned. "The boat can always go faster."

"Don't scare the boy. I can fly back if time gets short."

Tenzin floated out of the boat and Ben leapt across to the closest dry step.

"Thanks, Claudio."

"See you later," the young man called in English.

Tenzin took Ben's hand and led him down narrow pitch-black streets. Within minutes they were standing outside a small warehouse, its high windows glowing with a red-gold light.

Tenzin knocked once, then pushed the door open. They walked in to see a large, open workshop with a glowing-red forge at one end, racks of tools and equipment across the opposite wall, and a large worktable at the other. A worktable where a black-haired vampire held a woman sprawled. She was half-undressed and her hand clutched his long hair.

"Oscar!" Tenzin yelled.

The vampire's head rose, blood dripping from his lips and his fangs bared.

"You're late," he growled. His hands still pinned the woman down, but she was struggling.

Ben's lip curled and he reached for the knife at his waist. Tenzin put a hand out, halting him.

"I'm paying you to mint coins, not have sex with your engraver. Let Ruby go and show me what's finished."

6

————

RUBY SMACKED OSCAR'S MASSIVE SHOULDER. "Let me up, you beast. And get your hands out of my knickers. You got no sense of propriety, you don't. Sorry, Tenzin!"

Ben turned and faced the forge. "Maybe we should have waited for them to answer the door, huh, Tiny?"

"Why?"

"I forget I ask this of the woman who regularly climbs in my bed to stare at me while I sleep."

"You make it sound creepy, when really I'm just impatient."

Ruby continued to berate Oscar as she dressed. The old vampire muttered something under his breath and she quieted. Then he walked to the forge and waved them over.

"This gold," he said, motioning to a small table. "It's very soft."

"It should be the same composition as the originals," Tenzin said, picking up a button of gold from a shallow pan of sand where a row of buttons had been poured. She dropped it in the bucket nearby.

"It is," Oscar said.

Ben couldn't quite place Oscar's accent. He didn't sound or look Italian. Ben was guessing Spanish, but what would a Spanish glassmaker be doing in Murano? He had a large, smooth scar up the side of his neck, and his head was square as a block. Heavy black hair curtained a face that wasn't handsome but might be called compelling.

Oscar took a pair of clippers and snipped at the row of gold buttons, trimming them into neat rounds as he dropped them in the water. "The softness of this particular alloy means we'll have to do more deformation with the finished pieces than I originally planned."

"You saw the originals I brought. I trust your skills."

"I want some of the trimmings from the reproductions."

Tenzin cocked her head and watched him work. "No."

"I want them," Oscar said, dropping the trimmed gold into a small crucible where he'd melt it down again to make more buttons. Ben could see another pan of sand with round indentations where the smith would pour the next batch of molten gold. "I'm willing to subtract the value out of my fee. I'll even pay above market."

Now Tenzin looked curious. "Why?"

"I want it for a project. That's all you need to know," Oscar said. "Can we work something out or not?"

Tenzin said, "Fine. I'll talk to you about it when the coins are done."

"Good." He nodded toward Ruby and continued trimming. "She has the last two die sets done."

"Excellent."

Ben and Tenzin walked back to the worktable where Ruby was still tucking in her shirt. "Sorry about that, Tenzin."

"Forget about it," Tenzin said. "Ruby, Ben. Ben, Ruby."

"Oh, oi," Ruby said, dark brown eyes sparkling in her round face. She looked African, but every syllable she spoke screamed

London. Ben liked her smile, even when he caught the edge of tiny fangs peeking from her lips. "Pleasure to meet you, Ben."

Not a human. Interesting.

"Nice to meet you too." He held out a hand and she took it immediately. Ben was guessing Ruby was fairly young. Her mannerisms and slang said newly turned, and her hair was cut in a stylish, short afro held back with a deep purple scarf.

"So you're the engraver?" he asked.

"I am now!" She grinned. "Oscar taught me the engraving bit. I was an art student before... before."

"She's good," Oscar growled across the room. "She'll be better than me with practice."

"And this was very good practice," she said, pulling up the heavy metal dies with intricate carvings on the face. "Now keep in mind, the actual dies would have degraded over years of use, but we don't have time for that. These are the new ones, but like the other two sets, Oscar'll heat 'em and cool 'em a few times to soften up the edges before we strike the actual coins."

Tenzin nodded as if that all made sense. Ben was quickly catching up.

The original coins were over eight hundred years old. They would be scarred and deformed from time. Though gold didn't deteriorate like silver or bronze, some marks of age would be inevitable. The original coin dies used to strike them would have had variations too. So after producing the imitations, Ruby and Oscar were going to have to age them. Each coin would have to be just a little different, or the ruse would be obvious.

Ben picked up a die. Crude Arabic inscriptions around a central circle. "Are these supposed to be... What language is this?"

"The original Norman tarì were imitations of gold coins minted by Arab rulers," Tenzin said. "So they had Arabic or Kufic inscriptions."

"So the original tarì are copies of other coins?"

"In a sense," Tenzin said. "They were made of gold and the size was convenient. That's why they became popular for trading. Nobody much cared who struck them as long as their value held."

"So... we're making copies of coins that were already copies of other coins?" he asked.

Ruby laughed. "It's all so delightfully twisted, ain't it?"

Ben shook his head. "That somehow makes me feel better, but I'm not sure why. Ruby, this work looks amazing. I'm no coin expert, but you're really talented."

"Thank you very much, Ben."

Tenzin was looking at each and every engraving. "I concur. This is excellent work. Oscar has taught you well."

"Means a lot coming from you," Ruby said. "Thanks. I have a batch just out of the tumbler if you'd like to see 'em. Haven't been treated, but they're softened up."

Tenzin nodded. "Let's see."

Ruby took them to a round metal cylinder turned on an angle. "I'd use a proper tumbler for lapidary, but since we're going for a mix of wear, we didn't want anything too even. I mocked up this crude one with a hand turner, and we've been using all sorts of textures for grit. Sand. Polishing compound. Even rocks and metal bits. Small batches. Nothing too regular." She opened the side door and pulled out a coin from the milky liquid within. "Take a look at that then."

Tenzin held the coin in her palm, feeling the weight, then she flipped it end over end and caught it in the air. She held it up to the light and inspected it, then handed it to Ben and reached for another coin.

"It's good," she said. "The weight and wear look perfect. The client hasn't seen the originals in at least four hundred years, so he's not going to be crystal clear on what they look like. No photographic evidence exists, so we just have to get close."

Ruby nodded. "That's what Oscar said too. Mostly we wanted them to have the right wear."

"And the patina?"

Ruby tilted her head toward Oscar. "He's in charge of that. With the copper content of this alloy, I'm thinking liver of sulfur might be involved, but maybe waxes too. Not sure what he has in mind."

"It will look authentic," Oscar shouted. "How I make it that way is my business."

"Fine," Tenzin shouted back. "And you're about half-done?" she asked Ruby.

The young vampire nodded. "Give us another week or so."

Oscar yelled over the roar of the forge as he put another crucible in to heat. "Ruby will bring them to your house on Thursday night."

Ruby's face lit up. "Really, Oz? All the way to the main island?"

Oscar grunted. "Just stay out of sight. Tenzin, leave. You're distracting Ruby from her work."

"Fine." Tenzin walked over and punched his shoulder. The stocky man glared at her.

"What was that for?" he shouted.

"Just because you're a bastard," Tenzin said. "Don't bite your woman unless she likes it, Oscar. I have ways of finding out."

"She likes it." Oscar's eyes flicked up to Ben. "What's this one, anyway?"

"Him?" Tenzin glanced over her shoulder. "He's my publicist."

Oscar narrowed his eyes. "Right. Keep him away from Ruby."

"Ben's trustworthy. He's not going to poach your woman, you paranoid ass."

"She's an investment."

Tenzin punched him again. "Such a bastard."

☿

THURSDAY night, Ruby turned up just after dark in Claudio's small boat. With her was a battered leather briefcase that must have weighed more than a bit, because the boat rocked when she hoisted it onto the steps.

"Thanks, Claudio!" she said, waving at the young man before he disappeared down the canal. Then Ruby planted her hands on her hips and looked at Ben. "Gelato?"

"Uh..." He set down the book he'd been reading. "I think we have some."

"I don't care if you have some here," she said, grabbing his hand. "I want to go *out*. See the city. Get a drink. And definitely eat some gelato."

"Okay." Ben laughed and let her pull him down the entry hall. "Don't get off work much, huh?"

"Ugh," she groaned. "Oscar's great, right? I don't mean to whinge on. But he's really overprotective. Very possessive, you know? I just need to get out a bit. I'm not nine hundred like some people."

Ben tucked that one away and went to grab the key for the door. "Come on then. I'll be your trusted escort through the city."

Ruby winked. "Know every nook and cranny, do you?"

"Not quite, but I'm getting there."

He glanced up and wondered if he needed to tell Tenzin they were going. Then he spied the heavy briefcase sitting on the stairs.

"Is that...?"

"A bloody fortune in reproduced Sicilian tarì? Yes, it is." Ruby smiled. "And rather expertly reproduced if I say so myself."

"Let me take it up to Tenzin," he said. "Let her know we're going out."

Ruby was strolling along the entry hall, examining the marbles. "So you've got a mummy too, eh?"

"A mummy?" Ben resisted the urge to break into hysterical laughter. "No, not exactly."

He hoisted the briefcase and climbed the stairs to the second level, knocking before he pushed the door open.

Tenzin was stretched out on a thick Persian rug at the end of the *pòrtego*, the grand entry hall on the main floor of the house. She was on her back, reading a book in front of the arched floor-to-ceiling windows that lined the front of the house. During the day, they were covered with a heavy red velvet drape, but at night they reflected the lights glittering across the canal.

The rest of the *pòrtego* was sparsely furnished and looked more like a gallery than a room. The terrazzo floors were a soft gold color and the walls were covered in a red Venetian plaster, but the ceilings were the tallest in the house, which meant they were the most comfortable for Tenzin, who preferred flying to walking when possible.

Ben tapped on the door again and she waved him in.

"Ruby's here," she said, putting the book on the ground.

He walked over and set the briefcase down next to her. "Yep."

Tenzin grinned. "She brought the coins."

"Is this the part where I pour them over you in a river of gold while you laugh maniacally? Because I'm going to be honest, this bag is heavy and I'm wondering how comfortable that would be."

"No, no, no." She rolled over and grabbed the briefcase. "Ah," she said, peering inside. "Lovely."

It wasn't a river, but when Tenzin poured out the perfectly reproduced tarì over the rich wool of the Persian rug, Ben had to admit...

It was hot.

She spread them with her hands, a small sea of intricately etched gold coins scattering over the red, blue, and ochre of the rug. Ben knelt next to her and picked one up. The patina looked identical to the examples he'd seen online. Even to his experienced eye, the coins looked hundreds of years old.

"Amazing," he said.

"Come on," Tenzin said, pushing the coins into a pile. "It's not enough for a bed, but you can use it for a pillow."

He laughed. "A pillow?"

"Just..." She stood and pushed him down to the rug. "Do it. Everyone should lie on a big pile of gold at least once in their life, Benjamin."

"Did you read that on a motivational poster somewhere?"

"No, but maybe someone should make one with that on it. I find gold very motivating."

Ben lay down on the rug and put his head on the pile of gold coins, staring at the ceiling. The beams had been painted with tiny decorative elements in red and lapis blue. The rug was soft at his back. And the pile of gold coins...

Tenzin lay down next to him. "It isn't very comfortable, is it?"

"No." He picked up a coin and flipped it in the air. "Sleeping on gold does have a certain appeal though."

"Yes." Tenzin scooped a handful and let the coins run through her fingers. "Gold always does."

The cool metal warmed to his neck as he lay on it. "I think that's what it is," he murmured.

"What?"

"The gold. It's... warm. It's precious metal, but it's not cold. Diamonds are hard and cold. Platinum always feels mechanical to me. But gold..." He picked up a coin and balanced it on his nose. "Never tarnishes. It doesn't break; it bends. It's warm. More human than other precious metals or gems."

He turned to see her watching him with a smile flirting at the corner of her mouth. "What?"

Tenzin said, "I've always wondered when you'd find it. It's an honor to be here when you did."

"What are you talking about?"

"Your one true love." Tenzin laughed and rolled away when he grabbed for her. "Should I leave you alone?"

"Shut up."

"Wait, I can't leave you alone. Your one true love needs to go in the safe." She flipped a coin at him, and he caught it just before it hit his face. "Kiss your true love good-bye, Benjamin."

"You're ridiculous."

"You're the one philosophizing about gold."

He filled a hand with the coins and let them pour out onto the rug again, delighting in the soft sound. "Do you blame me?"

"Me?" She rolled to her knees. "Never." Tenzin flipped a coin up, caught it, and kissed it before she tossed it in the bag. "Not when I'm guilty of the same thing. Like recognizes like, my Benjamin."

He tossed coin after coin in the leather satchel, listening to each one clink. "Ruby is still here. Wants to go out for a drink and some ice cream. You want to join us?"

She wouldn't want to join them.

"No"—Tenzin confirmed his suspicion—"just be careful with her. Oscar is very possessive."

"Yeah, I got that." He frowned. "Everything all right there?"

"It's none of my business." Tenzin shrugged. "The girl doesn't appear to be unhappy."

"And if she was?"

Tenzin raised an eyebrow in speculation. "Ask her."

"Fine. Be cryptic." He rolled up to his knees. "You want to finish this and I'll play host?"

Tenzin's eyes danced. "That girl knows the city better than either of us, I'd wager. Don't let her fool you. She's smart and she's not nearly as innocent as she comes across."

"Probably not." He shrugged. "But she's fun. We won't stay out too late."

"Nothing stays open late enough to worry about," she said. "This isn't Naples."

"Very true."

The thing that delighted Tenzin most about Venice was the very thing that annoyed Ben. It was too quiet at night. There was little to no nightlife unless you took a boat out to the Lido or trolled the tourist areas along the Grand Canal. Still, he'd found a good gelato place just around the corner on the Calle de la Mandola, and there was a bar not too far from it in Campo Sant'Angelo that served a nice selection of cocktails where they could sit if they wanted.

Ruby was waiting for him when he came down the stairs. "So, permission granted?"

Ben shook his head and cocked an arm out for her to take. "Come on, you brat. Let's find someplace you can let your hair down."

ò

THEY were sitting in the Campo Sant'Angelo and most of the square was empty. Ben and Ruby had the place to them-selves, aside from a small group of what looked like retirees who were chatting in German on the other side of the restaurant. The moon had risen and the night was warm. The wine wasn't great, but it wasn't bad either.

The company, however, was stellar.

"So tell me about vampires in Venice," Ben said. "How long have you lived here?"

Ruby cocked her head. "Ten years now? Almost eleven, I suppose." She grinned and the points of her fangs peeked from her lips. "I came on holiday and I never left."

"Intentional?"

"Very much not."

"But you've stayed."

"Well, I've got Oscar, don't I?" she said. "Can't leave him. Not until he gets bored with me."

Ben's protective instincts pricked. "Do you *want* to leave?"

Ruby winked at him. "You're adorable, you know that? It's not what you're thinking. But when I first came, it wasn't under ideal circumstances. In fact, Oscar's the one who brought me up in front of the council here."

"So there's a council? Not just one VIC?"

"VIC?"

Ben shrugged. "My shorthand for vampire in charge."

"Ha!" Ruby laughed. "That's brilliant. Yeah, there's a council. It's not big. For an old city, there's not as many of our kind as you'd think."

Ben thought for a moment. "No nightlife."

She pointed a finger at him. "Right in one. That's it. There's a larger population on *terraferma*, but in the old city? Not many anymore. And the ones here are more like Oscar. Old, ornery, and like keeping to themselves."

"And he's the one who took you to them?"

"Long story, but yeah. And I'm grateful he did. What did I know about any of this, eh?" She looked around. "I would've turned these canals bloody if I'd had my way. Oscar reined me in. Looked after me."

"And you work for him."

She grinned. "Among other things. No worries, Benny. He's not a bad sort. I'm happy enough."

"So you're settled here?"

Ruby snorted. "God, no. I'd love to get out. Travel the world. That's what I was doing before I turned, you know? I'm an artist. I can't stay in one place forever, can I?" She sipped her wine. "But I've got time. Gobs and gobs of it now. So we'll see. I'm here now."

"Well"—he took his card out of his pocket—"if you ever make your way to America—and I'm still alive—give me a call, huh?"

Ruby took the card and put it in a pocket. "I'll do that. So you and Tenzin?"

He shrugged. "It's complicated."

"Friends?"

"Yes," he said. "Always."

"She's a bit of a legend, isn't she? Got the creeps the first time I met her. Stories Oscar told made my hair stand on end." She fingered her tight curls. "Even more than it is now. And that's saying something."

Ben smiled. "Yeah, I've heard a few of them too."

A chime sounded in Ben's pocket, and he pulled out his phone.

"The docks near San Samuele," he said. "Sounds like Claudio's picking both of us up there at midnight."

"Both of us?"

"That's what he says." He tucked his phone away. "Maybe Tenzin went out to your place."

"Could be." She lifted her wineglass. "We should probably get going. I know the way."

Ten minutes later, they walked through the twisted streets of San Marco again, their footsteps echoing in the deserted city. If it hadn't been so empty, Ben would never have spotted their shadows as they crossed the Campo Santo Stefano.

"We've got company," he said under his breath, knowing Ruby would hear. "Just passing the library now."

Ruby's head whipped around and back so fast he could barely see it. "Vampires. I don't recognize them."

Ben's eyes glinted. "Shall we see how well they know the city?"

"Can you keep up?"

He grinned. "Not even a little."

Ruby ran.

She kept to human-ish speed, but Ben still had the devil's time keeping her in sight. She sped past the church on the south end of the campo and ducked right across a small bridge, almost losing him in the maze of streets.

Their vampire trackers stayed with them. They were little more than shadows, but they drew nearer to Ben, bolder than they were with Ruby. They knew he was human.

He ran past an alleyway and felt an arm reach out and grab him. Ruby pulled him next to her while Ben struggled to catch his breath.

"What?" he panted.

Ruby looked troubled. "If they were residents, I'd know them. If they were simply curious, they'd have left us by now."

Ben heard them slinking down the street. If there had been any other foot traffic, he'd have never have heard their silent feet, but they were utterly alone. His pulse hammering, he looked toward the mouth of the alley. When he looked back, Ruby's eyes were narrowed on the pulse in his throat.

He snapped his fingers in her face and she looked up, baring her fangs at him.

"Not the time," he whispered.

She was right. These vampires were following them for some reason, and Ben was guessing he didn't want to find out.

"Pretend you're biting me," he said, tugging her closer.

"Do I have to pretend?"

"Do it!" he hissed.

The vampires crossed the alley just as Ruby bent her head to his neck. They paused, watching them.

A low laugh and one said to another, "This one likes all kinds, eh?"

The minute Ben heard the distinctive accent of Naples, he jerked back. He met the eyes of one of the vampires from Alfonso's court in the dim streetlamp, then he glanced at Ruby.

Oh shit.

7

"THEY CAN'T SEE US TOGETHER," he said. "Ruby, they're from Naples."

"Got it."

With a quick flip, Ruby climbed up the wall, the tips of her fingers clinging to the bricks before she leapt on the two vampires at the mouth of the alley. Ben drew his knife and ran for the one Ruby hadn't landed on, cursing himself the whole time.

Man versus vampire rarely went his way.

His advantage? The vampire wasn't looking to get away and didn't want to kill him. Ben knew that any of Alfonso's court seeing him with Oscar's apprentice would be bad news.

The vampire circled him, fangs down, his head cocked curiously at the human he'd been tracking. He said nothing. His dark hood was drawn up around his face, but Ben recognized him. He recognized them both.

Ruby had one vampire's face shoved into the cobblestones while the other circled Ben. If it had been faster, they'd both have been dizzy.

"What do you want?" Ben asked. Shit, shit, shit. Ruby could

keep that one down, but this one looked old and smart. He was no match for a vampire. His survival strategy consisted of avoiding violence and relying on charm and connections. "Does Alfonso know you're here?"

"He sent us to watch you." The vampire glanced at Ruby. "You keep curious company, Tenzin's human."

"What can I say?" he said. "I make friends easily."

"But your choice of friends... this says much."

"You think so?" Ben held up his hand, letting the vampire see his knife. "Listen, I'm prey, but I'm not easy prey. Is this really worth it? I met a cute girl. We went out for a drink."

The vampire laughed. "You're not as smart as they say if you think I'd believe—" His words were cut off with his head, which fell to the side and plopped on the cobblestones with a wet thunk a second before Tenzin landed next to Ben.

He let out a slow breath. "Tenzin. What. The. Hell?"

"I told Alfonso not to send anyone to watch us," she said, bending down to the one Ruby held. "Is that why you're here? To watch me?"

Ruby let go of the vampire's throat.

"Yes," he choked out.

"Filomena or Alfonso?"

"Alfonso."

"Thank you," Tenzin said graciously. "I appreciate your honesty. I will give you a swift death like your friend."

Ben's hand shot out. "Tenzin—"

She was already gone. She'd lifted the vampire from the ground, shoving Ruby off him, and flown straight up. Ben heard scuffling on the top of the nearest building, then quiet.

"Fuck me," Ruby breathed out. "She *is* scary as 'ell."

Ben sighed. "Yeah, she is. And she always kills them before I can ask the questions I want."

Ruby patted his shoulder. "They died clean."

For following orders, his conscience complained. He tried to ignore it. If Alfonso had ordered Ben dead, those vampires wouldn't have thought twice about following those orders too. He'd seen that truth in their eyes. They could have taken Ruby with ease if Ben hadn't been around to distract one of them. They'd have killed her and not batted an eye.

Ben looked at the wall Ruby had crawled up. "How did you do that?"

"Do what? Climb the wall?"

"You looked like fucking Spider-Man for a minute there."

She smiled. "It's not easy, but you could teach yourself if you want. It's called parkour. I started studying it while I was still human. When I became a vamp... way cooler."

"Parkour?"

"Parkour."

Tenzin landed in the alley again, a delicate spray of blood across her cheek. She walked over, nodded at Ruby, and picked up the head and the body of the other vampire. He could see her favorite sword, a curved Mongolian saber designed for combat on horseback, strapped to her back. Tenzin never went anywhere without that sword.

"Thank you," Tenzin said to Ruby when she landed again. "I am in your debt for protecting Benjamin."

"Hey," he said. "Standing right here."

"No problem," Ruby said. "And he holds his own pretty well."

Tenzin sighed. "I am hoping he gets over this desire to be human. He's much more vulnerable as a mortal."

Ruby laughed.

"That's enough, Tiny." Ben looked up at the side of the building Ruby had crawled up. "What are we going to do with these guys?"

"They were both from Naples, and Oscar would have told

me if anyone from Alfonso's court had permission to enter the city. They were fair game if any of the Venetians got them anyway."

"I'll tell Oscar they were threatening me," Ruby said. "He'll smooth over anything with the council. Venetians may be a quiet lot, but they don't like trespassers." Ruby nodded at the roof of the building. "You can dump their bodies out in the lagoon."

"Oh, I know a few places," Tenzin said. "I do so love that splash. You two, get to the boat. I'll meet you in Murano."

☿

TEN minutes of listening to Oscar berate Ruby was more than enough for Ben. He was ready to murder the cranky old vampire. Though Oscar didn't raise a hand to Ruby, he beat her with his voice.

"Enough," Tenzin said. "I don't need to be here for this. Punish your woman on your own time, Oscar."

Oscar turned and bared his fangs at Tenzin before he turned back to Ruby. "Go to your room," he snarled. "I don't want to see you until tomorrow night."

Ruby's normally vivacious expression was gone. Her face was a mask. She looked down and nodded quietly before she left the workroom.

Ben started. "Ruby—"

"Shut up," Tenzin said, slapping her hand against his chest. "Shut. Up. Oscar, we're leaving."

"I hope you like the coins," he said, throwing his hammer down and shutting off his forge. "Because they're the last job I'm going to do for you, Tenzin."

"Fine," she said. "I apologize if I caused any trouble."

"Don't bring that human around Ruby again."

"Just remember I have ways of knowing," she said in a low voice. "Never again, Oscar."

"Out of my house!" he shouted. "And don't come back!"

Tenzin pushed Ben out the door and down the street toward the dock.

"He is going to beat her," Ben hissed. "Hurt her. And you're going to just let him?"

"Oscar is not going to beat Ruby," Tenzin said. "He's going to shout and rail, but that's all he's going to do."

Ben scrambled into the boat and glared at her as she floated in. "Oh yeah? How do you know?"

"Because he almost killed a friend of mine once," Tenzin said calmly. "A woman who had been his lover. He lost his temper when she left him."

Ben sat down, shocked into silence.

Ruby... He felt sick to his stomach for leaving her there.

"So I cut Oscar's balls off and stabbed a knife through his neck." She held up two fingers an inch apart. "Very close to his spine. His balls took a long time to grow back. He won't hit Ruby."

Ben shuddered. They rode in silence all the way back to San Marco, then Claudio dropped them off and sped into the night with a casual nod.

"Tenzin," Ben said.

"What?"

"Oscar... Is that really the last job he'll do for you?" As much as Ben might not have liked Oscar at the moment, he was a good contact. A great artist, and a discreet one from what Tenzin had said. Losing his skills would be a shame.

Tenzin frowned as if she was confused. "The last...? Oh." She waved her hand and sat on the chair in the entry hall. "I think he says that every time we work together. This is not unusual. He'll be fine. He'll be doting on Ruby by tomorrow night and best friends with me when I deliver a shipment of that gold he likes as a bonus."

"What are they?" He finally asked the question that had been bugging him ever since they left Murano. "Why would she stay with him? He treats her like a child."

"Well, how should he treat her?"

"Not like a child!"

"But she *is* a child. To him, she's a child. Oscar is not her father or her sire, but he is her superior. And her lover. In his mind, that makes Ruby *his*. You may not understand it—"

"I sure as hell don't understand it, and I don't understand why she'd stay with him when he treats her like that."

"Ben…" Tenzin closed her eyes and sighed. "Most vampire relationships are not like your aunt and uncle's. You should have learned this by now. There are no saints in this world. No one acts completely out of the goodness of their heart. There is always self-interest involved. Oscar protects Ruby. Cares about her in his own way. Ruby feeds Oscar and learns valuable skills from him. They both get something from the other, or it would not be balanced."

"That doesn't look like a balanced relationship to me."

"He is in charge of her, *but* she gets his protection. It's balanced."

"And she's supposed to be satisfied with that?"

"They're not *mates*, Benjamin. Will they be someday?" Tenzin shrugged. "Perhaps. Probably not."

Ben sat on the chaise and reached for the bottle of wine he'd been drinking hours before when Ruby had first shown up with the gold. He pulled the cork out and drank directly from the bottle, then passed it to Tenzin.

"So how does it end?" he asked.

She took a long drink. "None of your business."

"But—"

"Not everything comes to a happy end, Benjamin." She reached over and patted his hand. "Remember that. We're vampires."

☿

BEN drove to Rome the next day. Tenzin didn't trust the coins on the train and neither did Benjamin, so he started early, rented a junky tourist car, and made the six-hour trip on his own. He pulled into Residenza di Spada just a couple of hours before sunset and grabbed a nap before Tenzin arrived.

When he woke, he was alone, but he could see Tenzin outside his room, perched on the small balcony that overlooked the interior courtyard. He opened the window and heard the quiet buzz of city traffic, not knowing whether the clamor of vehicles was comforting or annoying.

"You're being so well behaved," Ben said as Tenzin floated into his room. Since he couldn't float, he sat on the edge of the bed. "You actually waited for me to wake up this time."

She was frowning and silent.

"What's up?"

"How was your meeting with Filomena before you left Naples?"

"Filomena?" He rubbed the sleep from his eyes as Tenzin hovered in a corner. "Good, I guess. We flirted. Nothing much happened. But she seemed pretty progressive for a vampire."

"Instant read on her?"

He took a deep breath and lay back, closing his eyes as he thought. "I liked her. She's smart. Doesn't take herself too seriously. I found myself... surprised that she was Alfonso's lieutenant."

"Why?"

"One, she seems too independent for him. Two, he doesn't

seem like the type to have an independent thinker as his second-in-command."

"Which tells us…"

He stretched and rolled over. "It tells us she's either got him fooled, or there are more layers to the Mad Duke than we're seeing."

Tenzin nodded and crossed her legs on the end of his bed.

"Do you know who she reminded me of?" Ben finally said.

"Emil Conti?"

"*Yes*." Ben wasn't surprised Tenzin had picked up Filomena's similarity to the vampire in charge of Rome. "Old but progressive. The Naples court is too insular for her."

"I'm betting she didn't know Alfonso sent two men to follow you."

"I'd bet you're right. She had too much respect for you to piss you off."

"I think before we meet with Alfonso and give him his gold—"

"You mean, give him *your* gold that you very nicely forged for him?"

"Exactly. I think before we meet with Alfonso again, you should have another meeting with Filomena and… fill her in."

Ben narrowed his eyes. "What kind of trouble are you trying to cause, Tiny?"

"Benjamin, you know I only cause the very best kind of trouble."

8

BEN MET FILOMENA AT THE same restaurant where they'd had a drink before he left Naples. The vicious heat wave had not let up, but the breeze across the bay cooled the evening enough to make things slightly less miserable.

He spotted Filomena walking along the boardwalk. She was wearing a long summer dress that evening, which made Ben wonder where she was hiding her weapons. Wherever they were, he had a feeling he'd have a fun time finding out. It was a shame he had to talk about politics.

"Hey," he said when she came close. "Nice dress." He flipped one of the tarì at her, and her hand shot out to catch it.

Filomena held it in her palm. "Nice gold."

"Did ya miss me?"

"Wouldn't you like to know?"

She sat and slid a hand along his thigh until she'd leaned forward enough to brush his lips with her own. "Hello."

He tasted cherries and smiled against her lips. "Hey, Filomena?"

"Yes?"

"I want to give you a nickname. Can I do that?"

"If you call me baby, it might result in injury."

"No baby." His fingertips slid along her soft shoulder. "I'm going to think about it. I'm just warning you. A nickname is coming."

Filomena pouted. "If only I were too." She sat back and held up the tarì. "You got them."

"We got them. But we had some company—"

"What?" She straightened, all flirtation forgotten. "You had what kind of company?"

"The kind Alfonso sent. Anyone go on vacation lately?"

"That..." She closed her eyes and took a deep breath. "Was Tenzin very angry?"

"She wasn't happy. Which is why I wanted to meet with you before she sees Alfonso again."

"He'll claim he was protecting his interests."

"And she'll claim his sending people to follow her is an indication of distrust. And an insult to her reputation. Which, Filomena, you know it is."

She said nothing, torn between loyalty to her boss and realization that he'd made a significant misstep. "What do you suggest?"

"Would he apologize?"

Filomena snorted. "Never."

"Not even privately?"

"No."

"Then we're at an impasse."

"If..." Filomena's mouth pursed in concentration. "If the vampires who followed you were acting on their own..."

"But they weren't."

"But if they were..." She raised an eyebrow.

"If they were," he said, "it would change things, but they both claimed Alfonso sent them."

She smiled slowly. "But we're terribly dishonest creatures, are we not?"

Ben deliberated.

Tenzin had sent him to find out how much Filomena knew, but Ben knew he could also work this around to his benefit if he played his cards right. Filomena wanted to appease Tenzin and cover her boss's ass. And yet if word got out that Tenzin had allowed Alfonso to track her without consequences, it set a dangerous precedent.

"She'll give him the coins," Ben said, "but she'll need a higher finder's fee. It caused some trouble when she had to take care of them."

It hadn't—they hadn't heard a peep from the council in Venice about the two dead vampires—but Alfonso didn't need to know that.

"Of course," Filomena said. "I'm sure an additional fee could be arranged to compensate you for this unfortunate incident. As long as the transaction was agreed to privately. I'll guarantee the increased fee and the exchange will work out as previously arranged."

Private was a... fluid concept. Gossip in Naples would spread the word that something went down and that Alfonso paid the price for it. Not knowing specifics would allow both Tenzin and Alfonso to save face. On the surface, it was a perfect solution.

So why was a voice in head telling Ben he was missing something?

"I'll take your proposal back to Tenzin and let you know," he told Filomena. "I'm fairly sure that will be sufficient. And of course, if you didn't know about the scouts, I doubt anyone else did."

A little flattery never hurt.

Filomena's eyes flashed. "I would have known if they did."

They exchanged pleasantries for a few more minutes, but the playful banter had died when Ben mentioned Alfonso's mistake. Filomena's mood had turned from flirtatious to calculating. She chatted with Ben, but her mind was elsewhere.

They finished their wine and bid each other good-bye at the waterfront, and Ben walked back to his hotel alone. When he got to his room, Tenzin was reading a book on his bed.

"Fairly confident I'd be spending tonight alone, were you?"

"You're not alone." She patted his side of the bed without looking up. "You have me. And I'm far more entertaining."

"She didn't know about the scouts," he said, kicking off his shoes and stretching out on the bed. "And she wasn't happy about them."

"Interesting."

"She agreed to a larger finder's fee to compensate for our inconvenience."

Tenzin put down her book. "Well, that was clever of you. Nicely done."

"But she says he won't apologize."

She frowned. "So this is private? No public acknowledgement?"

"No mention from either party. Filomena will arrange the money. I have a feeling Alfonso is using public funds for this. Might not want his people to know how much he's spending to get these back."

"Very... interesting."

"Because?"

She shrugged. "We'll have to see whether this deal you worked out with her actually happens. If the exchange goes as planned... When?"

"Tomorrow night. Midnight."

"If it goes as planned tomorrow—we make the transfer and

Alfonso gives us a higher fee privately—that means Filomena is acceding to Alfonso's authority and allowing him to take security steps without her knowledge."

Yeah, Ben had a feeling that *wasn't* going to be the way it went down.

"And if it doesn't go as planned?" he asked.

"Then duck."

○̇

THEY met two of Filomena's people in front of Alfonso's nightclub the next night. She'd warned Ben that she wouldn't be coming herself, so neither Ben nor Tenzin was surprised. The two younger vampires led them through the popular club, openly baring fangs at humans who laughed and ran from them.

Ben looked around in sudden realization. "They think it's a game."

Tenzin said, "They usually do."

Ben, Tenzin, and their two escorts stepped behind a heavy curtain at the back of the club and descended stone steps where two more vampires guarded the entrance to Alfonso's court. The pulse of music pounded at his back, growing softer as they descended. As one, the two vampires opened the double doors for them and they stepped through, the damp earthen smell assaulting Ben's senses after the smell of cologne, alcohol, and sweat in the club above.

Tenzin walked behind him. He could feel her wary energy in the subtle press of wind against his back. He reached a hand back and gripped hers for a second before he released it. In his other hand, he carried a metal briefcase full of fake Sicilian tarì.

It was heavy, which meant he could use it as a weapon. Not a bad thing to have in your hands when you were walking into a giant den of vampires. The knives at his waist pressed into his skin, reassuring him with their cool presence.

The court was full that night. Dozens of dark-eyed vampires lounged on the steps around Alfonso's throne, others gathered in the shadow of pillars that held up the old Roman ruins. Filomena was one of them, her tall figure clad in a brilliant shirt of blue, yellow, and red. It glowed in the low light. Ben let Tenzin take the lead, coming up behind her, still carrying the gold.

Filomena stepped forward and said, "We welcome your return, Tenzin, daughter of Zhang Guolao. Sired of air. Mated to water, scourge of the Naiman Khanlig. Commander of the Altan Wind. Protector of Penglai Island. Patron goddess of the Holy Mountain, protector and scribe of New Spain. Friend of Don Ernesto Alvarez of Los Angeles." Filomena took a breath. "And we also welcome Benjamin Vecchio, ward of Giovanni Vecchio, scholar and ally of Rome."

As soon as Filomena said his uncle's name, silence fell in the court. He could feel the air in the room shift as vampires turned to stare at him.

Okay, so things were already going sideways.

"Lovely," he muttered. "Always nice to be the center of attention."

Tenzin spoke in Mandarin. "Stay close."

"This is the ward of di Spada?" Alfonso rose to his feet. "In my city?"

Filomena gestured toward Tenzin. "Tenzin is Di Spada's old partner, my lord. You knew that when you hired her. Is it any wonder she brings the assassin's son with her?"

"Not his son," Ben said quietly. "Not that it matters, I guess."

Alfonso was glaring at Filomena. "I will deal with your

insubordinate tone later. Tenzin, did you find what I hired you to find?"

Ben held out the briefcase to Tenzin, who took it. He suddenly felt naked and put his hands in his pockets, pressing his forearms against the blades at his sides.

Tenzin said, "I found it. I will expect the fee transferred to my account by the end of this night."

Filomena stepped forward again. "Did you not know that she had found the tarì, my lord? After all, you sent Patricio and Armand to follow the boy when he left your city so you could be kept abreast of their progress."

Suspicious murmurs from the crowd of vampires. Alfonso's lip curled up at his lieutenant.

"Silence, Filomena."

"Where are they?" Filomena asked, pressing forward as a dozen vampires moved to guard her sides. "Have your scouts not returned?"

Aaaaand any hope of getting out of Alfonso's glorified basement fled at that moment.

Ben glanced at Tenzin. Her head was cocked, watching Filomena with narrow eyes.

"What is she doing?" he whispered.

Tenzin said, "She's being very shrewd. Filomena has drawn me in. I can't ignore Alfonso's slight now."

"What?"

Tenzin flexed her shoulder and smiled. "She's maneuvered me into becoming her ally. Clever, clever girl. This just became interesting."

"I really wish you didn't sound so chipper right now."

"But it works out beautifully!"

"How?" Ben hissed. "How does this work out in any way that could be considered beautiful?"

Ben could see factions already forming as over half the

vampires in the room drifted toward Filomena while others gathered closer to Alfonso. In truth, the factions had probably lain beneath the surface for months or years. Or centuries.

"You spend the wealth of our city treasury to find a fortune you claim as your own," Filomena said, walking toward the throne. "You put corrupt humans in place and allow them to steal from your own people. What makes you better than the Romans who looted Naples in the first place?"

"I *am* Naples." Alfonso rose to his feet. "And you are nothing."

"I am the woman who will take this city from you!" Filomena said, drawing her sword. "And my people stand behind me."

With a surge, the vampires of Naples met in a clashing roar.

"Now is the time that you duck!" Tenzin yelled, shoving him behind a pillar and throwing the briefcase at his chest. "Here, hold this!"

Ben slid down the pillar, holding the briefcase. "Can't. Breathe."

That swing might have crushed a few ribs, but Ben listened to Tenzin. He had absolutely no dog in this fight, and he did not consider armed combat a fun way to hang out on a Saturday night.

He scrambled to a better location, knowing that in the rush to avoid eternal death most of the vampires had probably forgotten about the giant pile of gold he was holding, but not all of them would. Immortals were nothing if not opportunistic.

Ben noticed the first lurker as the vampire made his way toward the stairs. The stocky brown-haired man spotted Ben from the corner of his eye and grinned.

"Yeah," Ben said. "Can't imagine what you want, buddy."

The vampire jumped on him with stunning speed, reaching for Ben's throat as Ben swung his knife deep into his attacker's gut and pulled up. He twisted the knife around a few times until the vampire let go of his neck.

Quick. Messy. Ben's hands were covered in blood, but his throat and the briefcase were safe. The unexpected attack was enough to deter the vampire, who was only looking for easy prey before he fled. With a snarl, the immortal ran toward the back stairs, holding his bleeding gut.

Tenzin landed beside him. "Are you all right?"

"Yes, but—"

She took off again. Ben tried to make himself invisible while still keeping an eye on the fight.

It was clear that Filomena's allies had come prepared. Most were cutting down Alfonso's friends with quick chops and sweeping strokes from blades while many of Alfonso's allies were unarmed. It was an ambush. Ben saw mostly European blades, but Filomena carried a katana, and Ben even saw a few battle-axes.

Retro.

A few took the time to feed from their enemies, but most of the carnage was practical. Cut down. Take head. Go for the next one.

The second vampire who attacked him tried to grab him from the side. She launched in Ben's direction and latched on with all four limbs, slamming him to the ground before she attempted to dig in with clawlike fingernails. Ben twisted away, grappling with her superior strength while tossing away a butcher knife she'd stowed on her back.

He managed to roll far enough away to put a hard boot in her neck. The impact stunned her enough that Ben got in another couple of kicks before she hissed and ran away.

He crawled to another corner, dragging the damned brief-case with him. Tenzin was swooping over the heads of the fighters, one of the few air vampires in the room. Most of Filomena's people were, like herself, water vampires. Isolated from easy access to their element, the battle was dirty and bloody and crude.

It was hard to tell how long it lasted. All Ben knew was, by the time the third vampire attacked, he was sick. The smell of blood was thick in the air; he could taste it on his lips. He saw the vampire running and aimed a throwing knife at one eye. He threw it, hit the target, then sent three more into the twitching body before he walked away. He hadn't killed it, but it was on the ground and one knife had gotten close enough to the thing's neck that Ben doubted it would chase him.

"Tenzin!" he shouted.

She landed a few minutes later, her face flushed like a child coming in from play. "Are you hurt?"

"No."

"Is the gold safe?"

"Yes."

She frowned. "Then what's wrong?"

His throat was tight. "Is this almost done? I want to turn over this gold, collect our fee, and go home. Unless someone else is planning to attack us."

Tenzin's eyes took a slow sweep around the room, then she poked her head around the corner and reported, "Filomena has almost killed Alfonso. I think this is close to done."

Ben joined her, craning his neck around the pillar to see Filomena roar, her blouse drenched in blood, two swords in her hands. She whirled and struck at Alfonso, who parried with surprising speed. Alfonso had brute strength going for him, but it was clear who was the better swordsman. Filomena worked Alfonso across the dais until he was bent back over his throne.

"How does the throne feel now, you mad Spanish bastard?" Filomena screamed.

Alfonso tried to roll away, but she brought her blade down

on his neck before he could escape. Unfortunately, the blade didn't go clear through, and Alfonso's head listed to the side but didn't quite detach.

Ben winced and looked away.

"Unfortunate," Tenzin said. "She hit him at a difficult angle. She'll get it on the next—ah. Gone now."

The roar of the crowd told him that Filomena's allies clearly considered their side victorious. Since Ben didn't know which bodies belonged to which side, he couldn't judge just by looking at the carnage.

"We done now?" Ben said.

"I believe so."

He crossed his arms and leaned against what was now his favorite pillar, his boot resting on the edge of the briefcase with all the gold tarì. A thought struck him. "Hey, Tiny?"

"Yes?"

"Was Alfonso the only one who ever saw the original coins?"

Tenzin leaned against the pillar next to him. "Other than me, I believe he was."

"So there is now no one who'll be able to..."

"Correct."

He let out a slow breath. "Did you plan this out in advance?"

She shrugged. "Let's just say that it was time for Naples to leap into the twenty-first century. We just gave it a little nudge."

Ben heard Filomena giving some kind of inspirational speech in the background about the new Neapolitan republic and the end of foreign oppression as she stood over the bodies of the vampires she'd killed.

And Ben felt... exhausted.

He picked up the briefcase full of gold, handed it to Tenzin, and walked toward the stairs.

"Where are you going?" she called.

"Home."

The problem was, Ben wasn't quite sure where home was at the moment.

So he went to Tuscany.

9

THE HOUSE IN TUSCANY WAS out in the country, surrounded by olive groves and grapevines. The vines in midsummer were laden with thick-skinned purple fruit and lush green leaves. He walked through the vineyard during the day and ate the sweet, seedy grapes. He brought a blanket into the olive grove and lay in the afternoon shade, reading a book or napping. He ate sandwiches made from the bread and cheese he bought when he rode his old bike into town. He opened cans of salty sardines stored in the pantry and picked tomatoes from the garden the caretaker tended.

He drank a lot of wine.

When the sun set, Ben locked himself in his room and slept. He slept long and hard, and he tried not to think about blood or gold or pretty girls with deadly fangs. He stayed in the primitive wing of the house with no electricity and let his phone die. When it was dark, he slept. When the sun rose, he woke.

Ben knew he'd have to go back to Los Angeles eventually, but he wanted to take some time to think about his life.

What the hell was he doing?

Who was he?

A human? A vampire in training? A lackey or a leader?

Could he walk through a world where he was always seen as inferior because of his mortality? Would he be satisfied living in the human world again?

Was living in the human world even an option at this point?

Ben thought it would be Tenzin who found him eventually, but it was his uncle. Giovanni waited for him one morning a week or so after Ben had arrived in Tuscany, taking shelter in the library before Ben dragged himself out of bed.

His uncle said nothing at first. Then he stood, patted Ben's cheek, and said, "We'll talk tonight. I'm tired," before he left the room.

ō

BEN took a nap that afternoon and woke to the smell of steak smoking on the grill. He walked out and saw Giovanni manipulating the flame around two thick cuts of beef, searing them from the outside before he warmed the coals underneath them and left the steaks on the grill to finish cooking. There was an open bottle of wine on the table and two full glasses.

"Sit," his uncle said. "The meat is almost done."

The dinner was simple, which was all he'd ever expect from Giovanni, who had not learned how to cook more than the basics in over five hundred years of life. Meat, bread, wine, and a few tomatoes sliced from the garden, with olive oil poured over them. Ben sat and drank his wine, staring out over the orchards at twilight.

Ben looked at his uncle.

Giovanni was, objectively speaking, the most handsome man Ben had ever seen. When he was in high school, all the girls had a crush on his Uncle Giovanni. Every girlfriend he'd brought home had angled for a hint of a smile. It had annoyed him until his last girlfriend said Ben and Giovanni looked more like brothers than uncle and nephew. That had made his chest puff up at the time, but now it freaked him out.

Because it was true. His uncle used clothes and hair and glasses to age himself for humans, but if you looked carefully, Giovanni didn't look a day over thirty. He'd stay that way forever, and Ben was quickly catching up.

"I talked with Tenzin in Rome," Giovanni said. "You have both made a friend in Emil Conti."

"Huh."

"The new regime in Naples is decidedly more open and willing to work with him. Added to that, they've already been able to shed more light on the library theft. Zeno was invited down examine the documents they were keeping from Emil's people. Emil believes Zeno's status as a native Neapolitan and former clergy will be of benefit in building trust."

"You must have agreed to let him go," Ben said. "He's under your aegis."

Giovanni drank some wine and shrugged. "It will help clear things up for my clients."

"Right."

"And Emil is a good ally. Filomena could be as well."

"She's something, all right."

Giovanni was silent.

"It's not that she used me," Ben said. "It's that I was oblivious to it. I thought I was a bishop when I was a pawn."

Giovanni nodded. "I understand. But you won't be oblivious next time."

"*If* there's a next time."

They were both silent for a long time.

"There doesn't have to be," Giovanni said. "Not for any of this. You know that, don't you?"

Ben cleared his throat. "Be honest. Has living a normal life ever really been an option for me?"

Giovanni paused. "I talked to Matt and Dez before I left."

"Yeah?" Ben sipped his wine. "How are they? I haven't been by for dinner in too long. How's Carina?"

"Growing quickly," Giovanni said with a smile. "She starts school in the fall. Soccer too. She already has her first set of cleats and her very own ball. It's purple. She's very excited."

Ben felt his throat close up. He remembered when Carina had been born. Had listened to her hummingbird heartbeat when Dez had been in the hospital in Rome. And now Carina was buying cleats and starting school.

His heart began to race. It was all happening too quickly. His uncle looked like his brother. Babies were growing up and Ben was graduating. Casper was slower every year, and Isadora's hearing was beginning to go.

"Gio—"

"I talked to Matt and Dez before I left LA," Giovanni said softly. "The apartment over their garage is empty right now. You could rent it if you wanted. Matt has an opening at the company in his online security division. You are more than qualified for it. You could—"

"It's not the job thing," Ben said in a rough voice. "I'm not worried about... It's not the job."

"I know." Giovanni stood and took the meat off the grill. "I know it's not about a job."

Giovanni sat down again and poured more wine while the meat rested and the temperature in the hills dropped. A cool breeze drifted over the tops of the trees, sending a shush of sound through the valley.

"Who am I?" Ben asked. "Benjamin Amir Rios, bastard pickpocket? Ben Vecchio, ward of the famous vampire? Your son? Tenzin's... butler?"

"You're none of those things," Giovanni said. "Or maybe you're a bit of all of them. What is important is that you have the choice." His uncle leaned across the table and squeezed his shoulder. "The man you are, Benjamin, the man you're becoming... I am privileged to know him. Whatever you choose—whatever you do—I will be there. Beatrice will be there. You are ours. Maybe you don't have our blood, but—"

"What if I wanted to be an immortal?"

Giovanni's hand tightened, and Ben realized for the first time how much his uncle truly wanted him to say yes.

"Either of us," Giovanni said. "You know this. Either of us would consider it a privilege to sire you."

Ben blinked hard. "And if I wanted to get an office job, find a nice wife, and raise fifteen kids?"

"I'd be godfather to every single one," Giovanni said. "And we would watch them always. Protect them always."

"Why are you making it so easy?" Ben sniffed.

"Because I love you. I want you to be happy."

Ben started to laugh. "And yet I hear a 'but.'"

"But I also want you to be challenged. Excited and driven about whatever you do. Because you won't be happy unless you're challenged."

Ben put his head in his hands and gripped his hair. "Why can't you just tell me what to do already?"

"It doesn't work that way."

"Sometimes I wish it did."

"No, you don't." Giovanni dropped a slab of steak on his plate and passed the bread. "Besides Ben, if I told you what to do, you'd find a way to do exactly the opposite. Then you'd argue with me that your way was what I should have chosen to begin with."

He took a deep breath. "Yeah, you're probably right."

"Of course I'm right. Now eat your dinner. I didn't ruin it this time."

"Thank God for small miracles."

☿

THEY were kicking a ball back and forth the next night when Ben finally asked about her. "So did she go back to LA?"

Giovanni didn't need to ask whom he was talking about.

"I don't think so," he said. "She told me you needed human time."

Ben nodded.

"She also told me not to leave you alone too long because you're a brooder."

He rolled his eyes. "I'm fairly sure Tenzin thinks any reaction time over five minutes long is brooding."

Giovanni chuckled. "I'm not sure about that, but she does live in the moment."

"Has she always?"

"Well..." Giovanni stopped the ball with his foot. "You have to remember, she's the type of immortal that will get fed up with the world, then go sleep—figuratively speaking—in a cave for a century without thinking twice. So when she's awake, she's *present*."

Ben thought about that and it made an odd kind of sense.

"To get to be that age without going mad," Giovanni continued, "I think you have to live in the moment." Giovanni started kicking the ball again. "They're very different personalities, but if you think about Carwyn, he's the same way. He exists in the present. It's rare to get him ruminating about history. Vampires who ruminate about history tend to meet the sun because they become melancholy."

"You ruminate."

Giovanni nodded. "I used to. And how long do you think I would have lasted if I hadn't met Beatrice? Not long."

"Gio?"

"Hmm."

"Do you wonder? About me and Tenzin? About... whatever it is we are?"

Giovanni paused. "Not anymore. I love you both. Whatever you are... you'll figure it out, Ben. Both of you are simply more alive when you're together than when you're separate. I don't know what that means yet. I don't think you do either."

Ben let that one sink in for a while.

"It's okay," Giovanni said with a smile. "You don't have to know yet."

☿

THEY were playing chess and drinking wine the following night.

"I think I want to move back to New York," Ben said.

Giovanni paused, a rook held in his hand. "You want the town house?"

"No," Ben said. "I'd stick out like a sore thumb in that neighborhood. I'm thinking about a loft in Brooklyn."

"For?"

Several kicks under the table from Fabi, a few dropped hints from Tenzin, and lots and lots of sleep were starting to make things clear. "I want to do what you do," Ben said. "Or at least I want to try. But not with books. I can't spend that much time looking for books, Gio. I'll go crazy."

"Do you think this is a surprise to me?"

"I want to find art," Ben said. "Antiquities. Take on clients and find things for them on commission. What do you think?"

Giovanni paused and finished his wine. It took three more moves from both of them before he replied.

"You can't do it alone," Giovanni said. "Not in the immortal world. No matter what your reputation, skills, or connections, there will be some who only take you seriously if you have a vampire partner."

"She'd go with me. You know she would."

"So you're the brains and Tenzin is the brawn?" Giovanni tapped the table. "It has possibilities. You'd be in O'Brien territory."

"Would that be a problem?"

"I don't think so. You don't have political ambitions, and neither does Tenzin. If you gave them a cut rate for family and associates like I do with Ernesto, you'd probably be fine. Cormac is the one to approach. Talk to Gavin."

Ben nodded, growing more and more excited about the idea as he thought about it. "I can do that."

"They wouldn't like Tenzin living there...," Giovanni said. "Or maybe they would. If it would open a business relationship with her allies in Asia, they might not have a problem. She'd have to play nice sometimes."

Ben shrugged. "I can get her to play nice when necessary."

"You're possibly the only one who can."

"Do you think it's a big enough market?" Ben asked. "Could we make any money with it?"

"If you were good, you could make very good money, but we should consider it an offshoot of Beatrice's and my business to start. I'll refer clients to you when they need to find antiquities—"

"And eventually I'll refer clients to you if they need to find books."

Man and vampire both smiled.

"This could work, couldn't it, Gio?"

"Are you excited about the idea?"

Ben paused and really thought about it. "This feels right," he said. "More right than anything else I've thought of. I just have to keep Tenzin from forging copies of stuff we're hired to find."

Giovanni closed his eyes and turned back to the chessboard. "I'm pretending I didn't hear that."

"Good call."

"Don't do it again."

"I won't."

"You risk your reputation and mine, Benjamin."

"I get it. I get it. I'll keep her in line."

TO LADY FILOMENA De Moura

Immortal Guardian of Naples and the Second Partheno-pean Republic

NENA (I TOLD you I'd give you a nickname),

FORGIVE me for leaving your beautiful city so abruptly. I meant no offense, so I hope none was taken. The events that led to your rise were, admittedly, surprising to me, but I hope that Tenzin and I were able to assist you in our own way. I understand the collection of Sicilian tarì have been returned to the Neapolitan treasury. I am grateful that our small part in their recovery was satisfactory. (And the bonus was very much appreciated.)

As I have now discovered the delights of your city, I hope to return again soon. I understand you and Emil Conti are working toward smoother relations between the Neapolitan and Roman courts. I wish you both well.

Until our next meeting I remain...

YOUR ADMIRER,
    Benjamin Vecchio,
    International Man of Mystery
    Scourge of the _____ (still working on that one)

-✳-

DEAR BEN,

COME BACK TO NAPLES SOON. You will be welcome.

Nena

EPILOGUE

THE HUMIDITY WAS EVEN HIGHER than when he'd left two weeks before, but Ben was whistling when he saw the prow of Claudio's boat as it drew up to dock near the train station.

"*Ciao*, Claudio."

"*Ciao*, Ben."

He threw his satchel into the back of the boat and climbed in next to Claudio.

"It's still hot," Claudio said. "Even at night. It's not cooling off at all anymore."

"I know."

"You have your passport? Get it out. I'll take you to the airport right now. Get you out of this dreaded damp furnace."

"No, thanks."

Claudio shook his head. "Fine. Whatever you want. You're an idiot like her, I think. Come back in the spring. It's much nicer then."

Ben smiled. "You're the one who lives here, Claudio."

The young man shrugged. "Where else would I live? It's Venice. The greatest city in the world."

☿

BEN heard Louis's trumpet echoing down the quiet canal as they approached the house. Claudio let him out at the end of the Rio Terà dei Assassini and tossed his bag up to him.

"You have the key?" Claudio asked.

Ben held it up. "I made my own copy."

"I'll talk to you later then. Try not to die."

Ben blinked. "Okay. Is there an ambush I need to know about?"

"No," Claudio said. "I say that to all the humans I know who hang out with vampires." He waved and drifted off down the canal.

Ben watched the lights of his boat until they disappeared around a corner, then he turned and punched in the gate code before he twisted the key in the lock. Both the gate and the door swung open easily because he'd oiled them before they left Venice the last time. It was little stuff like that Tenzin always forgot to do.

"Honey," he called quietly when he stepped into the courtyard. "I'm home."

A faint sound of laughter echoing off marble.

Ben dropped his bag on a bench and walked to the turntable at the end of the entry hall. He picked up the needle and skipped to "La Vie en Rose," then he walked over and plucked the wineglass out of Tenzin's hand and set it on the coffee table.

Accusing grey eyes met his. "I was drinking that."

"I know," he said. "But you should be dancing."

"This is becoming a bad habit, Benjamin."

Ben pulled her to her feet and spun her out before he tugged her back and grabbed her around the waist as the trumpet solo started. After a few minutes, she relaxed in his arms and let him lead.

"I thought you'd go back to LA," she said.

"I missed your house."

She chuckled. "Good to know where your loyalties are."

"My loyalties are never in question," he said in a soft voice. "You should know that by now."

She didn't say anything, but her hand gripped tighter at his waist.

They danced silently around the entry, their feet shuffling along the checkerboard marble as the record scratched and echoed and skipped. The moon rose through the arched window over the stairwell and the ancient house breathed with the tide.

Minutes of peaceful silence were broken when Ben groaned, "Why is it so *hot?*"

"Heat wave," Tenzin said. "They say it's the worst in sixty years."

"That's just hideous and wrong."

"And yet, you're still forcing me to dance."

"You like it."

"I don't—"

Ben slapped a hand over her mouth so she couldn't argue. "Stop. Just dance. It's Louis. We always dance to Louis. That's the new rule." She bit his hand and he let go. "Ouch."

"It's so cute when you try to boss me around. Is this an absolute rule? What if a Louis Armstrong song happens to come on at an inopportune moment? If we're fighting for our lives, do we have to stop and dance?"

"We can be flexible in life-threatening situations."

The record switched to "Blueberry Hill," and they kept dancing.

"So," he said. "I did a lot of thinking in Tuscany."

"You brood."

"I was not..." He stopped talking so he didn't start yelling. *Take a deep breath.* "Thinking is not brooding. I was thinking."

"Fine. Whatever you say."

"And I figured out what you can call me when you introduce me."

Tenzin looked up, her eyes laughing. "Oh yes? Can I stick with life coach? That's my favorite so far. I was thinking about some other ones though—"

"No." Ben spun her round and round until she was laughing aloud. "I'm not going to be known as your life coach or your yoga instructor or your publicist."

"So what then?"

Tenzin took a wrong step and tried to take the lead, but Ben shook her arm until she stopped trying to push him around. "No. Don't do that, you'll just mess up the dance. Let me lead. I'm a better dancer."

"Fine." She relaxed and Ben stepped forward, dipping her until her hair brushed the ground.

He pulled her up. "Partner."

Tenzin blinked. "What?"

"You and I," he said, "are going to move to New York."

"Hmmm." It was a suspicious *hmmm.*

"We're going to find shiny, pretty things," Ben continued.

"I like that."

"And we're going to return them to the people paying us to find them."

"I don't like that so much."

"For a very generous fee."

Tenzin thought. She thought until the needle was bumping against the edge of the record, but Ben didn't stop dancing.

Finally, she asked, "Can we—?"

"No, we cannot make forgeries and keep the originals for ourselves."

She pouted. "You're no fun."

"I just need to know." Ben spun her out and tugged her back, the quiet lapping of the water in the canal the only accompaniment to their dance. "Are you in or out, Tenzin?"

Tenzin's eyes narrowed and the corner of her mouth turned up in a smile.

"In."

☿

TENZIN let Ben turn the record over and dance with her for another half an hour.

She was glad she let him figure it out on his own. It was much more satisfying to know he'd come to the same conclusion she had years ago. It was obvious after their trip to China that he'd be the perfect partner to treasure hunt with her. It had taken him a little while to come around, but he couldn't help being slow. He was human.

For now.

THE END

OMENS AND ARTIFACTS

Setting up shop as an antiquities hunter means nothing if you don't have clients. In the vampire world, Ben Vecchio is the subject of widespread speculation, but so far that speculation hasn't translated into work.

What Ben needs is a job. A big job. A profitable job.

A *legendary* job.

Finding the lost sword of Brennus the Celt, the mythical Raven King of the British Isles, would make Ben's reputation in the immortal world, but it could also draw dangerous attention. The Raven King's gold hoard isn't famous for being easy to find. Luckily, Ben has his own legend at his side.

PROLOGUE

N ew York City
2016

SHE STARED AT THE BLANK white wall, mentally placing the weapons she would hang there. The bustle of traffic was barely audible on the top floor of the factory on Mercer Street. The building was old but renovated with the highest level of care. Luxury with character, the agent had advertised.

But Tenzin didn't care about the luxury below her. She didn't care about the discreet doorman. She didn't care about the stunning view of the New York City skyline.

The massive loft had twelve-foot ceilings, a roof terrace, and nearly three thousand square feet for sparring. There was another two thousand square feet below them that functioned as office space and sometimes a basketball court for certain humans with insomnia.

Ben had chosen well.

It wasn't as spacious as her warehouse in Southern California, but if Ben insisted on living in New York City, then this would do. When the shutters closed over the giant windows during the day and Tenzin was alone, the loft almost reminded her of one of her favorite mountain caves in Nepal.

Almost.

But she couldn't decide how to organize her swords. Should she line them up in neat rows? Organize them by size? Arrange them in order of usefulness, historical era, or just make it random?

Such a large blank wall. So many choices.

Ben had introduced her to an entire television network that was focused on home and interior design, but there were few shows that spoke to her specific needs. It was rare for Americans to decorate extensively with weapons. And as a wind vampire, the wall needed to look good both from the ground and the air. She'd fixated on the question for weeks now but still wasn't sure what she wanted to do. She couldn't go out in sunlight, but she didn't sleep either.

Tenzin's surroundings had always been important to her. If she was going to spend twelve or more hours a day limited to the indoors, they had to be.

A polite chime echoed from the kitchen on the other end of the loft. Tenzin set down the hammer and nails she'd been holding, picked up a throwing dagger, and walked warily toward the sleek silver machine that sat on the counter.

"This is Cara." The delicate lilt of a woman's Irish accent filled the space. "You have an incoming voice call from Benjamin Vecchio. Shall I accept?"

Tenzin frowned and tried to remember what she was supposed to do. The voice didn't belong to a real person, Ben had told her. It was something called a "virtual assistant." Like a tiny day-person who lived in the computer. Tenzin found the whole concept very odd. If you were going to keep a servant, why not just hire a living one that could also provide blood?

"Shall I accept?" the voice asked again.

It might be a trick. Benjamin was in London and had no reason to call her.

And if he did call her, he'd probably ask what she was doing. Tenzin guessed "pounding nails into your walls so I can hang my knife and sword collection" wouldn't elicit a positive response.

"Shall I accept the call from Benjamin Vecchio?"

"No?"

"Very well," Cara said. "Sending Benjamin Vecchio to voice mail."

The voice went silent and Tenzin relaxed.

The polite Irish woman was hooked into the Nocht voice-recognition system that had been installed in the loft two weeks before. One of the Dublin vampires had flown to New York to oversee its installation and customization. "Cara" could run the computers, security systems, and communications. All without a vampire needing to touch a button. It was voice command. Everything was voice command.

At first Tenzin had been suspicious of the voice that came out of nowhere. It felt like she was never alone. As if she were being watched or monitored by something she couldn't see. The omniscience of the polite voice unnerved her.

But the first time Tenzin had shouted, "All I want to do is watch *Property Brothers!*" into the empty loft and the voice had answered, "This is Cara, and I'd be happy to assist you," Tenzin decided she and Cara could be friends.

Cara chimed again. "Benjamin Vecchio has left you a voice mail. Would you like to listen to it now?"

She narrowed her eyes. "Yes?"

Ben's voice filled the room. "Tenzin, I know you're there. The security monitor in the loft shows me there's someone small flying around the room, so it better be you. Do *not* put holes in my walls. I'm going to call again in five minutes. Tell Cara to accept the call."

Tenzin glanced at the open doors of the roof terrace and considered going out for a short flight just to spite him. She *was* being watched. How annoying. And efficient. Her paranoid nature was forced to admire Ben's cunning.

Cara spoke again. "You have an incoming voice call from Benjamin Vecchio. Shall I accept?"

"That was *not* five minutes." She eyed the terrace doors. Then she eyed the sleek silver box that housed Cara.

"Shall I accept?"

Tenzin flopped down on the Persian rug that covered the floor in front of the media center. "Fine." She tossed the throwing dagger end over end, catching it before it stabbed her face. "Accept call."

"Is Cara working?" Ben asked. "There weren't any hiccups in the system when I left. What took you so long to answer?"

"I was deciding if I wanted to talk to you or not."

He sighed. "Tenzin."

She smiled at the irritation in his sigh. He was so delightfully stuffy sometimes.

"If I'm calling you from London, there's a reason," Ben said. "So the next time I call, can you just answer so we don't have to waste ten minutes?"

"That's not true." She tossed the dagger again, higher this time. "You called the other day to ask me how my night was and tell me about your research at the library."

"What?"

"I am pointing out that there wasn't any reason for that conversation, so your previous statement was untrue." She caught the flipping blade between her palms. "But I know you are prone to hyperbole, so I won't hold it against you."

"Is Cara working or not?"

Tenzin called out, "Cara, are you working?"

Cara answered, "I can run a systems check if you would like. In order to run a systems check, all current operations will need to be ended. Would you like to end your voice call now?"

Ben started, "No, don't—"

"Yes," Tenzin said. "End call and... run systems check."

Ben's voice cut off mid objection, and Tenzin laughed.

A moment later, Cara spoke up. "I am currently running a systems check. You have an incoming voice call from Benjamin Vecchio. Shall I end systems check and accept call?"

"Sure." She flipped the dagger in the air again, catching it on the way down.

"Dammit, Tenzin, will you cut this out!"

"I think Cara is working correctly," she said. "But she had to cancel the systems check to answer your call. I hope you didn't mess up her programming, Benjamin." She flipped the dagger again. This time it went so high it stuck in the ceiling.

Tenzin winced. Ben wasn't going to like that.

"I'm in London, and I need you to fly over here. Can you just do that? Meet me at that house I rented last summer. I've got a line on something big. Something that could really get our name out there. Other than the Aztec artifact we recovered for that friend of Gio's, the phone has been dead for months. If we pull this job off, I don't think we'll ever worry about finding work again."

Tenzin curled her lip. "But... my weapons just arrived. I was hoping to hang them up before you got back."

"Do not put holes in my walls, Tenzin."

"You told me I could bring my weapons if I moved out here with you."

"You can hang and display *some* of them. Properly. With brackets mounted by an actual contractor. Not random nails pounded into my walls, Tiny. Put the hammer down."

She flew up and grabbed the dagger out of the ceiling, then landed on the Persian rug and brushed away the plaster dust. "I don't have a hammer. I have a knife." She looked up. "And the hole in the ceiling isn't even noticeable from the floor."

"What hole in the ceiling?"

"I suppose I can come to London, but can you have someone hang my stuff up while we're gone?" An idea struck her. "Cara, can you help me with that?"

"What hole, Tenzin? There wasn't a hole in the ceiling when I left."

Cara said, "What can I help you with?"

"Can you find someone to hang up my weapons while I'm in London?"

"What hole are you talking about, Tenzin?"

Cara said, "Let me look." There was a pause. "I can e-mail you a list of general contractors within a five-mile radius. I can also e-mail you a list of custom firearms cabinet builders. Is that what you're looking for?"

Ben was muttering curses. "There better not be any holes in the ceiling. So help me, if there are holes—"

"Send me a list of contractors," Tenzin said. "I don't own any guns."

"Very well."

"Ben, I'll see you in London in a few days." Tenzin tossed the dagger back on the pile. "Cara and I need to find a contractor, then I'll fly over there."

"Do not hire a contractor, Tiny. The loft is not yours, it's mine."

"Technically it's Gio's, isn't it?"

"Technically it belongs to a corporation that doesn't exist, and it doesn't matter because *do not hire a contractor without me!*"

"I'll see you in a couple of days," Tenzin said. "Cara, end call."

"Tenzin—"

"Ending call now," Cara said.

A soothing silence swept into the room along with a gust of wind from the terrace doors.

"Is there anything else I can assist you with, Tenzin?" Cara asked.

She didn't really want to hire a contractor. She wanted to hang the weapons herself. But it was so fun imagining Ben's face turning red, she decided to let him stew until she met with him.

Tenzin walked over to the blank wall again. "Are there any reruns of *Divine Design*?"

"One moment please... There are five episodes currently streaming online. Would you like to watch one?"

Tenzin grinned. "Excellent."

1

L *ondon, England*

BEN STEPPED OUT OF THE tube station at Ladbroke Grove and turned left, dodging the two laughing mothers in Eritrean scarves pushing strollers up the road. He ducked into the Tesco a block up. He wanted Indian food and beer, but he didn't want to order delivery or go out. He didn't want to talk to anyone. He could barely tolerate the brush of fellow shoppers.

He was in a foul mood.

It was cold and damp. The sun had set at four thirty, and the fog had fallen with the dark. Even more than the damp weather, hunger, and crankiness was the impatience of *waiting*. He'd been in a holding pattern since he'd spoken to Tenzin a week ago. He'd expected her two, maybe three, days after they'd spoken.

So far, nothing. Not a single blessed sign of her, and he was hitting a brick wall with his research.

He didn't have many friends in London. Gavin was in

269

New York at his new bar. He'd called the house in Rome and tried to get Fabi to come visit him, but the sun-loving girl's only response was a laugh. Even Tenzin seemed to be avoiding him. She was probably at home, tucked into their clean and spacious new loft, putting holes in the walls with manic glee while his own boxes sat unopened in a corner of the office.

Yep. Really foul mood.

Ben worked his way through the after-work crowds to grab a tray of lamb korma and a pack of Sharp's pale ale before he headed to the self-checkout. He didn't even want to talk to the clerk at the front of the store.

He'd spoken to every early Celtic collector who would respond to him. He'd interviewed several professors and dug into old land records, but until he could meet with Gemma—and hopefully Tywyll—he was stymied. And until Tenzin got to London, he didn't want to meet with either of those two, because he was more than happy to admit he was out of his depth when it came to teasing information out of very old vampires.

Why was the damn line taking so long? He craned his neck to look around the older woman in front of him.

One machine working. Perfect.

He'd met Terrance Ramsay for a drink the night after he'd landed at Heathrow. The vampire in charge of London was an old family friend of his uncle's. The VIC was also neck deep in dealing with massive vampire political shifts in the Mediterranean at the moment and didn't have much time to worry about lost treasures that no one born after 1000 AD really thought existed.

His tired gaze landed on two teenagers who ambled in, suspiciously close to a woman with a diaper bag and a stroller. Ben narrowed his eyes as they moved closer.

Dammit, he was going to have to talk to someone or they'd have her wallet in seconds.

Just then, the woman's toddler let out a high-pitched shriek and the boys changed directions, unwilling to mark anyone attracting that much attention.

Saved by the screaming two-year-old.

Ben moved three feet forward. Thunder rolled overhead, and outside the shop windows, rain began to pour down on the pavement.

Why had he picked London in winter?

Oh right. Gold and notoriety.

The gold hoard of Brennus the Celt was a tale draped in shadows and wrapped in myth. It was an urban legend among *vampires*, for heaven's sake. A legendary treasure of weapons and gold artifacts so beautiful that Viking invaders wept at the sight of it, which was what gave Brennus time to kill them and hide his treasure.

According to the rumors.

But no one knew what had happened to Brennus, ancient immortal chieftain of Britain, much less his treasure. Everyone had stopped looking for traces of him or it a thousand years before. That chapter of history had drifted into legends. Searching for the treasure was a dead end. If no enterprising vampire had found it in twelve hundred years, then it was lost to history.

Ben wasn't buying it.

He finally made it to the front of the line and swiped his card for his dinner and beer. He left the market and turned left, heading toward the quiet house on Oxford Gardens.

The house wasn't noteworthy in any way. Just another rental house on a street of nearly identical row houses. It had three stories and a back garden. It was close to a tube station. It was anonymous and nowhere near most immortal neighborhoods, which was exactly the reason he liked it. Half the owners on the street were part-time residents or in a constant state of refurbishment, which meant no one paid attention to the dark-haired American man who came and went at odd hours of the day and night.

Ben unlocked the heavy door and walked to the kitchen. He put the korma on the counter and the beer in the fridge. Then he went back to the entryway to kick off his shoes and peel off his damp overcoat. Clad in stocking feet and already feeling lighter, Ben returned to the kitchen and opened a beer.

Despite the disappointing news from the cartographer today, he was certain the treasure existed.

Ben had asked questions. Dropped hints. Listened to stories. Then he went where vampire treasure hunters didn't think to go. He looked in the human world. The tedious, daylit human world. He didn't look for a big treasure. He looked for one artifact. A weapon of such renown that it had been given a name by the Romans who encountered it.

Sanguine Raptor.

Ancient writers called it the Blood Thief.

It was Brennus's blade. The sword that slew thousands. Which might or might not be true. Ben was sure the sword existed, and he wanted it. He wanted that sword and the treasure that came with it. If he and Tenzin could find the treasure of Brennus the Celt, *they* would be the legends.

He'd found veiled mention of the sword in Tacitus's account of Agricola's governance of Britannia. He'd found another reference from a monk who'd traveled to Charlemagne's court just prior to the raid of Lindisfarne.

He popped the tray of korma into the microwave oven and leaned against the counter, drinking his ale and staring at the dark sway of damp trees in the back garden.

The Sanguine Raptor existed. The treasure existed. Ben

had even narrowed down the geographical area based on recorded Viking raids in the north and had several probable sites to start hunting.

He just needed that one thing.

One clue. One mention. One... anything that pointed him to its hiding place. He was hoping Tywyll, the oldest vampire in the British Isles, would be the one to give him that key.

He squinted as he watched the trees. Why were they moving so much? He set his beer down and walked to the garden door. The rain had stopped and it wasn't windy. In fact, he hadn't noticed any breeze when he...

A dark figure jumped from the tree just as he opened the door. His heart leapt and his stomach dropped.

"It's you." He let out a breath.

Tenzin grinned. "Did you miss me?"

The ugly knot of frustration loosened in his chest. "Yes." He pulled her into a tight hug. "What took you so long?"

"I had things to do." She squeezed him back before she ducked under his arm and into the kitchen. "What smells so— *Why are you eating food from a microwave?*"

He followed her back in the house. "Because you haven't been here to cook for me."

She picked up the box and gave him a dirty look. "This is poison."

He smiled. "I really don't think it is."

"What is wrong with you?"

"Did you put holes in my ceiling?" He rubbed his eyes, suddenly exhausted. "I expected the walls, but the ceiling?"

She narrowed her eyes and started opening cupboards. "Don't try to change the subject. Now sit down. You have rice and lentils at least. I should be able to throw something together."

She kept muttering as she looked in the refrigerator and

grabbed the one nod to fresh food he'd managed in London, a bag of mini carrots. Ben watched her bang around the kitchen, a smile on his face. The knots in his shoulders relaxed.

Tenzin was here.

Everything would be fine.

×

DESPITE THE STATE of his pantry, Tenzin managed to put together a pilaf dish that would make most people weep. And while she cooked, he pulled out all the research he'd put together and spread it on the table in the dining room. The journals and pictures. The property records and satellite pictures. As she cooked, he prepared to make his case.

"Tell me," she said, setting down two bowls of pilaf and grabbing the chair next to him.

"Brennus the Celt," Ben said.

"Didn't know him." Tenzin picked at her pilaf. "He was Carwyn's grandsire. Carwyn's mother, Maelona, was rumored to be the only surviving child of Brennus. She walked into the dawn almost a thousand years ago."

"But no one knows what happened to Brennus."

She shook her head. "Just rumors."

"And Brennus was rumored to have treasure stolen from the Romans. Welsh gold. Silver. Jewels and weapons."

Tenzin nodded slowly. "I have heard of this treasure."

Ben walked to the kitchen and grabbed his bottle of ale and another one for Tenzin. "Reports said that northern raiders were so in awe of Brennus's wealth that they were struck dumb at the sight of it." He walked back and handed her the beer before he sat again.

"Cheers." Tenzin tipped up her ale and drank. "And while the raiders were gaping, Brennus killed them. Chopped off their heads with his mighty blade."

"Yes. Now, before you start telling me it's a—"

"Legend. It's a legend." She shrugged. "Vampires have lots of legends, Ben. We get bored. We enjoy lying. We enjoy conning others of our kind when we can. It makes us feel superior."

"But Brennus's treasure wasn't *just* a legend. It existed at one time. Look." He shoved the journals to her. "The wealth of the chieftain Brennus was mentioned twice by Tacitus." He showed her another scan from the monk in the French court. "And in France by this priest. It was mentioned by multiple sources, not just one. Add to that the rumors in the immortal world and you have enough smoke that the fire has to exist."

She still looked skeptical.

Ben said, "Brennus's treasure existed."

"I agree, but that doesn't mean it *still* exists."

"I don't think it's been found and broken up. A gold hoard of that size would have been noted."

"Unless it was found by another vampire. We tend to keep quiet when we find lots of money."

"True, but—"

"And it might not be as big as you think. You have to remember, my Benjamin. Treasure in ancient Britain wasn't like treasure in the more civilized world. Brennus was a chieftain, not an emperor. He wouldn't have had a giant room filled with riches."

"Why not? Those did exist."

"But not *here*. Rome took most of Britain's gold." She looked out at the dark trees behind the house. "They took it far, far away. The gold Brennus was rumored to have might have been a single chest. It might have been next to nothing that he boasted of to make his enemies jealous."

"Was the Sanguine Raptor made up?"

Her eyes sharpened. "No. If any part of that legend is true, it's the Sanguine Raptor. I've heard too many details to doubt that. Rumors of it traveled all the way to Rome."

"What have you heard?"

"A Celtic blade made of the particular kind of iron Brennus had perfected. Very strong. Very flexible. Jeweled hilt."

"What style?"

"More a saber than a long sword. I'm not certain of that, but reports say that it was short—closer to the Roman gladius—and curved. Brennus forged his own iron. Earth vampire, remember?"

"So if the Sanguine Raptor existed, why not the rest of the treasure? According to legends—"

"Listen to yourself, Ben. *According to legends.*"

"Legends come from somewhere!"

She paused. "You're not wrong. All I'm saying is that *if* this treasure exists, it might not be on the grand scale it's made out to be. Is this really worth our time?"

Ben shuffled his papers together. He didn't need to convince Tenzin the treasure existed. After the past couple of summers, she owed him a job or two on faith. But Tenzin was a magpie and didn't like parting with her money. She also didn't like being bored. What he needed to do was convince her that looking for Brennus's hoard was worth the effort.

"This job, Tiny... You need to think bigger. It doesn't matter if it's *monetarily* worth it."

"Money always matters."

He folded his photos back into his notebook. "I'm thinking about reputation."

She grinned, her clawlike fangs glinting from the corner of her mouth. "I don't think my reputation needs any work."

He put everything in his folder and closed it. "Well, mine

does. I'm willing to lose money on this deal if it means my reputation gets a boost. And you might not be as reputable as you think you are."

She snorted.

"Face it," he said. "Right now you're known as an assassin more than an antiquities hunter. People would hire you in a heartbeat to get rid of their enemies, but they're not necessarily going to trust you with the family silver."

"Which they shouldn't." She leaned forward. "Because I would keep it all for myself if you let me."

"Which is why I need to build *my* reputation if we're going to be partners. If we finish this job—"

"Did someone hire you for this or did you come up with this idea yourself?"

He sat back. "Finding a client is part of the job."

"You want to find a client to hire you to find a treasure you have already picked out?" Tenzin rested her chin on her hand. "Benjamin, I'm not sure you understand what contract work is about."

"We *need* to do this, Tiny."

"Says who?"

"Me. You agreed to be partners."

"Yes, I did. But Brennus's gold is the definition of a wild-goose chase. Hundreds of vampires have looked for this treasure. Hundreds. Why do you think you can find it?"

"Satellite photos, human resources, and metal detectors."

Tenzin stared at him, then she threw her head back and started laughing.

SHE WASN'T LAUGHING at him. Not really.

Okay, maybe a little.

She was laughing more at his ego. Her Benjamin was bold.

"Satellite photos, human resources, and metal detectors."

Confidence had never been a problem for Ben.

"Fine." He glared at her as she wiped her eyes. "Laugh. But you're going to do this for me, Tiny."

How long would it take to talk him out of this crazy scheme? And was there anything she wanted to do before she returned to New York? She'd already visited the Harry Potter studio. She'd visited the ravens at the Tower. There wasn't much else—

"Are you listening?" he asked. "You're staying and you're helping me because you owe me."

She frowned. "What do I owe you for?"

He held up his hand. "Xinjiang." One finger. "Shanghai." Two fingers. "The freighter." Five fingers went up.

"That was years ago."

He held up his other hand. "Naples. Running for my life in Venice. Filomena."

"Hey! You walked into that one all on your own."

"Breaking into Hogwarts?"

He sure had a lot of fingers held up.

"I didn't ask you to come and get me from Hogwarts," Tenzin said. "I could have avoided those guards on my own."

"And I'm not even going to count the raccoon thing."

She pointed at him. "Raccoons are assholes. You know it. I know it. The whole world knows it."

"Fine." He picked up his beer. "But you owe me."

"But—"

"Don't even think about arguing," he said. "You're going to help me, Tenzin. Or..."

"Or what?" This ought to be good. She crossed her arms and waited for his worst.

Ben smiled. "I'll tell Giovanni you were the one who deleted his recording of the *King of Iron Chefs* 'Chen versus Sakai' battle."

Her smile almost fell. "You wouldn't."

His raised eyebrow said he would. Ben could be cunning when he put his mind to it.

"And the Chinese cabbage battle."

Tenzin's eyes went wide.

"Didn't know I knew about that one, did you?"

"I admit nothing."

Ben shrugged. "Doesn't matter when he already suspects you."

"Both those episodes are on YouTube!" she snarled. "He's just being stubborn."

"You know he hates watching TV on the computer."

Tenzin glared at him and stood. Damn conniving human.

She was so proud.

And irritated.

"You're going to help me," Ben said. "I'm meeting with Gemma tomorrow night. Now that you're here, I'm going to request a meeting with Tywyll."

She curled her lip. "That old man?"

"Is he any older than you?"

"I have no idea. Probably not." She was pouting. She knew it. Tenzin hated when Ben bested her.

Damn that *Iron Chef Japan* and its improbably entertaining kitchen battles.

Ben said, "Tywyll was a contemporary of Brennus. According to Carwyn, he was in Cornwall when Brennus was in southern Scotland, but they wrote to each other regularly and Tywyll considers him a friend."

"Considers? As in presently?"

"That's the other thing. According to Terrance Ramsay, Tywyll thinks Brennus is just hiding."

"Tywyll thinks Brennus is alive?"

"Yes."

Tenzin rolled her eyes. "Yes, he sounds like a brilliant source. Highly reliable."

"To be fair, no one witnessed Brennus's death or even heard rumors of it. It was always assumed that he burned up somewhere because he disappeared, but there's not any evidence of it. It's possible he's hiding. Haven't you ever hidden from the world?"

"I think my maximum was around a thousand years." She squinted. "Maybe two."

Ben opened his laptop again. "Well, Brennus has only been missing for twelve hundred, so it's entirely poss— Wait. Why are you smiling now?"

"I was just thinking that stealing treasure from a hidden vampire is much more entertaining than finding lost treasure from a dead one."

He shook his head. "You're twisted."

"You knew that already." She stood and cleared the dishes. "So when do you want to start?"

2

BEN WOULD LIKE TO SAY that the Swan with Two Necks lived up to its name.

It didn't.

"This place is a dump," Tenzin said.

"I'm sure its regulars think it's delightful, so try not to share that sentiment too loudly."

"Fine." She whispered, "This place is a dump."

He smiled and hooked an arm around her neck. "Come on. The old man said he'd meet us inside."

The floating pub creaked when they stepped aboard. Then it creaked when Ben opened the door. In fact, Ben had a hard time imagining how the building remained afloat unless Tywyll kept it held together by the sheer force of his amnis.

Which, according to his aunt, was entirely possible.

Tywyll was a water vampire who could easily be as old as Tenzin, if not older. His reputation left everything to the imagination. He was a loner. He was not ambitious. But the River Thames was *his water*. And not a single vampire in England— not even Terrance Ramsay—disputed Tywyll's claim on it. Ever.

He was sitting in a booth when they walked in. Ben knew it was him because every other eye in the place turned toward them, glanced, then nodded toward the back corner booth. They walked toward the small man with pale skin. He was dark-haired and his face was lined. Tywyll wore the uniform of a man who worked on the river. Sturdy pants. Worn shirt fraying at the collar. Heavy shoes. Flat tweed cap.

But his energy crackled. Ben knew he was approaching one of the most powerful vampires in Britain. What he wasn't sure of—what no one was sure of—was whether Tywyll would be a friend or enemy that night.

The vampire looked up as they approached and nodded toward the opposite bench. "Ye'd be Vecchio's lad then."

"I am." Ben thought about holding out his hand but didn't. He made sure his pulse was steady and his breathing even.

Tywyll turned his eyes on Tenzin. "And I'd bet my pint on ye being the windwalker."

"You wouldn't be wrong," Tenzin said.

"What're ye doin' with this 'un?" Tywyll nodded at Ben. "He's not yer sort."

"He's my sort if I say he is." Tenzin's eyes went cold. "Don't pretend you know me, old man."

Tywyll cackled. "Ye've as many years as me. Or maybe I have more. But fine. Say yer piece, young Vecchio."

Ben decided Tywyll would appreciate the direct approach best. This wasn't a vampire who wanted niceties and charm. "We're looking for the Sanguine Raptor," he said. "According to rumors, you and Brennus were contemporaries. Some say friends. Are they correct?"

Tywyll's eyes went sharp. "The Sanguine Raptor, you say? And what's that?"

Ben smiled. "Brennus's sword. A sword so famous Roman

historians mentioned it. Are you saying you've never heard the name?"

"Ah." Tywyll took a long drink. "You'd be asking after the *Fitheach Lann* then."

"The what?"

"*Fitheach Lann*, boy. The raven blade," Tywyll said. "You're looking for Brennus's blade and you don't even know the name of it?"

Ben filed the information away. Some of his immortal sources had drawn parallels between the real vampire Brennus and the mythical figure of Bran the Blessed in Welsh mythology. Bran, "the Giant King." The *Raven* King. In addition to the name similarities, the Sanguine Raptor was depicted as a curved Roman-era blade that resembled a *falcata*. More important to Tywyll's leading questions was the hilt, which was drawn as a stylized raven with ruby eyes.

"Forgive us, Tywyll. You're correct. The *Fitheach Lann* sounds like the sword we're looking for."

Tywyll narrowed his eyes. "And what greed possessed you to seek a sword not made for your hand?"

"We don't seek the Sanguine Raptor for ourselves. We've been hired to find it by someone in Brennus's line."

"Is that so?" Tywyll said. "And who'd be that 'un?"

Ben said, "That's between me and my client. We haven't been given permission to share that information. Not even with you."

"Ye've the look of truth. Or maybe the look of a good liar." Tywyll nodded and took a long swallow of his ale. "You don't have permission to say who seeks the sword. And Brennus didn't give me permission to share where he buried the *Fitheach Lann*, so I suppose we're at an impasse, ain't we?"

His uncle had said that Tywyll liked to play games, so Ben smiled. After all, games were supposed to be fun.

"So you know where it is?" Ben asked.

"Did I say that?"

"You implied it."

Tywyll's eyes glinted. "I might 'ave. Doesn't change that Brennus ne'er gave me leave to share that piece with you." He took another drink. "Not that ye'd be the first to ask about Brennus in the now and lately."

"Really?" Tenzin leaned forward, resting her elbow on the table. "Who else has been asking about Brennus?"

"Folks here and there," Tywyll said. "Been folks askin' about Brennus for centuries now."

Asking about Brennus, but what about Bran? Both were legends, but if the Sanguine Raptor belonged to Brennus, then the *Fitheach Lann* belonged to Bran.

"They're asking the wrong questions," Ben said.

Tywyll's eyes narrowed. "Are they?"

"They ask about his treasure, but do they spare a song for the Raven King?"

"Few do." Tywyll's eyes met Ben's and he smiled a little. "But humble folk still be hanging ribbons at the Raven King's tree."

"Is that so?" Humble could mean poor. But Tywyll was ancient, and in Middle English, humble meant "low to the ground." Were "humble folk" people of the earth? Mortals?

Humans were hanging ribbons at the Raven King's tree.

"Many looked for favor that way," Tywyll said. "Though only the wise'll find it. Brennus never put stock in trinkets and tricks. Not like the one come looking."

Tenzin pressed. "When?"

"Fortnight past." Tywyll took another long drink. "But he didn't have a coin for the new king's stone."

Trees and ribbons. Stones and kings.

Ben kept the smile contained. Barely. He didn't know if his pulse gave him away. Tywyll had given him the key, but he had to remain calm.

"That was foolish," Ben said. "You should always bring a coin for the Raven King's throne."

Tywyll cocked his head. "Ravens like ribbons, but they like silver more."

"I can hang a ribbon at the Raven's tree," Ben said, "But I'm happy to pass a coin to the riverman first."

"A coin for the river will never serve you wrong." Tywyll's eyes twinkled. "But save your silver for the king, young Vecchio. Do ye think ye know where yer headed then?"

Ben let the smile break through. "I do."

"We'll see if yer as keen as your auntie, won't we? She's a great one for a riddle."

"How about the other one who came asking?" Ben asked. "Did he like riddles?"

"The other liked flash and fire. Blood of the Raven, but none of the ken."

"Blood of the Raven?"

Tywyll nodded slowly. "Watch yerself, young Vecchio. Yer not the only one digging into the past."

Tenzin's eyes darted back and forth between the two of them. "Okay," she said, nodding. "Ben, I'm going to get a beer. Do you want one?"

He smiled. "Sure. Tywyll, what'll you have?"

"Another porter," the old man said. "Then ye can tell me all about how yer lovely auntie is faring out in California with that fire-starter she mated."

"BENJAMIN!" Gemma Melcombe, earth vampire and first lady of London immortal society, strode into the sitting room, hands held out. "I've been hoping you would make time to see me."

She was tall for her era, pale-skinned and blond with vivid blue eyes. No matter what Gemma was wearing, Ben imagined her dressed for a period film. She was the child of Carwyn ap Bryn, who was like another uncle to Ben. He'd already tried to mine Carwyn for information about Brennus, but the jovial immortal had been surprisingly tight-lipped. Ben was hoping Gemma would be more forthcoming.

"Gemma." Ben stood and kissed both her cheeks. "Thank you for meeting us. I'm sorry I didn't come around sooner."

At one point, Gemma had also been his uncle's lover. Ben thanked the heavens daily that hadn't lasted. He wasn't nearly fancy enough to be Gemma's adopted son.

Tenzin remained seated, paging through a coffee table book. "Hello, Gemma."

"Tenzin." Luckily, Gemma seemed amused, not offended. "Welcome to you as well."

Tenzin slammed the book shut and looked around the room. "You have opinions on decorating."

Ben thought he ought to be concerned about Tenzin's line of questioning, but he was too curious where it might be leading.

"I do," Gemma said, settling on the settee across from Tenzin. "I've been to several design schools. It's a fascinating subject, and of course, with our color perception being what it is, subtleties are easier for us to recognize. I heard you and Ben have a new place in Manhattan." She glanced at him. "What neighborhood?"

"SoHo." He sat down next to Tenzin. "We have a penthouse loft on Mercer. Built late nineteenth century. Great ironwork."

"And very tall ceilings," Tenzin added. "With roof access. I want to make a garden there."

Ben said, "You didn't tell me you wanted a garden."

"Well, I do."

Gemma said, "I'd love to see it. Is it renovated?"

"It was an artist's loft," Ben said. "The rest of the building was renovated a few years ago, but our seller used it as a gallery. So it's mostly empty, but the walls are in good shape. One bathroom. A little kitchen. The wood floors are redone. We have the floor below for our office and storage."

Gemma said, "It sounds like a wonderful space."

"But how should I hang my swords?" Tenzin said, looking intently at Gemma. "Should I try for something symmetrical or more utilitarian?"

Gemma seemed stymied by that one, but only for a minute. "I'd aim for eclectic but balanced. Have you thought about mixing art in with the weapons? I'm assuming your collection is drawn from several eras."

Tenzin leaned forward. "It is! And various martial traditions. Mixed metals as well."

"Then mixing the weapons with the art will create a gallery effect for the space." She glanced at Ben. "And also make the collection appear a bit more... decorative than functional."

In other words, mix art in with the sabers, or human company might get weirded out.

Thank you, Gemma.

Tenzin smiled and leaned back on the settee. "See? I knew she'd be the right person to ask. The television shows never talk about the right things."

The look on Gemma's face was Ben's signal to change the subject. "How are things, Gemma? I met with Terry last week, and he said the stuff going down in Athens been... interesting."

She raised a delicate eyebrow. "It's definitely a shift in power. And lower risk for Elixir poisoning could affect the blood-wine market, but we'll see. Vampires are cautious. So far, orders don't seem to be falling off."

Tenzin elbowed Ben. "Remind me to order some before we leave."

He frowned. "You barely feed as it is. You need blood-wine?"

Her teeth glinted in the lamplight. "No, I just like the taste."

Ben managed not to shudder. Blood-wine was exactly what it sounded like. Blood preserved in wine. The preservation process Gemma and Terry's winemaker had perfected served two purposes. It preserved blood for years without cold or anticoagulants, and it removed any trace of Elixir—a deadly vampire virus—from the blood supply. The good news was, reports from the Mediterranean indicated that Elixir was probably on the way out in the vampire world. This time for good.

Gemma asked, "How are Giovanni and Beatrice, Ben? I haven't been to the West Coast in years. And they seem to be hermits these days."

"They like their books," he said. "Unless I drag them to Italy, they're usually in Los Angeles or Chile. The quiet life suits them."

"Indeed." Gemma glanced over as a maid set down a tray with cordial glasses and two dark bottles. "Tenzin, would you like to try some of our new blood-port? And Ben, I've brought out the non-blood variety as well."

"Yes, please." Tenzin held out her hand as Gemma poured. "Ben, when are you going to ask her the real question?"

The corner of Gemma's mouth turned up. "You mean you didn't come here to talk about design ideas and try my new wine? I'm shocked."

"I came for that," Tenzin said. "He's the one with ulterior motives."

With a single look from their mistress, the humans standing in the corners of the room left, leaving Gemma alone with Ben and Tenzin. "Does this have something to do with your research in Exeter and the reason you wanted to speak to Tywyll? You've attracted some attention from certain quarters, Ben. I hope that's not a surprise."

"It's not. And yes, that's why I'm here." He wasn't surprised that Gemma knew about Exeter. He was a friend, but he was still a human under a foreign vampire's aegis who was traveling within Gemma's territory. "But my research project has something to do with your family as well."

Gemma looked less bored and more interested. "Is that so?"

"You know that Tenzin and I have started our own offshoot of Gio's business, right?"

"Hunting antiquities, I believe." Gemma spread her hands. "I wish I had a job for you, but right now I don't. If I need your services in the future, you can be sure I'll contact you."

"I appreciate that, but right now we're in the middle of a job. That's what the research in Exeter is about."

"Old land maps, Benjamin?" Gemma sipped her port. "One would almost think you're involved in *treasure* hunting."

"And get my hands dirty?" Ben winked at her. "Come on, Gemma. You know I'm a city boy."

"You think you fool me with your charm and wit," Gemma said. "And I'll let you continue the illusion. But don't forget, Benjamin Vecchio." Gemma glanced at Tenzin. "Like recognizes like."

He sighed dramatically. "Why must you think the worst of me?"

Gemma laughed. "Why do you think it's the worst? Don't forget who my mate is."

A barely reformed criminal, Ben thought. If anyone knew what it meant to tread the line between dark and light, it was Terrance Ramsay. Gemma pulled Terry over to the side of the good guys... most of the time.

"I'm hunting something," Ben said. "A sword."

"Oh?" Gemma's eyes flashed with something Ben didn't catch. "What sword?"

"The Sanguine Raptor."

Her mouth firmed into a line. "Do you like your life, Benjamin?"

"I'm a pretty big fan of it, yeah."

Her eyebrows rose. "Then quietly return whatever money you've been given, apologize to your client, and go home."

That was *not* the response he'd been hoping for. Tenzin sat still and silent at his side.

Ben shook his head. "That's not the way it works."

She said, "Brennus's treasure is not something to play with."

"So you're not going to try to convince me it doesn't exist?"

"No," Gemma said. "I'm going to tell you that searching for it could be your end."

Tenzin took a sip of her port. "That's excellent," she said. "A little too sweet for my taste, but it's very good." She stared at Gemma for a few more moments before she said, "Ben, we should be going."

Ben frowned. "What? We haven't asked her—"

"We should go," Tenzin said again. "Thank you, Gemma."

Gemma nodded. "Tenzin."

Tenzin stood and looked down at Ben. He felt his temper rise; he turned to Gemma. "Blood of the Raven," he said. "Tywyll mentioned the blood of the Raven was looking for the treasure. Brennus was the Raven King. You, your brothers, all of Carwyn's family are the blood of the Raven. Is that why you're shutting me out? Has someone in your family been asking about Brennus's sword?"

Gemma rose, and Ben was forced by drilled-in manners to rise with her.

"I'm sorry," she said graciously. "I don't know anything about that."

"Really? You don't know if anyone in your family has been in town asking about your great-grandsire's treasure?"

Tenzin pulled on his arm. "Thank you, Gemma. Good-bye. Thank you again for the wine. I'll send a messenger with my order before we leave the city."

"Of course." Gemma leaned over and kissed both Ben's cheeks. "Ben, it was so good to see you. Please give Giovanni and Beatrice my regards."

"I'll make sure to do that." He was pissed. So, *so* pissed. Gemma knew something and she was holding back. Tenzin better have a damn good reason for retreating, or she had a lot to answer for.

"Ben."

Gemma called his name, and he turned at the door.

"Leave it alone. I'm asking you to leave it alone." She sighed. "Even though I can tell by the look in your eyes that you won't. You're too much like your uncle."

"I take comparisons to my uncle as a compliment, Gemma."

"You should. But you should also remember something else." She smiled sadly. "Giovanni is a fire vampire with a reputation earned over many centuries and many battles. I know he has taught you many things, Ben. But you are not your uncle. And you are so much easier to kill."

Without another word, Tenzin pulled him from the room.

✕

USUALLY TENZIN LEFT him when he started down the stairs to the underground, but that night she didn't. She followed him to the High Street Kensington station, pulling out her own Oyster card for the tube. Ben didn't even know she had an Oyster card. She walked with him silently as he followed the signs for the Circle Line and racked his brain.

Gemma knew something.

Blood of the Raven.

Brennus's line.

Did Carwyn have siblings?

How many children did Carwyn have?

How many children did *Carwyn's children* have?

The train pulled into the station and Ben boarded, Tenzin walking silently behind. It was nearly ten p.m., and they were the only travelers at their end of the compartment. He sat down and stared out the black windows as the doors hissed closed, and Tenzin took the seat next to him.

Just how much "blood of the Raven" was wandering around Western Europe? Had Tywyll given whoever this mystery person was the same information about the Raven King's tree? Had they also discovered the stones in Dunino Den?

"...he didn't have a coin for the new king's stone."

No, Ben didn't think Tywyll had given the key to the other seeker. Still, the question remained—

"So, who do you think it is?" Tenzin asked.

"I don't know," he said quietly. "But Gemma does."

"She won't tell us." Tenzin stretched out her legs and crossed her arms. "The only people Gemma cares about are family."

And Ben wasn't family.

"Tywyll said the other one had 'Raven's blood.' I assumed it was part of Carwyn's family. Are there any other descendants from Brennus's line?"

She shook her head. "If there are, they're hidden. Brennus did live on the Continent for many years. He was originally from the Celtic tribes in the Carpathian Basin. My sire's men had occasional conflicts with them. That was the first time I heard his name. He had other children, but as far as I know, they were all killed in a massive battle around two thousand years ago. It was rumored that was the reason he went to Britain. After that, there was only Maelona and her sister. I don't know the sister's name. Then from Maelona, Carwyn."

"So as far as anyone knows, all of Brennus's blood is concentrated in Carwyn's line?"

"Yes. And Gemma would only care about protecting her sire's clan. She has no love for anyone other than her family and her mate. She has friends—your uncle, for instance—but she'd sell Gio out in a minute for her own blood."

Ben mulled it over as the train hurtled under the city. They transferred at Edgeware Road and walked across the platform to catch the train to Ladbroke Grove.

"There's something else she's not telling us," he said.

"I know." Tenzin tapped her foot. She hated being underground. "I may be more worried about that than whoever is looking for the treasure. She warned you away from it, and Gemma isn't overly dramatic."

"You've known her for a long time."

She shrugged. "When she was still with Giovanni."

"Hmm."

Ben stared at the blurred rush of the train as it came to a stop in the station. They entered again, this time with more company, so Ben stood silently while Tenzin leaned against the front of the compartment. Black windows underground turned to grey night as they resurfaced past Paddington. The city glowed with passing streetlamps while raindrops made dancing jewels on the windows of the car.

He took Tenzin's hand when their station was called. Sometimes, when she wasn't thinking about it, she forgot to keep her feet on the ground. Tucking her under his arm, Ben walked down from the platform and steered them up the deserted street. The only fellow walkers that night were two drunk men and a lone dog trotting up the middle of the road. Tenzin walked silently with him as they turned left and ambled down their quiet street, but she halted when they reached the gate before their house.

"Someone is inside," she said under her breath.

Ben palmed the blade concealed in his coat lining and looked around. There were no eyes on them, so he jerked his chin up. Tenzin took off, flying up and over the house as he approached the front.

He was at the top step when he heard the whistling. Someone was in his house. And they were whistling.

The front door was unlocked. He pulled it open and walked into the dark entryway. The light was on in the kitchen and he smelled... tea?

A short scuffle, a loud bang, then he heard Tenzin say, "I've got him."

Ben walked back to the kitchen to see a dark-haired Caucasian man sitting at the kitchen table, a teacup halfway to his lips. Tenzin's blade was at his throat.

The stranger's smile was crooked and his eyes were dancing. "I was only trying to make myself comfortable until you returned."

The accent was undoubtedly French. The energy was vampire. Ben didn't say a word. He sat across from the man—the vampire—who'd been foolish enough to invade his and

Tenzin's territory and set his hunting knife on the table. His pulse was low and steady.

"Allow me to introduce myself," the stranger said. "My name is René Dupont. And I do hope you won't tell Gemma I'm in town."

3

"WHO IS GEMMA TO YOU?" Ben asked.

René's eyes narrowed. "Who is she to *you?*"

"A friend," Tenzin said. "She's certainly never broken into our home. Ben, why don't you call Gemma now?"

A flash of concern in René's eyes when Ben pulled out his phone. "I wouldn't."

"Oh?" Ben asked. "Why not?"

"She won't thank you for it. My aunt has known I'm here for weeks. If she can deny it, she can leave me in peace. If she can't..."

"No offense, Frenchie, but your peace is not my problem." Ben unlocked his phone. Tenzin gripped René's hair and pulled his head back, exposing the slow pulse in his throat.

"We have a common interest!" René said.

"What's that?"

"The Sanguine Raptor."

Ben's eyes met Tenzin's. Her grip on the blade tightened, and a drop of blood spilled from René's neck. Ben held up a hand and her grip relaxed.

Slightly.

"What do you know about the Sanguine Raptor?" Ben asked.

"Not as much as you," René said, his eyes dancing again despite the blood that rolled down his neck to meet his collar. "I must confess, I was simply... curious at first, but now I'm quite fascinated. My father has spoken of Brennus's greatness for as long as I can remember. This is the first time I've actually been able to imagine the reality. Rumors are that you are close to finding it."

Ben shrugged. "So what? You think we want your help? You may not know this, René, but Tenzin and I do this—as in *professionally*. We're working for a client, and we don't need extra help."

René's face fell. His eyes were stricken. His shoulders slumped and Tenzin released her grip on his hair. She looked at Ben.

He rolled his eyes.

Tenzin dropped her sword and stood to the side, but her hand remained on René's shoulder.

Ben almost felt bad for snuffing out the vampire's excitement until René threw his head back and burst into laughter. His dark curls bounced around his head as he leapt to his feet and darted to the corner of the room. From the safety of his corner, René bit his lip and winked at Tenzin, who stood, her arms crossed, watching him with a blank expression.

"My dear human," René said with a smile. "Whyever do you think I would want to help *you*? I'm not going to help you find Brennus's hoard." His smile fell away. "I'm going to steal it."

...he didn't have a coin for the new king's stone.

So here was the one who put stock in trinkets and tricks. Even with Tywyll's warning, René had surprised him. Ben had been spotting cons since he was a boy, but he'd lowered his guard once he knew René was in Carwyn's clan.

He was getting soft in friendly territory. He'd have to change that.

Ben decided to play along. "So you're going to steal it from us? And how are you going to do that, René?"

René cocked his head. "Well, you may not know this, Benjamin Vecchio, ward of the great assassin Giovanni Vecchio, but I do this. As in *professionally*."

"You're a professional thief?" That was a new one. Since when did thieves advertise? "I've never heard of you."

"If you had, I wouldn't be very good at my job, would I?" René turned to Tenzin and pressed his hands together in front of his chest. "But you, my lady Tenzin. Daughter of Penglai. Commander of the Altan Wind. *You*..." His eyes heated. "The honor you have given me by marking my neck humbles me. I am at a loss for how I can repay you."

Tenzin frowned. "Are you trying to flatter me?"

"Flattery would be dishonest, while I speak only the truth."

Oh brother... Ben tried not to roll his eyes. "So you think you're going to steal the treasure from us?"

"Oh no. I know I will." René was still staring at Tenzin, and a smile teased the corner of his mouth. "Lady Tenzin, your human is impertinent."

Tenzin smiled, and her clawlike fangs became visible. "He is not my human."

René sucked in a breath. "Beautiful."

"Lethal."

"Is there a difference?" René's gaze swung back to Ben, and feigned merriment turned to swift calculation. "So he is not your human? I understand."

"I very much doubt that," Tenzin said. "Ben is my partner. I am not looking for another. You may leave now." Tenzin cocked her head. "But perhaps it is too late for that."

René's eyes narrowed and darted toward the entryway a second before Gemma roared into the house, her appearance causing the foundation to tremble beneath him.

René showed his first real emotion in the very odd night.

"Oh damn." He grimaced. "Good evening, Gemma."

✕

GEMMA MELCOMBE WAS SEETHING.

"You will get out of England, René. You will leave tonight and you will not come back."

René spread his hands in a pacifying gesture. "*Ma tante,* you are overreacting."

Ben and Tenzin were watching the show playing out in the living room. Ben started a fire and decided this was the best entertainment he'd seen in weeks. Tenzin grabbed two beers and handed one to him before she perched on the back of his armchair.

"You think this is overreacting?" Gemma's face was colder and more vicious than Ben had ever seen it. And the first immortal lady of London was regularly referred to as the Ice Queen. "I intervened for you years ago, René. You were a foolish boy then, and you're a foolish boy now. Nothing has changed."

Ben whispered, "What did he do?"

Tenzin said, "I'm not sure."

Gemma whirled on them. "You want to know what he did? He aided in the death of Terry's sire and *my friend.* He was part of a coup—"

"I didn't know they were planning those things!" René shouted. "For pity's sake, Gem—"

"You will get no more pity from me!" She bared her fangs. "It was unwitting. *Fine*. But isn't that typical? You bounce around the world, charming your way in and out of trouble. Leaving the most horrendous wake as you sail past the little people who are forced to clean up after you. Is that what Guy would want for you, René? Your father—"

"My father doesn't give a damn about me," René snarled. "He wishes he'd never turned me. He said so himself."

"Grow up." Gemma practically spat out the words. "He's tired of your antics. Just as we all are. Find something useful to do with your eternity. Then maybe your father will speak to you again."

Tenzin handed Ben a bowl of popcorn that seemed to appear out of nowhere.

"Where did you get this?" he whispered.

"Shhhhh."

"You're leaving tonight," Gemma said. She glanced at the clock over the mantel. "You have eight hours to get your affairs together, but you're leaving our territory *tonight*."

René kicked up his feet on the coffee table, and Ben kicked them off again.

The Frenchman glared and said, "I'm not going anywhere. I'm not afraid of Terrance Ramsay."

Tenzin snorted and beer sprayed through her hand.

"Gross," Ben said.

"He's not afraid of Terry," Tenzin said. "That's funny."

René said, "And I am not afraid of you either, Gemma. You may cluck like an angry hen, but at the end of the day, I am your blood." He shot an arrogant look at Ben. "You will not sell me out for these two."

"I don't care one damn about these two," Gemma said. "But

if you think I'm going to let my mate deal with you, you're very much mistaken." Her voice dripped scorn. "Terry *will* kill you, René. Because Terry keeps his promises. He'll kill you, and then he will hurt. He will feel regret. Sorrow. Not for you, but for *me*. For your father."

René narrowed his eyes.

"Do you think I'm going to let that happen?" Gemma's voice dropped to a whisper. "Do you think my loyalty to *you* will allow me to let my mate hurt?" She bent over his shoulder. "I will kill you myself, little boy, before Terry ever sees your face. I will kill you so he doesn't have to. You have eight hours, René. Make the most of them."

René's eyes locked with Benjamin's. His eyes narrowed and he pursed his lips in a sneering kiss.

Then—in a blink—he was gone.

Ben heard the night wind gusting down the hallway as the old oak door squeaked on its hinges.

SHE STARED AT THE FIRE, sipping the glass of wine Tenzin had poured for her.

"He's incurably charming," Gemma said. "That's most of his problem. He's also very smart and very capable."

"Is that why you followed us?" Ben asked. He hadn't noticed a tail.

"I *had* you followed, Ben. You'll be happy to know I made sure to put one of Terry's best men on it. I wouldn't want to insult you."

"Fine. Why did you have us followed?"

"Because René likes to play with his prey. It's as simple and as complicated as that."

Arrogant, interfering vampires.

"What does he do?" Tenzin said.

"He's a thief. More or less. A gambler." She sighed. "René is whatever he wants to be when he wants to be it."

"He's a hustler," Ben said. He knew René's kind. His mother *was* René's kind.

"Yes, he is." Gemma gave him a wry smile. "So is my husband, if we're being honest. The difference is, René doesn't care who he hurts along the way. And he's much more comfortable lying."

Ben asked, "What does he know about Brennus's treasure?"

Gemma took a deep breath and paused. She looked at Ben. Then Tenzin. Then back to Ben. "You won't leave this alone, will you?"

"No," he said. "Especially not now."

"Your research has attracted attention," Gemma said. "That's the only reason René is here. I don't know who hired him, but he'll have a client. He doesn't hunt for the sake of hunting."

Ben leaned forward, his elbows propped on his knees. "How much do you think he knows?"

"If I were a gambler... I would bet that René knows as much about Brennus's treasure as you do. I made inquiries after Tywyll brought it to my attention. He's been in London for weeks."

But he didn't give a coin to the riverman.

René didn't know what Tywyll had told them. That was Ben's bet. And Ben was a pretty decent gambler himself.

But Ben hadn't counted on someone shadowing his steps. René could easily have followed Ben's movements. He might know what offices and universities he'd visited. What books he'd borrowed. What experts he'd interviewed. With the proper use of amnis, René could get a fairly clear idea of Ben's movements so far.

Of course, René was also limited by daylight, so Ben had that to his advantage.

"Whatever you have planned," Gemma said, "I want no part of it. I have too much happening in my own city to seek drama elsewhere. My one word of advice is this: René—whether you like it or not—carries Brennus's blood. If you find anything and he can make a claim that supersedes yours, no vampire will be on your side, Benjamin. You're human. And your partner is from the East."

Ben said, "So hire me to find it for you. I promise my terms are very reasonable."

She raised her hands, palms out. "Not even for Giovanni's son. I refuse to involve myself in this, and I don't want you bothering my father either. Carwyn has more than enough to worry about at the moment."

He'd already interviewed Carwyn, who had been less than forthcoming and quickly changed the subject to far more entertaining things than treasure. The old earth vampire was good at that. Ben would go visit him for one reason and quickly find himself in the middle of some lunacy that had nothing to do with the original purpose of his visit.

One Christmas Ben had ended up herding sheep in nothing but his underwear. He still wasn't quite sure how that had happened. "Listen, Gemma—"

"*Don't* bother Carwyn," she said again. "However..."

Gemma seemed to deliberate again.

Come on, you know you want to help me.

Finally she said, "If you happen to head north..." She gave him a loaded look. "I imagine Max and Cathy would love to meet you."

Yes!

"Oh?" he said, trying to keep his heart rate steady.

"If you happened to be in Edinburgh," Gemma said. "I'm sure I could call."

Well, it appeared that Gemma knew far more about Brennus's hoard than she'd let on. And René must have really pissed her off.

Ben couldn't stop his smile. "I would *love* to meet Max and Cathy."

"It would only be polite," she said. "Considering your... ongoing connections to our family."

Score. Max was one of Carwyn's sons, and Cathy was Max's mate. She was also a fire vampire and chief of security in Edinburgh. Ben had been going to ask for an introduction anyway, but Gemma calling ahead more than took care of any political hoops. More importantly, if Ben could convince Max to hire them, he'd be in the clear over any claims René might make. Max was a generation closer to Brennus and would have a greater claim on any recovered artifacts.

"So Scotland?" Ben tried to look innocent. "What a lovely idea. I love Scottish weather in the fall."

Tenzin frowned. "Why?"

Ben slid from his chair and scooted over to Gemma, taking her hand and kissing it. "You're a peach, Gemma Melcombe. And no talk of bloody retribution will convince me otherwise. A *peach.*"

Gemma rolled her eyes. "God save me from charming men."

EDINBURGH, Scotland

THE ROLLICKING thump of Scottish punk filled the pub where Ben and Tenzin dodged drunken festivalgoers fleeing the more traditional concerts that filled the city during the Scots Fiddle Festival. Bagpipes clashed with electric guitars. A singer wailed into the microphone as drums crashed in the corner.

"I love this!" Tenzin yelled, earplugs stuck in her ears. He'd forced them on her a block from the pub.

"I'm glad!"

"I can't hear you!"

"I can't imagine why!"

He grabbed her arm after they'd procured two pints from the bar and made their way down a long hallway where the music was still clear, but less demanding. Max and Cathy sat canoodling in a corner booth.

Yep. Ben was pretty sure that was the word for it. Canoodling.

Tenzin stopped. "I'm judging them."

"Just because you're not a fan of public displays of affection doesn't mean they can't be."

"He looks like he's devouring her face. That can't be pleasant."

"Will you stop?" He tugged her hand. "I'm sure they'll cease and desist when we sit down."

Except they didn't. Or... not right away.

Cathy eventually came up for air. Ben could feel the heat of her skin from his seat across the booth.

"Sorry. Max has just come into town tonight. We haven't seen each other in four weeks."

Ben said, "If tonight's not a good night, we can—"

"It's fine," Max said, his voice rough as he pressed kisses

along Cathy's neck. "It's very nice to meet you, Ben. Tenzin, you too."

"I don't feel like we've actually met yet," Tenzin said. "Though I feel that I'm well acquainted with your mate's breasts."

Max lifted his head and looked at the hand resting under Cathy's sweater. "Oh. Sorry about that."

"I'm not," Cathy said. Luckily, she straightened her sweater anyway and faced them.

"Oh," Tenzin said. "You both have faces. Imagine that."

"Is she always this way?" Cathy said.

"Yes." Ben took a drink.

Cathy smiled. "Cool!"

Ben continued, "So Max, I've heard a lot about you. All of it is good."

"Well, that's nice to hear."

Ben said, "And Cathy, apparently you're a raging she-beast who will devour me and destroy my sense of dignity if I allow it."

"Ah!" Cathy said. "You've been talking to Deirdre then."

"How did you know?"

Cathy laughed and laid her head on Max's shoulder. "I love your sister, Max."

"It's to your credit that you haven't wiped her from existence, darling."

"I'm sure you tell her the same thing."

"Of course I do."

Tenzin looked back and forth between Cathy and Max as if she were watching tennis. "I like you. Well, now that you're not showing me your tongues. I found that episode rather disgusting."

"Thanks," Cathy said. "I'm not sure how I feel about you." She leaned forward. "Are your fangs always down?"

Tenzin leaned forward too. "Yes."

"How do you eat?"

"I suppose like everyone else. I don't remember *not* having my fangs down, so I don't know any other way."

Cathy frowned. "Fascinating. Can I ask how you—?"

"No." Max pulled Cathy back. "No, you cannot."

"You don't know what I was going to ask," Cathy protested.

"Yes, I do." He cleared his throat. "So, Ben, what did you want to talk to me about?"

Ben said, "You changed the subject so gracefully I barely noticed."

Max smiled. "Thanks."

"I sense they both have boundary issues."

"I heard you were a young man of sense"—the vampire finished his whisky—"and it appears the rumors were correct."

Max was one of the most human vampires Ben had ever seen. From his dress to his mannerisms, he struck Ben as a thoroughly well-adjusted immortal. All of Carwyn's humanity without as much comedy.

"Tenzin and I," Ben started, "have been heading up a new branch of Giovanni's business."

"I've heard a bit," Max said. "New York, right? Working in O'Brien territory?"

"We have an agreement with them, yes." He took a drink. "Unlike Giovanni's branch, Tenzin and I have cast a wider net. We're less focused."

"And by that you mean...?"

"We find things for people who are missing them. Not people. We're not casting the net that wide. But if it's a thing that can be found, we can find it."

Were his claims grandstanding and dubious optimism? Yes. Ben went with it anyway. No one got anywhere by being overly modest.

Max said, "And I'm assuming you have some experience in this?"

"Tenzin and I have been working together for about three years. Mostly word of mouth. You may have heard about our recovery of Sicilian tarí in Naples last summer."

"Oh!" Cathy said. "I do remember hearing about that. It was right around the time the Mad Duke bit it, right?"

"Yes," Tenzin said. "We were there for that."

"Exciting." Cathy's eyes lit up.

"I thought so. Ben, not as much."

There was so much he could say... but Ben bit his tongue. He sensed that Cathy and Tenzin had similar ideas of "fun."

Max shrugged. "I can't lie, Ben, this all seems very interesting. But I don't sense you need an investor, and I'm not in the market for any lost items. What do you want from me?"

"I want you to hire us," Ben said.

Cathy laughed. "He takes after his uncle."

Max laughed. "Whatever for?"

"We have information on an object that we believe might be highly prized by you and your family," Ben said.

"Oh?" Max said. "And what would that be?"

"The Sanguine Raptor." Ben took a drink and observed Max and Cathy's faces. Max's face was carefully blank. Cathy's was alight with excitement.

"Max, is that the sword—?"

"Yes." He cut her off with one word and an expression Cathy was quick enough to read.

"Oh," Cathy said. "That's interesting." Then she took a long swallow of her cider.

Ben waited. Then he waited some more.

Silence did not sit comfortably at the table.

"The Sanguine Raptor is... lost," Max said. "Arcane.

Despite some local wives' tales, it passed into legend centuries ago."

"And yet..." Ben wanted to speak carefully. He had no idea if René had come north. No idea if Gemma shared his meeting with Tywyll. "There has never been any proof that it was destroyed or stolen. In fact, *none* of Brennus's treasure was ever found."

Max smiled. "Don't you think it would have been if it existed?"

Ben shrugged. "I don't know. The Staffordshire hoard was found intact by a retiree with a metal detector. Anything is possible."

Max examined him, and Ben tried to regulate his breathing. His pulse. Any tell that might give Max more information than he wanted to share.

"So..." Max steepled his fingers with his elbows on the table. "You really think you can find Brennus's treasure?"

"I wouldn't be here if I didn't."

"You've some... clue that leads to gold missing for twelve hundred years?"

Ben said, "I don't want to get too specific, but... yes."

"If that's true, what do you need me for?"

"I told you. I want you to hire us."

Max leaned forward. "To fund you?"

"No. Just to hire us. We can negotiate a split for the treasure."

The corner of Max's mouth turned up in a rueful smile. "You're audacious, I'll give you that."

"This isn't about the money."

Max's smile turned patronizing. "Young man, *everything* in our world is about money."

"In my opinion, it's more about currency. And money is

only one kind of currency." Ben set down his drink. "Tell you what, do you have a five-pound note on you?"

Amused, Max pulled a slim wallet from the inner pocket of his jacket. He pulled out a five-pound note and set it in Ben's hand.

"There," Ben said. "I'm hired."

"That's all you want? Five pounds?"

"No, I want more than that," Ben said. "I want permission to search in this territory. Not only are you of Brennus's line, you're connected. If you and Cathy give your permission, the vampire in charge of this territory won't cause any problems for me."

Cathy said, "That's true."

"And you're certain Brennus's treasure is within this territory?"

Ben continued as if he hadn't heard Max's question. "I don't want to keep the majority of the gold for myself. I'll split it with you, and I think you'd find the split more than equitable."

"Why are you doing this?" Max asked. "The money?"

"I told you, it's not about the money."

"Then why?" Max cocked his head. "The sword?"

Ben smiled but didn't say another word.

"Do you truly think it's real?" Max asked.

"I know it is."

"You're not the first who has looked for it, you know."

"Brennus's treasure—and the Sanguine Raptor—are legends," Ben said. "I want to be a legend too."

Max smiled. "Now that is a motivation I can appreciate." He pulled out a hundred-pound note. "There. Add that to the five and you're officially hired. Ben Vecchio, I want you to find my great-grandsire's treasure or die trying."

Tenzin reached out and swiped the hundred-pound note. "He's not taking a death oath."

"Relax, Tenzin," Ben said. "I'm pretty sure Max is joking."

Tenzin's eyes fixed on Max. "Maybe. Maybe not. But words have power, Benjamin. And I'll take that oath before you do."

"Tenzin, you're not taking a death oath either."

"Exactly."

"Fine," Max said. "Benjamin Vecchio, I want you to find"—Max couldn't stop an amused smile—"the treasure hoard of my great-grandsire and bring it to me. If you don't succeed, you'll owe me twice again what I've paid you for this task."

"Those are terms you can agree to," Tenzin said. She held on to the note.

"Thanks so much." Ben held out his hand and Max shook it. "Looking forward to this."

Cathy clapped and a spark shot from between her hands. "And I thought this winter was going to be boring."

4

I T WAS AMAZING HOW EARLY the sun set in
Edinburgh in the fall. By four o'clock in the afternoon, it
looked like nighttime in California. Streetlights went on and
golden light rippled on the damp black stones that made up the
Royal Mile.

While the setting sun meant little for most humans who
tromped up and down the road between Holyrood and Edinburgh Castle—some tourists, some festivalgoers, some everyday
citizens of the old city—the setting sun had always meant something different to Ben.

Here there be monsters.

As a child, night was the time his mother let her demons out
to play, falling into the sad oblivion of the bottle. Sometimes his
father would come in the dark, shouting and throwing money at
her, tossing dire threats before he stormed off, forgetting about
the skinny boy until it came time for the next round of money
and recrimination. Junkies woke at night, their greedy, distant
eyes searching to see if a little boy had anything worth taking.

Ben had learned to hide before he could read.

Other predators roamed too. They were the ones who made

Ben's skin crawl. Their eyes weren't distant, and the greed was of a different kind. When Ben's instincts told him to run, he ran.

Now the monsters came in the form of friends and adversaries, immortal creatures who seduced with pale and beautiful faces. Tricksters who seemed more genteel than human predators... until you looked into cold eyes that saw you as food.

For Ben Vecchio, the night had always been owned by monsters.

He moved up Lawnmarket to the flat he'd leased in James Court. He'd rented it months before, anticipating a long-term stay in the city. With so many tourists around, Ben could be just another face in the crowd, but the flat itself was in one of the massive stone buildings surrounding an open courtyard. It was thick-walled and nearly lightproof. Once he'd ducked off the Royal Mile, Ben was concealed from most prying eyes. Tenzin was able to come and go at night, taking advantage of the black courtyards, narrow alleyways, and steep side streets that curved like ribs branching from the spine of old Edinburgh.

"Not that we'll be here much longer." His murmured words frosted the night air as he hummed a tune playing from one of the many pubs he passed. He didn't know where Tenzin was, but he was nearly certain that she'd be back at the flat unless she'd decided to disappear on him like she had the night before.

"Mr. Vecchio, isn't it?"

Ben paused when someone called his name. He turned, looking over his shoulder.

Well, hell.

"What a wonderful coincidence to meet you here." René Dupont leaned against the wall of Deacon Brodie's Tavern, two tourists, a man and a woman, hanging off his arms.

"René Dupont," Ben said. "What a surprise."

"Hello, my friend." René glanced up and down the still-busy street. "I see you are also here to delight in the sounds of the Scottish Fiddle Festival."

"Oh yeah," Ben said. "Every year. Never miss it."

René smirked. "So I thought."

Ben nodded toward the two humans, who were clearly under the influence of René's amnis. The couple looked like typical tourists, stuffed backpacks and crisp coats. One even had a camera hanging around her neck.

"New friends?" he asked.

René ran a finger along the woman's cheek. She smiled and sighed, leaning into his touch. "They asked me if I was interested in showing them 'another side of the city' when we were chatting at the bar. I decided to take them up on it." He lifted an eyebrow. "I don't think they were talking about a local tour."

Ben examined the couple, uncertain how to proceed. Mostly likely René would feed from the humans and be on his way. Sex might or might not happen. Every vampire was different, and some had no morals about seducing humans with amnis.

"Relax, honorable young Vecchio," René said. "I know who the enforcer is in this town. Cathy has burned me before, and I'm fairly sure she enjoyed it. Feeding guidelines are strict in this city no matter how willing the participants may be."

"They're under the influence."

René shrugged. "They were well on their way before they met me."

Cathy was a fire vampire, and it wasn't a secret that William, Lord MacGregor, the vampire in charge of Edinburgh, kept her around because of her ferocity. Edinburgh was a city that owed much to its reputation as a safe city for tourists, festival attendees, and students. MacGregor couldn't have any of them reporting assaults or strange attacks at night. Cathy made sure it didn't happen.

"What are you doing in Edinburgh, René?"

"I am visiting my uncle, of course." René smiled. "I love Max. Such a wonderful chef, if you get a chance to taste his cooking. Excellent taste in whisky. But what are *you* doing here?"

"Taking in the sights, of course."

"I do hope your alluring associate is with you." René glanced up and down the street again. Then overhead. "Should I be so lucky, my friend?"

"No," Ben said flatly. "I am pretty sure you'll never be that lucky."

"Oh, my dear human, has she rebuffed you?" René cocked his head. "Do not despair. It is likely your mortal body has little to tempt her other than blood. It is only natural."

Ben ignored him. Typical vampire superiority. "Why are you here, René?"

"There is a charming exhibit at the National Museum I was hoping to see. Jade ax-heads from the Italian Alps." He shivered. "I'm passionate about the Stone Age."

"Really?"

"I am only sorry I missed the Celts exhibit earlier this year. Did you happen to see it?" René's eyes gleamed.

"I did. Too bad you missed it. But then, you should probably get used to missing things."

René laughed. "You are so confident. In a way, it is endearing."

"Yeah, I hear that all the time." Ben clenched his hands in his pockets. "I'm super-endearing. Adorable even."

"I have no doubt." René shrugged off the arms of the tourist couple and stepped toward Ben. His voice dropped, and all pretense of amusement fell. "You are mistaken, my friend, if you think my interest in the Sanguine Raptor is frivolous or passing. I know you believe you know the location of Brennus's sword.

315

My intention is to find it before you. And if that fails, I will simply take it from you."

Ben smiled. "Do you think so?"

"I know it." René stepped within inches of Ben. He reached up, but Ben grabbed his wrist before he could make contact, yanking René's hand away from his face and forcing his wrist back.

"Not a good idea." No vampire would be making contact with Ben's bare skin unless he knew they were a friend. He'd learned his lesson on that one.

"You are quite strong for a human, aren't you?" René's eyes lit with mischief. "What can I say? I am so curious what all the fuss is about."

"It's good to wonder about things," Ben said, stepping back and releasing René's wrist. "Have a good night."

"Say hello to Tenzin for me."

"No."

"She'll smell me on your skin," René said. "I shall savor the thought until I see her again."

BEN SMELLED the cardamom and ginger when he walked in the door. "Tiny, you read my mind."

"Not lately," Tenzin called from the kitchen.

Ben blinked. "Wait... what?"

"How was New Town? Did it take long to walk?"

Ben hung his coat and kicked off his boots before he headed to the kitchen. "Have you been using amnis on me?"

"Of course not." She slid from the stove to the sink in her

stocking feet. "How was New Town? Did you find what you were looking for?"

"Yes." He walked over and spun Tenzin around, pushing her against the counter and trapping her between his arms. "Have you been using amnis on me?"

Her eyes went wide. "No."

His temper, held in careful check during his meeting with Dupont, spiked. "Dammit, Tenzin. You know that's not allowed. We talked about that when you asked to stay at the loft."

"You were talking in your sleep again." She patted his cheek. "I just put you back to sleep. Don't overreact."

He stepped away. Ben didn't want to know what he said in his sleep. At times like this, ignorance was bliss.

"Don't do it again." He reached over her shoulder and stuck a finger in the curry. "Hot!"

She slapped his hand. "Don't do that."

He sucked off the sauce that tasted something close to a spicy korma. "That's good. Lamb?"

"Yes."

"Where'd you get lamb?"

She went still.

He closed his eyes. "Tenzin, if you're snatching random sheep from some farmer, I need to know about it. And... I don't even want to think about where you may have cleaned—"

"Ha!" She grinned. "I got you. Max gave me the name of the late-night butcher he and Cathy use."

Oh thank God. Ben was trying to imagine scrubbing frozen sheep guts off the stones in the courtyard before the neighbors woke up.

"I'm glad you're finally getting the hang of this using money to buy food thing." He reached over her head and grabbed bowls and plates from the cupboard. The flat had come fully furnished, but the furnishings were sparse. Since it was just the two of them, it wasn't a problem. He hoped they wouldn't have company though.

"Speaking of company," he started.

"Were we speaking of company?" She leaned over and sniffed his jacket. "You saw the Frenchman."

"Caught that?"

She wrinkled her nose. "There's a cologne he uses. It's distinctive."

Ben sniffed his shirt. "I didn't smell anything."

"You wouldn't." She stirred the simmering pot. "So our friend René is in Edinburgh, is he?"

"He was disappointed not to see you." He set the plates out, put the bowls next to the stove, and opened the drawer for the silverware. He grabbed a spoon for Tenzin, which was the only kind of flatware she liked. "He knows we're here after the Sanguine Raptor."

"Gemma did warn us about that."

"I'm debating whether or not to call Max. René said he was visiting his uncle, but that may have been a lie."

She shrugged. "He's your client. This one is up to you."

That was the problem. Ben was still figuring out how to properly plan and run a job of this scale. He was sure he was capable of it... most of the time. But the majority of his past experience had been scrambling after Tenzin, cleaning up her messes. Planning and executing a job of this size took an entirely different perspective.

It was also a new way of operating for Tenzin, who had taken jobs in the past, but mostly for mercenary work. Hunting immortals required a slightly different skill set than hunting artifacts.

"Wine or beer?" he asked.

"Beer, but nothing dark."

"Got it." He pulled two bottles of bitter out of the cooler. "So, the Register House was good. I think I've narrowed it down enough to go for a drive tomorrow."

She heaped his bowl with a mound of fragrant rice, then spooned the lamb overtop before she served herself a smaller portion. "A drive to...?"

"I'll tell you in the morning," he said. "Right now we should enjoy this food, because I am starving."

"You're always starving."

"And you always feed me." He leaned over and kissed the top of her head. "No wonder we make such great partners."

THE WOMAN WAS TWENTY-FIVE, but her green eyes looked older. She was tall and leggy in a way that reminded Ben that the Vikings really got around back in the day. Her pale face was pretty and freckled. Blond hair whipped across her face from the sea breeze as she crossed the narrow street to the cafe, ducking in just before the rain came down. She paused at the door, looking for him. Ben looked up from the phone held in his hand, nodding at her over his steaming cup of coffee. Just another random student staring at his mobile phone and reading his Twitter feed in the bustling university town of Saint Andrews.

She spotted him and walked over, a set of keys clutched in her hand.

Excellent.

Ben looked around, but no one noticed the girl. The people she passed barely looked up.

People were so easy to distract now; all they did was look at their phones. Ben figured the only person who'd looked him in the face since he walked in the door was the woman who took his order at the counter.

Annoying? A little. But it made it much harder for a vampire looking for him to question humans later.

Thanks, technology.

The girl was named Susan. She was a student at the university and the sister of one of Max's day-people. She sat down in the chair across from him and tried to tuck her hair back into a bun. She wasn't too successful.

"Can I get you a coffee?" Ben asked.

"No thanks."

Ben had taken the train up the coast and stayed at a hotel in the town center after taking a cab into town. Classes were still in session, so the streets were busy and businesses were full. He'd made no secret of his presence in the city—if anyone was looking for him, they could find him—but he'd been wary about renting a car. He didn't mind people—okay, René—knowing he was in Saint Andrews, but he didn't want anyone to know what kind of car he was driving.

That was were Susan came in.

"The car is not mine. It's my neighbor's, and I sang her a story about my desperate and pitiful young American friend." Susan kept her hands and the keys folded on her lap. "So if you're trouble and don't bring the car back, Max and Cathy will know. The money you're paying me isn't going to cover the cost of a new car, even if it is just a Corsa."

He smiled. "You're telling me you haven't already called them?"

"Maybe."

"If you didn't, you're not as smart as I thought you were."

"Jarod asked Max. He vouched for you."

"What else did he ask?"

Susan rolled her eyes. "Do you think we're new? The less I know, the better. I don't even want to know your name. I want my money and for you to return the car by next week." Her eyes narrowed. "You're not a shitty American driver, are you?"

"Of course I'm not a shitty American driver." He reached his hand out, and she put the keys in it. "Kind of a shit British driver though. Whole thing about the wheel being on the wrong side of the car, you know?"

Susan stood. "Don't be an arse. Just because you know important people doesn't mean your blood doesn't run as easily as any other human's."

He held out an envelope that she grabbed and stuffed in her messenger bag. "All you need to do is keep quiet and pretend you never saw me," he said. "The car will be back in its parking spot in a week. And tell your friend thanks. Just don't use my name."

"Handy." She wrapped her scarf more tightly around her neck and raised her hood. "As I don't know your name. Don't crash the car, nameless American."

Ben couldn't help but like her. "Is this that rumored Highland hospitality?"

She curled her lip. "Does it look like we're in the Highlands to you?"

Without another word, she turned and walked out the door. The wind was so strong it took some leaning to push it open. Then Susan was out the door, and Ben had a car.

And coffee.

Glancing at the downpour happening outside, he decided he had enough time to finish the coffee.

FIVE DAYS LATER, he'd secured a completely different vehicle, an empty vacation cottage nearer the probable site, and all the supplies he'd need for a prolonged hunt. Nothing was under his name. Most of the reservations had been made over the phone. Supplies had been ordered online and delivered to the house. There was a small barn at the rear of the cottage that would work for storing the car. Ben would be working on foot, and he'd be working during the day.

He didn't care what Tenzin thought. Daylight searching was imperative.

He took the train back to Edinburgh after leaving the car parked where he'd promised Susan. The old Jeep had been stored at the cottage. He'd be able to take a cab or walk from the Leuchars train station depending on the weather.

By his estimation, the search for Brennus's gold should take three days in the field. He hadn't seen a hint of René Dupont anywhere around Saint Andrews, but that meant little. Ben had been making an effort to show up at the normal tourist sites in town and making himself known as a regular at a number of markets and cafes. If René was following him, Ben wanted to be the one placing the bread crumbs.

The announcer's voice woke him to the approaching station. "Next station, Haymarket."

Ben roused himself from a light nap and realized he'd be getting into the city just after dark. He knew Tenzin barely slept. What was René's habit? Most older vampires didn't need a full twelve hours of sleep a day, but most did sleep. This time of year, vampires had fifteen full hours of darkness to play with. Ben had only nine hours of light.

Why had he planned this trip for the winter? The lack of tourists and the busyness of the university town suddenly seemed to pale in comparison to the luxurious hours of daylight

—and dry weather—he would have had available during a Scottish summer.

Of course, it also meant he had Tenzin as a resource with longer nights. And since Tenzin did *not* sleep, winter meant a happier and less housebound partner.

He gathered his backpack and exited the train at Waverley station. A crowd of evening commuters barely let him pass by before they crowded on the train heading north out of the city and toward Dundee. Unsurprisingly, it was raining. He lifted the hood on his jacket, tucked his phone in the inside pocket, and walked up the hill and toward the flat where he hoped some food would mysteriously appear.

Up the steps and up the hill. Dodging loitering tourists, brisk businessmen, and the ever present pipers on the Royal Mile, he trudged up the damp street toward the dark shelter of the north passage to James Court. He ducked in and entered the code for the doorway, pulling open the heavy door and letting it close behind him.

Ben let out a breath. Silence.

The cold stone walls blocked out the bustle of people and automobiles, pipers and vendors.

As he walked up the old spiral stairs, he heard a sound he hadn't been expecting.

Laughter.

Male laughter.

The laughter went silent as he approached the door. Quiet shuffling. His key went in the lock.

Ben walked in with his hand on his knife. When he saw who Tenzin was entertaining, he felt no urge to remove his hand, but he did have to restrain himself from pulling the blade.

Tenzin had been cooking again. But this time her guest was René Dupont.

5

WELL, THIS SHOULD BE INTERESTING.

Tenzin set down her spoon and wondered just how wise her Benjamin had grown.

"You're back!" she said brightly.

"I am." His face was... not so bright.

But that was fine. He needed to scratch a bit of the brightness off if he wanted to survive in the immortal world.

"René found our flat," she said.

"I can see that."

"I invited him for dinner."

Ben set his messenger bag down on the armchair and leaned his shoulder against the large stone chimney on the opposite side of the room. "You invited him for dinner," he said. "Were you that hard up to find fresh blood?"

René's mouth turned up at the corner. "Witty."

"Curious," Ben said.

"I am no vampire's meal."

"Bet you wish you were," Ben said. "Why are you in my flat?"

"I understood I was invited."

"Not by me."

Tenzin tried not to roll her eyes at the posturing. They were both so young. They were like two roosters puffing out their chests. Obviously she needed to intervene before the spurs came out. "I invited René to our flat when I found him feeding —very indiscreetly, I might add—in the pub where we heard the loud music."

Ben said, "That could literally be any pub in the surrounding area. You have told me nothing."

"I invited him here"—she ignored his boring disapproval and continued—"so we could have an honest discussion about the Sanguine Raptor."

René looked disappointed, though his smile hid it well. Ben looked quietly outraged.

"Why?" Ben asked.

"Because he wants it." Tenzin stepped between Ben and René. "Look at him," she said to Ben. "He's clearly not a swords-man. Watch the way he moves; he has no sense of balance. He'd be pathetic with a blade."

René stood and began cursing at her in quiet French, but Tenzin put a hand on his chest and shoved him back in the chair.

"So he doesn't want the blade for himself," she continued. "He wants it as treasure. You heard him speaking with Gemma. He's not sentimental, even with his immortal clan. Which means he has a buyer for the treasure. Which means we should find out who they are and see if we can make a deal with them." She glanced over her shoulder. "I mean, I'm fairly sure I know who it is already, but I wanted to confirm."

René curled his lip. "I changed my mind. I don't find you charming at all."

"Yes, you do." Tenzin smiled. "You don't want to, but you do. It's the power."

His silent glare said everything Tenzin wanted.

She knew there were always some vampires, both male and female, who were drawn to her because of her age and elemental strength. It was like a magnet. For some, the attraction was pure instinct. For others, it was calculation. Either way, it taught her to be circumspect.

She turned back to Ben. "If you want me to kick him out, I can. But I made enough for three, so it's up to you."

"No." René stood and smoothed the front of his jacket. "It is up to *me*. You disappoint me, Tenzin."

"You wound me, René."

A smile forced itself to his lips, and Tenzin changed her opinion of him in an instant. René was more complicated than she'd initially judged. He *was* attracted to her, but it wasn't calculation. Or not entirely. Despite her suspicions, she liked him a little.

"I see your game," he said quietly. "I decide not to play it."

"Come now." Tenzin walked over and flicked a minuscule piece of lint off his shoulder. "You were playing a game too."

"I suspected you would be a horrible liar," René said. "And you are."

"I know," Tenzin said, making her eyes as wide as possible. "Which is why you should probably practice with a blade more. You favor your left side."

"You think?" The Frenchman wrapped his cashmere scarf around his neck and shrugged on his coat. "*Au revoir, ma petite*," he said. "We will meet again." He glanced at Ben. "Tell your human his clumsy attempts to mislead me were not successful."

"I'll be sure to do that," she said. "Good-bye."

Without a backward glance, he walked to the door and left the flat. Tenzin waited until the heavy metal door to the passageway swung shut.

"Well, at least he's not one of those villains who always has to have the last word," Tenzin said. "Those are so annoying."

"Did you find out what you wanted?" Ben slid his hunting knife back in its sheath and walked to the counter. "And did you *really* need to invite him into our flat?"

She sprawled on the couch. "It seemed like the thing to do at the time."

"I'm making tea. It's freezing out there. Do you want some?"

"Please."

Ben filled the kettle and set it on the stove before he turned around and leaned his hip against the counter. She could see the smile flirting at the corner of his mouth. "So you're a bad liar, huh?"

"Pathetic. Didn't you know that?"

"Ha!" Ben shook his head and let the smile break through. "Did you find what you wanted?"

"No, but I will. He'll contact whoever hired him, and I'll figure out who it is." Tenzin floated from the couch and over to the windows. She glanced outside before she closed the heavy wooden shutters. They blocked out the lovely twinkling lights from the streetlamps and signs, but they helped keep the flat warm too. Buildings of this age were chilly in the best weather. In the damp cold, they could be miserable.

"And his threat about following me?" Ben asked.

"Empty. I was tracking him since nightfall. He hasn't left the city and he can't fly. The most he got was that you took a train to Saint Andrews."

Ben smiled. "Good."

"Are you set up wherever you need to be?"

He nodded. "You staying around here for a couple of days?"

"I want to watch the Frenchman for a few more nights. He reacted too perfectly. I'm either getting more psychic, he's really that predictable, or there's something we're not seeing. He's not dumb. He's smart, and he's played this game longer than we have. We shouldn't underestimate him."

The kettle whistled and Ben filled the teapot. "Fine. I'll be working during the day anyway. You won't be able to help. Might as well stay around here and see what he's up to."

She smiled. "And that's all you're giving me about your brilliant plan?"

"Hey, turnabout's fair play." He winked at her and grabbed two mugs for tea. "It's not like you've been Miss Let's Share All the Details in the past."

"Does this mean I'm going to get trapped on a submarine crossing the ocean back to New York?"

"If everything goes according to plan? Yes."

"Good to know you've worked through your issues on that," she said in Chinese.

He answered in kind, setting a pot of tea on the table. "Be quiet and drink your tea, you wide-eyed innocent."

"THIS?" Two nights later, she was staring at... She didn't know what it was, exactly. All she knew was that it made the most alarming noise when she approached it. "What is this? This is your brilliant plan?"

Ben tromped into the cottage, mud up to his knees, bundled in plaid, and clearly in a foul mood. "Did I ask you? Give me a minute to get warm before you start interrogating me."

"What is it?"

He hung the contraption on a hook by the garden door as he sat and tried to remove his mud-encrusted rubber boots. "That is the Garrett ATX metal detector," he said, yanking off one boot.

"Waterproof. Thirteen different sensitivity levels. Seven hundred thirty pulses per second."

Tenzin's mouth dropped open. "You're using a... a metal detector? To search for one of the largest caches of gold in immortal history?"

"The size of the cache is only rumors." He yanked off the second boot. "And yes. I'm using a metal detector. It worked in Staffordshire."

"That was an exception, not a winning business break-through."

He leaned against the wall, and Tenzin could see how tired he was. "Tiny, I'm exhausted. I'm not getting into this with you tonight. What did you expect me to do? Hire a friendly neighborhood earth vampire to walk the grid with me?"

"Yes, because that is an excellent idea. Unlike a metal detector, which is not."

He straightened and stretched his shoulders back. "No."

"Why not?"

Ben said, "First, I'd have to work at night, making me more conspicuous to vampires. Second, I'd have to tell someone else the treasure is here—"

"*Probably* here."

"Definitely here." The first smile broke through his exhaustion. "Go look in the bread box, Tiny."

Tenzin walked over to the small kitchen and opened the wooden box where she smelled stale bread.

"See the teacup in there with all the loose American change?"

She found the teacup. "And?"

"Shake it out. You expect me to do all the work for you?'" He rose to his feet and stretched. His sweater rode up, exposing the pale line of his stomach and the dark line of hair on his abdomen.

He really was becoming annoyingly tall. Tenzin looked away and back to the coins in the cup. She poured them into her hand and felt the moment it touched.

Gold.

She smiled and put the other money back, letting the single gold coin settle in the palm of her hand.

There was nothing like the energy gold emitted. Some would call her superstitious, but they weren't as old as she was. They hadn't seen the eternal metal as she had. Hadn't felt it surrounding them.

The paltry treasure hoards of the modern age were nothing in comparison to those of kings and empresses of the past. Tenzin had walked in rooms layered in gold, had drunk blood from solid hammered goblets, had eaten food sprinkled with its dust.

She'd taken a king for a lover who painted her body with gold dust just to see her outline on silk sheets after they'd made love.

The weight of the small coin made her smile. To the less-experienced eye, it would appear Macedonian. It wasn't. It was early Gallic, and in excellent condition.

She asked, "Where did you find it?"

"Near the bank where the stream branches." Ben took a towel and rubbed at his hair, which had grown damp with the evening mist. "I decided to keep going with my grid for the time being, but I'm focusing on the search areas closest to the stream. If the geological surveys are correct, there's a limited area where any cache of significance could be buried."

"Unless it's in a cave formed by an immortal," Tenzin said. "Those don't show up on geological surveys."

"Tenzin, I'm not calling an earth vampire to help us look."

"Why not?"

"It's just one more person knowing that we're looking in this location." He draped the towel across his shoulders. "And the last thing we need is someone blabbing—"

"I could probably..." She paused. Ben would most likely *not* approve of looking for a rival vampire and using them to search before dispatching them.

He frowned. "You could probably what?"

"Nothing." She glanced at the nonsentient machine he'd been using. "Your machine sounds very interesting. Tell me more about it."

His eyes narrowed. "No."

"What?" She made her eyes very big again. It had worked well with the Frenchman. "You don't want me to know about the machine?"

"You know that's not what I'm talking about." The eye trick did not work with Ben. He rose and walked toward her. "Whatever you were thinking just now. No."

"I don't know what you're talking about."

"I'm sure you don't." He grabbed a can of beer from the cooler and cracked it open. "Isn't my metal detector nice?"

"Yes, very nice." She smiled, but he did not look reassured. "And, of course, vampires wouldn't be able to use something like that. Excellent planning, Benjamin."

SHE RESTED THAT DAY, meditating and watching over Ben as he slept. But the next night, she flew over the search area while Ben was making notes on his grid. She was glad he'd spent a few days turning up nothing. He was learning one of the cardinal rules of treasure hunting: Most of it was boring. Patience was rewarded; daring was not. Tenzin had the patience of a hunting cat. When she was focused on something, she could wait as long as necessary for her prey to reveal itself. And riches were her favorite kind of prey.

The countryside was deserted and high fog rolled in off the North Sea. She flew over the trees and ducked between them to land in the wooded glade of Dunino Den. She breathed deeply; the ancient energy of the wood surrounded her, and she understood immediately why Ben had been so certain of this location. The air felt heavy, and the wind spoke to her, removed from the roar of modern life and humanity. This was an old place.

Trees, brush, and exposed rock marked the tiny corner of wild. Moss hung heavy from trees and lichen decorated rocks. The stream had swollen with the recent rain, and the sound of rushing water filled the air along with the scent of moldering debris. She walked up the den, letting her fingers flutter over the ribbons and beads tied among the bushes. Wilted flowers, leaves, and lovers' tokens hung on an ancient stump at the center of the glade.

"Humble folk still be hanging ribbons at the Raven King's tree."

How had Tywyll known Ben was thinking of this place?

She passed the old stump and walked beside the exposed limestone that bordered the natural amphitheater. Her fingers traced the crosses and symbols inscribed on the rock and she floated up to investigate. Some artist had added the visage of a gnarled face with a wide nose and full beard. The scowling face emerged from the rock, a silent and disapproving witness to the pilgrims who offered their gifts. She floated up the stone steps cutting through the twin outcroppings and let the night wind speak to her.

"Ravens like ribbons, but they like silver more."

She reached the top of the steps and saw the pool in front of her. It was a round ceremonial well. The holy men who came later would have taken it for their own purposes, but Tenzin spotted the hollowed-out footprint at its edge. To the immortal eye, it was clear evidence of an earth vampire.

Brennus?

But Ben had said this was a Pictish site.

"...he didn't have a coin for the new king's stone."

That phrase was the key. Those were the words that had made Ben's eyes come alive. Tenzin had heard *king's* but had Tywyll been saying *kings?* Who were the new kings? Would the Picts have been the "new kings" to an ancient like Brennus?

The new kings' stone...

Tenzin wandered up the path with the wind whispering in her ears.

The new king's stone.

The new kings' stone.

She walked the narrow lane between the woods and the churchyard, drawn to the graves that dotted the deep green grass. She passed an old headstone with the penitent's face worn away by time. A mourner was carved into the edge of the granite, her hood smooth and worn by water and wind. Past the headstone in the moonlight, Tenzin caught the shine of silver.

"...he didn't have a coin for the new kings' stone."

She stepped closer and bent to inspect the coins, careful not to move any of them. Currency from all over was piled on top of the lichen- and moss-covered rock. Silver and nickel mostly. Some copper. Some brass. It wasn't a gravestone, it was a standing stone or the stump of one. The ground was cleared around the stone, as if someone had cut back the grass around the base.

What was this place? A holy tree. A ceremonial well. A standing stone.

A place of ritual. Of spiritual power. A natural amphitheater.

Dunino Den was a place of holiness, ritual, and authority.

Her eyes fell to the standing stone covered in coins. In offerings.

In... tribute.

"You should always bring a coin for the Raven King's throne."

Tenzin went to her knees before the old stone and scraped back more of the grass to bare the soil. She sank her hands into the packed dirt and bent, putting her mouth to the ground. She held back the instinctive revulsion at the taste of earth against her lips so she could concentrate on breathing out the air that would speak to her. She exhaled, forcing her amnis into the ground with her element.

Then she closed her eyes and waited. Her hair hung around her like a curtain, brushing the grass and gathering water as she waited.

She waited.

Her breath crawled along roots and under rocks, seeking tiny spaces to possess. It traveled along grains of rock and rotting vegetation. It traveled down.

Down.

Down.

Tenzin sank into her mind. Dug her fingers into the ground and let the air within her connect to the night and the blackness and the space in all things. She felt the night birds move over her and the wind moving the trees. She dissolved into her senses and the amnis within all things.

She waited.

Until the air she'd breathed from her body found the hidden places she'd been seeking. It crawled and explored, tasted and gathered secrets. Then the air came back to her, whispering tales of gods and treasures.

The new kings' stone.

The Raven King's throne.

Tenzin started awake from her trance, tasting the soil on her lips. She sat up and put a hand on the strange rock, her eyes wide and her mind racing.

"Brennus," she whispered. "You clever bastard."

6

———

BEN WOKE THAT AFTERNOON, HIS body rolling into the beam of light that cut across the bed in the west bedroom. He could hear Tenzin in the front part of the house, moving with her familiar lightness, a fluid combination of walking and flying that marked her presence to his ears. He lay in the angled light and let the sun warm his face.

It was no coincidence that he'd chosen this room for his bedchamber, just as it was no coincidence that he slept better in the day. Sun meant safety. For the past week, he'd been working days, searching the glade and streambed, and he'd been restless at night until Tenzin had arrived. His sleep had completely turned around, and it felt good to enjoy a long nap in the afternoon sun.

He heard the kettle whistle and knew Tenzin had put the tea on, which meant she knew he was awake. He enjoyed one last stretch in the sunbeam, a scratch on his belly, and then he rose, unfolding his limbs from the short bed in the cottage. He threw on a flannel shirt and made his way out to the kitchen, forcing his hair into submission under a knitted beanie as he debated for the hundredth time whether or not he should shave it all off.

"Good evening," Tenzin said. "Or afternoon, I suppose."

"You went exploring last night." He slumped at the kitchen table, still not quite awake, and rubbed his eyes. "When did you get back?"

"Six or seven?" She filled the teapot and Ben enjoyed the rising aroma of bergamot and black tea. "You were in your room scribbling, so I decided not to interrupt you. Then I think you fell asleep."

"I haven't been sleeping at night," he said with a yawn. "And I've been working during the day, so yeah. A bit exhausted."

She turned toward him, and for a moment, her eyes were so sharp with pain his breath caught in his chest.

"Tenzin?"

The moment dissipated like steam in a cold room. "I do miss sleep. Sometimes I miss sleep."

Tenzin wasn't one to complain about... well, anything. Not seriously. She only whined to annoy him or tease.

"I didn't know you missed it," he said carefully. "You don't get tired though, do you?"

"It's not physical. I meditate to rest," she said, turning back to the cupboard and getting two mugs for tea. "But I don't get tired. Not like humans do. Not in my body. Just my mind."

"I think anyone would. I'm glad meditation helps."

"But sometimes..." Her eyes drifted again. "Sometimes you need more. You need a break. Most of the past century was a break for me. I went into the mountains with Nima and I just... was. I didn't see anyone. I didn't talk to anyone."

Ben remained frozen. It was so unusual for Tenzin to speak about her past, he feared the slightest movement would break whatever strange spell was causing her to confide in him.

"Giovanni had left me," she continued. "He'd become tired of mercenary work. I was too. The human world became violent on a different scale. Wars were global. Everything was changing so fast. I decided to take a break."

"In Tibet. With Nima."

"Yes. Most of us do, you know."

"Take a break?"

"Yes. Very old vampires become tired or bored or over-whelmed. We debate going into the sun. Some of us do." Her eyes met his. "But then others who are still hungry for life... we sleep. Not as humans do. It's a kind of stasis. In my longest stasis, I became a living idol. My cave became a shrine, and I fed from those who came to pray to me."

"No one tried to harm you?"

She shook her head, and her eyes became less dreamy. Sharper. "The humans thought I was a goddess. Because to them, I had always been there. Never moving. Never aging. But I wasn't asleep. If something had tried to attack me, I would have protected myself."

"But nothing did."

Tenzin poured the tea and added a twist of lemon to hers and milk to his. She walked over and sat at the kitchen table across from him. "No, nothing did. They left treasure for me. Beautiful things. Many of them are still in that cave."

Ben tried not to salivate at the thought of a hidden treasure cave in the Himalayas. "The humans didn't take the treasure?"

"Of course not. They were offerings," Tenzin said, leaning closer. "Offerings to a god. To take them would have been... unwise."

...he didn't have a coin for the new king's stone...

Ben sipped his tea. Put the mug down. Thought about their strange conversation and the growing knot in his gut. "You're not just feeling chatty, are you?"

Tenzin shook her head.

His conversation with Tywyll leapt to his memory. *"Brennus didn't give me permission to share where he buried the* Fitheach Lann, *so I suppose we're at an impasse..."*

Past tense. Or so he'd thought. "Tiny, if you're saying—"

"Brennus is alive," she said. "He was never killed. You found his treasure, but you found the Raven King too."

BEN SAT with his notes and charts and maps spread in front of him. Pictures and drawings. Old survey maps and handwritten accounts. Small mountains of paperwork and notes. Over a year's worth of research.

Tenzin sat across from him. "You have to leave it."

But he couldn't. He'd done too much work. He had a client. His *first* client. A client who had hired him to find the Sanguine Raptor, the *Fitheach Lann,* or whatever old vampires wanted to call it. And now he had René Dupont in Edinburgh. He didn't have time to restrategize.

And it was just one sword...

He could leave the treasure if Brennus was still alive. All he needed was one sword and his reputation would be established. He'd be twenty-four and his reputation in the immortal world and the antiquities collecting market would be set.

He pulled at the hair that had escaped from his hat. "One sword, Tenzin."

"Stop it," Tenzin said. "You don't know what you're asking for if you try to unearth him."

"Weren't you the one who got more excited at the idea of stealing from a living vampire than a dead one?"

"That was when I thought he was hiding in Fiji or had started a new life in South America. I didn't think he'd actually be *in stasis* with the treasure we were hunting. I won't let you do this, Benjamin."

His anger began to simmer. "*Let* has nothing to do with it."

Tenzin bared her fangs. "Do you not understand what I'm telling you? I was in stasis. I would have attacked anything that tried to disturb me. It would have been automatic. But Brennus is not resting peacefully in a cave where penitents feed him. He is resting in a barrow of his own making. An ancient king with his wealth gathered around him. He has not set traps to deter thieves, he *is* the trap. All anyone would need to do is disturb his treasure and he would wake. And he would wake hungry."

Ben tapped on a map of the churchyard, an X marked in the spot where the standing stone sat. He'd made notes and taken pictures of its location, but he hadn't connected the stone to the king. He'd been too focused on the well and footprint at Dunino Den.

"Ben, are you listening to me?"

The Raven King was an earth vampire. He could burrow anywhere. And an ancient holy site that had crowned kings and was then protected by new druids—as Brennus probably saw the holy men who founded the church—would have seemed perfect. No one would be disturbing his rest. The earth was verdant. There was water nearby.

"He's not dead." Tenzin's voice rose. "He *will* be hungry. The first thing that unearths him will be food for that hunger. He will be ravenous. Animallike. Out of his senses. There will be no reasoning—"

"We can bring an animal with us," Ben said quietly. "An offering. If he wakes, he'll feed from that."

"If he wakes, he'll want human blood."

"You don't know that."

340

"I have been in stasis, do you understand?" she shouted. "Leave this alone, Benjamin. I forbid it."

He glared at her. "You don't get to *forbid* me from doing anything," he said. "I am not your servant. I am your partner. And if I think the risk of trying for the sword is worth it—"

"Don't you understand?" Her eyes were wild. "It's just treasure! It's a *metal sword*. There are a million swords in the world. They are like stars in the sky."

"Says the woman who has a reputation to fear and the wealth to back it up. I'm not you, Tenzin. I need this."

"This treasure is not worth your life when you are so fragile."

"So now I'm fragile?" He sneered.

She flew over the table and grabbed him by the shirtfront. "You know what I mean!"

"And you know why I need to do this!"

She was hovering over him, her face inches from his, but Ben refused to be intimidated. Her fangs had cut her bottom lip, and he could smell the metallic scent of her blood. Her fingers were cool against his neck, but her breath was hot.

"I am not yours to command," he whispered.

Tenzin was not his mistress. Not his employer. He brought just as much to this business as she did, and this was *his* job, not hers.

"You're insane," she said, shoving him back and returning to her chair.

"No, just determined. And flexible. I received new information about the mark—thank you very much—but I'm not giving up the job."

"This is not a con."

"I know that."

"Brennus will kill you."

"Or maybe I'll kill him."

Tenzin snarled. "Foolish boy! Do you think I have no honor? Brennus is a warrior of legend. Father of your friends. Do you think I would let you slay him while he rests?"

"Is he an honorable warrior or an animal with no reason?" Ben asked. "You can't have it both ways, Tiny. If he attacks me, I'll defend myself."

"And you'll die."

"Says you."

"Says common sense," Tenzin said. "You're not thinking clearly. You're too focused on the gold. You need to—"

"You need to stop treating me as a child," he said. "I'm not one. You think I've never stolen anything from someone more powerful and dangerous than me? Think again."

"Not. Brennus."

"You don't even know this vampire."

"I know his type."

Ben took a deep breath and closed his eyes. "This is useless. I'm not asking your permission. I'll dig during the day. It'll offer another layer of protection. If Brennus wakes—"

"And you think the church is just going to let you dig up the area under a historic standing stone for... what? Fun? Bribes? What's your plan here?" she asked. "You need to have permission to dig during the day. I'm not going to be with you, so we can't use amnis."

He paused and thought. She had a point. He couldn't dig during the day without attracting human attention. The area was sparsely populated, but it wasn't deserted. And he couldn't dig at night, not when the monsters had free run of the countryside.

"Dawn and dusk," Ben said. "I'll scout the location today at dusk. Before the sun goes down. Get a reading on how deep it is, then come back just before dawn and dig. It can't be that deep, and he's in stasis. He might even be sleeping. Not everyone is a day walker."

"You're a fool," Tenzin said.

He waited, because calling him a fool wasn't saying no. And Ben knew Tenzin was partly right. This was his job, but he still needed her help.

"If you're determined to do this," she said, "dawn and dusk are the only times that might work."

He was wary of her agreement. "So you're coming with me?"

"After the sun goes down?" Tenzin sat back down, her arms crossed over her chest. "Of course I'm coming with you. You're my partner. And I'm your only chance of not getting killed."

✕

BEN DRESSED and put on his boots, grabbing the last of the sunlight while he could. He left a disapproving Tenzin at the cottage and followed the stream up the wooded path that led to the church, his metal detector bulky under his coat. He'd gotten a few odd looks over the past week, but nothing from anyone who wasn't a passerby. None of the few residents in the area seemed to pay him any mind. And though he'd walked around the churchyard, he hadn't once seen anyone coming from the church building.

With that expectation, he was more than a little surprised to interrupt an old woman when he climbed the top of the stone stairs leading up from the glen.

"Hello," he said, a friendly smile plastered on his face. She didn't look like a tourist. Her clothes were old and worn. They looked homemade. "I didn't expect anyone out this late. How are you today?"

The old woman had a stooped back and bright blue eyes. Her hair was tucked under a scarf, but he could see flyaway grey curls escaping the edges.

"I am as I am," she said. "But what are you?"

It was impossible to hide the metal detector from her keen eyes. He shrugged and decided to play it casual. "Just... out for a bit of fun."

She smiled, and he saw she had a tooth missing from the front. "You're another after the Raven King's gold."

"Another?" he asked. "Has someone else been by?"

"Now and then they wander by," she said. "Those of the earth and the air."

Was she talking of the fairy legends surrounding the den? Local legends were part of what had led him to this place, so it wasn't a surprise that she mentioned them. Or was she talking about vampires? *Those of the earth and the air?* There was no way of telling without provoking more questions.

Ben maintained the casual veneer. "So, do you have any advice for the new guy?"

The old woman cackled and pointed to the well where reeds grew long. "Have you made your prayer to the old gods yet?"

His smile fell a little. "I'm not much for praying."

"That's too bad." She stooped down and brought out a pair of trimmers from the pocket of her coat. "A well-placed prayer will never do you wrong." She clipped at some of the greenery around the well. Ben didn't know enough about herbs or botany to know what she was clipping, but she put it in a shallow basket by the edge of the water. "But then, I suppose a machine like you have is very modern."

Something about the woman made him want to linger, but he saw the sun dropping quickly. "Well, you have a good—"

"Don't forget"—the old woman straightened—"be back inside at sundown. No treasure is worth getting snatched and carried away, eh?"

He paused. "What do you mean?"

"Snatched by the Raven King, boy." Her eyes lost some of the merry and bright. "Tales is tales for a reason. Seven years, they say, to be dancing in the Raven King's court. But I've never seen a one return, have you?"

Snatched by the Raven King? Perhaps Brennus wasn't in the kind of stasis Tenzin imagined. "Have people been lost?"

"Here and there," she muttered, bending to her task again. "Seven below, seven on earth, and seven for the people of the air. Everyone knows that."

"Right." Ben didn't usually dismiss folktales, but these sounded like a bastardized explanation for people going missing around Brennus's mound. He'd have to remember to tread carefully. "Well, I'm off. Have a good night."

She waved at him but didn't look again. "Remember, not after the sun goes down, boy."

"Yeah, thanks. I'll be careful." He turned and walked up the path. Within seconds, the old woman was lost to his vision and nothing but fading sun and green trees surrounded him. He walked the path through the churchyard, looking for the stone he'd earlier dismissed. He caught sight of it and paused to look around before he stepped over the fence.

He circled the stone and turned on the metal detector, casting his eyes again to see if anyone watched him. He felt exposed in the graveyard, the speckled stone monuments watching like silent sentries as he swept the grass with his beeping contraption that felt so very out of place in the still and dimming evening. Just as it had been the past few days, no one interrupted him. No one disturbed him when the heavy mist turned into a drizzle and the machine gave its first beep.

Ben listened with a practiced ear.

Gold.

His heart leapt in his chest, and he itched to find a shovel. A spade. Anything to start digging immediately. But he stopped, paused, and marked the first hit with a golf tee. Then he went back to work, walking a grid around the stone.

He hit again. Another tee.

Again. Another tee.

In the space of twenty minutes, he marked the ground with twelve green tees, barely visible unless you were looking for them. Twelve green tees outlining a circle of roughly twelve feet across. And at the center was the standing stone with the pile of silver coins at the top. The markers backed up what Tenzin had told him.

Benjamin Vecchio had found Brennus the Celt.

7

TENZIN FLEW OVER HIM AFTER the sun had set as he walked back down the stream, over the fields, and toward their temporary home. Some nights Tenzin wondered if Ben realized he lived his life like a vampire. He only rested during the day, when immortals were confined. He did most of his work at night unless he had to visit human establishments. He thought in terms of power dynamics, threats, and allies. He was a vampire in all but biology and durability.

She watched him shut the door of the cottage, then she flew into the woods and checked the rabbit snares she'd set the night before. Seeing two animals hanging in the traps, she grabbed them, stowed the snares in the bushes, and flew back to the house. She cleaned the animals and buried the innards in a shallow hole. Some scavenger would come and dig them up if it had need of them. She eyed the skins but had no real use for them and no method of tanning available at the cottage.

Pity. So much in the modern world was wasted.

Leaving the skins hanging on a fence, she took the carcasses back to the house and thought about what Ben had in the cupboards. Carrots and potatoes would be enough to add to the rabbits. She'd seen some overgrown herbs in the garden.

She could hear him banging around in the cottage, shucking off his soiled boots and jacket, humming under his breath. His human habits were oddly comforting.

Home. They made her feel at home. It was an odd, but not unwelcome, sensation.

"Ben." She kicked at the door until he opened it. "I found dinner."

He glanced down at the rabbits and raised a curious eyebrow. "So you did." He looked up. "I found Brennus."

She sighed. "Are you sure you're not going to change your mind on this?"

"Positive." He ushered her inside. "What can I do for dinner?"

She'd table the discussion about Brennus's gold until she was feeding him. "How are you at identifying herbs?"

"Uhhhhh." He frowned. "What are herbs again?"

"Ha-ha." She handed him the skinned rabbits.

"Thanks?" He walked them over to the sink.

"Cut those up and put them in a stewpot with some chopped potatoes and carrots," Tenzin said. "I'll get the herbs." She headed for the back door and paused. "I will miss your appetite."

He looked up from the bloody rabbits. "Huh?"

"Nothing."

NOTHING.

Sure, Tenzin.

Ben ignored her sly insinuations about his mortality because it was no good arguing with her. Tenzin was determined that really, secretly, he wanted to be a vampire.

He really, honestly didn't.

The pot was bubbling on the stove and Ben was looking over the diagram he'd drawn in his notebook when he heard the door open. "My best guess, the hoard starts at about a meter down."

"That matches my feeling about the place too." Tenzin walked over to the stove and fiddled with the flame before she threw some green things in. "But it will go deeper."

"Into the sandstone?"

She nodded and stirred the pot. "I need to know if the sword will be enough."

Ben didn't answer too quickly. "I think... if he wasn't living, I'd want it all. At least to recover it. Even if we handed over the majority of the treasure to Max, I'd still want to recover it. But if he's alive, it feels more like stealing."

"But you still want the sword."

"I still want the sword."

"And that's not stealing?"

He let out a long breath. "Yes. But... I'm not keeping it. We can always tell Max to give it back if Brennus decides to return to the world, can't we?"

"We can."

"And as long as we get that one artifact—that one thing—people will know I found the treasure."

Tenzin said, "They're going to wonder where the rest of it is unless we tell them Brennus is living."

He shook his head. "Not our secret to tell."

She smiled and crossed her arms. "You have a very nuanced sense of honesty."

"You probably deserve some credit for that, so don't judge."

"I'm not. I find it entertaining."

He closed his notebook and rose to walk to the kitchen. "We hand the sword over to Max and let people wonder. 'Do they have the treasure? Are they hiding it?' If it works out the way I hope, it'll only get people talking more. We both know how much vampires love to gossip. The more people talk, the more likely they are to hire us."

"If for nothing else than curiosity," Tenzin said.

Ben frowned. "That's fine as long as they pay us too."

"They'll pay us," Tenzin said. "No one cheats me. Being an assassin gave me a reputation for that."

Ben held in a shudder. "Has anyone tried?"

"Yes." She glanced up. "They're dead now."

Why was he not surprised?

THEY ATE. He slept. Ben wanted to be ready to search before the crack of dawn. Tenzin would be able to join him until the sun rose over the horizon, which meant they had a fair amount of light without direct sun. It would be the best time to search, though he'd be vulnerable. He didn't know how long they'd have to dig in order to find the sword. He was only praying that Brennus hadn't followed medieval tradition and buried himself grasping his sword.

If that was the case... Yeah, they were pretty much screwed.

He'd laid out every piece of equipment and checked it twice. Probes and shovels were about as high tech as it got when it came to actually getting gold out of the ground. He briefly debated calling a trusted earth vampire to come move ground, but knew it would just make everything more complicated in the end.

This was something he had to do. Him. Ben Vecchio.

And his mad, miniature partner.

He slept deeply. Tenzin had promised not to leave the cottage until he woke. He dreamed of lying in the sun in the barley fields by the house in Florence. The wool blanket was at his back and the heavy heads of grain bent with the wind, brushing his bare skin as a warm body stretched beside him. Stretched limbs and the scent of honey. He rolled to the side and reached out—

"Ben!"

He woke with a gasp, automatically gathering the sheets around his body. "Dammit, Tiny, I'm naked."

"No, you're not." She patted his cheek. "Wake up."

He blinked and glanced at the clock. "It's not time." His voice croaked, and he coughed to clear it. No sun. No barley field. He was in Scotland, and it was cold and damp and they had to go tromp around in the mud to dig up an early medieval sword.

Ben rubbed his eyes. "Why did you wake me up? My dream was way better than—"

"We have to go. Someone is at Brennus's barrow."

"*What?*"

BY THE TIME he reached the churchyard, Tenzin was already there, staring down at a pit opened in the field next to the standing stone.

"What the hell?" he muttered. He still felt half-asleep, and this was like a dream. The moon was full and low in the sky and a drifting fog covered it, making the whole graveyard glow with an unholy light. Tenzin stood in the moonlight, her hair loose around her shoulders. She hovered over the ground, examining the pit.

Ben ran up to her, barely stopping before he fell in. "Who is it? How did they find the site? Is it gone? What happened?"

Tenzin glared and held up one of the golf tees. "Did you have to put out a flag?"

"A flag?" His mouth dropped. "Those? You could barely see them in the grass."

"No, *you* could barely see them, human. But you're not an earth vampire, are you?"

Well, an earth vampire would certainly explain the giant hole in the ground. Most of them could move dirt like Ben moved furniture. The edges of the pit were smooth. The sides were steep. He resisted the urge to dig through the loose piles of dirt that cluttered the grass.

He couldn't see down into the darkness of the mud and mist. "Who is it?"

"*Merde.*" A quiet, desperate curse drifted from the bottom of the pit.

Ben and Tenzin exchanged a look.

"René," he said.

"René."

"Stop staring," René hissed from the bottom of the pit. "Help. Me."

Ben put his hands on his hips. "Do you think he found Brennus?"

"Oh yeah."

"Do you smell any blood?"

"Not yet," Tenzin said. "There is a not-surprising amount of... restless energy, however. It's only a matter of time."

"So he's not awake?"

Quiet, whispered curses in French met Ben's ears. Apparently René didn't appreciate their casual conversation at the edge of his grave.

"Well, that's what you get for trying to steal my treasure," Ben said. "Think twice next time, René."

"You bastard human piece of *aaaargh—*"

Tenzin said, "I think Brennus is awake."

A strangled, gargling sound came from the bottom of the pit. Ben backed away slowly, but Tenzin's hand shot out and grabbed his arm.

"Don't run," she said calmly. "Stay right where you are."

"Are you nuts?"

"You can't see him, but he's watching you. If you run, he'll chase you."

Ben couldn't pull away. She had his arm in an iron grasp. A scraping sound came from the pit. Then the earth moved beneath him, and the ground bulged like a fountain churning living soil.

Rising from the darkness was a hunched figure with dirty auburn braids falling down his back. He was lean, nearly skeletal, and his skin was marked with swirling patterns and spiral scars. He hunched over a kicking figure that was struggling to break from the iron grasp of the monster who held him.

Brennus the Celt was feeding from René. As Ben and Tenzin watched, his flesh swelled and filled in, like a dry sponge soaking in water. René kicked and twisted, but Brennus didn't seem to notice, nor did he release the vampire from his grasp.

Ben had never seen anything more frightening.

"We should stop this," Tenzin said.

"Why?" Ben whispered. "In the grand scheme of things, it's him or us and I vote for—"

"Brennus." Tenzin's blade was at her side.

Shit!

She called in Latin, *"Ecce tuum sanguis."* Behold your blood.

The monster paused, flexed his shoulders, and turned toward Tenzin. But instead of Tenzin, his eyes locked on Ben.

Well, that was sadly predictable.

With a curled lip and a snarl, the emaciated vampire leapt from the earthen pit and attacked. Ben didn't even feel him collide. He was standing; he was on his back.

Brennus was poised over Ben, his fangs bared. Blood dripped into the gnarled red-brown beard that fell down the ancient's tattooed chest. But while he crouched over Ben, his head was yanked back and a bronze blade pressed against his throat. Ben blinked to clear the dirt from his eyes. He tried to take a breath, but the ancient's weight lay on his chest, his hands planted by Ben's shoulders. Brennus snarled and snapped his teeth but was held back by Tenzin's grip and the sword at his neck.

Tenzin continued in Latin. "This one is *not* your blood."

Brennus blinked, and Ben saw a shadow of reason return to vivid blue eyes.

"Sida," he growled in a cracked voice.

"We don't use that name anymore, old man."

It was both fascinating and frightening to behold. As Ben watched, Brennus's cheeks grew less hollow and his lips plumped red as René's blood worked through his system. Ben began to see a shadow of the king he must have been. He wasn't as old as he'd first appeared. Perhaps forty in human years. He was barrel-chested and shorter than Ben, though probably tall for the men of his time.

"Why have you woken me?" Brennus managed to croak out, also in Latin. At the movement of his throat, Tenzin's blade pressed into the flesh. It sliced, but no blood dripped out. The vampire had none to spare.

"We did not wake you. A child of your blood did that."

Brennus's lip curled like a great hunting cat; his eyes still locked on Ben's neck. "You are not of my blood. Why are you here?"

Ben knew the question was directed at him. Brennus might have been mad with hunger, but he wasn't completely without reason. Ben reached down, managing to work his hand into the pocket of his trousers and grab the gold coin he'd collected from the streambed days before.

"I come to pay tribute"—he held the gold coin in front of Brennus's eyes—"at the Raven King's stone."

Brennus blinked. "Ravens like ribbons...," he muttered.

"But they like silver more." Ever so slowly, Ben scooted away from Brennus. He wiggled out from under the vampire's body and knelt on the grass. He didn't run. He held the gold in front of the vampire, who watched the coin as it glittered in the moonlight.

"Can I offer my gold to the Raven King?" Ben flipped the coin over, and Brennus blinked.

Abruptly, the vampire's eyes moved from the coin to Ben's face. "Who are you, mortal?"

More and more reason returned to his eyes.

"I'm the son of a scholar," Ben said. "But I am seeking the Sanguine Raptor." He caught himself. "The *Fitheach Lann*," he said. "I came looking for the Raven's blade."

"What need have you of my sword?" Brennus asked. "Are you a knight?"

They were still speaking in Latin, and Ben had never been more grateful that his uncle considered it God's language. At the time Brennus was buried, his English—if he even spoke it— would have been barely recognizable to Ben's modern ears.

"I seek the blade for one of your children," he said.

"That one?" Brennus curled his lip and nodded toward René, who was groaning and twisting in the dirt.

"No. The one I serve is the son of Carwyn ap Bryn, who is the son of Maelona, your child."

A flicker of recognition. "This vampire is the son of Maelona's child?"

"Yes."

Something worked behind Brennus's eyes, and Ben caught a flicker of who the old king might have been when reason still ruled him.

"How fares my daughter, mortal? Do you serve her as well?"

Well, shit. This probably wasn't going to end well.

"Maelona walked toward the dawn," Tenzin said before Ben could speak. "She had joy in her life and in her blood. She only looked for peace."

Tears filled Brennus's eyes and dripped down his cheeks.

Ben said, "But Maelona's son is alive, and he sired many children. And they sired children. Your clan is all over the world now."

"I care nothing for conquest," Brennus said. "I only wish to rest in the earth." Brennus blinked and his head darted up. His nostrils twitched and his eyes closed. "There is a creature roaming the woods. Release me, sida. I will hunt this beast and regain my strength."

"Will you attack this mortal?"

"I give you my word I will not."

Tenzin caught Ben's eye and he nodded. Slowly, he rose and walked to Tenzin's side. When Ben reached her, Tenzin released Brennus, who ran into the dark woods without a backward glance.

"Please tell me it's a deer out there," Ben said.

"Pretty sure. Though Brennus may end up hunting cows for all we know."

A low moaning sound caused them both to turn.

"Are you still on the ground?" Tenzin asked.

René rolled over and Ben winced. The vampire's throat looked like mangled meat. His neck had been gnawed on, and his face was pale from blood loss.

"Need blood." René's eyes lit on Ben.

"Don't even think about it," Tenzin said. "You've caused enough trouble tonight."

"How was I supposed to know he was alive?" René's voice was barely more than a wheezing rasp. He wouldn't heal until he got some blood, but Ben didn't have any urge to help him out. He didn't even let Tenzin drink from him, not that she needed blood very often at her age.

"How were you supposed to know he was alive?" Ben asked. "By doing your research, asshole. And not just following after us like a dog looking for scraps."

Despite his pale face, René curled his lip and bared his fangs.

"Give it up, René," Tenzin said. "I hardly think this performance is going to impress the Ankers."

Ben cocked his head. "Is that who he's working for? But why would they want—"

"Tell you later," Tenzin said. "Besides, René doesn't care what the Ankers wanted the sword for, do you René? This was just a job to you."

Ben said, "He's hired help. And not very good at it."

The hate flared in René's eyes, but Ben was feeling cocky with the vampire on the ground. He squatted next to the Frenchman, close enough to taunt him but far enough to stay out of grabbing distance. "If you're very nice, I'm sure Tenzin can fly to the house and get some blood-wine for you."

René looked between Ben and Tenzin, then he nodded slowly.

"But you're not getting the good stuff," she said. "I don't like you that much." Then she knelt over him and plunged her blade into his shoulder, digging it into the ground and pinning René to the grass as he screamed in pain. "I can't trust you to be civilized when you're this injured. I know you'll understand when you're more rational."

Tenzin flew off, and Ben sat waiting in the cold churchyard, a giant pit on one side, a cursing vampire on the other, and a ravenous ancient hunting in the woods.

Well, he definitely wasn't bored.

René continued to spew vile threats, but Ben had seen how deeply Tenzin's blade had penetrated. René wasn't getting off the ground, especially as weak as he was from blood loss.

And considering what was hunting in the woods, Ben knew he should probably be more worried.

Thanks, adrenalin.

A few minutes later, Ben heard rustling in the bushes. He placed his hand on his hunting knife and took deliberate breaths to calm his pulse as Brennus walked out of the trees. His tension eased as the vampire drew nearer.

Brennus was no longer the hunched figure that had emerged from the earth. His skin was flushed and his red hair and beard dripped with water. He must have splashed in the stream, because though his chest and arm muscles were filled in, Ben didn't see a drop of blood.

More important to Ben, reason had returned to the vampire's arresting gaze. He stood at the edge of the churchyard, surveying the land and watching the human and vampire who stood before him. He frowned at the pinned René.

"Is there a reason he has a sword in his shoulder?"

Brennus was still speaking Latin, so Ben replied in kind.

"Tenzin went to get him some blood. She didn't trust him not to kill me."

"She is wise," Brennus said. "Are you a day servant for the sida?"

"You mean Tenzin?"

"Yes."

Ben made a mental note to look up the word *sida*.

"I'm her partner," Ben said. "We work and travel together."

Brennus nodded. "In my time, it was not common for our kind to copulate with humans, though perhaps it is more acceptable now."

"What? No! No, it's not like that."

Brennus looked skeptical. "Truly? Because I thought..."

"Nope."

"Are you sure?"

Ben blinked. "Yes. Quite sure."

"Because she's very possessive."

"I'm her *partner*."

"I see," Brennus said, still looking unconvinced. He stretched out his arms and twisted his torso like an athlete warming his muscles. "Well, the world is always changing. What year do they call it now? Who is the human king? What language does he speak? And by what name shall I call you?"

Ben tried to sort through the barrage of questions. "No king," he said. "Not right now anyway. Uh... most nations are kind of past the whole king thing."

Brennus frowned. "No kings?"

"Nope. We're trying democracy right now."

Brennus snorted. "Good luck to you."

"And my name is Benjamin Vecchio. So I guess you can call me that."

"Well met, Benjamin Vecchio. In my time I had many

human slaves, and I rarely killed them. Humans were protected in my household and considered honorable and necessary."

Really?

"That's... good to hear," Ben said. "But I am not Tenzin's slave."

"Where did your partner—as you call her—go to hunt?"

"Not far. I'm sure she'll be back soon." Ben gestured at René. "He's not in good shape."

"He will live." Brennus went down on one knee and patted René's shoulder. "My thanks, blood of my blood. You have fed your sire and restored him to health. The honor is yours."

Ben noticed how grateful René looked.

So, *so* grateful.

He bit back a smile as Tenzin landed, carrying a bottle of the blood-wine she'd ordered in London.

Brennus said, "Ah sida, your... partner was just informing me that this land has no king."

"No, it has a queen, but she is nothing but a puppet. Common people make the laws and enforce them."

Brennus shook his head. "Madness."

"I know," Tenzin said. "I try not to think about it too much."

Brennus motioned to René. "What shall I do with this one?"

"He is of your line," Tenzin said. "I have brought blood to heal him, but you may do with him what you would. He *is* the one who woke you from your rest." She glanced at Ben.

Okay, yes. Clearly, waking an ancient vampire from sleep was a bad thing. Lesson learned.

René's eyes looked panicked for a second before his face turned stoic. He looked... resigned. Ben almost felt sorry for him.

"Despite his unwise actions, I approve of his courage," Brennus said. "Though he disturbed me, I will let him live."

Tenzin held the bottle of blood-wine toward René but pulled it back at the last second. René whimpered.

"Brennus," she said. "I would offer this blood-wine to you first. It is only proper."

"You honor me," Brennus said. "But I have no desire for wine."

"It is blood preserved with wine."

"Blood preserved in a glass bottle?"

"It keeps for many years," Tenzin said. "No rotting or spoiling."

"I must try this blood." Brennus took the bottle, tipped it up, and took a drink. He smiled. "That is far more pleasant than whatever beast I drank from in the field."

"Probably a cow," Ben muttered.

"Indeed not," Brennus said. "For the blood of the cow is second only to the blood of man. This was a strange and hairy white beast with a long neck and unpleasant disposition."

Oh shit. Well, the neighbors' llamas had lived a long life. Probably.

"But this blood-wine is excellent. *Most* excellent." Brennus crossed his arms and narrowed his eyes, watching as Tenzin bent down and offered the rest of the wine to René. "So, Benjamin Vecchio, tell me why you were here when I woke from my rest."

Ben said, "As I told you, I came to look for your sword." *And steal it.*

"Because one of my line has need of it?"

In a very loose sense... "Yes."

"Very well." Brennus inclined his head regally. "I will consider your offer. What will you give me in exchange for the use of my sword?"

Well... damn. What did he have to offer a legendary immortal Celtic king?

A metal detector?

Money?

"Uh..." Ben had a feeling none of those things were going to impress Brennus very much. He looked desperately at Tenzin, who was trying to tell him something with her eyes, but it wasn't making any sense.

He'd found the Sanguine Raptor. He had survived the ancient vampire who guarded it.

Now how on earth was he going to keep it?

8

———

POOR BEN. HE LOOKED SO confused. Didn't he realize Brennus had already told him what he wanted?

Should she let him dangle for a while longer or just make the offer herself? It had clearly slipped Ben's notice.

She waited a few more beats. Just when Ben started to look truly desperate and Brennus started to look annoyed, she decided she'd waited long enough.

Besides, the Frenchman was starting to knit back together. In a few minutes, he'd be able to talk.

"A case of the wine," Tenzin said. "Twelve bottles. Nearly the blood-weight of two humans. Think of it, Brennus. You can keep this wine with you as you rest. When you wake, you will be able to drink as you will and rise in control of your hunger."

It was exactly what the old vampire had been thinking. Tenzin knew, because it was one of the first things that occurred to her when she first consumed blood-wine.

Brennus smiled and nodded at her. "Very well. I will give loan of my sword to this human if he vows to pass it into the safekeeping of my kin in exchange for this fine wine you have shared with me tonight." He looked around. "This world is not to my liking. I believe I will retire again."

René finally rose to his feet, holding his throat as he spoke in a rasping voice. "Chief Brennus, father of my line, pay no attention to this human. *I* am your kin. I am René, son of Luc, son of Carwyn, son of Maelona. I also seek the Sanguine Raptor."

Ben said, "But he works for one outside your bloodline. He only wants the sword to get rich."

"Is this true?" Brennus asked.

René glared at Ben. "No more than this one seeks the sword for his own glory. He is a hired thief, nothing more."

Brennus looked at Ben. "Were you given money to seek the Raven King's blade?"

Tenzin wanted to speak, but Ben's expression was calm and confident. He stepped forward and held out the gold coin he'd first used to captivate Brennus when he'd been out of his wits.

Something in Tenzin's chest ached. Ben stood, bold as a crow, smiling in the face of an immortal just barely in control. Maybe it was naiveté. Maybe it was pure guts. But there he stood, holding a token out to the legendary king like a knight on a quest. He didn't look away. Didn't shy from Brennus's power.

"I was offered a token," Ben said. "A gesture of good faith like the token I offered at the Raven King's stone."

Brennus said, "For if there is nothing staked, then what do we risk?"

"Exactly," Ben said. "Brennus, I give you my *word* that I will put your sword in the hand of the one who shares your blood. Who wants it to protect and *not* to sell as treasure." His hand held steady, the gold coin in his palm.

Brennus paused and looked between Ben with his bright face and outstretched palm, and René, holding his neck with a wary expression and blood dripping between his fingers.

He put his palm over Ben's coin. "My faith is in you. I will have your word on this gold that when I rise again, the Sanguine Raptor will find its way back to me."

She saw the brief hesitation. Saw Brennus's reaction to it. The old vampire understood in an instant what Ben thought but wouldn't say. *Would Ben still be alive when the Raven King finally woke?*

A slight smile touched Brennus's lips. "Mortal, your fate is clear to all but you."

Ben said, "I give you my word. I will do everything in my power to return your sword to you. And I will leave it in hands I trust."

Brennus nodded. "Very well, human. We have an agreement between us."

René shouted, "What is this?"

Brennus pinned him with a single look. René fell silent, but his eyes remained on Ben.

Nothing good would come of this. Though they had saved his life, Ben had made an enemy and bested René at a game the Frenchman thought he'd walked into as a winner. Tenzin would have to keep an eye on René Dupont. No doubt he'd be keeping an eye on them.

Brennus reached down and plunged his arm into the soil. The earth rippled and flexed beneath his hand. Then, slowly, the ancient king pulled the Sanguine Raptor, the raven's blade, from the old churchyard in Dunino Den. The blade was blackened iron, its single edge curved like the line of a horse's back. The sharp tip ended less than an arm's length from the hilt, which was a stylized raven with ruby eyes.

Tenzin stared at it and *wanted* it.

Damn Ben Vecchio and his insane idea about professional ethics. The sword Brennus held reminded Tenzin of the falcatas on the Iberian Peninsula.

She didn't have a falcata, and her sword wall was now incomplete.

Brennus held the blade out to Ben, who took it by the hilt, showing the sword the respect it deserved. She'd trained him well.

"Cool your gaze, sida." Brennus's eyes cut to Tenzin. "This blade is not for you."

"A pity," Tenzin said, "for I would wield it well."

"No doubt you would." He held up a finger to Ben. "A loan, human. That is all I will grant you."

Tenzin didn't watch as Ben and Brennus exchanged polite words about the Sanguine Raptor. She didn't listen to the stories Brennus told or the questions Ben asked.

She watched René Dupont. And she waited.

BRENNUS THE CELT, legendary chieftain, warrior of renown, father of one of the largest clans of earth vampires on the planet, sank into the ground with so little fanfare that Ben had to pinch himself to make sure he wasn't dreaming. The immortal sat on the ground, a crate of blood-wine beside him, and nodded at Ben before the ground opened up and swallowed him like a wave taking a swimmer into the deep. For a few moments, the earth shifted and shook. The ground pulled in, constricting the churned dirt until it lay smooth and even with the rest of the graveyard.

Then everything fell silent.

The standing stone where humans had laid offerings sat in the same position, though the earth around it was bare of grass. Ben walked over and placed his hand on the stone. His feet barely made an impression in the dirt. Brennus had disappeared as if he had never risen. If Ben didn't have the raven sword in his hand, he probably would have thought he was dreaming.

He felt a gust of wind at his neck. He turned when he heard the scuffling start behind him. There was a blur of bodies, then everything stopped.

Tenzin straddled René on the ground, one hand on his chest and her bronze blade at his throat. "Don't even think about it."

"That sword is mine," René said. "I am the one descended from Brennus. I unearthed the treasure—"

"After I was the one who found it," Ben said. "You were following in my tracks, René. Don't pretend you did the work on this."

"And don't think I don't feel the weight of gold in your pocket," Tenzin said. "Brennus grabbed you, but not before you took a few trinkets for yourself."

"They are nothing to the Sanguine Raptor."

"That may be," Tenzin said. "But you're not walking away empty-handed."

"I want that sword!"

"Not. Going. To. Happen." Tenzin pressed her blade against the still-healing gnaw marks on René's throat. "You don't want to test me on this, Dupont."

René's eyes cut toward Ben. "You cannot always protect him."

"You're a fool if you think he's an easy target," Tenzin said. "But beyond that, you should know that making an enemy of this man"—she nodded toward Ben—"makes you so many enemies, you don't even want to think about it. Do you know who he is?"

"I know he is the spoiled—" René broke off when the sword pressed harder.

"I don't like it when people insult my friends." She bent

over and licked at the line of blood dripping from René's neck. "But if you want me to cut you more, go ahead. You taste good, René." She straddled his body, her hold intimate. "No wonder Brennus drank so much."

René bared his fangs, but his eyes were hot on Tenzin.

He likes it. And so does she.

The quick bite of annoyance stabbed his gut. Ben walked over and pressed the tip of the Sanguine Raptor into the ground near René's ear. Looking down on the vampire, he said, "I won this round. No doubt you'll win others. Don't make us enemies, René. That's not what I want."

"You're so magnanimous when you're the one holding the spoils," René said. "I do wonder if your heart will be so generous when I am the one who wins." His eyes darted to Tenzin, who was still bent over his neck, sniffing. "Can you make her stop doing that?"

"Maybe. I promise nothing. " Ben tapped Tenzin's thigh with the flat of the sword. "Tenzin, he's not dinner. At least, he's not dinner *tonight*."

She looked up, her eyes fixed on René. Her hair fell over her face. Her fangs and lips were red with blood. The Frenchman's eyes locked on her.

"René."

"Yes?"

"Don't threaten my friends," she whispered. "I don't like it."

René nodded a little. "I understand."

Tenzin arched up as she straightened, her movements unabashedly sexual. Anger twisted in Ben's belly, but he quashed it. Without another word, she floated off René's body and came to rest at Ben's side. René took a deep breath, then he sat up, brushed off his hands, and stood.

He looked at Ben. A little longer at Tenzin. He glanced at the horizon and ran without saying another word.

"Well," Ben said. "He'll be having nightmares about that for a while. Or sex dreams. Could be either."

Tenzin laughed. "He is amusing."

"That's certainly one way to think of him."

The sky was just beginning to glow, and Ben was carrying a sword nearly as long as his arm. He decided taking refuge in the cottage was the right move. He walked back over to Brennus's stone and drew a pound coin from his pocket, placing it on the moss- and lichen-covered rock with the other coins resting there.

A scraping sound near his feet made him look down.

Lying in the dirt was the gold coin Ben had found near the stream days before. He bent down and picked it up, flipping it in his fingers. It was warm, as if someone had been holding the piece of gold in the palm of their hand.

"Thank you," he said quietly. "I will keep this."

The earth said nothing.

"PLEASE."

Tenzin stared at the Sanguine Raptor, her chin in her palms, her eyes pleading with him.

"No."

"Please, please."

Ben twisted the wooden vises to the table in the cottage, then he placed the padded alligator clips in them and set the sword between the rubber tips. "Tenzin," he said, "this sword is being cleaned and taken to Max. I cannot believe what good shape it's in." He shook his head and put his hands on his hips. "I don't even see any rust. This is amazing."

"He probably waxed it."

369

"Stop pouting. Do you think he had it wrapped? He must have had it wrapped."

"Yes." She was still pouting. "It's beautiful. Please, can I have it? I will give you so much gold."

He forced the smile back. "Aren't you the one who told me there were so many swords in the world?"

"But I don't have one like this. All I'm going to see on my sword wall is the space where this should be." She looked up, her eyes shining. "Please, Benjamin."

He shook his head. "Are you making yourself cry right now? I didn't even know you could do that."

"Dammit, Ben! I really want this sword!"

He laughed. He couldn't help it. He sat down and stared at the Sanguine Raptor. It *was* beautiful. Once he'd had time to examine it, he saw why it was so legendary.

The balance was exquisite, even after two thousand years. The quality of the iron was exceptional; he was going to have to research early Celtic iron forging, because there was something different about the quality of the metal. The hilt was worked with copper and gold details, and the stylized raven's eyes were true rubies. He'd thought they might be garnet, but no. Rubies. Delicious cabochon rubies. It was no wonder Tenzin was trying to guilt him into giving it to her. It would be the crown of her collection.

"I'm not going to lie," he said. "I want to keep it myself. But that's not what we're doing here."

"But Ben"—she floated over and settled on the chair next to him, leaning into his shoulder—"I have stolen things so much less wonderful than this. This is worth stealing. It's worth pissing off lots of people. You'll be fine. I'll protect you."

"Nope."

She threw her head back and groaned. "This is so much worse than I imagined!"

"Suck it up, partner. You didn't have this reaction to the idol we found. What's going on?"

Tenzin rolled her eyes. "The idol was small and ugly. It didn't have anything shiny on it. It definitely didn't have *rubies*."

"Old-world snob."

"*Rubies*."

"I didn't know you liked rubies so much." He patted her shoulder. "I'll have to remember that."

"I'm thinking of something very painful happening to you right now."

"This was the agreement," he said. "No copies. No duplicates. We return the original artifact to the client without forgeries of any kind. How else will clients trust us to deal straight with them?"

"I have never been known for straight-dealing! You're spoiling my reputation as an unpredictable, chaotic force of nature. This could ruin me."

"So dramatic. I'm sure people will still be terrified of you. And don't forget, we do get to split the finders' fee."

She snorted. "What, the hundred and five whole pounds Max gave you for volunteering to find this sword? Do I even want to know how much money we lost on this job?"

Ben tried not to wince, but it was difficult. "It's coming out of my trust. Don't worry about it. The boost to our reputation will all be worth it in the end."

It better be. He didn't want to think about how much money he'd lost. Spending months on this research hadn't come cheap. Equipment and paying off archivists didn't come cheap either. Of course, some of those relationships would continue. The next time he was in the UK for work, he'd be able to—

"You know." Tenzin broke into his thoughts. "I bet if I was working with René, *he* would let me keep the sword."

Ben cut his eyes at her. "René would let you do all sorts of things I don't want to know about. But he wouldn't let you keep this sword unless you outbid the original clients. Then he'd stab them in the back to give it to you, making an enemy of the Ankers. What is that about, by the way?"

"I think they wanted it for leverage. I haven't found out why yet. But would it really be so bad to piss off the Ankers? They're nothing but an entire clan of spies. People probably piss them off all the time."

"Since I am human and don't really want to die at the hand of one of their many assassins, yes. Yes, it would be."

She put her head on his shoulder. "I really want the sword, Benjamin."

He patted her dark hair. "Learn to say good-bye, Tiny."

"I'm terrible at saying good-bye to things I love."

Oh Tenzin. Ben sighed, because she was right. Tenzin was a collector. Of things. Of people. It was one of the reasons she tried not to get attached at all.

"I know." He turned and kissed the top of her head. "There will be other swords."

"I bet you say that to all your partners."

"Only you, Tiny. Only you."

9

E *dinburgh, Scotland*

"YOU FOUND IT," MAX SAID, eyeing the sword with a blank expression. "I didn't think you'd actually find it."

Cathy was staring at the sword in abject horror. "Oh... Not good."

This was so far from the reaction Ben expected, he felt like screaming. He'd showed up at Max and Cathy's town house bursting with pride. He'd waited in the sitting room trying to stay cool, but it was difficult.

He'd found the fucking Sanguine Raptor.

Tenzin had come with him but seemed far more interested in looking at the books on the coffee table than engaging in the conversation. She was still pouting about not being able to keep the sword.

"I don't understand," Ben said. "What's going on? What's not good?"

He'd spent over a week painstakingly cleaning the sword in preparation for handing it over to Max. He'd used dental picks to clean the hilt, tested each of the jewels and cleaned them too. Then he'd coated and waxed the blade. Polished and waxed the hilt. He had a scabbard specially made with stitching that complemented the design of the hilt while still being serviceable.

And he'd fought off Tenzin's pleading the whole time.

Now Max and Cathy were looking at the Sanguine Raptor like it would bite.

"What's the problem, Max?"

The vampire's face was pale. "And you said Brennus is alive? You saw him?"

"Yeah, but like Tenzin said, I wouldn't go trying to find him again. He wasn't real happy about being woken up. He's probably moved his resting place by now, and he's back in stasis. I wouldn't go spreading the news that he's alive or anything."

Ben and Tenzin had debated telling Max, but there was no way of getting around the fact that out of the legendary treasure in Brennus's hoard, they'd only recovered one sword.

Ben knew the sword was more than enough to establish his reputation, but he also didn't want Max thinking he'd been cheated. Now Cathy was rubbing Max's shoulder like someone had died.

"Do you want it?" Cathy asked in a low voice.

"Of course I don't," Max hissed. "I never have. The power you have is more than enough. Ioan knew if our clan amassed more we'd only become a target."

Ben was completely lost.

"You could do it. It would be bloodless. You know the MacGregors—"

"This is not about the MacGregors. It's about me."

374

"Then we don't tell anyone you have it," she said. "There will be rumors, but we can deny—"

"Are you kidding me?" Ben finally shouted. "What are you talking about?"

Max looked up at him. "Can't you just put it back?"

"Of course I can't put it back! Do you understand what we went through to get it in the first place?"

"You told me you were going after the treasure," Max said. "No one can know—"

"The whole reason I searched for this thing was so vampires *would* know! So they would talk about it. And you're going to act like it's some kind of embarrassment? What is wrong with you guys?"

Max shook his head. "Ben, you don't understand."

"No, *you* don't understand," he said. "You don't understand what it's like trying to make a decent reputation in a world that constantly underestimates you. You don't understand what it's like depending on other people all the time. To live off someone else's success. I worked my ass off to find this thing. I risked my life and I invested money—asking nothing from you but permission—so that I could have a job on my résumé. And not just any job. A massive job. A *legendary* job. And now you tell me you're going to pretend it didn't happen and—"

"Do you understand what you found?" Cathy yelled. The room heated in a second. "Do you know what this sword means?"

"Ben." Max rose and put a hand on Cathy's arm. The room cooled back down. Max's normally gregarious face was lined with worry. He looked... older. Less like himself and more like a vampire to be frightened of.

Max said, "The Sanguine Raptor is not just a sword. It's... Excalibur. It's Durendal. It's Tizona."

"I don't know what that means," Ben said. "It's a *sword,*

Max." Ben stepped closer. "It's not like some magical creature appeared out of nowhere and handed it to me out of a lake or..."

Max's eyebrows went up.

Ben put his hand over his face. *"Shit!"*

Max and Cathy were both nodding silently. Tenzin started laughing behind him.

"It's funny," she said, "because it wasn't out of a lake. It was out of the ground. He pulled it out of the ground and gave it to you."

Oh, he was screwed.

Max shook his head. "I didn't think you'd find it. I'm sorry, Ben. I thought you would find treasure. Something that would stoke the legends and make for great stories to spread around. You'd get more work. I'd add a few things to my collection, but nothing... nothing like this. I didn't truly believe it existed until you showed it to me."

Ben closed his eyes and sat on the edge of the sofa. "What does this mean?"

Max lifted the blade from the desk where Ben had placed it and drew it from the scabbard. He held it balanced in his hand, his arm stretched out. Then he brought it closer and looked at the tooled iron, the jeweled hilt.

"It really is extraordinary," he murmured.

Max put it back in the scabbard and walked to the sofa, putting the blade on the table in front of him. Cathy sat at his side. Tenzin put the coffee table book to the side, and Ben turned and slid onto the sofa next to her.

Why couldn't it ever be simple?

"This sword," Max began, "is the sword of the king of Scotland. The vampire king. The Raven King."

"Brennus."

"The king who would return, according to immortal legend among Scotland's vampires. There aren't many of us, but the old ones—including Lord MacGregor—do abide by the tradition. MacGregor has never been crowned or taken any title other than the one he was born with. He's a steward only. On the day the Raven King returns, I have no doubt he will bend his knee and hand over his authority to the bearer of this blade."

Ben shook his head. "It's not my blade."

"Tell me," Max said, "as exactly as you can remember it, what Brennus said to you."

Tenzin asked, "Do you want it in English or Latin?"

Cathy said, "English please."

"Ben said, 'I give you my word that I will put your sword in the hand of the one who shares your blood. Who wants it to protect and *not* to sell as treasure.' And Ben offered Brennus a token. A coin he'd found from Brennus's cache. Then Brennus put his hand over Ben's coin and said, 'My faith is in you. I will have your word on this gold that when I rise again, the Sanguine Raptor will find its way back to me.' And he took the coin."

Despite the seriousness of the situation, Ben found it amusing that Tenzin also included dramatic voices in her retelling. He was also slightly in awe that she remembered their words *exactly*.

"Then Ben was thinking about the fact that he's mortal and will probably be dead when Brennus finally gets around to waking up—"

"You don't know that's what I was thinking," Ben said.

Tenzin gave him a look that clearly said: *Whatever, dude.* Then she continued. "So Brennus said, 'Mortal, your fate is clear to all but you.'" Tenzin turned her eyes back to Ben. "Did you get *that*?"

"Be quiet and finish the story, Tiny."

Cathy held a hand up. "Can I just say that the two of you are fascinating to me? I'm not really sure what's going on, but it's very interesting."

Max said, "Finish *please*."

"So finally Ben said, 'I give you my word. I will do everything in my power to return your sword to you. And I will leave it in hands I trust.' And that was it. Brennus told him they had an agreement and then he gave him the sword and basically disappeared."

"Just that?" Max asked. "There was no exchange or formal pledge?"

"Tenzin bribed him with blood-wine," Ben said. "Other than that, no."

Max let out a long breath, and Cathy patted him on the shoulder. "Sorry, sexy. This one is on you."

Ben said, "What does that mean?"

"It means that Brennus didn't give the blade to *you*," Cathy said. "He gave it to Max with you as Max's agent. If he'd given it to you, then Max could bow out and you'd be stuck being the vampire king of Scotland."

"I'm not a vampire!" Ben said.

Cathy nodded. "It would certainly be an awkward and probably very short reign."

Tenzin said, "I would kill people for you. Just so you know."

"Thanks," Ben said. "So that's the deal? Whoever holds the Sanguine Raptor is the vampire king of Scotland?"

"Yes," Max said. "But I have no desire to be king. William—Lord MacGregor—is an excellent and fair ruler. Gemma is already in power in London. Deirdre and Carwyn have massive influence in Dublin, even though Murphy is in charge. If I was the ruler here, our clan would be far too visible. We would be seen as too powerful and we'd become a target. It was one of the reasons Ioan never sought any kind of position. Gemma is the only one of us interested in ruling, and she's still more of a co-executive than a queen. If I become king here..." He sighed and put his hands over his face. "You see why we cannot reveal that the Sanguine Raptor has been found."

Ben frowned. "No. I really don't. Not at all." The answer was so obvious to Ben he didn't know how Max and Cathy hadn't already thought of it. "All you have to do is tell people that Brennus is alive."

Max's head shot up. "What?"

"Whoever holds the Sanguine Raptor is like... the heir of Brennus, right?"

"Yes."

"But Brennus isn't dead. People just think he is. Which is why immortals have tried to find the sword, right? Because whoever has the sword would be the king."

"Or the queen," Cathy added. "There's no requirement the vampire be male."

Max said, "But you said we shouldn't tell anyone Brennus is alive. You promised—"

"Nothing." Tenzin picked up another coffee table book, this one entitled *Maximum Storage, Medieval Space*. "We didn't promise Brennus we'd keep his secret. I don't think he'd really care if anyone knew. If anyone is foolish enough to try to find him and wake him up, that's on their head."

"And let's be honest," Ben said. "René Dupont will tell his clients that Brennus is alive. It's the only excuse he has for not retrieving the treasure. Word is going to spread."

Cathy turned to Max. "He's right. If Brennus isn't dead, then there's no need for a succession. Edinburgh continues to be ruled by a steward of the absent king, and they can just fight over that position if they want to. William will love it because it cements his authority, and since you're a descendant of Brennus's, you can keep the sword in your own armory. Tavish can guard it. It'll give him an excuse to never leave the estate. He'll be the 'Keeper of the King's blade' or something like that. He'll love it."

Max was rubbing his jaw, but his face didn't look quite as pale. "This could work."

"It will work," Tenzin said, paging through the design book. "Vampires, especially old ones, are highly resistant to change. Cathy, are you the designer here or is Max?"

"Me," Max said. "Why do you ask?"

"I need to hang some weapons," Tenzin said. "And I'm just not sure... I'm looking for ideas."

"What type of weapons? Swords? Spears? Do you have any armor?"

Tenzin sat up straighter. "I do have some very nice Kozane armor from Japan, but it's in storage."

"Really?" Max said. "I'd love to see it. As for weapons, it's always nice to vary your presentation. How many rooms are you thinking of? If you need ideas, you *must* come visit the castle. My brother and I inherited an armory."

Ben watched Tenzin's eyes light up and knew he'd lost her. She'd been obsessing over her wall of swords for weeks, and she'd finally found someone who seemed as enthusiastic as she was about decorating with deadly things.

He turned back to Cathy. "So that's it?"

She nodded. "Leave it to me. Max hates politics, and everyone is afraid of me. I'll smooth things over with William." She grinned. "Congrats, kid. You just found your first big treasure."

"And everyone freaked out about it."

She shrugged. "At least you know it'll get everyone talking."

"That's what I wanted."

Cathy ran her fingertip along the length of the ancient sword. "It's beautiful, Ben. Be proud. Be very proud." She clapped her hands together. "Now, there's just one more step to finish this deal."

"Oh yeah?"

"We've got to drink on it. I hope you like whisky."

Ben smiled. "I knew I'd love this country."

✕

BEN AND TENZIN stayed in Edinburgh for two more weeks. They were present when William, Lord MacGregor, steward of Edinburgh, saw his king's sword for the very first time. Despite their initial fears, MacGregor showed no sign of posturing or political gamesmanship. There was only a quiet wonder at hearing the news that Brennus was alive in the world. The Raven King still lived. If anything, his legend had only grown bigger.

Ben shook MacGregor's hand and accepted the vampire's thanks for the recovery of a national treasure. And... the honorary title.

"You said you wanted a title," Tenzin said. "Well, now you have one."

"Master of Iron doesn't actually mean anything, Tenzin."

"It means we need to work on your sword skills, Benjamin Vecchio, Master of Iron in Lothian."

"It makes me sound like I do laundry."

She rolled her eyes. "It's an honorific to say thank you. 'Scribe of Penglai Island' doesn't really mean I'm a scribe, but that's one of mine."

"Commander of the Altan Wind?"

She cocked her head. "Okay, that one means something, but it's not as polite as Master of Iron."

Tenzin had forced herself to be gracious at the various receptions and parties they attended with Max and Cathy, but Ben caught her eyeing the Sanguine Raptor with covetous glances every time she was in the same room with it.

He probably ought to warn Max about that.

"Why don't you have to get dressed up?" He squirmed in his new kilt. The wool itched against his skin.

"I am dressed up." She looked down at the black pants and tunic. "This is embroidered silk."

"And it looks so much more comfortable than this," he muttered.

"You look very handsome." She adjusted the plaid over his shoulder.

Don't say it...

"All the women will want to have sex with you."

"Thanks, Tenzin."

Despite his discomfort with the breeze on his legs, attending the banquet and accepting the title and ceremonial dirk Lord MacGregor gave him felt... big.

It wasn't just that every immortal in Edinburgh was talking about the recovery of the Sanguine Raptor or the beauty of the historic blade. Ben felt part of something bigger.

He'd found something that was missing and returned it to those who valued it. He'd brought a lost thing home. Ben hadn't realized that would mean something to him, but it did.

Ben and Tenzin attended the banquet in honor of the Raven King's throne where William MacGregor, immortal son of Brennus's most trusted counselor, kissed the blade Max held and pledged to watch over the immortals and humans of Scotland until the time that the Raven King decided to finally return. They danced at midnight in a castle outside the city, and when they left, Ben was a Master of Iron in the Scottish court.

×

BEN AND TENZIN spent two full weeks at Max's castle in the Highlands. Tenzin forced Ben to take a million pictures while she took notes and nearly swooned over Max's collection of axes. Ben would have said her adoration was embarrassing except that both Max and his cranky brother Tavish seemed slightly besotted with the tiny air vampire with the bronze blade.

They laughed. They talked.

They drank a *lot* of whisky.

"I love this place," Tenzin said one night. They were sitting on the floor of the dagger room.

Yes, there was a room full of daggers. Every size and shape you could imagine. Ben was starting to worry that Tenzin would never want to leave.

"We have to go back to New York," he said.

"But why?" she whined. "I could live here, and you could call Max when you need me for something."

He nudged her shoulder. "You'd miss me too much."

"I would not."

"You would. Also, I don't think Max and Cathy get cable here. No HGTV, Tenzin."

Her eyes went wide.

"I don't think they even have Wi-Fi, so no YouTube either."

Tenzin made a face. "Never mind. I'll just come visit their weapons. Besides, Cara would miss me if I lived here."

"You do know she's not an actual person, don't you? It's an artificial intelligence program. There's not an actual person living in the walls or anything."

Tenzin shook her head. "I hope you don't say that at home. You'll hurt Cara's feelings."

"Not a person. No feelings. Artificial intelligence."

Tenzin rose and gave him a disapproving frown. "I expected more kindness from you, Ben."

"Are you joking? I can't tell if you're joking."

She walked out of the dagger room.

"Tenzin?"

Yeah, it was definitely time to go home.

EPILOGUE

BEN FLIPPED THROUGH A MAGAZINE while Tenzin placed the last sword at the top of the wall.

He flipped again.

She floated down to the ground and surveyed her handiwork. She'd have to make Ben take pictures and send some to both Max and Gemma. The two had been instrumental in the overall design scheme of the loft. Both had urged her to retrieve her armor and shields from storage, and the Ngoni and Indian shields made excellent additions.

Maybe she could convince Ben to build a dagger room in the loft.

He let out a small huffing sigh and flipped another magazine page.

Tenzin's eye twitched. "Cara," she called. "Please play music."

"What music would you like?"

"Enya, please. Just play all the Enya you have access to."

Tenzin found there was nothing that induced rage in Ben faster than the soothing sounds of the Irish singer. But lately, anything was better than Ben's silent pouting.

"Cara, stop music," Ben growled.

"Cara, play Enya."

"I do not understand," Cara's smooth lilt intoned. "What music would you like me to play?"

"Enya." Tenzin stared at Ben. "Shuffle. All."

Ben threw down the magazine as a wave of New Age voices filled the room. "What is wrong with you? You know I hate that music."

She batted her eyes at him. "You seem tense."

"I'm fine."

"Really? Because you seem tense." She gestured at the wall. "You haven't even complimented my decorating."

She was quite pleased with the contractor Cara had found. He wasn't cheap, but he was fast and he didn't ask inconvenient questions. Over the past month, she'd planned and placed most of her sword and shield collection. Her armor had been unpacked and mounted in the corners of the loft. Tenzin found she quite liked the idea of hollow warriors guarding their territory. She hoped it would make guests uncomfortable enough that they wouldn't stay long.

"Well?" she asked, gesturing to the length of the wall. "I think Ruben and I are going to start on a conservatory for the roof garden next."

He picked up the magazine again. "That's not decorating. That's easy access to things that can kill your enemies. Useful, I'll grant you, but you're not exactly curating Monet."

Tenzin narrowed her eyes and flew over to Ben, picking him up by the back of his shirt and hoisting him into the air while he kicked and twisted.

"Put me down!"

Flying with Ben when he cooperated was a challenge. Flying him when he was trying to twist away was almost impossible.

"Do you want to break your legs?" She nearly dropped him. "Stop flailing like a child."

"Put me down, Tenzin!"

She tossed him into her alcove and threw the magazine he was still clutching to the ground.

"You will stop this," she said, glaring at him. "Or I will hurt you."

Ben was red in the face, but he couldn't quell the urge to look around her small loft area. "This is smaller than I thought."

"I am not a very big person."

His head almost touched the ceiling. The loft itself was just over six feet tall and open to the rest of the house, but curtains were hung for when she needed privacy. There was a railing but no ladder. The only way to get in was to fly. There was a simple pallet on the floor with rugs and furs from her home in Tibet. There was an altar in the corner where she meditated and lit incense, and a small loom she'd built. Other than that, it was empty save for a few piles of books.

"Sit," she said.

Ben sat. His eyes were drawn to the loom. "You weave."

"Yes."

He stared at the blank wall across from him. "I didn't know that."

"There's a lot you don't know about me, Benjamin."

He was silent again.

"Why are you so angry?" she asked. "You're making everyone around you miserable."

"The only person I see is you."

"Not true." *Wait, was it?* "Don't dismiss Cara. She's a part of this family too."

At least that made him crack a smile.

Thinking back, Tenzin realized she'd rarely left the loft during the previous month. While she'd been video-chatting with Max and Gemma, ordering around Ruben the contractor, and seeing to the decoration of the loft, he'd been brooding in his office. She didn't know if there were pictures on his walls, and he still hadn't unpacked his books.

"Ben," she asked. "When did I become the well-adjusted one?"

"I don't know," he said. "It's so wrong."

"It is. I am the strange, frightening vampire and you are the human that everyone likes. This partnership isn't going to work if we try changing that now."

He nodded.

"You need to get a life here," she said. "Make friends. I don't need many people, but I'm not you. The O'Briens have invited you over on several occasions. You need to stop making excuses."

The O'Briens were the immortals in charge of New York City. They were an unruly clan of earth vampires who distrusted most outsiders but had been cautiously friendly to Ben because of his connections to Carwyn in Ireland.

Also, he had money. Which they liked.

She said, "You can only make work excuses for so long when you're not working."

Bingo. The pained look on his face told her what was really bothering him.

"They're going to call," she said.

"You keep saying that"—he picked at the edge of her rug —"but it's been a month."

"A month, Ben. A *month.* You are working with vampires here. Think about how most of us perceive time. A month is nothing."

He groaned and banged his head against the wall. "This is driving me crazy."

"You don't need the money. Not really. But you do need to relax."

"I don't know how to do that," he said. "My whole life has been busy. School. Training. Studying. Working with Giovanni. More training. More studying."

"Do you think Gio works all the time?"

"Yes." Ben shrugged. "He works as much as he wants."

"*Now* he does. But when we were working together, there were some times where we'd only work three or four months out of the year. That's contract work, Ben. Sometimes you wait for work. Sometimes you wait a long time. And other times you'll have jobs coming from everywhere."

"So how do you deal with it?"

"If you're a hermit like me, you don't care." She shrugged. "If you're *you*, you... go to a party with the O'Briens. Or fly to LA for a few weeks. Travel to Rome and see Fabi. Drink whisky with Gavin. But you *leave the house*."

He sighed.

"Or...," she said. "I'm going to physically hurt you at some point."

He smiled. "Got it."

She nodded toward the ledge. "Get out of my loft. It's too crowded up here with you in it."

He looked over the edge. "Sorry, but unless you have a rope ladder, you're going to have to help me down. I'm not breaking my legs because you had a temper tantrum." He raised his voice. "And for God's sake, Cara, stop playing Enya!"

"Stopping shuffle now," Cara said.

Ben shook his head, muttering, "Passive-aggressive New Age music" under his breath. "Cara," he said, "play the Real McKenzies. Shuffle all. Volume level forty-five."

In a few seconds, the sound of pounding drums and angry bagpipes blasted through the loft.

Tenzin grinned. "This is like the music in the pub!"

"I know!" he shouted. "Now will you get me down from here?"

She flew them both down to the main level and set Ben on his feet.

"Don't pick me up again," he said. "You know I hate that."

"Are you going to stop pouting?"

"I was not—"

"This is Cara." Cara paused the music; her voice—the volume still turned up to forty-five—filled the room. "You have an incoming call from Daniel Preston in York, United Kingdom. Shall I accept?"

Ben frowned. "Do you know a Daniel Preston?"

"No," Tenzin said. "But I have a feeling that he knows you."

Ben's smile lit up the room. "Cara, accept call."

THE END

THE BRONZE BLADE

"You may call me Tenzin, if you like."

A girl. A mother. A slave. A monster. A survivor. Descended into madness. Forged in fire and darkness, she became one of the fiercest warriors the immortal world had ever known.

But in the beginning, there was a girl.

The Bronze Blade is a stand-alone origin novella in the Elemental World series. **It contains violent themes of abuse that may not be appropriate for all readers.**

FOREWARD: COMING TO TERMS WITH WRITING TENZIN

When I set out to write Tenzin's origin story, *The Bronze Blade*, many years ago, I did so to exorcise a nightmare. For months, I'd been dreaming about Tenzin's origin and I desperately wanted to rid this story from my head. For a long time, I debated publishing it. It felt violent and horrible and cruel.

In the end, and at the urging of trusted writing friends, I decided to publish. Readers were fascinated by this ancient vampire with the mysterious past, and I wanted to explain to them a little more about who Tenzin was, where she came from, and how she arrived into my mind.

At the time of publication, many of those same readers were frustrated—some even angry—that I hadn't given her more story, not knowing that I had an entire series planned for her and Ben.

This novella is only a glimpse of a formative part of this character, and not nearly the whole of her. But I do feel that it is an important part, so I wanted to include it in this anthology, especially as it pertains to understanding Tenzin's reactions to certain situations and her relationship with her sire.

For readers who are sensitive to sexual abuse or violence, this is not a mandatory read to understand who Tenzin is. You will understand enough through hints in the other books where she came from and what she went though. So I leave that choice up to you.

In the end, I still have questions.

I often wonder why so many readers love and relate to Tenzin. How could a five-thousand-year-old vampire touch people so deeply? How could readers find her relatable? Or even sympathetic at times?

After spending many years with Tenzin in my head, I think her immortality and otherness reveal deep and often difficult truths of what it means to be human, and particularly what it means to be a woman.

For that, I'm grateful.

Elizabeth Hunter
October 2019

PROLOGUE: TELL ME A STORY

For every girl who has been lost
And to every one who has survived

"I want you to tell me before I die."

The old woman's eyes were bright with fever, but her grip was strong as she held the immortal's hand. Tenzin gently uncurled the fingers from around her palm before she dipped the cloth back in the scented water, the aroma of eucalyptus suffusing the room in her sire's house where Nima lay.

"There's time," she said softly.

"No. There isn't."

"You're being dramatic." Tenzin brushed the white hair from Nima's forehead, remembering when the hair had been shining black and the forehead smooth. Nima had always been proud of her fair skin. Had teased Tenzin that following her into the darkness had kept her young. It wasn't true, of course. Nima had been her human companion for over seventy years. She'd sheltered Tenzin and protected her during the sunlight hours, even though the immortal no longer needed to sleep. It was Nima who had dealt with the humans. Nima who had fed her rare thirst. "Always so dramatic," Tenzin said again, stretching out next to the old woman on the bed, pressing Nima's forehead against her cool cheek. It burned.

Her body fought to live even as her life drifted away. Nima was dying. Tenzin knew it. She'd known this day would come. It always came. But for the first time in a thousand years, the loss angered her.

Nima whispered, "I'm sor—"

"Don't apologize again. We're past that now."

"Please tell me."

"Why?" Her heart ached. Of all the stories that Tenzin could tell her, the fantastical tales she could spin, why did her friend ask this of her? Tenzin could tell her about the rise of the pyramids and how the moonlight shone off the snow that topped the Holy Mountain. She'd watched the Great Wall being built and hovered silently over a stage in Vienna as Mozart played. "Let me tell you a beautiful story."

"I don't want that. I want *your* story."

"You don't."

"I do."

Tenzin tried not to sigh in frustration. "Why do you ask this of me?"

"Why do you hold it back?"

Tenzin's brow furrowed. "I am no longer that girl."

"I know you're not."

"It was thousands of years ago. I barely remember her."

"Don't lie to me now," Nima said, her voice stronger. "Not now."

They waited in silence as the soft voices of her father's servants passed in the hall.

"Why do you want this burden?" Tenzin whispered. "It is not a good story."

"I want it *because* it is not a good story."

"Human, why do you search for meaning in pain? There is no meaning in pain. It is. You endure it. That is all."

"I am dying, Tenzin. Give this to me. Let me know you as you were." Nima's voice fell soft as she leaned her head on Tenzin's shoulder. "Give me this burden, and I will take it from you. Not all of it. But some. Give it to me, and I will take it with me when I go. Then, there will be just a little less darkness for you."

"I am darkness."

"You were." Nima took a deep, rattling breath. "But I see light for you now. Give this to me, so there is a little more."

There was no light for her—she knew that—because Tenzin loved the darkness. But that, she would never tell Nima. Let the woman believe there was some kind of happiness for her to come. If that would ease her pain, Tenzin would give her that.

"Are you sure you want my story?" she asked.

"Yes."

"Then I will tell you. But you must promise to stay awake, my Nima, so the nightmares do not come until I am finished. And when they do come, I will wake you, so you will see that nothing is real. Do you understand?"

"Tell me. And tell me the truth."

Tenzin thought for a moment, then said, "I will tell you, and you will decide if it is the truth."

Nima took another deep breath and said, "Tell me a story."

She stared into the rafters of her sire's house on Penglai, and a dragon stared back at her, surrounded by clouds and holding a pearl in his mouth. His gold eyes glistened in the low lamplight and, as she stared...

Tenzin heard the sound of cold wind as it swept over Northern plains.

The sound of the night breeze shaking the trees.

The low bleating of goats and a child's laugh.

"A long time ago," she began, "there was a girl..."

1

THE GIRL

The girl didn't rush to the goat pens. Despite the chill in the spring wind and the late hour, she walked slowly, rhythmically patting the baby tied to her hip. She sang a low song for the fussy child, patting his back as she followed the path toward the pens where the mother goats were meant to drop their kids. The raiders had been there that day, but some of the goats would be left. They always left some. Then they rode away on their stout ponies, fat and feasting on the village's food.

Seasons would pass. The herd would grow. The caves would fill with storage jars again.

Then the raiders returned.

As long as the girl could remember, it had been like this.

The last time they'd come, she couldn't even find the energy to hide what little she owned. She had been alone and sick, the only survivor of the fever that killed her man and her daughter. It had been spring that year, too. The raiders had come and taken the dried meat the girl's mother had brought and hung from the thatch roof in her small hut. They didn't pay her any attention. She was still too weak to notice. Thin and sallow, she'd lain on a pallet near the fire, the skins her man had given as a wedding gift were piled over her emaciated frame. The raiders took some of the skins, the meat, and a string of shells the girl had collected from the riverbed. Then, they left.

She'd survived.

Fortunately, First Wife had noticed her and taken her to her husband to give him the children the other woman could not. The next winter, when her belly grew swollen, the girl did not sing. Nor did she pause in her work to place her palm against the kicks that grew stronger with each passing moon. The Old Woman told her she carried two babes, but the girl paid no attention. She would birth in the spring, like the goats. And the child would belong to the man and First Wife, also like the goats.

The Old Woman was right, of course. There had been two. Two living boys with eyes like their father.

Her new husband had been pleased that his blue-green eyes, uncommon among their tribe, had been passed on to the two children the girl had born him. It was a sign of his ancestors' favor. The straw-haired people had long ago wandered back to the west, but their blood had mixed with those tribes who had stayed. So the girl's babe bore the startling eyes that shone blue-green in the twilight, as did the other child who rested, fat and pampered, in First Wife's arms.

The child she carried had been born alive, but small. And so silent, the Old Woman thought he would probably die. No matter. First Wife had already taken the oldest boy, red-faced and screaming, to show her husband. They were pleased with the healthy male, and told her she could keep the other for her own if she wanted it.

She wanted it. She wanted *him*.

The girl's arm tightened under the round bottom of the little boy on her hip, and he turned his eyes toward her, no longer fussy, but content and cooing, reaching for the long plait of hair that hung over her shoulder, gnawing on his chubby fingers. He was still small, but healthy and tough, crawling around their hut so quickly, he'd almost rolled into the cooking fire more than once.

The walking path wound through the bottom of a ravine, close enough to the village to check the flocks easily, but far enough out that the low grass still grew. The goats had stripped all the pastures near the huts.

The baby reached over and pulled at the girl's lip, tugging at the corner of her wide mouth until she turned and caught his fingers between them, pretending to bite while the boy let out a high pitched giggle.

Perhaps, if he hadn't giggled, they might have been able to escape, but she heard the panicked bleating too late.

The ravine opened up to her right, and the girl saw them, standing in a close circle under the pale moonlight. The boys in the village had said they were all gone, but they'd been wrong. The raiders remained. She tried to disappear among the rocks, but one had already turned and spotted her, no doubt searching for the unexpected laugh that drifted on the night wind.

Her heart raced, but the baby paid no heed. He continued to babble and throw his arms out, reaching for the goats. He liked the animals and wanted to be let down to play.

The girl panicked.

"Tsh, tsh, tsh," she tried to soothe him, throwing a blanket over his face as another one of the men turned. She heard shouts in a language she didn't understand. She noticed a pool of blood that the men were standing around. She tried to look away, but her eyes were fixed on it, along with the pile of grey and white bodies that lay in the middle like so many stacked stones.

She turned and ran.

By now, the baby had picked up on his mother's panic, and

he was crying, clutching the side of her breast and burrowing his face in her tunic.

"*Mama!*" he cried, his voice thin and high in the dry Northern air.

"*Tsh!*"

Every stone in the path, every branch and root, reached up to trip her as she ran. She heard a noise above her, like a great bird of prey, but she didn't look back. She kept running.

Then, impossibly, she couldn't. The path fell away beneath her churning feet as some monstrous thing grabbed her shoulders. A pale hand reached down and yanked at the sling her child rested in, and she felt it come loose.

No.

No!

"Ma! Mama!"

His screams reached the girl's ears as she rose higher and higher in the sky. She heard the baby's cries of pain as he tumbled back to earth, and the last glimpse she caught of her son was his vivid eyes, shining bright with tears in the moonlight as his tiny arms reached up.

"*Ma!*"

She didn't breath until a sharp yank on her hair let loose her fury and pain. The girl screamed long and loud, kicking her legs and biting at the arm that held her. She kept screaming as the creature dragged her higher into the starry sky.

Then something struck her temple, and everything was black.

WHEN SHE WOKE, it was in darkness and her arms were bound together with twisted strips of leather. She'd been left in a tent that reeked of old animal hides and rot. Stones dug into her cheek, and she could feel something—probably blood—dry and crusted at her temple. Her lips were split. She could see nothing, because black hair hung over her face.

The old women talked about it, occasionally. Sometimes, the raiders took more than goats. Sometimes, some or all the girls in a village would disappear. They were never seen again. The raiders were men, after all. And what could one small village do? That was the reason girls didn't wander at night. But First Wife had wanted to know how many goats the raiders had left them, and the girl didn't argue.

Mama!

She squeezed her eyes shut, trying to rid her mind of his terrified cries.

Ma!

Despite her physical pain, the bitter tears had not fallen until that moment.

She heard someone walk into the tent, then her arms were jerked up, and the bindings bit into her wrist. He grunted and brushed the thick mane of hair away from her face, muttering under his breath.

It was one of the raiders. His hand was cold when he pushed her forehead back to examine her. His grimy fingers lifted her lip to check her teeth, then he pulled off the tunic she still wore, though it had been ripped in many places and barely clung to her frame. She shivered in the sudden cold. He was a tall man, and stocky. He looked her up and down, seemingly satisfied by her appearance. His dirty mouth turned up at the corners, and the girl's stomach churned with a dreadful fear.

It wasn't a man at all, but a demon from childhood nightmares.

Fangs hung over his lip, and his gums were stained red with blood. His skin was pale and bloodless, but the eyes were like two black pits, reflecting her own panic back to her as she trembled before him.

A high keening sound came from her throat. In the back of her mind, she saw her son's eyes, wide in the moonlight, glassy with tears as he reached for her. Would someone find him? When she didn't return, would First Wife send another to check? Perhaps, the baby would crawl toward the pens where he played, and someone from the village would take him.

Probably, he was dead. At least he had been spared whatever horrors this demon would inflict on her.

The monster barked out some words she didn't recognize, and slapped the girl's face until she quieted her cries. Then he grunted and reached for something in a pile behind her. It was another tunic, which he pulled over her head, snapping the bindings on her wrists with two fingers. He was inhumanly strong. The girl wondered how easily he could snap her bones. He pushed the hair back from her face and tugged on her arm until she stumbled after him.

As she walked through the camp, the girl wondered what she had done to deserve this fate. Perhaps, she had been too happy once. Perhaps she had tempted the gods, as her mother had warned her. The gentle man who once met her eyes had died. The girl child had died. The boy would die too, if he was not dead already. Surely, it would be better to die before Fate caught her in some other net.

She was not afraid of death.

They passed two raiders, standing around a fire. They eyed her with blatant glee, but she ignored them, staring at the red flames that tossed sparks into the night air.

Fire was too uncertain. People fell into cooking fires all the time, but they didn't die unless the wound became angry and swollen. Then, a fever might take them. She needed something more than fire.

Perhaps they were near cliffs or a river. Either one would be a more certain way to die. And the girl knew she would rather die than exist for whatever purpose the demon chose for her. She did not know her child's fate, but she knew her own. Life was short and brutal for those who lived on the plains, and she'd lived longer than many.

She burned with the need to find a quick death.

The raider pulled her past some tents. They were thick and heavy, low to the ground, with no flaps to let in light. She saw no cooking fires and no women or children. The camp reeked of blood and spoiled meat. Filthy rags hung over the backs of the tents; some of them seemed to be washed, but only a few.

As they approached the largest fire, the monster turned to her and slapped her cheek again. The girl didn't make a sound. Her mind was occupied with how she might kill herself as quickly as possible. Perhaps if she angered the creature—

"Tshhh," he hissed, putting his finger over her mouth. He wanted her to be silent. He lifted a brow, looking at her as if she was dumb livestock, then he said it again. "Tsh."

She gave him no response, purposely making her eyes as dead as possible. He scowled at her, but the girl didn't care. Then he turned and continued walking toward the large fire in the middle of the tents.

The camp was not large, she saw no more than a dozen tents. There were no houses like the mud and thatch roof huts her people had built by the river, but a few of the tents were larger and sat higher off the ground. She saw a grouping of ponies near the largest tent. The animals were decorated with bright cloth saddles and beads in their manes. The girl had only ever seen ponies from a distance and had always wondered how the nomads rode them. But the one who had grabbed her had come from the sky.

Perhaps these monsters also rode some monstrous birds, as well as the four-footed, stomping beasts.

Her captor had hooked an arm around her neck as they walked. A few men parted before him. She saw two more raiders nodding at him with respect. Whatever he was, the demon that held her was a being of some importance.

The girl ignored all of them, until she saw a metal blade at the waist of a man nearby. It was not unlike the scooped stone knives she'd used to clean animal hides with her mother. Her hands were no longer bound. She watched as the knife came closer. Her fingers trembled.

As she passed the man, her hand darted out, yanking the knife from his waist as she twisted her thin frame from under her captor's arm. There were a few wretched laughs around her as some of them noticed.

Before the monster could grab her again, she fell to her knees, bringing the sharp edge of the blade up to her throat and pressing in. She felt it bite, and her mouth spread into a relieved smile, but before she could drag the knife deeper, her hand was yanked back and the snickers turned into roars of laughter around her.

Her captor knocked her to the ground with a cuff to her temple, but the girl didn't go down quietly. She screamed and clawed to her hands and knees, scrambling toward the knife that had fallen into the dirt. Her captor kicked her stomach, but she kept going. Her only thought was the sweet relief of death that waited on the edge of the bronze blade.

He yanked her up by the hair, and the knife fell from her fingers. Her dark eyes followed it down to the dirt where it landed, blade dug into the earth, out of her reach as he lifted her up by the neck. Then he tossed her toward the fire with inhuman strength as the men around him laughed and hooted.

The girl tumbled to the ground, rolling into a ball to avoid the flames. Flames would not be enough. They would only bring her pain that might weaken her from cheating Fate's plan. She let out a low grunt when she hit a pair of leather wrapped legs. Her tumble halted, she looked up into the eyes of the most fearsome creature she'd ever seen, all the more terrifying, because he looked nothing like a monster.

His eyes were cold and beautifully sloped; his long hair was pulled back into a neat topknot. His face was severe, as if sculpted from rock, and his skin was the soft brown of newly dried clay. From the length of his beard, he was old, but not a single grey hair touched his temples.

He looked at her for a long moment, then he looked up and the other men fell silent. The girl understood immediately. He was their chief. Or god. Perhaps the beautiful monster was a god come to earth, though his legs certainly felt solid. The chief said something to her captor in a low voice. He responded in the same mysterious language. They went back and forth for some time, with another voice—a younger one—occasionally sounding between them.

The chief did not sound pleased. After a few more heated moments, the girl felt herself yanked up by the hair again, then she hung in front of the god-like creature as he peered into her eyes. She did not break her stare, but met his eyes boldly. After all, she didn't want to show respect; she was hoping the monster would kill her. Quickly.

There was a faint lift at the corner of his eyebrow, then he said something to the girl she didn't understand. She didn't know how she was so certain he was speaking to her, but there was not a doubt in her mind that it was so. He put a hand to her jaw, then gripped her neck, and a wave of dizziness washed over her. Her head swam and her eyes closed. The raucous sounds of the monsters' camp picked up again, and she thought she heard more cackling laughter. Or perhaps it was only the fire popping.

As the wave of numbness swept over her, the voices drifted to the back of her mind.

She didn't know, and for the first time, she didn't care. She was peaceful. Swimming in oblivion. The last thing she remembered was a sharp pop at her neck, and then she knew nothing else.

~

As SHE WOKE, she curled around him. Her child's little warm body was wrapped in her arms, and he clung to her. She was warm, and morning thirst pressed against the back of her throat. Her boy smelled sweet, as if he'd spent the day playing at the edge of the river in the sun while she washed their clothes. She pulled him closer, pressing her lips to his neck to nuzzle his skin.

But as she drew closer, the burning in the back of her throat became a fire. She clutched the child when he began to struggle in her arms. The girl felt an aching in her jaw, and she stretched her mouth open as her teeth lengthened. Long. Longer. Her mouth dropped open in pain, her nerves woke, and then everything—

EVERYTHING woke.

Pain.

Like a crackling fire along her skin, spreading and digging into her as she curled her shoulders, no longer aware of the body in her arms. No longer aware of her own breath. Her body was an open wound.

Worse than the fever. Worse than giving birth. Like nothing she could have imagined.

She knew she was dying. Her eyes closed against the agony, she threw her head back and howled. Her mind was consumed by the burning in her throat. Her belly. She opened her eyes, but there was only blackness around her when she heard it.

Th-thunk.

Th-thunk.

Th-thunk, th-thunk, th-thunk.

The sound was the beating of a primal drum. The call of panicked prey. Her jaw ached, and hunger tore at her throat.

Th-thunk, th-thunk, th-thunk, th-thunk, th-thunk, th-thunk.

Her lips felt for the soft thrumming of the vein. Then her mouth dropped open, and she plunged her teeth into the flesh, biting down hard as her prey squealed. She rolled over it, trapping the creature under her as she drew even deeper, desperate for the relief the hot liquid splashed against her tongue.

Sweet.

The sweetest taste that had ever crossed her lips. Richer than honey from the hive. It splashed her lips and washed down her throat until the flesh ran dry. Then she sucked at the vein, licking her lips for the last precious drops.

She rolled to her back, staring into the nothingness that surrounded her before her eyes closed again in relief.

As the pain ebbed from her limbs and throat, the girl blinked back into awareness.

She was still surrounded by the scent of animal skins and blood, only it smelled far, far worse. She wasn't dead, but she was still in the monsters' camp. Something heavy lay over her arm, but she couldn't see.

She pulled away and crawled to the edge of the tent until she came to a piece of animal skin that was not stretched as tightly as the others. She pushed the flap out until a low beam of light shone in. It was still blackest night, but even a sliver of light was enough. She could see perfectly in the darkness.

She turned back to see what lay with her, and her mind seized.

It was a child. No more than six or seven years, the small body lay crumbled in the center of the tent, his throat torn out, as if an animal had attacked it. Shaking, she crawled over to him, flipping him over with shaking hands until she could see the lifeless brown eyes.

The girl lifted shaking fingers to her mouth and felt the long, curving fangs that pressed against her lips.

Her mouth dropped open in a mindless roar.

She screamed, and she didn't stop.

2

THE MONSTER

They called her Saaral. It was the word for woman in their language. She thought. She was the only female in the camp except for the human women they would occasionally capture and kill.

Human women, she came to realize, were very breakable. If she'd wanted to live, she might have felt grateful to the solemn chief who had made her a monster.

But Saaral didn't want to live.

She'd lain in the tent that first night, shaking and weeping as she held the cold body of the boy she'd drained of blood. She would not move until the hunger struck her again, and that was just before the dawn began to break. She fell into blackness with her stomach twisted in knots.

And woke with another struggling victim. This time, it was an emaciated woman. Her hunger didn't care. By the time she realized she'd killed again, the woman lay with dead eyes staring into the blackness of the small tent where they'd thrown her.

The third night, it was a goat.

Then another child.

Then a pig.

A man.

She vomited up the blood from each kill, only to lap it from the dust when the hunger took her again.

The fourth night she woke in darkness, Saaral tried to hang herself. But though the leather strips she twisted around her neck held and her body hung loose from the tent supports, she did not die. She did not even lose consciousness. And that was the way the girl learned that she no longer needed to breathe.

A few nights later, she snuck out of the tent and found a dull blade stowed in a bedroll. She cut her neck from ear to ear, feeling every inch of the knife as she searched for death. She lost her vision at some point, but woke the next night with her captor grunting between her thighs, her healed throat was burning with hunger, but the flesh between her legs burned with pain. She raged and screamed, beating him with her fists, knowing it was useless. Then she turned her face to the side, and blood ran behind her eyes.

She didn't try to speak.

The girl they called Saaral was passed from tent to tent after that. Mostly, it was her captor who fed her and raped her. Other times, it was one of the men who seemed to please him. She never saw the frighteningly beautiful chieftain again. Within the small camp, her captor led the men. Most of them were human, but they followed the monster's every command.

Saaral spent most of her first summer searching for death, only to be disappointed. Once she learned the sun could burn her, she tried to crawl outside, but exhaustion took her before she reached the searing rays. Her captor tied her from that night on.

His name was Kuluun, and he was powerful. His fangs were thick and long. When they weren't covered in blood, they glowed like small white blades in the night. Saaral tried to smother him once. He'd looked like he was sleeping. He wasn't.

Kuluun laughed and slapped her across the tent. Saaral felt her jaw unhinge, then slowly shift back into place. Then he tossed her to one of the humans who had pleased him by driving a small herd of ponies into the camp the night before.

The human kept her for two nights. On the second one, Saaral snuck out of the tent, tying a rope from her neck to one pony's saddle before she kicked it and hoped her head would pop from her body before anyone noticed she was gone.

Kuluun caught her before she reached the edge of camp, dragging her back as the men laughed around her. Her rage-filled screams were shredded by the wind as Kuluun beat Saaral in front of the fire until the blood ran from her back and she fell silent. Then she felt her back knitting together as she lay in the dirt and he raped her again.

By the time the leaves began to change, the hunger for blood had eased, and Saaral had stopped screaming.

When the first snow fell, she gave up any hope of death.

THE MONSTERS CALLED themselves the Sida, and they could fly.

Not like birds. They moved through the air as if they were swimming in invisible streams. They caught rivers of wind that carried them over the plains, often dropping from the sky to capture and kill the way that Kuluun had taken her that first night. There were only three of them. Kuluun, along with his brothers, Suk and Odval. Their chief, the monster who had bitten her neck, and another of their brothers were traveling on other parts of the plains. It was Kuluun who was in charge while they were gone. The others in the camp were humans who followed the Sida, hunting and offering up captives and animals to the monsters as if they were gods.

Saaral knew they were not gods, for she was one of them now, though she could not fly and she barely held control of her body and senses.

Why they had decided to keep her, instead of killing her like they did most women, was a mystery. Why was useless. She was one of the Sida, even if she was unwilling. She began to listen to the language, though she still spoke to no one. She listened when she washed clothes for the camp. She listened when they growled and grunted between her legs. She listened as she roasted the meat they ate and when she rode next to them as they moved south to warmer places. She listened to everything.

The humans rode ponies, like all raiders did. The ponies also carried the tents and skins that they used to shelter themselves from the sun.

The tents weren't like the large dwellings made by the people of the plains, who moved from place to place with their families and animals. These tents were far smaller. For shelter, not living. Kuluun burrowed into the ground like an animal, then put the low tents over the opening, sometimes he buried himself completely with dirt before the sun rose. Saaral often woke to find herself buried next to him or one of his brothers, when Kuluun let them borrow her. It terrified her. But as winter grew more bitter, Saaral grew stronger and more coordinated. She watched how Kuluun moved. How he fought with Suk and Odval. She watched silently from the dust, though she still did not speak.

Soon, there were more.

Seasons passed. The band grew. Some of the humans who followed them, the strongest and most vicious, were turned into monsters as she had been. And though Saraal was raped nightly, she never grew heavy with child. Kuluun made children his own way, picking the humans who pleased him most to turn into Sida. The new Sida were given the fattest captives to drink while Saaral was fed just enough to keep her alive. This was the way she learned that the best blood made the Sida stronger. She was never given the best blood.

As the new Sida were made, Saaral was given to each in turn. She was long past protesting their lust, even feebly. She lay nightly as the monsters took what they wanted of her body, then tossed her back to Kuluun's tent like a dirty skin. If he had no other task for her, she was bound until the next night. Usually, she was put to work washing their blankets or cleaning their tents.

Saaral no longer thought of herself as human. She didn't remember the name her mother had given her. She didn't recognize the land they passed through. One day, she looked into a river on a moonlit night, noticed her reflection, and realized that she still looked the same as she had the summer after her son was born, though she'd seen more than ten winters under Kuluun's hand. The only difference was her eyes, which were some light color she barely recognized. She couldn't see clearly in the moonlight, but they were not the rich brown her human husband had admired.

Saaral was not surprised. She was no longer human. She was a monster, too.

She looked over her shoulder at one of the humans near the fire, her eyes seeing clearly in the dark.

Though she was thin and weak for a Sida, her senses had been honed. She no longer clenched hands over her ears when the animals were near. Her stomach did not turn at their scent. She had become accustomed to her new body, though Kuluun limited her to pony blood, keeping her just short of starving, so she did not become too strong.

But though she wasn't strong, her senses were as keen as any other Sida as she watched the human.

Saaral remembered laying with him when he was only a young man, his black hair thick and shining in the lamplight. He had not been as cruel as some. Now, there was grey in his hair, and his shoulders were stooped. Soon, she knew Kuluun would give him to one of the new Sida, who would drain his blood until he was only a husk.

She put down the clay dish she was washing in the sand near the riverbank where they had camped.

The man looked up. "Saaral?"

She didn't speak, but crouched down in front of him. She lifted a hand to his temple, tracing the silver she saw there as her eyes dipped to his neck.

"What do you want, Saaral? You know that Kuluun told the men not to touch you without his permission." A small smile lifted the corner of his mouth. "Are you trying to get me in trouble?"

Saaral still said nothing. She never did. As far as most of the men knew, she was mute. Kuluun was the only one who had heard her speak because he forced her to ask him for her nightly ration of pony blood. He liked to hear her beg, and blood was the only thing Saaral would beg for.

But now, she wondered why.

Why beg, when she could simply take it? She might not have been strong for a Sida, but she was still far stronger than the humans. There was no one around to see. Neither Kuluun nor his brothers was even close.

She leaned forward in a crouch, letting her senses absorb the delicious scent of fresh human blood. Her fangs were already down, aching to bite.

"Saaral?"

She wished he would be quiet. She had no desire to hear

him talk. Or cry. Slowly, she brought her eyes to his. Then she put a finger over his lips and whispered, "Tssssshhhh."

The rough sound left her mouth like a hiss. The human's eyes widened for a moment, and he opened his mouth to speak. Saaral clenched her hand around the nape of the man's neck, and she felt it.

Like a current of air, her will caught his and held.

Quiet.

She thought it, and the man fell silent. His watery gaze was locked on hers.

Interesting.

Give me your neck.

He leaned forward, offering up the wrinkled skin to her mouth. Saaral bent and took.

As the rich blood hit her tongue, the human arched his back and let out a grunt of pleasure.

She pulled her mouth away and scowled. She had no desire to please him. Had this human cared about pleasing her when he'd used her body like a vessel? Her hand tightened on his neck as she remembered the terror of her first years in the camp. The man's grunts of pleasure turned into whines of pain. His mouth dropped open, so Saaral sent the thought again.

Quiet.

He said nothing, frozen in fear. She took his neck again, taking gulps of blood fresh from his body. Live blood. She could feel her body grow strong as the old man grew weak. Her energy mounted. Her senses came alive. She could feel tiny currents of air teasing her skin. Her hair. The night wind caressed her body with eager fingers. Her skin grew flush and pink as she drank.

The human's heartbeat slowed.

Then stopped.

Saaral looked down in disgust. Surely he had more blood than that! Her hungry eyes swept the creek bed, only to see that none of the other humans was about. In the back of her mind, she knew Kuluun would not be pleased, but she ignored the fear for a moment, reveling in the rush of energy and strength. For a moment, her toes left the ground, and something she thought might be laughter bubbled in her chest.

Then her feet came back to earth, and she cocked her head, considering the lifeless human body that lay in the dirt. She bent down and threw it over her shoulder. Jumping easily across the stream, she worked her way back into the brush where the branches of the trees grew thick and no goats could graze. Then she found a small clearing and stopped. She tossed the old man's body to the ground and began to dig.

In a few minutes, the hole was deep. Saaral barely felt the exertion. She kicked the body into the hole and buried it, brushing the earth from her hands as she stood.

Then, she calmly walked back to camp. For a moment, she considered walking away as she did every night, but where would she go that Kuluun would not find her? He told her every night.

"If you leave, I will fly out and find you. Send one of my sons in every direction until they track you down and drag you back. Then I will bind you in my tent every night. I will bury you when you sleep, so you wake with the earth in your mouth."

If there was any threat that Saaral feared, it was waking with the earth in her mouth. It struck a primal fear into her that bordered on madness. She froze even at the thought, and Kuluun knew this.

But as she crossed the river, she saw him. His glare chilled the blood in her stomach, and she suddenly felt like vomiting up every drop of blood she'd taken. He knew. He would be able to see her energy. See the flush in her face. See the life in her eyes.

In the blink of an eye, Saaral ran.

She ducked back into the copse of trees, darting this way

and that, running under the branches where the monsters could not sweep down from above. But in too short a time, the trees ran out and she faced a broad meadow. She could hear them behind her, the humans crashing through the brush, the swirl of Sida above. She had nowhere to turn. Going back into the brush put her in the path of the humans. Going forward put her at the mercy of Kuluun.

She felt her fangs drop, and she ran into the meadow.

Perhaps, the blood of the old man would make her strong enough.

Perhaps, she would make the distant stand of trees that promised shelter.

Perhaps—

"I told you, Saaral."

He grabbed her by the hair.

"No!" she screamed, her voice rang thought the cool night air. "Let me go!"

Kuluun swept her up, jerking her closer as she struggled against his hold. She tried to reach for the blade at his waist to cut off her long braid and release herself, but she couldn't reach. He saw her trying for the knife and backhanded her, causing her vision to blacken and stars to flash at the edges of her vision.

"I told you."

"Just let me go." She twisted and fought, desperate as she hadn't been since the first night she'd been taken. "Please, Kuluun," she begged. "Let me—"

He cut her off and pulled her to his face, baring his teeth and hissing in her face. "You are mine. You do what I tell you. You drink what I give you. And you will not forget it again."

Then Kuluun shook her so hard, her brain rattled and she heard the bones in her spine crack. Her body fell dead as she lost the feeling from her neck down. Her limbs hung loose, flapping in the cold wind as Kuluun circled and turned back to the camp.

She stared helplessly at the stars, letting her mind go blank.

Dark.

Quiet.

In the blackness, her senses clarified.

Everything in her stilled. She focused on one sensation.

One thought.

She enjoyed the feeling of the wind in her hair.

SAARAL WOKE with the earth in her mouth and a burning hunger in her belly.

She tried to scream. She tried to struggle. But as she desperately dug her way to what she thought was the surface, a hand plunged into the earth and grabbed her neck. It twisted until her spine cracked again, and she lost the ability to move. Then she lay still and terrified in the darkness as distant voices walked away from her, leaving her alone.

She panted, the dust creeping into her lungs until she was forced to close her mouth. Forced to stop breathing. She lay in the silent earth, unable to move as her body, starved of fresh blood, slowly repaired itself.

Hours later, the voices approached again, but they did not come close. She could hear the screams of human captives. She heard children crying and men laughing. The humans had gone on a raiding party that day, and Saaral recognized the sounds of fresh slaughter. Her throat burned in hunger, but she had no relief. Little by little, the feeling returned to her legs.

She felt a hand reach down for her, testing to make sure she remained in her living grave. Then it withdrew, and she was alone again.

She closed her eyes and tried to imagine the wind.

Nights passed.

Weeks.

Months.

Saaral woke every night with the earth in her mouth. She did not move. She no longer struggled. She never spoke. She left her body, watching from above as Kuluun, Suk, or Odval checked her each night, sometimes giving her pony blood to keep her alive, sometimes giving her nothing. Always twisting her neck so she was captive to her own useless body as they had made her captive to the earth.

And she watched from above as they dug her out, raped her, then buried her again.

As the months went by, she watched more often from away, leaving the prison of Saaral's body and drifting above, rising out of the tent and into the skies above until she was part of the darkness. The moon spoke to her. The stars embraced her. The night wind whispered its secrets as her seasons in the earth passed.

By the time Kuluun dug her out of the ground, Saraal had become nothing.

3

THE MADNESS

Saaral watched her flit around the tent as Odval painted between her legs. The laughing creature pointed silently, mimicking the look of pained pleasure the Sida wore as he found his release.

"Ungh, Saaral," Odval said. "So tight. Not like the humans."

Odval was so hairy, Saaral wondered whether he'd needed to wear clothes when he was human. Perhaps he had run naked like a pony. He had that much hair.

"Give me your neck."

Wordlessly, she tilted her head back. Then the laughing creature's eyes flashed with rage, and she drew a hand across her throat, glaring at Odval as he took her blood.

Saaral lay silent and weak on the floor of the tent. Odval tied his trousers and lifted the tent flap, but not before tossing a skin of pony blood toward her. It lay in the dust. Saaral stared at it, wanting to reach for it, but not giving Odval the satisfaction of seeing her eat.

Saraal would let no one watch her drink. No one but the laughing creature who followed her around the camp.

She had come to Saraal soon after Kuluun finally pulled her from the earth. Saaral did not know how long she had been buried, though she knew they had moved many times. Those flights were her only sliver of life. When Kuluun or one of his brothers would carry her still body in the air as they moved camp, she would feel, for a brief moment, the wind in her hair. She had glimpsed the laughing creature on one of those flights. Saw the corner of her grey eye peeking from behind a cloud. Then she was gone.

She'd appeared again in the moonlight, creeping into camp to sit next to Saaral as she washed clothes in a stream. It looked like a girl around her own age, but Saraal was suspicious. No one else reacted to her, though. They ignored the creature just as they ignored Saraal.

It followed her everywhere. Through the tents. By the cooking fires. She even hovered in the corner of the tent when Kuluun or one of his brothers rutted with her, making faces or looking bored. At first, Saraal was afraid. Afraid that the laughing girl would be captured as she had been. Eventually, she realized that no one saw the creature but her.

She must have been an older Sida because she could fly. She hung in the air and swooped like a joyful bird. One night, Saaral began to talk to her as she washed the clay cooking pots in the sand.

"What is your name?"

"My name?" The creature looked confused for a moment, then she looked up at the full moon. "You can call me Aday."

It was a name from her human language, and it made Saraal smile. "You're a Sida like me."

"Yes." Aday's smile grew wide. "And no."

"What do you mean? Why can no one can see you except me?"

"Can't they?"

"You know they can't. That's why you mock them."

Aday didn't respond; she flew up in the air when Kuluun approached Saraal, towering over her.

"Who are you talking to, Saraal?"

Saraal put on the dead expression she wore for him. "No one."

Aday came back, hovering behind Kuluun and mimicking his angry stance, hands on her hips and eyes narrowed in anger. Saraal saw her, and an unexpected laugh left her throat.

"What is wrong with you?" Kuluun asked. "You don't speak to anyone but me."

Then Aday began to sing, though Kuluun ignored her.

"Not true, not true!" Aday's voice floated in the wind. "She talks to me, you old goat."

Saraal felt it again, a burst of laughter so high and clear she thought it must be coming from someone else. Kuluun backhanded her. But Saraal didn't stop laughing because Aday kept singing.

"Old goat! Hairless goat! Do your balls drag behind you, old goat?"

Kuluun glared at the laughing Saraal. "What is wrong with you? Disgusting bitch."

"*She's* disgusting?" Aday flew over and hovered in front of Kuluun, but he paid her no attention. "Do you like it when the other goats lick your sagging balls, Kuluun? They must get so dirty in the pony shit."

Saraal couldn't stop laughing. Tears came out of her eyes. She didn't even feel it when Kuluun's fist connected with her jaw. The pain was inconsequential. The joy of hearing Aday insult Kuluun made any pain he inflicted a pleasure.

Suk must have heard Saraal's peals of laughter because he

wandered over and pulled Kuluun's arm back, stopping him from hitting her more.

"What's wrong with you? It's my turn with her tonight. And I'm tired of fucking a dead thing. Leave her alone, Kuluun."

The glowering Sida wiped spittle from his mouth, his fangs cutting the back of his hand before he swung at his brother. "Shut up, you stupid shit, or you'll get no turn with my woman tonight. She's mine to do with as I like."

Suk cocked his head, watching Saaral, who was still giggling on the ground.

"What is wrong with her?"

"I don't know." Kuluun kicked her, but Saraal just rolled in the sand, laughing.

"She's mad. You've made her mad with your stupid punishment. I told you. She'll be no good to anyone now."

Odval wandered over. "At least she's laughing. Maybe she'll be a better fuck now that she's mad."

"I doubt it."

Odval shrugged. "I don't care. I'll take her if you don't want her anymore."

Kuluun punched his brother. "She's mine. You get a turn with her when I say so."

"Fine," Suk said, pulling Odval away before the brothers began fighting again. Saraal just watched them from the ground, smiling when she caught Aday behind them making rude gestures. Soon enough, the brothers wandered away, and she began washing the cooking pots again.

Some of the human women who belonged to the other Sida wandered over to do their chores alongside her, but no one spoke to Saraal.

The human women the Sida collected—those they didn't kill right away—thought of her as a mute. She wasn't human so she couldn't be trusted. But they knew she was a captive too, so she wasn't respected. They treated her with fearful disdain. There was no friendly chatter as the women did their chores, like Saraal faintly remembered from her human life.

The brothers had made many children over the years. Saraal would guess there were over fifty of them. Maybe more. But none was very strong. Not like Kuluun, Suk, and Odval had been. And the brothers were growing weaker. Saraal could sense it. Like water sapping from a leaky skin, every time one of the brothers sired another child, their strength depleted. She wondered what their own sire would think of it, but then she never saw him. He was only a rumor, like the sun.

As if reading her mind, Aday came to sit across from her.

"Who is their master?"

"Kuluun and his brothers?"

"Yes."

"They call him Jun. I never see him. Only once, when he made me."

"What do you remember of him?"

She thought back to that night, but the memory had become more and more hazy as the years passed.

"He was frightening."

Aday glanced around at the human women, who were staring at Saraal. She hissed like a snake, but the humans paid no attention.

Then she asked, "Do you think Jun keeps women, too?"

"I don't know."

"How many other children does he have? Many? Like Kuluun and his brothers?"

"I don't know."

"You don't know much."

Saraal shrugged, oddly hurt by the insult from the laughing creature. "I don't ask questions."

The women stood and walked away from her, moving downstream, though they kept their eyes on Saraal. She bared her fangs and they sneered. They also walked faster.

"You *should* ask questions," Aday said. "You never know what they might answer if you do."

"Why does it matter?"

Aday floated to her, curling around so that she could whisper in Saraal's ear.

"If you don't know how many there are, you don't know how many you'll have to kill..."

"I can't."

"You can." Aday floated above her as Saraal washed her clothes in the creek. She was wearing Suk's cast-offs, which were huge on her, but not as bad as Kuluun's or Odval's. "Why couldn't you?"

"I'm not strong enough."

"Not yet." Aday swooped down and hovered over the running stream, her long hair floating in the breeze, lifted by unseen currents. Saraal stared at her longingly. What would it be like to fly? To soar over the earth and feel the wind holding her body as a mother carried a child?

For a moment, she hated Aday. Then the moment passed and she thought about what the other woman had said.

"I'm not strong enough because I only drink pony blood. The others drink from the humans they capture."

"And why do you drink what they give you, Saraal?" Aday's grey eyes were playful. "You took from the vein once. Don't you remember?" The woman's seductive voice whispered, "How sweet was the blood on your tongue? Do you remember how it made you strong? You could join me, you know..." Aday did a slow flip in the moonlight. "You're older than most of them now. And you could be stronger. If you drank enough from the humans, you would fly, too."

A chill wrapped itself around her heart. "And if Kuluun saw it. He would break me."

Until I become nothing again.

"You're not nothing," Aday hissed.

"I am."

"You're not."

"I'm—"

"Not!" Aday sang out, swinging her body up over the water, dipping a hand in the current. "Not, not, not!" she sang some more. "You are mighty, my girl. A warrior in slave's clothing. A wolf hiding in the brush."

She hummed an old song Saraal thought she remembered her grandmother singing when she was a child. How the laughing girl knew it, she had no idea. They were many mountains away from her tribe. So many seasons had passed that her son would be old.

If he'd lived.

"Go away, Aday." The thought of her green-eyed boy pulled forgotten sorrow from her chest. "I'm tired of you tonight."

Without a whisper, the flying woman disappeared, and Saraal looked up to see two human women watching her, their eyes wide and frightened. She bared her fangs. It was easy to frighten the humans, and she didn't like their company anyway. They were more fearful than sheep.

She plunged her hands back into the freezing water. It was spring. Thin shoots of grass fought their way up from the earth, only to be ripped up as the animals fed. The water ran clear and ice-cold from the mountains.

It would take many hours for her clothes to dry. They might not even be done by the next night. No matter. She didn't feel the cold. Often, Saraal wondered why she wore clothes at all.

Then she would catch a glimpse of one of the human captives, who were tossed naked into piles as they were drained. Like stacks of wood. Jumbled pottery shards. Waste. Their clothes were gone. Wool was not wasted on the dead. Then Saraal would wrap her torn clothing around her more tightly and shove the image from her mind.

She bent over, and her braid dipped in the water. There was a flash of memory, as the stream gripped her hair, pulling it.

"No! Let me go!"

Kuluun grabbing her hair, yanking it as he captured her, dragging her into the darkness.

The water swirled around the long braid. A stick caught in it as she stared.

A new leaf.

Saraal could see quicksilver fish dart to the surface, cautiously testing the black threads that hung in the water like some alien weed, then darting back into the shadows.

How long had she looked into the dark water? She stared at her reflection, the glittering sweep of stars behind her head. The black night beyond.

Nothing.

Saraal let herself absorb the dark sky as she felt her body dissolve, until the stars shone through her and not around. Her hair—that loathsome rope that had bound her to her captor—drifted in front of the vision, marring her view of the sky.

She sat back on her heels, searching the camp.

Kuluun was drinking from a human at the edge of the fire, four of his sons surrounding him. They hoped for his cast-offs. Usually, Kuluun would let them feed after him. If there was any blood left.

Odval was in the corner, fucking a human woman who no

longer cried. He'd kept her for almost a week. The woman's eyes were dead. He would drain her blood soon. Saraal felt relief on her behalf. Odval had no gentleness in him.

Various other Sida strolled around the camp. Some drinking. Some fighting. Others polishing weapons or saddles, since most of them still rode the ponies they stole from the humans. They weren't strong enough to fly.

Saraal's eyes finally fell on Suk. He was leaning against a rock, sharpening his bronze sword on a black rock they'd found in a human's bag. It was smooth, and when you wetted it, was excellent for sharpening blades.

She walked toward him, feeling bold.

"Saraal." He eyed her. Suk was not as dumb as Kuluun; he wasn't as powerful, either. But if there were any kind of challenge to the leadership of the tribe, it would be Suk and his keen eyes. He saw far more than his brothers.

"What do you want, Saraal?"

She was silent, eyeing his sword.

"Did your invisible friend leave?" He looked amused. "You're not talking right now?"

She held out her hand toward the blade.

"No." He looked around and tossed a sharp-sided stone toward her. "Use this."

She ignored the rock that hit her chest and kept her hand out, eyes on the bronze.

"No, Saraal."

She sat down across from him, saying nothing.

Suk continued sharpening the blade on the wet rock, dipping it into a jar of water when it dried. He studiously ignored her.

Scrape. Turn. *Scrape.* Turn.

The metal caught the edges of the cooking fire the humans tended.

Scrape. Scrape. Scrape.

Suk sat back and sighed. "You really want my sword, don't you?"

She said nothing but thrust her hand toward the blade again.

"For what? You're not going to try to kill yourself again, are you? You know it doesn't work."

Saraal narrowed her eyes, still not speaking.

Finally, Suk shrugged and held out the sword.

"Fine. But don't mar your face. You're in my tent tonight, and I don't want to find extra blood for you because you're healing."

Saraal didn't even stand up. She sat across from Suk, eyes on the ground, holding the blade in her hands. Then she reached back, grabbed onto her braid, and cut.

The sharpening stone worked. The sword sliced through her think shank of hair with ease. Saraal immediately let out a sigh of relief, then she brought the blade back to her head and cut again.

Over and over, she grabbed fistfuls of her thick black hair, cutting it as close to the scalp as she could.

She left nothing to grab.

As she lifted the piece behind her ear, she felt it—just for a second—her son's tiny fingers twisting in the black strands as he nursed from her breast. Then the bronze blade sliced through the last of the girl's hair, and he was gone.

WHEN THE WARM SEASONS PASSED, the flying girl did not leave Saraal. And despite her misgivings, she began to trust her appearance. It was never predictable. Aday would alight on the top of a tent as Saraal passed by on her way to whatever stream, creek, or lake they were camped near. She could keep Saraal company on long nights when the others ignored her. She didn't question it when they began having conversations, though Saraal was always cautious what she said.

No matter how Aday coaxed her to rebellion, Saraal was resolute. This was the fate she had been granted. She would exist for as long as she existed. And perhaps, if death finally found her, her ancestors would be pleased. Or if not pleased, they would at least grant her rest.

Rest was all she longed for.

Some nights, Saraal thought she could lay for a thousand years, staring at the sky and listening to the wind. The night was her blanket. The stars, her family. They wrapped her in their precious silent glow, even when the camp erupted in violence around her.

"Psst!" Aday hissed in her ear. "Go! Run now!"

Saraal blinked and let her eyes come back into focus. She was laying on the edge of the camp, hidden behind some rocks as the other Sida feasted on the humans from a village they had ravaged. They were becoming more and more violent as their numbers grew. Fewer captives were allowed to live. Whole villages were being wiped out. For some reason, Saraal knew this was wrong. Some instinct from her human life told her so, but she pushed back the feeling and turned her eyes back into the night. She didn't care about the humans. Why should their lives be any easier than hers?

"Saraal! You stupid girl! Where are you?"

She heard Odval's voice drift on the wind. He was quiet, trying to remain quiet, anyway. She didn't respond, but she didn't move, either. Aday stayed with her, crouched on the top of the rocky outcropping, watching Odval approach with narrow eyes.

"There you are."

He said nothing else, pulling her by the ankle until she was away from the rocks. Then he shoved up her tunic and began to untie his trousers. "The human women die too fast."

Aday sneered. "And you care if they're dead?"

Saraal only turned her face to the side and stared at the stars. At least she could still see them; Odval hadn't pulled her into the tents. She no longer allowed herself to wince when they raped her. She felt the pain each time, because her body renewed itself with every sleep. Her skin would bruise and mottle, but in minutes, the marks would be gone. Her flesh would tear if they were too rough—as Odval usually was—but by the next night, her body bore no trace.

She lay still and stared into blackness while he fucked her.

Aday appeared, hovering over Odval's shoulder, as if she was perched on his back. Then she rolled off and lay next to Saraal. Reaching out a tentative hand, the girl squeezed her cold fingers. Then she rolled to her side and met Saraal's eyes.

Her fangs ran down, and Saraal realized, for the first time, that Aday's fangs were beautiful. Curved like tiny twin blades. Delicate. Like a hawk's claws, they curved back into her mouth.

Saraal lifted a hand and let one finger run down the girl's fangs. She felt Aday's lips move.

"Kill him, Saraal."

Odval grunted and groaned. He was almost done. Finally.

"I can't."

"Yes. When he leans down to take your blood. You must strike first; he won't be expecting it. Strike first and bite him. Drain his blood. It is older than yours. Powerful. Drink and be strong. Then you will kill him."

"Sida cannot be killed."

"You know they can. You've seen Kuluun kill the younger ones. You know how."

"I can't—"

"You will take this." Aday's hand ran down Saraal's side to the dagger that she had concealed beneath her breasts. It was a bronze blade, like Suk carried, but shorter. She had found it among the bodies while she was scavenging. She knew she shouldn't have kept it—Kuluun would be very angry —but Aday has teased and coaxed until Saraal had hidden it away.

"You will take this, my girl, and you will kill Odval. Slice the back of his neck. Sever his spine, then drink every drop of his blood. When you are finished, you must cut off his head."

As Aday spoke, Saraal could see the blood-soaked vision. It tempted her. She could scent the blood in her nose. Feel the rich syrup on her lips.

Saraal reached for the dagger. Or Aday did. She didn't know anymore. She felt the girl's hand close over her own.

"Good, Saraal," Odval rasped. "*Ungh.*"

They pulled the dagger from its sheath as Odval neared his release. His eyes were closed, lost in his own pleasure.

"Give me your neck," he said. "I want to drink."

"Don't let him," Aday whispered. "Do it now. Reach up and—"

"Yes!"

Saraal hadn't ever moved so fast, not even when she was running from Kuluun. Odval was still spilling inside her when she grabbed his hair and pulled his head forward, plunging her fangs in his neck as her dagger sliced across the back of his neck.

"*Aaaargh!*" Odval's inhuman scream shattered the night. But there were too many screams that night. The village was being systematically massacred around the fire as the Sida roared and laughed and feasted.

His legs stilled as she took great, gulping mouthfuls of his blood. Only a strangled whine came from his throat. No one would hear them at the edge of the camp.

"Good," Aday whispered. "Very good. How does his blood taste?"

So sweet, she wanted to weep. It was sweeter than human blood, sweeter even than the child she'd killed her first night. Odval's blood should have tasted like piss and dirt and pony shit, but it didn't. The Sida's blood held none of the filth of his personality. It was the most delicious nectar to ever pass her lips.

"Saraa—*gghhll...*" Odval choked as the lifeblood poured from his body. Saraal tugged his head to the side and met his mouth in a murderous kiss, biting off his tongue and spitting it out before she sucked the blood that he tried to cough up.

So much blood.

It filled her. Fed her. Saraal felt as if she would drift away from the earth as she took it, but Aday lay at her back, curling around her body and crooning her approval as Saraal drained Odval.

Finally, when he lay still, she pushed his body away, shoving her tunic down until she was covered. She ripped the sleeve from his shirt and wiped his bloody seed from her legs, then kicked at his lifeless legs when she stood.

Saraal took a deep breath and looked up. The stars were brighter now. The sounds from the camp clear and clanging in the cold air. The other Sida were fighting. It would last until dawn as each warrior tried to prove himself the strongest. She let her eyes drift down to Odval, who lay weak and silent at her feet.

She knelt beside the once mighty giant, licking his cheek where a dribble of blood had escaped. Then she spoke directly to him for the first time, and her voice was low and smooth, resonant in her own ears.

"What should I do with you, Odval?"

He said nothing.

"Perhaps I should bury you like this and dig you out

tomorrow night, break your neck again, so you can't move. Maybe you'll have more blood to give me then."

A high whine.

"No?" She lay her cold cheek against his and spoke in his ear. "I should do that, Odval. Perhaps it is *your* fate."

Aday lay in the grass next to Odval, her hands folded casually behind her head. "I think you should find a human even bigger than him to rape *him* every night. I think he would like that."

"No..." Saraal whispered, her mind suddenly clear. Aday was right.

She *could* kill them all.

"I don't want to drag him with me. He's so big and ugly." She sat cross legged in the grass and cocked her head at Odval, who watched her with silent, panicked eyes. "What will happen when I cut off his head?"

Aday sat across from her and shrugged. "I don't know. He'll die. You've seen how Kuluun does it. Just leave his body somewhere the others won't find it. Won't it burn up in the sun?"

"Of course."

Saraal rolled Odval to his stomach and began cutting the hair at his neck and tearing his clothes to expose his skin. "Do you remember?" she asked the silent monster. "Do you remember how you liked to take me this way when you kept me in the ground? I wouldn't even be awake from my day rest when you'd dig me out, Odval. Then you'd shove my face in the dirt and fuck me like this, so I woke with dirt in my mouth and dirt in my cunt." She leaned forward, shoving his face in the rocks and dust. "Have some dirt before you die, Odval. You do not deserve a warrior's death."

His skin was pale and bloodless from her feast. It didn't even bleed when she began to cut. His body spasmed for a few moments, then he was still as she finished, hacking at his head until it rolled from his body. Saraal sat back and smiled.

Aday sat next to her and held her hand.

"You need a better sword. How do you feel?"

Saraal felt her body float slightly off the ground. Her smile grew wider.

"Strong," she said. "I feel strong."

4

THE FIRE

No one ever asked about Odval.

After his death, Kuluun eyed her with suspicion, but Saraal knew he didn't mind that one of his brothers—who were really his rivals—had disappeared.

Suk, however, wasn't pleased. He treated her more harshly than he had before, and he never allowed her to spend the day in his tent.

The brothers had moved north again, following the warm weather to more heavily populated areas along the hunting routes. They moved at night, and their ferocity did not cease.

Villages were emptied, then burned. It was a waste, she thought, to destroy the hard work of the humans. Stupid. But then, Kuluun was never all that bright, and now he had a cheering group of sons who all praised him, no matter what he did. Odval's children had given their loyalty to Kuluun, as well. And Suk had never sired as many children as the others. More and more frequently, Saraal would see him keeping his own company with his dozen or so sons and the humans they had collected.

Saraal also kept to herself, with Aday's more silent presence keeping watch. She tended her own meager belongings. She serviced whichever brother shoved her into a tent. She didn't speak to anyone except Aday anymore.

She had also started drinking human blood.

"You can make them forget," Aday whispered to her one night, months ago.

"What?"

"Do you remember the human you killed? So long ago, before Kuluun put you in the earth. Do you remember?"

How did Aday know about that? Saraal had never told her. She avoided the memory, instinctively shying away from something that had felt so good, then gone so wrong.

"I don't—"

"You can force your will on them. The humans." Aday slid closer as they sat beside the cooking fire. "You've seen Kuluun do it. Suk does it all the time. You have only to touch them, and you can control them, my girl."

She remembered. She remembered the human falling silent. She'd thought it, then he had done it. She'd felt the trickle of energy leave her and go into him. The same pricking heat that ran over her skin now when the wind stroked her.

It had woken after Odval, like a long-forgotten friend. After she'd taken his blood, the wind came to her more. It wrapped around her and held her. She had only to stand in its bracing power to feel her body strengthen. At one point, she'd even experimented with hovering off the ground. But as time passed, her new friend grew quieter. She could no longer hover.

Saraal was not surprised by this. She had become accustomed to disappointment.

"You must drink from the humans to be strong. Then the wind will be at your command, as it is for Kuluun."

"How do you know?" Saraal asked.

"I know." Aday's grey eyes were lit with mischief. "And you do, too."

She did.

Saraal tilted her head and listened to the camp. It was a relatively quiet night. A few women were busy around the cooking fire, and the others were entertaining the Sida.

"That one," Aday whispered, nudging Saraal's side. "Drink from that one."

'That one' was a fat old human Kuluun had decided to spoil. She must have been someone important in her village because she had immediately began ordering the other women around once she'd been captured. Kuluun doted on her as if she was one of the wild dog puppies that followed their wandering tribe. She slapped and intimidated the other women into doing what she wanted. She ignored Saraal.

"I don't think she would taste very good," Saraal said with a shrug. "She has to taste dirty since she fucks Kuluun and seems to like it."

Aday rolled on the ground with laughter, but still managed to say, "Just look at her, though. So fat. He gives her the best meat. She has plenty of blood to spare."

The woman walked past her, carrying a bowl of stew. No doubt she was heading toward Kuluun. Though Saraal and the other Sida didn't need food to survive—she'd learned that when she was in the earth and given nothing more than pony blood—they did eat some. An empty stomach triggered the same pains in a Sida belly as a human one. Luckily, a small meal lasted long in their stomach; Saraal relieved herself only rarely.

But she enjoyed food, and she wanted some of the stew. More, she wanted some of Kuluun's woman's blood. Aday was right; it would be rich. The woman was plump with life, like the berries she remembered once grew along the riverbanks near her village. In the summer, they swelled fat and red like the woman's cheeks.

Saraal caught the woman's eyes and held out a hand. Sneering, the woman came closer.

"What do you want, Saraal?" The human knew not to ignore her completely, as Saraal suspected everyone knew what had really happened to Odval.

She held out a hand, and the human huffed out a sigh. "This is for Kuluun. Tell one of the others to get a bowl for you." Then she curled her lip. "I'll allow it, even though it is my own meal."

"She eats the meat of a razed village and boasts," Aday said. "Maybe you *should* kill her."

Saraal shook her head, the ghost of a smile turning up her mouth.

The human's eyes widened and she stepped back, but Saraal was too fast.

One touch.

That was all it took, and she felt the faint energy leave the tips of her fingers, which were banded around the woman's wrist. The energy wound up the arm, the neck, until it grasped the woman's mind like a viper and sank its teeth to hold on.

"Should I tell her to come back?" Saraal asked Aday.

"No. He will know you hold her mind. Do it now."

Bend down and give me your neck.

"Wait. Take her behind the tent," Aday said softly. "You don't want the others to tell Kuluun."

Saraal stood and took the woman to an empty tent. Then she gave the command again.

Give me your neck.

Wordlessly, she tilted her head back and Saraal felt her fangs grow long. They pricked her own tongue before she folded herself down and sank her teeth into the soft neck of the human.

441

Bliss.

It wasn't as sweet as Odval's blood, nor as rich, but the human's blood was pure and clear, like water from a spring stream. She drank in, not thinking until she felt a hand on her shoulder. It was Aday.

"Not too much," she whispered. "Now heal her neck and tell her to forget."

"How do I heal—"

"Think, Saraal. What heals you if you have a cut?"

Her own blood. It was something she'd learned accidentally after Kuluun had beaten her bloody. The areas where her blood trickled into her wounds closed faster. Saraal pricked her finger with a fang and spread the red blood over the bite marks in the human's neck.

Within minutes, they were closed.

"Now, tell her to forget." Aday's voice sounded bossy to her ears.

Saraal stood up and met her eyes. "I know what to do, Aday."

"Do you?"

She glared at Aday and turned to the woman, tugging on the thread that connected them.

Forget this. Forget the tent. Forget my bite. You're back at the cooking fire and taking a bowl of stew to Kuluun.

She thought that would work. If it didn't, she'd find out soon enough.

The human ducked out of the tent and Saraal heard her scurry away. Her ears were open. Her eyes took in every corner of the dark tent, which belonged to one of Suk's older children.

She inhaled deeply and escaped into the night.

"How do you feel?" Aday asked, as they walked along the dark edge of the camp.

"Good."

"Only good?"

Saraal shrugged. "Good is enough."

"No, it's not." Angry fire lit Aday's eyes. "Good is never enough. Nothing is enough for you. This starts tonight."

"What are you talking about?" Saraal was annoyed and wanted to remain unnoticed for a while. As much as the other Sida were avoiding her, she still didn't want to court Kuluun's wrath.

"What am I talking about?" Aday was grinning like a madwoman, her curling fangs and cloudy eyes alight with humor. "You're walking on air now, my girl. And you're not going to stop."

"I KNOW... YOU'RE... DRINKING... IT!" Each pause was punctuated by a fist as Kuluun straddled her, holding her to the ground as her ears rung and her eyes swam. "I saw you flying. I smell you on her!"

Flying was probably an exaggeration. The most she could do was hover. But Saraal had no doubt that Kuluun could smell her on his human, who became very affectionate when she was bitten. Who knew it could be a pleasurable experience for humans? Saraal found the touching distasteful. She only humored the woman because she enjoyed the blood. Unfortunately, it was the woman's moan of pleasure that alerted Kuluun to Saraal's drinking. Or at least, confirmed it. He'd grabbed her from her tent as she woke and taken her to his.

Kuluun's fist caught Saraal under her ear, and she felt a trickle of blood leak out. She'd have to drink extra later. If she was still conscious.

But she wasn't going to stop drinking.

"Ungrateful bitch! I should have killed you years ago."

How was Kuluun still so strong? With all the children he'd sired, he should be weak. Saraal guessed it was a combination of brute force, blood gluttony, and pure hate. It occurred to Saraal that he was so enraged, he might actually kill her. If he took off her head...

"And if you think I don't know what you did to—"

He broke off when he heard the sound of pony hooves in the distance. Saraal heard them, too. In fact, she'd heard them before Kuluun did.

Interesting.

The humans were in camp that night. They'd taken a village during the day, and they were enjoying the spoils that night. Cooking fires roasted fat spits of meat. Sida laughed and women cried. No one should be approaching the warriors' camp that night. No one should have been coming that fast. No one—

Kuluun muttered a curse and stood. There were cries of surprise. Then cries of pain. Kuluun left the tent in a blur.

Saraal curled into herself and stared into the shadows. Aday came to rest beside her, stroking her back.

"Not long now." She stroked Saraal's messy cap of hair. "Soon, you'll be strong enough to kill him."

Saraal said nothing. Her mouth was swollen, but already healing. She felt two teeth come loose as the new ones grew in behind them. She'd lost so many teeth over the years from the brothers' fists, she was surprised her body still produced them. Luckily, her fangs were rooted. She'd still be able to feed.

The sounds outside the tent were chaotic for a few minutes —ponies snorting, humans crying, grunts and the metallic clang of weapons. Then, it died down and there was silence.

"What is happening?" Saraal quietly asked.

"I don't know."

"That sounded like fighting."

"It was. You should get up," Aday said. "Leave."

"I... I'm sore. I'll just wait a few moments."

"Leave, Saraal."

Aday's voice was growing panicked, but Saraal's eyelids were starting to droop.

"In a minute. Promise..."

It happened occasionally. If she bled too much, her body would shut down and repair itself in sleep. She always woke the next day with barely a bruise, no matter how violent the beating. She could feel her tongue grow thick, her eyelids droop.

"Leave! Leave now!"

"Can't. Can't..." She remembered a rhyme her mother taught her. It was a playful song she was supposed to sing when she was hurt. To distract herself from the pain. So much pain...

"Saraal, you must get up. Wake up. Run now!"

She was drifting. She should get back to her tent. Back to safety...

"RUN!"

Why was Aday so loud?

Saraal gasped awake when someone grabbed her neck and pulled her up. Her eyes flew open at the clash of scents.

"What is this?" There was a commotion outside the tent, then the whole low structure was torn away and Saraal was tossed in the air.

Aday was screaming and flying in circles over her head. The creature was enraged.

"No! *No no no no no!*"

Saraal could do nothing, bloody and broken, she hadn't had time to heal. Hadn't had time to plan. She landed in a pair of burly arms. Who held her? She had no idea, though there was something oddly familiar about his scent.

"What is this creature?"

"We found her in your brother's tent. She was talking to herself."

445

"Why would a human..." There was a long pause, then whoever held her yanked her back by the hair. He cursed. "I thought it was a boy. She didn't used to look like this."

"What should we do with her, Temur?"

Silence. Saraal forced her eyes open, only to find herself looking into a pair of black eyes. Demon eyes. They flared red with fire.

But no...

No, it was only a reflection of the fire burning through the camp. She could smell the smoke. She blinked and her eyes cleared. The dark eyes still stared.

"She's one of us. Sida."

"A female?"

The man grunted. "Kuluun said he wanted a wife, as he'd had when he was human. A mate who would be like him."

Saraal started to laugh. High, hysterical laughter burst from her bloody lips. Her belly shook with it. The pain tore through her, but she couldn't stop laughing. The men kept talking over her laughter.

"What have they done to her?"

"A better question might be, what *haven't* they done?"

One of them threw her over a shoulder and started walking. Saraal kept laughing as Aday flew behind, hovering and scowling at the two men as they talked.

"She's mad."

"Clearly."

"Should we just kill her now? It would probably be a mercy."

"No. She's a child of Jun."

"Directly sired?" Saraal stopped laughing at the surprise in the man's voice. Was it so unusual for Jun to sire children?

"Yes. My father turned her himself."

The other man let out what sounded like a curse, but in a

language Saraal didn't recognize.

"I know," the man carrying Saraal said. "Kuluun has always been stupid."

"What a waste."

"Well…" The two men stopped at a tent. Saraal could see it through one swollen eye, which was also aching, trying to heal. The tent wasn't like others she knew. It was round, stretched skins wrapped tightly around stakes driven into the ground. It was so tall that a man could walk upright under it. The roof was rapidly taking shape as humans bustled around, setting up camp in a familiar rhythm. The roof was made of more skins and blankets. Richly woven and heavy, they would keep out even the smallest sliver of light. The tent flap was thrown open and a human woman stepped out.

"Tend to her," the man carrying her said. He stepped inside the tent and put Saraal on the ground. "Wash her and find some new clothes. She won't need much to heal, just some blood. You or one of the girls may give it to her. She is a child of Jun."

The human nodded with respect. "I will feed her my own blood, Master."

Aday lay next to her and stroked her back. Saraal sighed and said, "Should I run now, Aday?"

"I don't know."

"Tell me if I need to, please. I'm going to sleep now."

"Stay awake for a while longer. Feed from the woman, so you can be strong."

"Should I kill her?"

"No."

A pair of knees hit the floor in front of her face.

"Listen to me," the dark-eyed Sida said. "I have let you shelter in my tent. My humans will feed you. You will not kill any of them. They are my property, not yours. Do you understand?"

His hand reached over and tugged her short hair. Saraal hissed and he let go, but he still glared at her.

"I know you're mad, but do you understand me at all?"

Saraal curled her lip, revealing a vicious fang.

The other man was standing at the tent flap. "I don't trust her. She needs to be guarded."

"I think if we feed her, she'll become more lucid. She's barely conscious right now."

Aday stretched out on the ground and threw an arm around Saraal's waist. "We're not mad. Why can't they see that? There's a difference between madness and anger."

"Put a guard on her, Temur. Or put her in the ground."

Saraal screamed and rolled away. She felt her body leave the ground as she scrambled to move away from the man called Temur. She had to get away. Far away. Away from the ground. Into the air where she could dissolve into darkness. If she could only become nothing, perhaps they would leave her alone. Perhaps—

"Stop!"

Four hands pulled her down from the corner of the tent, where she was trying to tear through the skins. They pushed her down to the ground, holding her arms and legs. The screams froze in her throat. Saraal let her body go dead. She let her limbs fall still. Then she closed her eyes and turned her head to the side, spreading her legs to that it would be over more quickly.

The man who'd been standing by the tent flap grunted. "I think we know one of the things they did to her."

"Are you surprised?"

"No."

"Obviously, they buried her, too. My guess is that is what caused this. So let's not mention the ground again. Eh, Roshan?"

The man's voice dropped. "She's powerful. Do you feel it? Even in her condition—"

"I know."

They slowly let go of her arms and ankles, and Saraal curled into a ball again. Safe. She went to the black sky in her mind and flew, humming a tune her grandmother had taught her.

A soft hand stroked her head. "Girl, we will not bury you."

She rocked back and forth, and Aday sang along with her. "Do you understand?"

She felt a wrist pressed to her mouth. She didn't think; she just opened her mouth and drank.

Sweet, sweet, sweet. Sweeter than Kuluun's woman, even.

Someone pinched her nose and pulled her away from the wrist.

Saraal gave into her instincts and slept.

WHEN SHE WOKE, the tent was empty. She was healed. Her hair was clean and her clothes were fresh. She looked down at herself, barely recognizing what she could see. She opened her senses, but she couldn't hear Aday anywhere.

The tent flap was partially open, letting fresh air invade the stuffy shelter. Saraal crept closer and peeked out.

Half the camp was gone. Tents burned. Animal and human bodies scattered. A huge fire was burning in the cooking pit. Though she smelled humans around, she did not hear any screaming. Voices drifted from around the fire, so she crept closer, staying in the deep shadows. The moon was full and the air smelled of smoke, roasted meat, and blood.

"—too much attention. Our father is not pleased."

"What does he care if the humans die?"

Kuluun was still alive, but clearly was being questioned by the Sida called Temur. Saraal recognized him now. He was the other Sida who had been there the night Jun had sired her. He'd been there, but had left with Jun. Years had passed, but now Temur was back. And Saraal could hear the anxiety in Kuluun's voice. He was trying to mask it with arrogance, but she could hear through it.

"Jun doesn't care about the humans. He cares about discretion. You have become a terror over these plains. Stories spread. They spread about the god who flies, burns villages, and steals food. They spread along the trade routes where they meet stories of a god in the west who commands fire from heaven. Do you want this god to hear of us?"

"Who are we to fear some myth from the west?" Kuluun scoffed.

Temur's voice rose. "Are you so stupid you think we are the only of our kind? Jun commands this place, yes. But there are others, Kuluun. I have seen this Sida from the west, and he is frightening to behold. You kill with a sword, but this immortal kills with fire from his hands. He and Jun avoid each other, and you are testing your father's patience with your actions."

Saraal heard a low murmur and realized that many other Sida were also listening. She peeked around the corner of the tent and saw Kuluun and Temur staring at each other from across the fire. Kuluun's sons stood at his back, but Temur had his own men, and they looked far more dangerous. Saraal also noticed that many of Kuluun's sons were gone. Where there had been thirty or forty before, no more than a dozen joined him now.

Had they fled? Or had something else happened to them?

She allowed herself to drift on the edge of the gathering. Unfortunately, Temur must have caught her scent.

"And what have you done to the woman?"

Kuluun puffed up his chest. "What do you care what I do to my woman?"

The crowd had parted when Temur's eyes landed on her.

Saraal tried to run, but the man from Temur's tent, Roshan, was there. He must have been able to fly, because he appeared out of nowhere to block her escape.

"You've driven her mad, you idiot. *Jun's child*. You told Jun you wanted a woman. He gave you one. He made an immortal for you, and you have driven her to madness with your cruelty. Humans are one thing, Kuluun, but she is a Sida. Not a human for you to play with."

Kuluun's eyes narrowed on her. "What has she said to you? Saraal lies. Constantly."

"She says nothing. She talks to herself. She laughs at nothing and bites like an animal."

"She is *my* woman. It's none of your concern."

Rashon herded her to the edge of the fire. Kuluun's eyes found hers, and Saraal curled her lip.

Temur laughed. "Yes, she's obviously your woman! Well done, Kuluun."

"What are you going to do to me?"

Rashon released her arm, but stood behind her, clearly prepared to grab her again. Now that she was closer, she could see that Kuluun and Temur were not simply talking. Kuluun was bound and two of Temur's guards stood behind him. His sons were pale and frightened, their eyes darting between their sire and the new Sida with the powerful energy and the longer sword.

Temur was as tall as Kuluun, but leaner. His figure was striking and Saraal saw the human women who remained eyeing him appreciatively, so she guessed they considered him handsome. To Saraal, he exuded a threatening power.

"I'm not going to do anything to you, Kuluun." Temur stepped around the fire, eyes fixed on his brother, and a smile curled the corner of his mouth. "I promised Jun that I'd do nothing to you without consulting him. And he is away in the east somewhere. I have no idea when I will see him again. So Kuluun, I may have killed your children. I may have burned your camp. But I will do nothing to *you*."

Then Temur's gaze left Kuluun and swung over to Saraal. He nodded once and she felt a weapon pressed to her side. She turned, and Roshan met her eyes. He said nothing, but pulled out her hand and slapped the handle of a bronze blade into her palm. Then he closed her fingers around the hilt and stepped back.

Saraal looked at Temur. His eyes told her nothing. Luckily, at that moment, Aday came to her side.

"They give you a weapon to kill him, my girl." Aday's voice was gleeful. "You may kill him so they don't break their word to their master."

Kuluun started, but Temur's men held his arms. "What are you doing?"

"I told you, brother," Temur said. "*I* will do nothing to you."

"You gave her a weapon, you ass!" Kuluun screamed. "You can't give her a weapon!"

"She is a child of Jun. A female, yes. But a warrior by his blood. Are you saying you never trained her with weapons *as all his children must be trained*?"

"She's crazy!"

Temur bared his fangs at his brother and hissed, "She wasn't when he made her, was she?"

"She killed Odval! We never even found his ashes."

Temur looked at her with new respect. "Well, then giving her a weapon hardly seems necessary. I suppose at this point, I'm merely curious what she can do with it."

Saraal approached Kuluun as if he was a banquet laid before her. A harvest feast, like those she remembered as a girl. Temur's men stepped away. Kuluun's sons deserted him, clearly understanding where the power had shifted.

She stood before him, and he vibrated with anger. "You stupid bitch. You won't do anything. You're a mindless sheep. Too stupid to even—"

In a blur of movement, Saraal bent down and cut behind Kuluun's knees, slicing the tendon as if she was preparing a goat for the spit. He cried out and fell to the ground, but Saraal immediately grabbed the tongue out of his mouth and pulled, cutting it off as he retreated into enraged gurgles. He spit up blood, and Saraal did not waste it, licking up his chin to capture it before she bit his neck.

She heard the crowd behind her, but she ignored them. Aday was at her side, coaxing her on.

"Yes, yes, yes," she crooned. "Powerful blood. You will be strong, my girl. Drain him. Kill him like Odval."

She drank and drank, latching her fangs into his neck and sucking as he tried to jerk away. She plunged the short sword into his kidney and held him still. She could hear laughter around her, but she didn't stop.

Eventually, his veins ran dry. Saraal pulled away and looked down. The front of her new clothes were dripping with blood. She could feel it falling from her chin, smeared over her face. Her hands dripped with it; she had stabbed Kuluun over and over any time he tried to move. When she pulled away, his body fell to the ground and Saraal turned to Temur, licking the blood from the fingers of her free hand.

Her voice was rough and wet when she spoke.

"Fire destroys us?"

"Yes," Temur said, glancing toward the burning pit.

"Good to know."

She turned, hefted Kuluun's body over her shoulder, then tossed it into the fire. It jerked and sputtered, but soon went up in flames. Saraal watched it for a few minutes, then turned and walked away, still gripping the bronze blade.

5

THE WARRIOR

"You've got to stop killing Kuluun's children."

Saraal lifted her eyes when Temur swept into the tent. "Why?"

"I let you kill him because he was defiant and a problem. But you're killing off perfectly good warriors at this point."

"Do I have to tell you what he let those 'perfectly good warriors' do to me after he turned them?"

Temur sat across from her. Saraal was cleaning her blade. No doubt, there were still traces of blood on it from Kuluun's fat son, who had laughed when he ripped her hip from the socket as he raped her. Her leg had hung useless for almost a week because it was winter and blood was scarce. It had been a painful healing.

His fine mouth was frowning. "Enough, *tseetsa*. Or I'll stop your lessons."

Temur was born farther west than Saraal's people. She didn't understand the language he spoke to her sometimes, but she was learning. He'd told her *tseetsa* meant bird. It was not a bad name. Better than Saraal. He told her she should choose her own name, as he had done. Perhaps she would use *tseetsa*.

"I'll stop," she said quietly.

"For now," Aday whispered from the corner with a secretive smile.

She was quieter now. Still present, but often Aday kept to the side, particularly when Temur was with her. She didn't rage or make faces when Temur stayed in her tent. Temur wasn't as rough as other men. He was quiet when he took her. He used softer hands. Once, she'd even felt stirs of pleasure under him, but he finished and rolled away, so Saraal hadn't said anything.

Most importantly, he didn't share her body with the other men. The others didn't ask. Not even Rashon, though he was Temur's most trusted warrior. Saraal was surprised by this, but then, she was learning every day how different Temur was from Jun's other sons.

"But if we ever find Suk," Saraal said, "I'm killing him like I did his brothers."

"Suk and his children fled. They haven't made any trouble."

"I warned you," Saraal said in a low voice, "Suk is different. He's dangerous. And mean. Not as mean as Odval, but close."

"He's always been weak."

"But smart."

Temur shrugged and stretched out next to her. "I suppose."

He lay quietly like that for a while, watching her methodically clean and sharpen her sword.

Scrape. Scrape. Scrape.

It was the same sword she'd killed Kuluun with. During the day, she slept with it under her pillow. More than once, Temur had cut himself on its edge, but he never said anything about it. She knew he kept one with him, as well.

His hand reached up to play with the raw edges of her hair, which was slowly growing out. "What is my *tseetsa* doing tonight?"

"This. Then a lesson with Rashon."

"He's a good teacher."

"He doesn't trust me not to hurt him when we spar."

Fingers tightened on her hair.

"Good. Neither do I."

"I wouldn't hurt you, Temur."

Aday whispered, "Not while he still has things to teach you."

His smile was slow and wily. "My *tseetsa* speaks with secret eyes."

Saraal didn't disagree.

She had stayed in Temur's camp, even though they'd never tried to bind her. She'd stayed for the same reason she'd stayed with Kuluun. Where would she go? She couldn't fly yet. Not like Temur and Rashon. With a steady diet of fresh human blood—which she didn't need to drink nearly as often as pony blood—she was starting to get her flying. She could hover at will, but no more than that. Temur said there was something she was missing. If she could hover, she should be able to fly. There was some link her mind needed to make the jump, and she just wasn't seeing it. Until she did, she would learn other skills.

Temur taught her hand to hand combat. He said he trusted no one else to do it. Rashon taught her weapons.

Their band of Sida had moved on, north and east until the forests surrounded them and the air changed. They were closer to where Saraal's human home had been. She guessed. There was no way to be sure. So many years had passed that nothing seemed clear anymore. Temur and his men were raiders, like Kuluun. But unlike him, they didn't destroy where they raided. When she had enough skill, she went along with them. She quickly became one of Temur's best. Temur's Sida were far more like the raiders Saraal remembered as a child. They came. They took. They moved on. They did take humans, but no more than they needed in order to survive. No villages were burned, and no one took the children.

For this small mercy, Saraal was grateful.

After she'd killed Kuluun, the nightmares had started. She'd never dreamed before. Not after Jun had made her Sida. She was awake; she was asleep. There was no memory or consciousness during day rest. Her mind was completely blank. But after Kuluun had died, she'd dreamed of killing him. Then different dreams came. She dreamed of the child she'd killed the first night she had woken as a monster. His dead eyes blinked at her and his silent mouth gaped.

"Mama?"

She woke screaming, even though the sun still shone. After a second of terror, she was dead to the day again.

It was the first time it had happened, but not the last. Sometimes, Temur was with her, and she roused him, too. Once, he had stabbed her, not understanding that she was the one screaming. She'd blacked out in pain, but when she woke, the wound in her stomach was already healed, so she didn't speak of it.

Throughout it all, Aday was still with her, but she was more of a quiet shadow than she had been. A guardian. She watched and warned Saraal sometimes. She was the one who told Saraal which of Kuluun's sons needed to be killed. After she reminded Saraal of all the man's wrongs, she cheered when she killed them. One by one, Saraal was killing any man who had touched her. There were many, and some were very skilled. She needed her lessons from Temur.

"What do you want?" Saraal asked Temur, who was still laying beside her.

His hand slid up the inside of her thigh and cupped her between the legs. "I want this."

"This" was never as quick with Temur as it had been with Kuluun or his brothers.

"Rashon will be waiting," she said quietly, though she set her sword to the side and lay back as he began to remove her leggings.

"Rashon can wait," Temur said. "While I enjoy what is mine."

∼

THE SWORD CLATTERED to the ground, and Rashon leaped on her, pressing his dagger to the back of her neck.

"You're dead. Again."

Saraal sneered and shoved him off. She'd bested him the night before, and he seemed intent on teaching her a lesson that night. He'd been vicious. He'd fought dirty. And he'd been winning. He had her pinned to the ground, her face in the dirt and his hips held her down. He was holding onto the back of her hair, which had grown past her shoulders in the years she'd been with Temur and his warriors.

She needed to cut it again.

Saraal twisted around and tried to kick him in the balls. He blocked her, but he didn't notice her hand, which had crept back and under his hip. She grabbed onto his testicles and pulled. Hard.

Rashon screamed and slammed her head into the ground, over and over, but Saraal did not let go. Her grip was unyielding. She squeezed harder. She felt his blade press into her spine, and she twisted. Eventually, the blood dripped into her face and she couldn't see. But she could still feel his balls in her small hand, and she would not let go. Rashon's blade left the back of her neck, then he yanked on her hair as he was pulled off. Saraal let go of him and immediately rolled into a crouch.

Temur was holding Rashon by the hair. The Sida was guarding his sore testicles and his fangs dripped blood where he'd bit his own lip.

"I'll kill her!" he growled. "You won't stop me this time!"

"You'll do nothing," Temur said, shaking Rashon by the hair. "You were sparring. You came to a draw. You're finished."

Until the next lesson. Saraal eyed Rashon with suspicion.

Aday whispered in her ear. "He'll kill you the next time you fight."

Temur must have agreed with Aday because he said, "And you're done giving her lessons. You've taught her all you can, and obviously, she's strong now. You're finished."

"But—"

"Go." Temur slapped his child on the back and smiled a little. "Find a human to tend what is sore. Leave Saraal alone. My orders, Rashon."

Rashon limped away, and Temur grabbed Saraal from her crouch. Then, without a word, he held her and took to the air. She sucked in a cold breath at the shock of the wind. Then she closed her eyes and allowed herself to feel.

Cold ripping air did nothing to calm her blood. She could feel her heart beating in excitement. Could feel her mind racing. Within moments, Temur had landed them in a thick stand of trees, out of earshot of his Sida children.

"What were you doing?" he hissed.

Saraal cocked her head, surprised by his anger.

"We were fighting."

"You almost ripped his balls off, Saraal. They would have grown back. Eventually. Do you know how painful that is?"

She sneered, "You've seen me naked, Temur. Do I have a pair I don't know about? He'll be fine. He was fighting dirty. I fought dirtier."

"You can't do that to my men. You've already killed all of Kuluun's children. My men are off limits to your rage."

"Then they shouldn't pin me down and put a dagger to my neck."

"You will show respect!"

"To who?" Her chin lifted. "To you? Fine. To Rashon? No."

Temur's eyes flashed. "He is my second in command."

"And I, as you so often remind me, am Jun's child."

His eyes narrowed. "So you are."

For once, it didn't sound like a compliment.

Saraal did everything she could to soften her voice. "I meant no disrespect to you. Perhaps it is better that I avoid Rashon. He does not like me or trust me."

No one liked her except Temur. And Saraal often thought he only liked her because he could fuck her. But she knew he didn't trust her. She could see his eyes cutting to her every time she mastered another skill. The long sword. The bow. The spear. Would he still put up with her once she could fly?

Because Saraal knew in her gut, once she could fly, she would be stronger than Temur. She sired no children like Temur did. Her strength was growing as his waned with each new warrior he made on his father's orders.

Temur stepped closer to her, and his eyes narrowed. "Give me your neck."

Saraal took a step back. In all their time together, all the times she had allowed his body into hers, he had never taken her blood. He'd never even asked.

"No," she said in a small voice.

"No?" His eyes were starting to glow in anger again. "You don't tell me no, Saraal."

"I don't want you to bite me."

"I wasn't asking."

Her heart began to race, and she saw Aday peeking from behind a tree. "Why are you doing this?"

"Respect, Saraal."

"I give you my body anytime you want it." She hated the quiver of fear in her voice. "I give you my respect. I don't want to give my blood. If you're hungry, take a human."

"I don't want a human."

He was closer. Boxing her in. She looked to the sky, but she could not reach it, even though it called her.

"Don't. Do. This." Saraal clenched her jaw and turned her head to the side when Temur backed her up against a tree. His large body pinned her in.

"Give me your neck, Saraal."

She had allowed him to touch her. She had grown to enjoy it at times, since Temur seemed to care. She'd begun to reach for him, which he enjoyed even more.

"Please, Temur," she whispered, dread coating her throat. "Don't do this thing."

He bent down, put a hand to her throat, and sunk his fangs in her neck. Saraal closed her eyes at Temur's groan of pleasure. The small portion of her heart that had softened to him died, even as the sensual pleasure of his bite washed over her.

"*Tseetsa*," he groaned. "So sweet." He tugged at her clothes. She did nothing to stop him. He pushed her leggings down and untied his own, then he lifted her against the tree and slid his body in hers. The pain wrapped around her heart as he took her.

She saw Aday leaning against a tree on the other side of the clearing, watching them both. Her mouth sneered, but her eyes reflected Saraal's pain.

"Just like the others," Aday whispered. "I told you. He is just like the others."

When Temur was finished, he kissed her neck and licked

the drops of blood from it. Then he kissed her again and ran a soft hand over her hair.

"That was good, Saraal. I can feel you in me now." He put his arms around her and took off into the air. Aday followed them. "I can sense you now. This is good."

But he hadn't offered his own blood to her. No, Temur didn't offer that kind of trust. After all, she might have been Jun's child, but she was still just a woman. That much had always been clear.

He flew them back to the camp, and left her at her tent, walking off in the direction of the humans. His hunger was piqued now. He would probably drink from at least one more human. Possibly more. And then he would fuck some human women. He usually wanted three or four in a night if his blood was running. Saraal was just glad he didn't seem to want her again.

She was distracted, but it still wasn't an excuse. By the time Saraal sensed him, she was already in her tent, and Rashon had her by the neck.

"Let's see what makes you so special, little bird," the monster whispered, then he cut her throat before she could scream.

ADAY WOKE with the earth in her mouth.

Enough.

She could sense the girl with her. The girl didn't feel the wind as she did. Didn't sense her power. The girl was broken. There was no repairing her this time. She huddled, terrified as the dirt became her grave.

Enough.

Aday felt the air around her, even underground. She felt

the fine particles flowing through the soil, just as they flowed through the trees and the water. She knew there was no place the air did not live. No place she could not draw power. None. She had felt it long ago when she woke beside the girl. Felt it when she followed her through her years with Kuluun. With Temur. She had given the second a chance, but the girl had not found her power. Had not flown. She still didn't understand.

Enough.

She could hear Rashon over her, stepping on the earth, leaving footprints over the spot where he'd buried the girl after he'd raped her viciously. After he broke her neck. After she was close to death. Rashon knew Temur would punish him. Taken by his own rage, he had forgotten it, but as the sun set and the moon rose, he remembered again.

Aday closed her eyes and pictured what she knew of Rashon's tent. She had been in it many times, choosing a weapon from his chest before practice. She focused on one she had seen him polish, a new blade with a vicious curve that he'd picked up from traders in the west. It was new. It would be near the top of the chest. Wrapped in good leather, if she had to guess.

She would claim the blade. It would be hers when she killed its master.

Aday held her breath, but sent a curl of energy out, touching the air that permeated the soil. The air moved and shifted, pushing the soil down and lifting her up through the thick mass, obeying her command until she lay at the surface, naked and dusted in dirt, her body perfectly healed as she knew it would be.

She heard Rashon rifling through the chest, his back to her. She rose, her feet light upon the ground as she felt the wind cushion her. It swallowed the noise of her steps. It hid her movements from her enemy until she'd picked up a dagger he had laying beside his pallet.

Without a word, she went to him. He sensed her a second before she struck. He turned, mouth open, eyes gaping in horror at the monster she had become. The monster they had made.

Aday struck swiftly.

She drove the dagger through his throat so he could not scream. Drove it all the way through his neck until it pierced his spine. Then she yanked it back and forth, making sure Rashon's backbone was severed. His body gave a jerk, but that lasted only a few seconds as she hacked off his head. Aday shoved it to the side and wiped away the blood that had spattered on her face. She kicked his body away from the chest and searched for the curved blade.

She smiled when she found it. The sword gleamed in the low lamplight. Its handle was wrapped in fine leather, and the bronze blade was burnished to a sheen. It was hers. Hers alone. Rashon had traded for it, shown it to others, but he'd never spilled blood with it.

"*Saraal*," she whispered, giving her sword the dead girl's name.

She slipped out of the tent in the early evening light. The moon had not risen, and the black sky conspired with her to block out the stars. No one saw her when she moved to the next tent.

The warrior was feeding from a human when he saw her. His fangs were down and his body hard. The girl had stopped struggling, but the bruises on her body showed Aday how she'd been used.

He sat up, but Aday had already moved. Flipping in the air, over his head, to land on his back. The blade swept out, slicing easily through the thick cords of the Sida's neck, cutting it cleanly before he could make a sound.

It was a good sword.

Aday sat with the body between her legs, staring into the dead eyes of the woman. Her lips were split open. Her eyes were black. She tipped back her chin, baring her throat to Aday.

Enough.

She brought the blade to the woman's throat and gave her a quick death, then she moved to the next tent.

She killed a younger Sida next, one of Temur's newest children. Then an older one, who she'd seen eying Saraal with lust. He'd wanted her. And Aday knew it was only a matter of time before Temur would start passing the girl through the camp.

By the time she'd killed five warriors, the bodies were beginning to be found. She could hear cries of surprise and anger. Somewhere in the distance, Temur yelled out for the girl.

She's gone, Aday thought as another warrior's blood dripped cool down her breast. *There is only me now.*

"Saraal!" he yelled. "Come here *now!*"

Aday stepped out of the tent and saw torches coming toward her. She flew straight up, avoiding the fire, before sweeping down and grabbing a burning stick from one of the humans who guarded the warriors during the day. He gasped when he saw her and fell to his knees. She flew over the camp, touching the flame to the tents as she passed.

Like a row of dead trees, the tents went up in flames, and she smiled when she heard the cries of the warriors inside as they met their end.

A few had taken to the air to look for Saraal, but the girl couldn't fly, so they were looking down. Aday could, so she snuck up behind them, the wind holding her aloft as she overpowered the flying Sida and took their heads.

One.

Two.

Three.

She laughed at how easy it was, in the end. They were finished. All but a few of Temur's warriors were dead. A couple had fled into the trees with the humans. Most were burning in their tents. Aday took a deep breath and reveled in the smell of death around her.

She was almost finished.

She saw Temur heading toward her, so she dropped to the ground out of respect for the girl, who had cared for him in her own way. Aday watched the Sida as he landed across from her, his camp burning in the background, humans and animals still running for their lives as the air filled with smoke.

"Why?" he yelled, bloody tears running down his face. "What have you done, Saraal?" His hair was singed and his clothes black.

"You killed her."

Aday began to walk toward him. She could hear the girl somewhere, whimpering in protest.

"What are you talking about? You killed my sons! Their sons. When I would not let them touch you." He screamed into the night, *"They feared your madness and I trusted you!"*

Aday shook her head. "You shouldn't have."

Temur's face melted in rage, and he flew toward her, his sword held out. Aday met him in the air, embracing him and kneeing him in the gut at the same time. She was stronger than Temur. The girl didn't know it, but she did. She'd known for some time. He folded over in the air, and when she put the knife to his neck, she felt surrender wash through him.

His children were dead.

His camp in flames.

"I trusted you," he said quietly, the wind muffling his words.

"No, you didn't," Aday said, pressing her cheek to his as she held the knife to the back of his neck. "Not really, Temur. You killed her last night. You didn't even know."

"Finish it, *tseetsa*," he murmured, dropping his sword as she flew them higher and higher. He put his arms around her, and held on. "Fly me to the stars and finish it."

Aday heard the girl screaming as she pressed the blade to Temur's neck and cut. She would give the girl that. Temur would die quickly. His eyes closed as the curved blade caught his neck. With one pull, his head was gone. She held his body, dripping blood onto her chest as she flew to the clearing where he had forced the girl to give up her blood. She landed there and set Temur's body down, stretching across it as his blood flowed into the earth where the girl was buried.

She lay there, wrapping his arms around her back to see if she could feel what the girl had felt for him, but there was nothing. No energy. No comfort. She wondered if there ever had been, or if the girl's feelings were an illusion.

The moon rose over Aday as she held Temur's corpse and the stars watched. Then she felt herself leave her body again, absorbing the black night. She surrendered to the space inside, letting the darkness fill her. Claim her.

And when the sun rose, Aday smelled Temur burning over her from her hollow in the earth.

EPILOGUE: THE HEIR

She left the plains and flew far, taking shelter in the mountains. She felt the sun rise and set from beneath the earth. Seasons passed; her hair grew long again. And when the frost came, she left the cave where she had sheltered and drifted among the humans, feeding on more than the birds and small creatures that populated the dark. The bronze blade never left her side.

She found clothes. She learned languages. She flew. She hid. Few noticed her, and those who did avoided the small woman who wore men's clothes and wandered the trade routes at night.

She crossed the plains again, tracking Suk and his sons. When she found them, she killed them in their tents, then she set fire to the last of those who held the girl's memory.

She became no one. Nameless. Though she passed others of her kind on the trade routes, she did not speak to them. She only engaged them if she needed to defend herself.

She existed.

Then one night, she realized she felt something. Not in her body, in her mind. It was a feeling that had crept up on her, as much a result of her years on the earth as the length of road she had traveled.

She was tired.

She found another cave, higher in the mountains where the winter was long. Bright flags rippled from the trees, like colorful birds dancing in the wind. She found a cave where humans had been. A small statue sat at the back in a niche, hidden from the light. She crawled next to it and lay down, stripping off her clothes to cushion her flesh from the rocks, rubbing snow over her body to clean it.

She lay down with the bronze blade under her head, and for many seasons, she did not rise.

Humans came to her, first frightened, then curious, then reverent. She was high in the mountains, but the tribe who tended the small statue came regularly. She didn't move, but they fed her, reaching out to touch her gently. She caught them with her mind, so they held out their wrists, letting her drink as she needed. She never took too much.

A tree took root near the mouth of the cave.

She watched as the years passed. Her eyes rested on the tree. Each day, it grew a little more. Each night, she watched its progress. The humans came. They brought finely woven blankets and laid them over her, so she did not feel the bite of cold. They brought food for her to fill her stomach, though she did not eat. She existed on blood, and she survived.

Years passed, the tree grew tall as a man. The humans brought polished stones and purple shells. Bits of carved bone and pottery.

When the tree was as tall as the mouth of the cave, they brought brightly colored beads and rings made of a shining metal that did not tarnish. Her bronze blade grew dull beneath her head, but still, she did not move.

To them, she was a god. Never aging. Never moving. Many

years passed, and they whispered to her. Dreams and prayers. They asked for wisdom. For blessing. For answers to questions she did not know. She listened and thought about their lives, these humans who tended her. She listened, and when she was tired, she closed her eyes.

ONE NIGHT, she woke and he was there, sitting at the edge of the cave, perusing the treasure the humans had brought. There were jewels and scrolls. Colorful blankets and food. Intricately painted pots. Pounded metal vessels and carved wooden screens. The humans had painted the walls of the cave with beautiful designs they hoped would please her.

She sat up and spoke for the first time since the tree took root.

"Are you here to kill me?"

Her sire looked up from the scroll he had been studying. "Why would I do that?"

"I killed your sons."

Jun shrugged. "Then they deserved to be killed."

"Did you make more?" she asked, her rusted voice dripping with scorn. "Shall I kill them, too?"

Jun looked at her, then smiled. Then his smile grew wide; he threw his head back and laughed. The cave echoed with it. His beautiful face was suffused with glee.

"You are my finest warrior," he said when he stopped laughing. "Who would have thought?"

She narrowed her eyes, suspicious. "How did you find me?"

"It took many years. You are a rumor in these mountains. A legend. The Sleeping Goddess. They tell stories of you on the roads. I followed the legends when I decided to look for you."

"Why did you decide to look for me? Do you want to fight me?"

"No, my daughter." He shook his head. "To tell the truth, I do not know which one of us would win."

Her eyes flashed with arrogance. "I would."

"You might." But the glint in his eyes told her that Jun did not believe her.

Despite her pride, she had to acknowledge he was probably the greater warrior. Power poured off him in waves. The air around him was suffused with it.

"You asked me why I wanted to find you," he said after some silence had passed.

"Yes."

"I am tired of wandering. I am going to an island with others of our kind. Do you want to come with me? It will be a place of peace and reason."

"Why?"

"I am tired of war," he said. "Aren't you?"

"No, why do you invite me to come with you?"

He stepped closer, but she did not shrink back. She never would. Never again.

"You are my only child," Jun said. "Clearly, the most worthy. You are the only being left in the world who speaks the language of my birth."

She blinked. "Have so many years passed?"

He smiled sadly. "Yes, they have."

She thought about his offer. Then she said, "You do not know me."

"And you do not know me."

"I have no desire for a master," she said. "I will not answer to another again."

"I will always be your sire."

"I do not know what it means for you to be my sire," she said. "Do you?"

He stared at one of the paintings on the wall. "I thought I knew what it meant, but perhaps I didn't. Perhaps you will teach me."

"No," she said. "You will learn, or you will not. I do not think it is my place to teach you."

"I think..." He paused and turned to her. "I think I would like to sit with you and talk. Someday, I would like that."

"Perhaps," she said. "But not today. Today, I will stay here. I am still weary. I will stay here until I am not."

Jun paused and watched her, then he rose and gave her a small bow.

"If this is what you want, I will hold your treasure until you join me."

"Treasure?" She had grown to like beautiful things as the humans surrounded her with them.

"You are my child, and a warrior of legend now." His chin lifted with pride. "I am honored to give you half of everything I have gained, daughter. Until you come for it, I will hold it in your name."

"I have no name."

"Yes, you do," he said, turning to leave. "Those who worship you call you Tenzin. They believe you show them the wisdom of their god, for to them, you exist in perfect harmony."

She thought back to the humans who cared for her. They offered their dreams and secrets to her. If she offered them anything, then she was grateful.

"Tenzin?"

"Yes," he said. "Tenzin. It is your name if you want it."

Tenzin?

She tried out the name in her mind, and the wind whispered that it was good.

The girl looked at her father, who waited on the edge of the cave.

"You may call me Tenzin if you like."

Penglai Island
Present day

TENZIN STRETCHED out next to Nima, whose breathing was the only sound in the room. Her heartbeat was slow. Her breath shallow.

"I told you, my Nima." Tenzin stroked her silver hair. "It is not a happy story."

Nima said nothing. At some point, her eyes had closed. Her frail body had gone still. The mortal's life was slipping away.

"There will be no nightmares for you," Tenzin whispered, placing a soft kiss on the old woman's wrinkled cheek. "Not anymore."

Nima had shown her love. For years, even when Tenzin had been ungrateful. Even when she'd been angry or petulant. Nima asked for nothing and gave everything. Like the humans who had made her a god, Nima had been faithful.

So Tenzin would do the same.

She held the woman as she took her last breaths on the earth. She washed her body and sang the song she had sung to the father of her child—the song she had sung over her own mate's body. Tenzin held Nima until her sire came and took the mortal's body to be burned as Nima had wished.

Nima's body was put to flames by the Immortal Woman. It was a great honor for a valued member of her father's household. Then her ashes were scattered in the gardens of Penglai, and her friend became everything and nothing on the earth.

After eight days of mourning, Tenzin lay down in her room at her father's house as servants and immortals hurried around her. Nima had occupied an important position in her father's house. None of the humans were immune to her loss, but each one honored Nima in his or her own way. Mostly, by quietly continuing the tasks she had given them.

But Tenzin was tired. And though she no longer slept—not even during the day—the immortal lay in her bed, reached under her pillow, and felt for it.

It was there, as it always was. Aday's blade was heavy and smooth to the touch. Shaped by time and battle, it lay like a lodestone in her hand.

She clutched the bronze blade and closed her eyes.

Tenzin held the old sword in her hand, and she rested.

THE END

Turn the page for an exclusive three-chapter preview of Night's Reckoning, the next adventure in the Elemental Legacy series.

PREVIEW: NIGHT'S RECKONING

A special preview of the newest book in the Elemental Legacy series, Night's Reckoning, *available on November 26, 2019 at all major retailers.*

CHAPTER ONE

Ben was expecting the punch, but that didn't make it hurt any less. It landed on his jaw; snapping his head back. His skull cracked on the edge of the metal chair where they'd tied him up.

He was sitting in an old warehouse on the run-down edges of Genoa taking their vicious punches with his ears open, ignoring the taunts of the humans around him. The men had grabbed him when he'd been snooping around the warehouse near the railroad tracks.

Exactly as he'd planned it.

One vampire stood with the humans, silently watching Ben as he tried to ignore her. The humans he wasn't worried about. The vampire was another story.

"I hear she keeps him on a tight leash," one of the men said. "I'm surprised he got this far out of Napoli."

The vampire was female and petite. In Ben's experience, a vicious combination. She stared while Ben tried to look beaten and miserable.

"Poor boy." Her voice purred. "Little puppies who wander too far get kicked by the bigger dogs." Her voice was a whisper that begged for his attention, drawing him in, seducing him, exactly as she wanted it to.

Ben narrowed the one eye that wasn't already swelling shut and concentrated on the pain to resist the lure of her voice. Hits to the face he'd put up with for the job. Kicks to the ribs were hardly anything new. But if the vampire touched him, she would be able to use *amnis*, the electric current that gave her elemental power and control over humans if she wished it. Ben would do nearly anything to escape his brain being messed with. It had happened before, and he wasn't a fan.

He'd been told he had natural resistance to amnis, but resistance wasn't immunity.

"What does Piero want with him?"

The vampire's purring voice turned hard. "Shut your mouth if you want to keep your tongue, human."

Ben tried to see which man was talking. It was the bombastic one, the tallest in the group with three days' worth of beard and a sweat stained polo shirt clinging to his chest. The man had fists the size of Iberian hams and they felt just as solid.

It didn't matter. *Piero*. Ben had a name. One down, one to go.

The human puffed his chest and angled his shoulders back. His chin went up. "I don't work for you."

"You stupid mortal," the vampire muttered. "Of course you do."

"Piero gives me orders. I don't even know why he brought you to Finale—"

The man's voice cut off with a strangled gurgle.

And a place. The corner of Ben's mouth turned up. That was quicker than he'd thought. *Gotcha.*

The humans in the gang started shouting at the vampire, who released the man's throat from her iron grip and let him slide to the floor.

Ben silently released his wrists from the restraints he'd loosened an hour before, minutes after they'd tied him up. The humans weren't very good with knots.

As the men shouted at the small vampire in defense of their friend, Ben moved, slipping from his bonds and easing into the shadows between stacked pallets in the warehouse. The whole place smelled of sardines and motor oil, not a good combination.

"Stefano, where's the kid?"

More shouting in loud Italian. Their accents didn't sound like Genoa. Much farther south, if Ben had to guess. Not Naples. Sicily? Calabria maybe. His client would want to know. The vampire wasn't Italian. Ben was guessing French.

As he crept away, he listened for her movements. She was the only one he was really worried about. The floor was cold against his feet—hard packed dirt with cracked concrete near the door. They'd taken his shoes and he had no idea where they'd put them.

"You idiot!" Another yelled. "Piero is going to take your balls!"

"He's a skinny foreigner. Find him, you shit! He can't have gotten far."

Ben slipped into a shadowed corner and climbed up the plastic wrapped pallets, clinging with his fingertips and toes to the edges of the wrapped cans and waiting for the first man to come to him.

A dark-haired human looked into the narrow corner but didn't notice Ben halfway up the wall. He turned around, and Ben immediately fell on his back.

Ben locked his elbow around the man's throat and covered his mouth to block his muffled yell. Once his mouth was covered, Ben chopped the edge of his hand against the man's throat in a swift slicing gesture, bringing him to his knees and driving the breath from his lungs.

Ben released his hold and the choking man clutched his throat as Ben quickly drew his fist back and aimed for the temple. His fist made contact, the man's head snapped to the side, and he fell in a solid thunk.

Ben quickly rifled through his pockets, grabbing his wallet and the knife and gun in his waistband. He felt for an ankle holster but didn't find one.

Shoes? He needed shoes.

Damn. This guy's were too small.

"Topo, where are you?"

"By the door!"

"Luca?"

Nothing.

Ben looked at the man he had to guess was Luca. He'd wake up eventually and he would deserve the massive headache.

Now with one hundred percent more weapons, Ben crawled on top of the stack of pallets and surveyed the warehouse. His head was throbbing, but he needed to eliminate the human threat and avoid the vampire.

He'd have to crawl down eventually to reach the door. He crawled over two more stacks of pallets and dropped to the ground. Three more humans and he'd have a clear shot at the door.

The second man nearly walked into Ben. He turned into the alcove where Ben was waiting and his eyes wide, but Ben put the knife to his throat before he could yell.

"Shhhh." Ben put a finger to his lips. "The baby's sleeping."

The man cocked his head, confused. "Wha—?"

478

Crack. Another fist to the temple. Another snapped neck and the human fell to the ground with his eyes rolling back.

And his shoes were still too small. What was with these people? Did they all have miniature feet?

Ben kept the knife out. There were three more wandering around, not counting the vampire.

Where was the vampire?

He had the door in sight when he nearly ran into two of the men. One reached for his gun, but Ben kicked it before he could raise it. The man muttered a curse and reached for his knife, while Ben dodged the other man's grasp.

They weren't expecting Ben to be so fast. They thought they'd wounded him. They'd thought he was broken.

Gotcha, suckers.

Silence was useless now. The men were shouting as he fought them off. He grabbed the unarmed man by the shoulders and brought his face down to his knee. Ben felt the spurt of blood from the man's nose.

The scent of blood lay like bitter copper in his mouth. His own skin was broken. One man rolled on the ground, holding his hand to his face as blood poured out, and Ben turned to the other man, who was now a little more cautious. It was the original ringleader, Stefano, whose throat was still red and raw from the vampire grabbing him. He was bent to the side, still limping.

His voice was hoarse. "Who are you?"

Ben touched the corner of his split lip and flinched. "No one important."

Before Stefano could ask another question, Ben brought his foot up and swiftly kicked him in the gut, knocking the man to the ground. Then Ben walked over and kicked Stefano's temple, snapping his neck to the side and making his eyes roll back.

Ben examined the two men on the ground. Making a swift decision, he grabbed Stefano's shoes and slipped them on his feet, leaving the laces untied. They were a little big, but they were better than nothing.

He ran for the door. He was nearly home free when the vampire appeared.

She appeared few yards away from Ben, moving so quickly he nearly didn't see her. She stomped her foot on the ground and a crack split the floor. Ben's foot fell into the earth and he felt the pulse of power through as the dirt tightened around his foot.

Earth vampire. He added that to the file.

"Hey there." He kept his knife out and reached for the gun he'd slipped in his pocket, never taking his eyes off the vampire walking toward him. "Ben Vecchio. How you doing?"

"I know who you are."

She wasn't angry. She was curious. Her head was angled to the side and she examined him like normal people examined an interesting specimen at the science museum.

"I'm just trying to get out of here," Ben said. "I have no desire to start a fight."

"You've already been in one." Her voice was still barely over a whisper and Ben was starting to wonder whether she had some physical disability that affected her voice.

Contrary to human mythology, changing into a vampire didn't cure all your ills. It didn't make you younger or heal anything other than the most recent injuries. If you were missing an arm before you turned, you were still going to miss it. If you were deaf as a human, you'd be deaf as a vampire. Nerve damage could be cured and immortality cured all but the most severe eye problems. But a damaged voice? You'd live with that for eternity.

"I'm not looking for a fight," he repeated. "I just want to go home."

480

"Do you?" She met his eyes and her fangs fell. "And who would miss you if you didn't go home, Ben Vecchio?"

He raised the gun. "I don't know you. I am a human under vampire aegis. We have no quarrel. Let me go."

Her mouth was halfway between a smile and a pout. "If you're under vampire aegis, you should know that gun won't do anything to stop me."

"I know if I hit your spine, you'll be out of commission until nightfall tomorrow." He glanced at the ceiling. "You'll be safe in here. I won't even have to feel guilty. No direct sunlight. Whoever might find you during your day rest, that's not my problem, is it?" He really wished Luca had a semi-automatic he could steal, but he was still a decent shot with a revolver. "I'm an excellent shot. You don't want to take a chance. Let me go."

She smiled. "I'm not going to kill you. I was simply curious."

"Oh?" He kept the gun trained on the vampire's neck as she moved.

"Curious what she sees in you."

Fuck. Ben knew exactly who *she* was and just the reminder pissed him off. He cocked the gun. "Let me go."

"I don't poach." She came closer. "But I wonder if a taste—"

The gun went off and her long hair blew back. Ben could see a red line where the bullet had passed by her neck.

"Back off," he said in a low voice. "I won't miss again."

"You didn't miss that time. Interesting." She blinked and smiled fully. "I do see what she sees in you, Benjamin Vecchio."

Without another word, the vampire ran out the door and Ben heard it creak from the swift gust of air.

And his foot was still stuck in the ground. "Really?"

Wiggling it back and forth, Ben managed to work it out, but only because Stefano's shoes were bigger than his foot. He left the right shoe stuck in the ground and limped to the door.

Ben was almost there when it swung back, revealing a thin

481

man leaning against the wall, pointing his gun at Ben with a shaking hand.

Ben glared at the man. "You really want to do this?" He raised his revolver and the man lowered his gun.

"No, I don't—"

"Are you Topo?"

The man nodded.

Ben kept his voice low and walked toward him. "Okay, Mouse, the rest of them are out. The vampire's gone. You want me to punch you or shoot you?"

The blood drained from his face. "Are those my only options?"

"You think your boss is gonna be satisfied if you just run?" He nodded over his shoulder. "She knows you were here and walking when she left."

Topo's face crumbled. "I guess... shoot me. Left leg?"

Ben was certain the man was going to go for the knock out. "A bullet? You sure?"

The man pointed to his eyes. "The doctor, he says if I take any more punches, I could lose an eye. I used to be a boxer."

"That sucks."

Topo shrugged. "It's only a nine millimeter."

"Still a bullet, man."

Topo hesitated. "Maybe... you could break a few ribs?"

It was a solid option. It wouldn't put him completely out, but with enough bruising, his boss would believe Ben got past him. After all, he'd already taken out all the other brutes.

"If you're sure."

Topo put the safety on his gun and tossed it to the side. "Yes."

Ben didn't hesitate. He smashed his fist into Topo's ribs, punching him until the man was falling to the ground and Ben's fist felt like hamburger.

Damn. He really wished he'd just gone with the bullet like Topo wanted. His knuckles would take weeks to heal.

Ben finished Topo off with a swift kick to the side. He looked at Topo's feet and bent over. "Hey Mouse?"

Topo could only blink. He was gasping for breath.

"I hate to do this, but I'm gonna need your shoes."

For more information or to preorder the book, please visit my website, ElizabethHunterWrites.com.

THE ELEMENTAL LEGACY SERIES

Now available at all major retailers in e-book, paperback, and audiobook!

Midnight Labyrinth

He's one human caught in a tangled maze of theft, politics, magic, and blood.

In other words, it's just another night.

Benjamin Vecchio escaped a chaotic childhood and grew to adulthood under the protection and training of one of the Elemental world's most feared vampire assassins. He's traveled the world and battled immortal enemies.

But everyone has to go home sometime.

If you're a human in a vampire's world, nothing goes according to plan.

When a map to the mysterious fortune of notorious privateer Miguel Enríquez falls in the lap of Ben and Tenzin, only one of them is jumping at the opportunity. Tenzin can't wait to search for a secret cache of gold. Ben, on the other hand, couldn't be less excited.

All Ben knows about Puerto Rico is what he hears on the

news and a few lingering memories of his human grandmother. Going back to his roots holds zero appeal for the carefully constructed man he's become.

In the end, the lure of hidden gold can't be denied.

Blood Apprentice

~

Darkness comes for everyone, and some fates are inescapable.

For over a thousand years, the legendary sword Laylat al Hisab—the Night's Reckoning—has been lost in the waters of the East China Sea. Forged as a peace offering between two ancient vampires, the sword has eluded treasure hunters, human and immortal alike.

But in time, even the deep gives up its secrets.

Night's Reckoning

When Tenzin's sire hears about the eighth century shipwreck found off the coast of southern China, Zhang realizes he'll need the help of an upstart pirate from Shanghai to retrieve it. And since that pirate has no desire to be

in the middle of an ancient war, Cheng calls the only allies who might be able to help him avoid it.

Unfortunately, Tenzin is on one side of the globe and Ben is on the other.

Sign up for my newsletter for information about this series and more upcoming releases!

ABOUT THE AUTHOR

ELIZABETH HUNTER is a *USA Today* and international best-selling author of romance, contemporary fantasy, and paranormal mystery. Based in Central California, she travels extensively to write fantasy fiction exploring world mythologies, history, and the universal bonds of love, friendship, and family. She has published over thirty works of fiction and sold over a million books worldwide. She is the author of Love Stories on 7th and Main, the Elemental Legacy series, the Irin Chronicles, the Cambio Springs Mysteries, and other works of fiction.

ElizabethHunterWrites.com

ALSO BY ELIZABETH HUNTER

The Bronze Blade

The Scarlet Deep

A Very Proper Monster

A Stone-Kissed Sea

Valley of the Shadow

(December 2019)

The Irin Chronicles

The Scribe

The Singer

The Secret

The Staff and the Blade

The Silent

The Storm

The Seeker

The Cambio Springs Series

Long Ride Home

Shifting Dreams

Five Mornings

Desert Bound

Waking Hearts

Contemporary Romance

The Genius and the Muse